All Good Women

Valerie Miner

•

ALL GOOD WOMEN

THE CROSSING PRESS / Freedom, California 95019

Jacket Illustration by Gwyneth Jones
Photograph of author by John M. Burgess
Printed in the U.S.A. by McNaughton & Gunn
of Ann Arbor, Michigan

Lyrics from "I'll Be With You in Apple
Blossom Time" printed by permission of
Jerry Vogel Music Co., Inc., co-owner of
the copyright, 501 5th Avenue, NY, NY 10017.

Lyrics from "Hold Tight, Hold Tight" printed
by permission of Mills Music, Inc.

ISBN 0-89594-250-X

First published in Great Britain 1987 by
Methuen London Ltd.

For Helen

Acknowledgements

Many people have been generous with their time, ideas, experience and support during the five years while I was writing this novel. As a Baby Boom daughter, I was a product of the Second World War, but not a participant in it. So let me first thank some of the older women who have shared their experiences with me; these include Mary Miner, Dorothy Bryant, Margaret Johnson, Tillie Olsen and Peggy Webb.

Marge Piercy proved to be the best of artistic comrades, generously sharing her research and insights regarding a period about which she was also writing.

My research into the lives of Japanese Americans was greatly enhanced and stimulated by Sandra Uyeunten, who teaches Asian American Studies at the University of California, Santa Barbara. Also very helpful was Jere Takahashi, who teaches in the Asian American Studies Program at the University of California, Berkeley.

For background about the Jewish refugee children, I am indebted to the patient assistance of Ruth Wolf, of Birmingham, England – former secretary of the Midland region of the Refugee Children's Movement Limited.

Many thanks go to those friends who read entire drafts of the novel and provided invaluable feedback. These people include Paula Gunn Allen, Sandy Boucher, Candace Falk, Jana Harris, Deborah Johnson, Helen Longino, Eve Pell, Susan Schweik, Madelon Sprengnether, Sandra Uyeunten and Peggy Webb.

Over the years I have worked with five fine student research assistants who chased after elusive details and provided new perspectives – Katy Irwin, Lori Katz, Jean Mandel, Stacey Ravel and Elizabeth Shelton. I am also grateful to Ida Dunson and Rosario Guerrero who administered the Undergraduate Research Program at the University of California, Berkeley Women's Center.

Many librarians and archivists have facilitated my research. In particular I would like to acknowledge Lynn Bonfield at the San Francisco State Labor History Archives, Carole Leita at the Berkeley Public Library and

John Slonaker at the US Army Military History Institute in Pennsylvania.

Among other writers, scholars and Second World War veterans who have been very helpful are Allan Bérubé, Nat Gould, Judy Grahn, Marlene Griffith, Mary Mackey, Daphne Muse, Heather Reid and Roberta Yusba.

All Good Women is a novel. All the characters are fictional. In fact some of the immediate settings, such as the Lion's Head Camp and the London refugee office, although informed by historical data, are creations of my imagination.

Finally, I deeply thank Elsbeth Lindner and Leslie Gardner for their faith in this project over the years.

What your Mother tells you now
in time
you will come to know.

Mitsuye Yamada, *Camp Notes And Other Poems*

And still we wear our uniforms, follow
The cracked cry of the bugles, comb and brush
Our pride and prejudice, doctor the sallow
Initial ardor, wish to keep it fresh.
Still we applaud the President's voice and face.
Still we remark on patriotism, sing,
Salute the flag, thrill heavily, rejoice
For death of men who too saluted, sang.
But inward grows a soberness, an awe,
A fear, a deepening hollow through the cold.
For even if we come out standing up
How shall we smile, congratulate: and how
Settle in chairs? Listen, listen. The step
Of iron feet again. And again wild.

Gwendolyn Brooks, 'Gay Chaps At The Bar'

Chapter One

●

Spring 1942, San Francisco

AMERICANS SURRENDER ON BATAAN

●

RAF BOMBS LUBECK

●

BRITISH LAND IN MADAGASCAR

●

AMERICANS DEFEAT JAPANESE AT MIDWAY

'She's going to hate this. She's going to hate us,' said Moira, her damp eyes on the faces of the two friends beside her as she steered down Borden Street. Her cheeks were flushed and her normally bouncy red hair straggled over the padded shoulders of her green polka dot dress. 'She'll never talk to us again.'

Three years, thought Moira. The four girls had shared a house in San Francisco like family for three years and now they were being split apart.

Gently, Ann squeezed Moira's chin and moved her friend's face back in the direction of traffic. 'She'll feel even worse when we don't make it alive.'

Ann's voice was low, as if she had one of her headaches. Teddy noticed that Ann's olive skin looked even darker at times like this, as if the migraine cast a shadow.

'Maybe Moi's right,' drawled Teddy, who always sat near the window when they borrowed Randy Girard's Studebaker so as not to block the view since she was the tallest of the four women. Three women, now that Wanda was being interned, arrested, imprisoned, evacuated with all the other Japanese Americans. None of the words sat well with Teddy, who was feeling especially blond today. She thought of those thin, grey men who hid behind FBI files, sidling up to the house to protect the USA from Wanda. Ridiculous, the curfew which meant she had to be home before eight o'clock every night and the order that all her people had to turn in 'contraband' such as binoculars and cameras. The orders became crazier and crazier and now this; now they were taking Wanda away.

'Moira,' scolded Ann, pointing again to the road. 'This was your idea, remember?' She spoke with affectionate exasperation. 'You were the only one clever enough to find out where the bus was leaving from.'

'It's just that Wanda can be, you know, so private,' Moira worried, 'and she's not exactly going off to college while we wave pompons.' She grew quieter. 'Where's she going, anyway?'

'I told you yesterday.' Teddy tried to steady her voice. She didn't want to be short, but Moira's frenzy left no room for anybody else to be agitated. '"An assembly center", whatever that means.' Teddy spoke directly to the two gardenias she had brought for Wanda and her mother, Mrs Nakatani. Their warm sweetness saturated the car, enveloping them all in a spring which refused to dawn this foggy April morning. If she closed her eyes and inhaled the heavy perfume, she could pretend this was all a dream, that Wanda had never left home, that they were all sleeping safely in the Victorian house on Stockton Street.

Yet, thought Teddy, this was as irrevocable as Mr Nakatani's death. Suicide, not death. She was just becoming aware of the importance of precision. Words cut sharply during a war.

It was because of his suicide that Wanda left Stockton Street to return to her family. And it was just three weeks after the funeral that the Nakatanis received the family 'evacuation' order. Teddy had seen her friend once in the last month, on the day Wanda and her brother Howard moved their family furniture into the Stockton Street basement for safe-keeping, for 'the duration', whatever that meant. What was unimaginable in December when war was declared – that Wanda would be seen as an enemy – was only one part of the craziness now. Everywhere she turned Teddy saw headlines screaming 'Jap' this or 'Jap' that. 'Jap Invasion of West Coast Expected'. All San Francisco Japanese merchants were holding 'Evacuation Sales' hoping to sell their goods before the windows were smashed. Wanda told her some boys had scrawled graffiti outside her uncle's cannery, 'Rome, Berlin, Tokio' and 'Down with Slant-Eyed Spies'. Wanda said she was lucky the Nakatanis could store their furniture. Many of her friends had lost money selling precious belongings to unscrupulous second-hand dealers. So they had crammed as much furniture as possible into the basement and into Wanda's room.

Moving day had grown more painful with each load, as if they were taking things away rather than moving them in. Moira, Ann and Teddy stayed around to help. The storage turned into a funeral, each of the pallbearers silent until the tables and bed frames were laid in the cellar. Teddy remembered Wanda on the first day of typing class four years before – the shy, determined girl, so pert in her red suit. She had aged ten years these last two months.

Moira spotted the dispersement center as they passed San Angeleco Avenue. The large, gravelled lot was crowded with growling Greyhound buses. Such confusion: babies wailing and women squeezing 'just one more' parcels on to the buses, past the drivers who stood, arms across their chests, shaking their heads. Policemen hovered everywhere, watching. At the far end of the lot, one bus roared; the doors shut and it began reluctantly to roll, gorged with people and furniture and bundles of food.

'Oh, no, we're going to miss her,' shouted Moira. Frantically, she swerved Randy's car to the curb and switched off the ignition. 'They said they wouldn't leave until 10.00. It's only 9.30.'

Ann followed swiftly. 'Moira, I don't believe you. Where did you develop this abiding faith in the United States government?' She shook her head and rubbed a muscle at the base of her neck. She didn't believe herself. This wasn't the time to argue with Moira. They had to find Wanda before it was too late.

Too late. Ann thought of Uncle Aaron's last letter. They were taking Jews to camp, he said. Don't believe the newspapers. He'd heard rumors of torture and . . . worse. At first Ann had thought he was exaggerating, suffering from the root paranoia that would hit anyone whose land was under siege. He was, after all, Mama's brother, the child of highly dramatic Galitian Jews. In this instance, Ann preferred the cool Frankfurt reason of her father's family. Yes, she dismissed Uncle Aaron impatiently. After all the Americans had kept diplomats in Berlin until last December. But as time passed and the next letter confirming their safe arrival in Amsterdam never came, Ann grew less and less confident of her doubt. This uncertainty was even more frightening because it made her believe that, with her crazed premonitions of terror, Mama had been right all along. Ann had to admit she was as scared of madness as she was of death. When the two of them coincided like this – when only through delusions could you see danger clearly – she was terrified. Her migraines had been terrible these last few weeks. Despite the fire splitting up her neck, it was Ann who saw Wanda first.

At a window seat, near the back of bus number five, sat Wanda, her eyes closed, seemingly oblivious to the turmoil in the parking lot and the cacophony on the bus. Likewise silent were her mother beside her as well as her sister Betty and brother Howard in the next seat forward. Their muteness raised a wall of privacy between them and the other eight families in the grim vehicle.

Wanda was thinking of Uncle Fumio burning memories of Japan – photographs, letters and diplomas – trying to create an innocence against the inevitable charges of subversion.

'*Ba-ka-ta-re*,' Papa had said. 'Stupid. Stupid to burn these pieces of paper. You cannot change who you are. All they need is one look. They will know your family does not come from Stockholm, Fumio.'

Papa would not destroy his documents. He waited, bitterly, for them to take him as they had arrested so many of the older Issei immigrant generation. And it was them – the FBI men, not his family – who found him, holding the note in his rigid hand. His body they could retain. But his spirit, his Japanese American spirit, had already been evacuated elsewhere.

Since Papa's suicide, Wanda had moved as if in a trance, preparing to leave her home for the resettlement communities intended to hold tens of thousands of Japanese Americans. Sometimes she questioned what held her together. She looked over to Mama. Was there an unstated pact between them that they would not fall apart? At night, alone in bed, Wanda couldn't help wondering how her father had done it, considering where he had purchased the poison, how long he had planned his exit, how he had convinced the family to go to Sebastapol for the day, what he was thinking when he saw them off in the morning. Had the poison hurt? Was it all finished quickly? She mulled over their last evening again and again, but there had been absolutely nothing unusual. Sometimes Wanda was filled with admiration for Papa's courage. Sometimes she was furious with him for leaving them – as he had always done – to go his own way. Then, she became angry at the government for killing his pride. Lately, she had felt overcome with grief and despair. What could she do – about Papa? About the evacuation? Was she becoming like her uncle and aunt?

'*Shikata ga nai*,' Uncle Fumio said. 'It cannot be helped.' Each day this month, she felt stunned by the good deportment with which people accepted the move. Of course those who fought back met severe punishment. That man in Oregon who protested the curfew was thrown into solitary confinement for months. And in a way, Wanda was relieved to escape the hostility that had surrounded them since Pearl Harbor. Personally, her only persecution had been contemptuous glances in the shops and on the streetcars. But Joyce Shimasaki had been cut with flying glass from her front window. Mr Hata's nursery had been vandalized. The FBI had randomly ransacked homes for months. She did know she was glad to be with her people, apart from the Caucasians. Safe on her way to what the government described as 'havens of refuge.'

After Papa's death, the hardest part had been leaving the house on Stockton Street. She kept intending to return after they moved the furniture. But there had been a thousand delays until she realized that consciously taking leave of the house would be the ultimate violation, the real arrest. The way she had left – to tend to Mama's grief, to mourn Papa – had been a private movement in a time of deep numbness. The evacuation was an extension of that separation, spreading into a great public affliction. To leave Stockton Street fully aware that she could not return would fill her with uncontrollable rage. Instead, she telephoned. She hoped that Teddy and Moira and Ann would understand. But how could they when she, herself, did not understand? What was happening to her? To all of them? Perhaps when she awoke, the bus would have taken her back to Stockton Street. She longed to curl up on the lumpy old couch in the front room and hear Moira singing from the kitchen. She longed to step out into the small back garden and dig in the fresh, brown earth with Ann. She longed to sit quietly with Teddy at the dining room table, both of them lost in thought over steaming cups of coffee.

Wanda looked out at the gravelled lot now and remembered the stories from Moira's and Ann's parents about Ellis Island. Was being deported the same as immigrating? She should ask Emma Goldman, now there was a woman who knew both sides of the tale. Surely it looked the same. Next to bus number four, an old man was being frisked by two tall Caucasian policemen while his family stood quietly by, waiting for 'permission' to enter the bus. Over by the entrance, she watched a camera crew filming departing groups. The government was recording its own crimes. This was madness. Well, what did she expect?

Moira and Teddy raced after Ann, across the gravelled lot. Teddy noticed with dismay that the gardenias were browning on the edges where she had touched them.

They reached bus number five and waved frantically to Wanda, whose face had turned to rock. Finally Howard noticed them, grinned and swivelled to his sister. Wanda looked out and smiled thinly.

'I told you we shouldn't have come,' panted Moira, the color rising up the right side of her neck. 'She's mad at us.'

'No.' Ann spoke heavily. 'She's mourning. It's good we're here.'

'Can you come down?' Teddy shouted.

Wanda looked closer, as if staring might catch edges of an echo. Truthfully, she had heard Teddy. 'Can you come down?' Did she mean would they let her, or did she have the spirit to leave the bus, knowing she would have to climb aboard again?

'Can-you-come-down?' Teddy repeated, shaping the words carefully so Wanda might lipread.

Wanda shook her head. She stared past them, trying to re-enter the numbness of a few moments before. Oh, why had they come? How had they found the place? Of course if they hadn't come she would never have forgiven them. But she could have dealt with that later. Now their presence forced her to open up, to see them, to hear the familiar voices, to feel all the loss and confusion and anger that she was trying to evade in order to survive in one piece.

The bus sputtered into ignition although one family was still loading suitcases. The old mother spoke rapidly in high-pitched Japanese to her two sons who were approaching with a bulging duffle bag, marked with the family number.

Ann waved to Wanda, her left hand in a wiping motion.

Moira blew kisses to Wanda, Howard and Betty. Mrs Nakatani

huddled in a shadow.

Suddenly all heads on the bus turned toward a tall figure in the aisle.

'It's Teddy,' shouted Moira, amused. 'Look, Ann.'

Inside the bus, an astonished driver caught sight of a blond head in his rearview mirror. 'Hey, hey, how'd you get on? *You* can't be in here.'

'I was helping Mama-san with her parcel,' drawled Teddy, nodding to the old woman who had been calling nervously in the yard. 'And I came to say good-bye to some friends.'

'We're leavin' any minute.' He raised his voice and stared at her firmly through the mirror. 'So you'd better make fast farewells or you're off with the rest of 'em.' He had an Oklahoma twang and Teddy noticed he looked like her brother Virgil around the eyes.

She turned to Mrs Nakatani and bowed. Then she pinned the gardenia on the woman's beige wool coat.

Wanda fought back tears as her mother nodded stiffly and said, 'Thank you, young lady.'

But Wanda could not stand and come so far as the aisle. Teddy reached over, squeezed Wanda's hand and gave her the other flower. Teddy sniffed, wiping her navy sweater sleeve across her eyes. 'Bye, Wanda. Will you write to us when you can?'

'Yes.' Wanda struggled to contain an affectionate smile. If she didn't contain it, who knew what would flood out. She would write about this in her diary tonight; then she would sort out the emotions.

'I mean it, lady,' barked the driver, opening and shutting the door several times as if flexing his muscles.

'Bye, then,' said Teddy. She winked at young Betty and rubbed Howard's shoulder, upset with herself for not bringing them presents, also. She strode down the aisle, too choked to look back at Wanda.

The bus moved the minute Teddy stepped down. So she didn't have a chance to join the others in shouting good-bye.

Wanda looked out to Ann and Moira, waving back slowly.

Then, as the bus passed Teddy, in spite of herself, she blew a kiss.

The three women stood in silence, watching the Greyhound haltingly follow another bus off the lot and then down Borden Street.

Ann and Moira turned toward the car. Teddy held back a moment, with an urge to wave to all the people on the remaining buses. Eventually she caught up with them.

'I know you'll say it's naive,' Moira was talking to Ann, 'but I can't swallow my fury about the unfairness, the bloody injustice! I mean what would Wanda or poor Mr Nakatani – of all people – have done to "threaten the national security"?'

Teddy found it odd to refer to Wanda's father as 'poor Mr Nakatani'. He seemed the toughest person she had ever met.

'Exist.' Ann answered in a voice that was colder than she intended because she admired Moira's indignation. She wanted to say more, but the headache had taken over now, with nausea as well as excruciating pain.

'You're not naive,' exclaimed Teddy. 'You're a good person.'

'That's the trouble,' Ann cut through. 'Goodness is worth nothing now. We're all so innocent. We're all good women.'

'This is the end of the house,' declared Moira. Tears streamed down her hot cheeks as she unlocked the right side of the Studebaker and walked around to the left. Once seated, she lost control, leaning her head on the steering wheel and sobbing. 'Poor Wanda. Poor Wanda.'

Ann rubbed her friend's shoulder.

'Everything is over for us, too,' cried Moira, 'the house, everything.'

Ann looked out at the decaying street and the faded sign over the old bottle factory across the alley. The sky was a milky grey – as if April shunned violated countries.

'No, it's not,' said Teddy angrily, rolling down the window for fresh air. She recalled holding on to Virgil's leg, years ago, to keep him from falling out of the truck somewhere in Arizona. She felt a sudden relief in her lungs as she whispered, 'Nothing's over.'

Chapter Two

●

Spring 1938, San Francisco

GERMANY MOBILIZES

●

FORTY HOUR WORK WEEK ESTABLISHED IN USA

●

CHOLERA EPIDEMIC RAGES IN INDIA

●

ITALY SENDS GOOD WILL MISSION TO JAPAN

●

JAPAN BOMBS CANTON

Moira walked the block three times before she looked up and found the shingle hanging from a second floor window: Tracey Business School. They weren't exactly grabbing customers. How did this bode for their promise of 'One Graduate/one job'? Moira was counting on Tracey Business School and today's entrance was not auspicious.

Green, should she have worn this green dress or something more sober, like the white blouse and black skirt? She wanted to start out right. Tracey Business School was a means to an end. It got her out of Los Angeles, away from her parents and the depression she had felt in the year since high school when she had sat at so many soda fountains waiting to be discovered by a movie producer that she had gained 10 pounds. Now a slimmer, more determined Moira was beginning a new life in San Francisco and she resolved to subordinate her temperament to the task at hand. 8.10. Did she have time to comb her hair? Well, in this game appearance was important.

Staring critically into the mirror, she saw large green eyes; a small, slightly too-pointed nose; a full, heart-shaped mouth, which when she smiled revealed straight teeth, unless you looked to the left and noticed the two that overlapped. The red hair was her greatest asset. She reached up her skirt and pulled down her satin slip. There, she stepped back, admiring the effect. Drool on, Tyrone Power.

8.15, she had better get a move on.

By the time she reached room 105, she could hear clattering typewriters. Calm down, Moira, this isn't Immaculate Conception High School. The old wooden door squeaked loudly. A few heads turned, but most of the girls concentrated on their typing. A skinny woman stood at the front of the class, tapping a pointer on her broad oak desk. Moira smiled at the teacher, who frowned and nodded to a seat at the back. Moira walked with as much poise as she could summon – Katharine Hepburn spurning Spencer Tracey – and sat down in a desk next to a pretty, olive-skinned girl.

The girl turned, smiled briefly, and, by the time Moira had the composure to smile back, the girl had returned to work.

The skinny teacher didn't seem to be paying any attention to Moira as she stood in front, tapping out the rhythm on her desk. She looked like an army sergeant. Shouldn't let the thinness fool her, she was probably total sinew under that ridiculous grey tweed suit. Why did she pull her hair back in such a tight bun that it made her look old? What was she really – fifty, fifty-five? Not a trace of make-up. No accessories, not even a brooch and didn't all old maids wear brooches? Enough Moira, you don't want to get scared away the first day. She looked around the room, which at first had seemed filled with blond actresses. No, Moira inhaled and counted again, there were only four or five blonds in the room – if you included that woman with the dirty blond colour. Moira wished she didn't fixate on fair women. She knew it was a silly obsession, but she couldn't help it.

The dirty blond girl was interesting. Tall and strong, you could tell even when she was sitting down. She had a nice face – hardly pretty, but gentle and easy. Not your average secretary. Moira wondered about her talent for making friends with outsiders.

'For those of you who were late.' The toothpick was speaking to the back wall, but Moira knew she was being personally addressed. 'We have been doing an initial exercise to test coordination and reflexes. Now we will spend 5 minutes having people introduce themselves.'

'Connie Bently.'

Moira missed the next couple of names because she was staring at the girl in the middle of the first row, a beautiful Oriental girl. Moira had never had a friend who wasn't white. Would this girl talk to her? She was quite stunning and Moira admired the neatness of her outfit – the simple, trim lines of her red suit. The color was terrific with her shiny black hair. What kind of shampoo did she use? Moira pulled a pencil from her handbag.

'Wanda Nakatani,' the Oriental girl said.

Moira wrote down the name, wondering if she spelled it right. She took a closer look at the blond women and none of them appeared to be movie material. Too thin or egghead. Then the one with the dirty blond hair spoke. Moira wrote down, 'Teddy Fielding'. Teddy, what an unusual name, and she talked with a drawl. Was she Southern? Moira had always been interested in the South, ever since *Gone With The Wind*. The neighboring girl touched Moira's shoulder, whispering, 'Your turn.'

'Moira Finlayson.' Moira raised her head.

'Ann Rose.' Her neighbor followed. Moira wondered if she were Jewish, with such black hair and dark skin. She seemed a very sympathetic person. Moira peeked at Ann's typing exercise and observed that she made it all the way down the page whereas a girl in front of them had only finished the first line. Yes, this one would be worth getting to know, too.

'Miriam Schwartz.' 'Penny Lentman.' 'Dorothy Buckley.' 'Amelia Freitas.' 'Eleanor Mirelli.' 'Eve Smithson.' 'Gloria Porter.' 'Julia Tripp.'

Moira sighed back in her chair. This would be an adventure. Lots of new girls. A strange, witchy teacher. And what could be so hard about a little typing? If she could sew and knit – not that she did either brilliantly – she could type.

'Very nice, very nice,' said Miss Fargo. 'Now let's try that exercise again. Insert the paper carefully . . .'

Moira watched Ann Rose put the sheet behind the black roller and twist a knob on the side of the typewriter. Nothing to that, she decided, managing to insert three sheets of paper crookedly. She missed the rest of Miss Fargo's instruction.

Ann whispered, 'Put your fingers like this and type "asdfghjkl;".'

Moira jotted down 'asdfghjkl;' under the names Wanda Nakatani, Teddy Fielding and Ann Rose.

'No talking, please,' Miss Fargo called. Ann simply concentrated on the typewriter. Moira resolved to follow Ann's reactions to Miss Fargo.

Moira remembered being petrified how to act in grade school until she found the secret: she picked the smartest girl and copied her behavior. Susie Fitzpatrick was not only teacher's pet, but most popular girl in school. Moira noticed that Susie never talked when Sister was watching but rather waited until Sister's back was turned or she had left the room for a moment. Then she noticed that Susie always did her homework right away. Susie didn't have to fret about the delays which imprisoned Moira every night about seven o'clock. On the playground Moira saw that Susie didn't go out of her way to make friends, but neither did she spurn anyone. She wasn't a snob. And she certainly didn't suffer from shyness. It never occurred to Moira why Susie knew things naturally and Moira, herself, had to learn them. She just practiced being Susie Fitzpatrick.

At Immaculate Conception High School Moira continued to observe her friends and to compete with them. Sometimes this got out of hand. She had stolen Maria Ramos's boyfriend and then realized that what made him attractive was that he was Maria's. Moira defeated Elizabeth Getz in spelling, not because she cared about the spelling bee – in fact since then she had forgotten all the hard words like 'Philippines' and 'vacuum' – but because Elizabeth considered the spelling trophy worth seeking. Was she envious of her friends? No, Moira was afraid it was crazier than that. She didn't know how to live. Outside the rivalry, she was paralyzed with fear or boredom. She continued to compete until she could act anyone's part. Finally, Sister Lawrence noticed Moira had a gift; she was a magnificent actress. This was something for herself alone. Of course all the girls used to talk about John Barrymore, but none of them were serious about acting. Susie wanted to be a nurse. Elizabeth was going to marry a millionaire. Maria wanted to work at Woolworths. So the acting was Moira's alone. And she was going to succeed.

'Break ladies,' Miss Fargo called. 'Five minutes break.'

'Hello, my name is Ann Rose.' The girl across the aisle smiled.

'Yes, I remember from the go-round. My name is Moira Finlayson.'

'Finlayson.' The darker woman smiled. 'That's Scottish, isn't it?'

'How did you know? Most people think it's Swedish or, oh, I don't know, Outer Mongolian.'

'Well, I make a habit of collecting unusual names. Your family's from Scotland?'

Moira glanced at her watch: three more minutes. She started to explain and found herself revealing more than she intended. 'My parents met at MacBrides, that's a department store in Glasgow. Dad worked in the stockroom and Mother was a salesgirl. Mother had these hopes of coming to America, where it would all be different.' Moira paused, checking Ann's face to discover she was following closely. 'They chose California because my Dad – funny I've never called him that out loud – had lung trouble. Turned out to be tuberculosis. He died a year after they got here. Three months after I was born.'

'Sounds tough,' Ann sighed, 'for everyone.'

'Yes, Mother had a hard time, but she didn't want to return to Glasgow a failure. She met Daddy, my step-father, and they settled in Los Angeles.' Moira heard her voice shaking and changed the tone. 'It's almost time to return to our fascinating work. How about lunch tomorrow? I mean I have an appointment today, but tomorrow?'

'Good.' Ann nodded solemnly. 'I'll look forward to that.'

'Asdfghjkl;' 'asdfghjkl;'. Ann liked Moira. She had learned that a lot of girls who wore make-up and frilly clothes simply used their femininity as protective covering. Moira was bright and ironic. Ann suspected she would need friends to get her through two years of Miss Fargo's lectures. Poor woman, what a caricature of the cold spinster. Yet she couldn't be more than forty-five. Must be difficult to teach office skills to a group of women twenty years younger, most of whom wanted to be someone very different from their stern, gaunt teacher. Ann imagined herself ten years from now visiting Miss Fargo with her diploma in classics.

Ann wouldn't have selected Moira out of a crowd. She looked Irish with that red hair and the freckles. Ann remembered Mama's stories about the Catholics in Europe, the worst anti-Semites. Why was she so conscious of race this morning? First day defensiveness. She couldn't help noticing that there was only one other Jewish girl, Miriam Schwartz. She looked around the class now. Well, what's-her-name Lentman could be Jewish, even with the blond hair and blue eyes and turned-up nose. Papa had warned her not to type people. 'Jews come in all sizes and colors,' he said, 'as do Gentiles. Besides we're in America now, where things like that don't matter.' Ann wondered often about her father's capacity for self-deception.

She sat straighter in front of the typewriter, aware of the strain at the base of her neck.

'And now the top row ladies, "qwertyuiop", "qwertyuiop", 'qwertyuiop'. Let me hear it evenly, tapping to a regular rhythm. Practice. Practice, it's all in the rhythm.'

Ann obeyed, 'qwertyuiop', 'qwertyuiop'. She had always been obedient. A loving daughter. A model student. She recalled how Mrs Bird punished the second grade class, making everyone sit with folded hands. Ann obeyed and half an hour later Mrs Bird exclaimed to the whole class what a good girl Ann was. Here she sat, after all this time, with her hands folded on her lap. Imagine, said Mrs Bird. Imagine, Ann did try, but it always seemed smart to follow directions. Occasionally Ann felt as if she were born middle-aged – ever responsible and even-tempered. No one would guess she had these terrorizing headaches. 'qwertyuiop', 'qwertyuiop'. She hoped for some sentences, at least words, by afternoon. 'qwertyuiop', 'qwertyuiop'.

Ann was supposed to be grateful Papa was subsidizing business school. In fact she was grateful for the extra money because – with her part-time salary – it allowed her to move to Turk Street. Her throat caught at the thought of Turk Street; she *had* to forget the incident. After all, she had not been harmed; she had screamed so loudly the intruder had fled. Still, it was hard to sleep at night, imagining the man creeping in the side window with the paper bag over his head. All she could remember for the police were those big white hands with the long, well-manicured nails. She would like to move from Turk Street, but not so long as the only alternative was back to her parents' flat.

Ann nodded encouragement to Moira. Funny how this connection had become so important to her in the space of an hour. Ann had dreamed all her life of a few deep friendships. She thought she had found this in Ilse Stein in the third grade and then again with

Carol Sommers in high school, but she had lost both of them.

What an exaggeration. She knew exactly where Ilse Stein was. Aunt Ruth had written last year to say she was playing concerts all over the East Coast. She had even sent an address. Of course Ann could get back in touch. They had corresponded for years after Ann's family left New York. They promised passionately to stay in touch. They were going to be room-mates at Barnard. They even talked about their majors and the color of their bedspreads.

Concentrate, how could an intelligent person concentrate on 'qwertyuiop'? Humility, Ann, humility.

Could you count on anything remaining stable? She mourned for Ilse, but she knew they would never recover the old trust. Look at Mama, who hung on to the past like a drowning woman clutching an anchor. Sometimes Ann frightened herself by looking in the mirror and seeing Mama's hazel eyes. She even had the same brown speckle in her left eye. Spots on the eyes, now what did that portend? Did she really believe in things being portended? No more and no less than she believed in prayers. From moment to moment you had to believe in something. Thinking about Mama always caught her in these conundrums. Mama, Mama. How had she changed from that big, warm woman who banished all her children's troubles to a heaving mass of sobs and, finally, of silence? Was it Papa's fault? Surely Mama could have said, 'No, David, we are not going to America' or at least 'We *will* teach the children Yiddish.' Instead she strained to create an all-American home for him, unable to contain the confusion and grief and rage. The Yiddish slipped out – first as she talked to herself cooking supper or hanging out the wash, then in small endearments. So Ann was Chanela or Hanna or Anna when Papa wasn't around. She picked up a lot of the language when Mama was conversing with her friends, before the friends stopped coming in person and Mama began to conjure them.

'That's it, ladies.' Miss Fargo's voice cracked above the clatter. 'Lunchtime. Let's rest those fingers a while.'

The cafeteria was a cold, damp room in the basement. Ann's stomach turned as she considered what might have been boiling for years in the huge tureens. She was disappointed Moira couldn't eat with her. She noticed that several tables were already filled with girls chatting and laughing. They all seemed quite stylish. She looked down at her straight green skirt and plain pumps. Perhaps she should dress up more tomorrow. But it would take more than a colorful dress to fit in. These girls had a carefree verve. Actually, they were probably just as nervous as she. That tall, skinny blond woman at the front of the line looked as if she might die of shyness. What about Miriam Schwartz? Ann wondered. She turned and saw her gossiping with the Lentman girl. Now, how did she know they were gossiping?

'Excuse me.' Ann had run her tray into the one in front of her. She looked up to see it belonged to the Oriental student. The girl smiled self-consciously.

Ann smiled back. 'You look familiar.'

Wanda blushed. 'Aren't you Ann Rose from Lowell High School?'

'Yes.' Ann looked at her quizzically.

'Wanda Nakatani. I was the year behind you. My brother Howard was in your class. And I heard you speak at his – rather your – graduation.'

'Oh, yes, I remember Howard. What's he doing?'

'Soup or sandwich?' demanded the woman behind the counter.

'Sandwich,' Ann replied cheerfully. 'Egg salad please.' She paid the cashier and said to Wanda, 'Shall we sit together?'

'Oh, yes, I'd like that.'

Ann thought how much Wanda resembled her brother. Why hadn't she recognized Wanda? Of course seniors didn't talk to juniors. Now she regarded Wanda as a long-lost sister. 'I remember, you were interested in journalism. And you wrote poetry, too.'

Wanda nodded. 'Still do. In fact I had quite a lot running through my head during those gruesome typing exercises. Got to do something to preserve your sanity.'

Anna gobbled the rest of her sandwich, surprised at her appetite.

Wanda could barely conceal her pleasure about eating with Ann Rose, the girl she used to admire from a distance. 'Is your father still at the factory?'

'Good memory. You'll make a great writer. Yes, but he got promoted to foreman last year. Mind if I smoke? Would you like one?'

'Go right ahead,' said Wanda, 'but no thanks.'

Ann watched the smoke rise. She noticed Wanda biting her fingernails. First days were tough on everyone. 'Who were your friends at Lowell?'

'Oh, you wouldn't have known them.' Wanda grew shyer, intensely aware of the differences – Ann a year older and the school brain – but she had resolved to be more forthright with people in this new course. 'Emmy Yamamoto and Sarah Murdoch.'

'I think I knew Sarah. Wasn't she in art studio?'

'Yes,' Wanda said. 'She knew your friend Carol Sommers. Whatever happened to Carol? I always thought she was going to New York to make it big.'

Ann inhaled sharply. Then she stubbed out her cigarette and looked at her watch. Hell. She thought everybody knew. She considered excusing herself to the lavatory and then caught the panic on Wanda's face. She breathed deeply; if she told this story often enough, she might start believing it.

'She did go to New York.' Ann could smell the anger in her sweat. 'And it was very hard for her.' She struggled to hold back the tears.

Wanda wished she hadn't asked.

'Too hard,' Ann blurted. 'They found her in a bathtub, with her wrists slit.'

'How tragic for you.' Wanda reached for her hand.

Ann looked up, startled. No one had really consoled *her* in the year since Carol's death. 'Such a waste.' 'So sad for her family.' 'If we had only known, we might have been able to help her.' But no one had acknowledged Ann's feelings. She was only a friend.

Wanda watched Ann carefully.

'Yes.' Ann's voice was steady.

'I remember how close you were.' Wanda forced a smile. 'I always envied your friendship. The two of you going to football games together. And didn't you have the same coats – dark brown with black collars?'

'Yes.' Ann smiled, herself. 'Yes, she was a good friend and I miss her.'

'I'm sorry.' Wanda pulled back her hand. 'And I'm sorry I brought it up.'

'No, no,' Ann began, 'it's fine. You didn't know. . . .'

A buzzer rang. The two looked at each other. 'Like being back at Lowell,' they said in unison and laughed.

'Except that we have the same teacher all day.' Wanda shook her head. 'What a Lulu.'

Upstairs, they parted for their desks. 'Lunch tomorrow?' Wanda asked boldly.

'It's a date if I can bring another girl, Moira.' Ann was cheerful. She had no good reason to refuse – only a nagging sadness about

Carol. Well, best to get her mind off that. They would talk about other things tomorrow. Ann had hardly asked about Wanda.

Wanda walked back to her desk grinning. She was in the same class with the famous Ann Rose. Howard would be pleased. And Mama would be very impressed. Perhaps this would stop her questions about whether Tracey was the right place. Wanda could hardly believe it. Throughout high school she had wanted to *be* Ann Rose: the beautiful, brilliant girl who didn't know she was the awe of teachers and students alike.

'Asdfghjkl;qwertyuiop'. What would Mrs Longnecker say when she found out her star writer was taking secretarial lessons? Of course journalists had to learn to type. Wanda felt another pang; how could she tell Mrs Longnecker she was still working at the cannery? She thought she would get a job on a newspaper any day. But one look at her Asian face and editors said, 'No, that position was filled yesterday . . . an hour ago . . . in the last five minutes.' Sometimes the rejection panicked her. Maybe she was crazy – there were few enough women and no other *Nisei* she knew – who became reporters on the mainstream papers. Sometimes the rebuff focused her. She would show them. She would go to college. Meanwhile, the first step was getting out of the cannery and a decent secretarial wage.

Wanda listened to Miss Fargo's slow, precise instructions which made her feel as if she were in the first grade. Had she been especially slow and simple with Wanda?

Relax, Wanda. Tonight you can tell Mama about your suspicions and Papa about the day's adventures. The difference between her parents' temperaments always amazed Wanda – Papa so optimistic and energetic about American possibility and Mama low key, resentful about the broken promises. Maybe it was because Papa, coming from a poor Yokohama family, was used to hardship, while Mama left her middle-class comforts out of love for Papa and hopes of starting a new life. Wanda considered how they had met in a small socialist circle in Japan and carried their ideals across the Pacific. Surely they would never breach their class difference in Yokahama. First in Seattle and now in San Francisco, they held to their beliefs about a workers' state and shared wealth, but they found few *Issei* following such politics. Thus they had made more white friends than many Japanese–American families. They lived inside and outside the *Nihonjin* community. The Nakatanis, Wanda shook her head, were always iconoclasts. Maybe the distinction between her parents was that Mama was more conscious of her children's sacrifices. She had no tolerance for bigotry, yet as a Japanese lady she hadn't built up adequate defenses. Papa saw himself as a pioneer and was prepared for hardship.

Wanda thought about the time Howard came home crying because he couldn't join the same Cub Scout troop as his Caucasian friends. Mama was so furious Howard feared *he* had done something wrong. 'What kind of democracy is this, Yas, where children are not equal?' Wanda still wondered if Mama would have been exercised about the Brownies. Well, the boy was most important, that was that.

'What would you have us do, Miné?' Papa addressed Mama in Japanese. 'Return to Japan before our dreams are realized?'

'*Our* dreams? You are welcome to them. Yes, sometimes I think it would be better to return to Yokohama. At least we would only suffer poverty – and not this mad bigotry.'

Papa shook his head again. 'Wait, Miné, you'll see. Our people will become great Americans – scientists, writers, doctors – our own son.'

Mama pursed her lips and returned to the kitchen. She was a dutiful, if sometimes irritated, wife who allowed Papa the last word.

Traditions, it was hard to follow which traditions they would keep. Wanda: her very name was atypical. Most of her *Nisei* friends had Japanese names or at least more sedate Anglo names. But Mama insisted on naming her daughter after a favorite English teacher in Japan. 'Wanda Nakatani' – sometimes Wanda thought there were too many 'a's' in the name, that it left her too exposed; sometimes she liked the name's distinctiveness, which camouflaged her own bashfulness.

Wanda marvelled at the way Mama – who thought religion was a wasteful, deluded indulgence – put flowers by her parents' photographs on the anniversary of their deaths. A few Buddhist practices were all right, Mama finally decided; at least she hadn't converted to Christianity like Uncle Fumio. And if English was spoken when Caucasian guests were present, Japanese was the main language between Mama and Papa. Wanda grew up speaking English with Howard and Betty and her friends and almost understanding her parents' Japanese. Her life, like her name, was half

Japanese and half American. Half not Japanese and half not American. She was an amphibian, her mobility versatile to compensate for the lack of belonging. All the legacies were contradictory. She inherited from her parents a deep idealism about achievement as well as a grave fear of failure.

Papa had not quite fulfilled the prediction about himself – not yet, he was always quick to say. While most *Issei* in California farmed or fished, Papa still loved lumbering. He loved the sharp scent of evergreen forests and the independent life and the possibilities of fortune. Not until he was forty did he join his brother Fumio at the fish cannery.

Wanda admired Mama. Where would the family be without her? While she wished Mama were softer, she was grateful Mama hadn't imprisoned her in origami and Buddhist practices and a marriage arranged by the *Baishakunin*. Mama had cleared a way for Wanda to have more freedom than she had. She insisted her daughter make a variety of friends. Sometimes Wanda felt as if she were standing on Mama's shoulders, as if each generation of women in her family were supposed to stretch further. Mama's contribution had been immigration to this strange country. Now Wanda was supposed to make an independent life. But if you led an independent life for your parents, you were not independent. At times Wanda envied cousin Keiko who, although she might feel suffocated by convention, was spared Wanda's own confusion.

"'As we, as we, as we . . . .'" You should have that down, ladies. Shall we try a longer word? Put your right index finger on the "h", now the fourth finger of that hand on the "o", now the pinky on the "p". That's it. Try "hop hop hop hop". Then put it together. "As we hop. As we hop. As we hop.'"

Wanda suppressed a smile. Really, if she thought this was embarrassing, how must stern Miss Fargo feel up there dictating to all of them? She didn't look like she had had a good hop in forty years.

She would record this in her diary tonight. Wanda found that as soon as she told her family stories, they lost flavor. The diary was Mrs Longnecker's greatest gift. Wanda had filled the fancy, engraved green book years ago. Now she was on her fourth volume, making sense of things in her own words – her crush on Martin Kogowa; her ideas about Roosevelt. In addition to testing out emotions and opinions, the diary was a good place to meditate.

When she was sitting alone in her room with a cup of tea writing, she seemed to leave her body. She lived on the page. Wanda was afraid to feel too good while she was writing, afraid that she didn't deserve the happiness. She told herself she wanted to be a writer because so many social issues needed to be addressed. This was true, but there was also the sheer satisfaction of writing.

Miss Fargo was just two girls behind her now. Wanda tried to relax. She would forget Miss Fargo's original coldness to her. Probably everyone found her too formal. 'As we hop. As we hop. As we hop.' She continued typing at the same, even pace. Miss Fargo stood over each girl and pointed out errors. But, Wanda noted proudly, many of them couldn't get the letters straight while she hadn't made a single error since the '*Aw* we hop.' on the first line. Maybe Miss Fargo would overlook that when she saw the rest of the sheet. 'As we hop. As we hop. As we hop.' Wanda continued. She could smell Miss Fargo's carbolic soap now. Of course she wouldn't wear perfume and she would need something strong to remove ink from her fingers. Maybe after class Wanda should inquire about the correct brand of soap. She grimaced at her own eagerness to impress.

'Miss Nakamani,' Miss Fargo stood over her.

Wanda looked up, absurdly wondering for a moment, whether it was correct military procedure to keep on typing and talk at the same time. Maybe she should type out her response?

'Your work is indeed very neat. And save for that unfortunate mistake on the very first line, you seem to be doing fine. However,' Miss Fargo bent lower, as if she were being confidential, 'I wouldn't wear such bright colors if I were you. They create a distraction in an office. I rather suspect you'll want to blend in as much as possible.'

Wanda's cheeks turned the color of her suit. Blend in? Would she say this to any of them or was she saying that, as an Oriental, Wanda should try to be inconspicuous? How should she respond? 'Yes, Mam'? 'Thank you'? Her fingers took over typing. 'As we hop. As we hop. As we hop.'

It was so ironic – she had started wearing red because it *did* make her stand out, because it countered her preternatural shyness. At the mirror this morning, she worried about how unJapanese she looked. Was it her? Well, she wasn't going to dress for the sake of cliché. Yet every time she wandered from the norm, she fretted the balance between stereotype and authenticity.

Miss Fargo criticized the next girl for several spacing errors. See, Wanda, she's critical of everyone. But she hadn't commented on anyone else's clothes. Wanda wanted to scream and cry at the same time. It made her angry to be angry like this. She really hated to believe that people disliked her for race reasons. Her first instinct was to give the benefit of the doubt. Then she was surrounded by an immobilizing depression, a cloud of similar memories. Now her fingers grew stiff; she was furious at this silly exercise. Angry at all the white girls in the room obediently typing, 'As we hop. As we hop. As we hop.' How could she go on? The diary. She would write about it in the diary. Yes. She would write about distraction. 'Blend in. Blend in.' Wanda regarded her sheet now. 'As we blend in, blend in, *bland* in.'

Wanda leaned against the streetlamp at the bus stop. Closing her eyes, she pretended to store all her worries in a high cupboard. If she still hated Tracey Business School by the end of the week, she could quit. She imagined shutting the door to the cupboard. She let a long breath run through her body.

'Hi.'

Wanda didn't want to be sociable. The voice was from a tall woman. Wanda tried to guess who it was.

'Say, aren't you from the business school?' the voice added quickly.

A slight drawl, were there any Southerners in the class? Wanda opened her eyes and registered a thin, blond woman wearing a faded flowered blouse and a blue skirt. She didn't remember her at all. Embarrassed by her reverie, she stood straighter and extended her hand. 'Yes, I'm Wanda Nakatani.'

'Pleased to meet you. I'm Teddy Fielding.'

Teddy's large hand was roughly textured. Wanda considered the woman's kind, open face. Any other time she would have been pleased to meet her. Could they postpone this until tomorrow?

Teddy, too, seemed embarrassed after the enthusiasm of her own initial greeting. 'I don't know, I don't have much to say, except I thought it would be good to talk to someone from class. I was too shy at lunchtime.'

Wanda smiled, here was someone more scared than she. 'Where are you from, Teddy?'

'Oh, Renfrew Street.'

'I meant, where are you from originally? I noticed your accent.'

'Oh, yeah, some time ago, seven years or so, my family came out from Oklahoma.' She held herself tighter.

'The Dustbowl?' Wanda asked, trying to temper her amazement. She had never met an Okie before.

'That's what they call it. That's what it was like – all the dust you could eat.'

Wanda laughed with her. She felt her resistance lift. 'I've read a lot of articles about people from the Dustbowl. I wonder how genuine they are?'

'I don't tend to read much. Once you've been through it, you don't want to read about it. I have some nice memories of the country between here and there, but the leaving was hard and the travelling was tough and I'd as soon read a good mystery story.'

'I guess you don't know Dorothea Lange either?'

'No, there were a lot of people who came out from Oklahoma. Thousands.'

'Five hundred thousand.' Wanda hated herself for correcting Teddy. 'And Dorothea Lange, she's a photographer, oh, well, forget it. . . .'

'Now hold on, I have seen some of her pictures, in magazines. Very dramatic.'

Wanda smiled gratefully. 'What did you think of Miss Fargo?' So much for the cupboard.

'She's an unpredictable one. Seemed nice enough at the beginning, calling us all girls and saying she would help us find jobs. But then she seemed unnecessarily strict and said hurtful things. Like,' Teddy blushed, 'well, I guess the reason I spoke up in the first place was that I wanted to say you looked snazzy in your red suit. I admired it when I walked in and I was surprised when Miss Fargo was mean about it. I think she did it out of ignorance.' Teddy swallowed hard.

'Ignorance?'

'Because you're Oriental. I think she's prejudiced. Hope this doesn't make you feel bad. Probably shoulda kept my mouth shut.'

'Not at all.' Wanda watched her closely. 'It makes me feel good. I thought the same thing. And I'm glad you liked the suit. I stayed up until 2 a.m. finishing it.'

'I figured you sewed it. Looks nicer than what you see in the stores. My Mom sews all our clothes too.'

'*All* your clothes? How many are there?'

'Ten kids including me. Of course she's not the only one who sews. Jolene learned and Amanda is taking lessons from Jolene.'

'What about you?'

'Me, no, I'm all thumbs around tiny things like stitches. That's why I'm surprised I could type. But then I'm OK at the piano too.' She shrugged.

Wanda laughed and noticed Teddy watching her closely. 'Are you the oldest?'

'No, two older brothers. But I'm the top girl. So it amounts to the same thing. And you? Your family?'

'I have an older brother and a younger sister.'

A bus approached and they both squinted after the number. Sixteen. Wanda and Teddy stepped back slightly and the bus rattled past them.

'Why are you at Tracey?' Wanda asked. 'What's your secret ambition?'

Teddy looked puzzled. 'Guess I just want to be a secretary. Always been keen on an office job. And you?'

'Some day I hope to be a writer,' Wanda answered, and tried again. 'What I meant was what do you imagine yourself doing in ten years – if there are no obstacles?'

'No obstacles.' Teddy smiled. 'Can't hardly imagine. Let me see, yes, I'd be working in a company, with lots of people around.'

Wanda tried not to look disappointed. She cringed at her own snobbishness.

'Say, do you guess the other girls in class will be as friendly as you?'

Wanda laughed. 'I hope they'll be friendlier.'

'I guess when we break through the ice everyone will be pretty easy. But, I wonder about Miss Fargo. It could be a cool spring in that room.'

Wanda smiled. 'I think we're going to be friends, Teddy. At least we worry about the same things.'

Teddy looked embarrassed and agreed. 'How about coffee before school tomorrow? That is if you like to get up early.'

'Yes,' nodded Wanda. 'I got here at 7.15 today.'

'I got here at 7.0,' grinned Teddy.

Wanda waved to the approaching bus. She boarded, got a

window seat and waved to Teddy.

Teddy waved back, smiling and wondering how long she would have to wait for another number sixteen.

Chapter Three

Spring 1939, San Francisco

SPANISH CIVIL WAR ENDS

The Grapes Of Wrath PUBLISHED

NYLON STOCKINGS APPEAR

'Now is the time for all. . . .' The words clapped steadily from Teddy's typewriter. She enjoyed this instrument as much as the piano, even with this familiar exercise Miss Fargo assigned to show how much progress had been made in one year. 'Now is the time for all. . . .' She sat tall in her chair and brushed the light brown curls from her high forehead. A vague discomfort settled as she recalled the player piano plonking on Market Street last night. Would typewriters ever do this? Just press a button and the words would tap honky-tonk or ragtime or swing? She hoped not because she liked the sensation in her long fingers and the rapid configuration of words against the page. Miss Fargo always praised her typing accuracy and neatness. The teacher encouraged her to speed up if she wanted a 'decent job'. 'You could get a plum,' the woman advised almost warmly. Teddy appreciated the encouragement although she didn't want to work for one of those fancy lawyers. She had more in mind a lively business or maybe a department store.

Still, Teddy worried whether she had made the right decision about typing school, when she could be earning a wage for the family now. She would have passed up the church scholarship if Mom hadn't insisted she take it. Pop said Teddy was crazy spending even more time behind a desk. When Pop got work on the docks, he was fine. But when he was laid off, he missed Oklahoma powerfully. He would curse his decision to come to Northern California where his old army buddy promised him shore work. He should have tried to farm in the Valley like so many of their friends. When Pop was laid off, it was always the same pattern; he'd say he was going to put extra time into fixing up the house and then he'd get sloshed. He would shout at the top of his lungs or grow sullen as an angry boulder. He would eat into Mom's nerves and into her savings in the broken green coffee pot. How would they have made it without the unsteady wages from her brothers' construction work? Several times this year, she had offered to quit Tracey and go back to housekeeping full-time, but Mom insisted one of her children was going to make it.

Teddy surveyed the fourteen straight-backed women playing different tunes to those identical lyrics. She held an easy fondness for each of them, from Gloria, who was as sweet and formless as a melting Hershey bar, to stern Miss Fargo. She checked on Moira, Wanda and Ann – feeling content about life in their North Beach house. Had they known each other a whole year? Yes, it was last spring when they met here. Such a year: making friends closer than she ever expected. Imagining a truly free life for herself. Watching her own family grow larger with Hank's wife and baby moving into the Fielding house. Sun washed through the side window now, drenching the front desks in a pool of yellow light. The rain had ended. Teddy sat straighter, forward from the damp sweater hanging on the back of her chair. At least it would be a dry walk home tonight. Maybe they could stop at Clooney's to toast spring.

'Now is the *tame*' Damn. Where is that eraser? Easy, Moira, don't press too hard. Remember the hole in the last page. That's it, light, brisk strokes. What did old Fargod say, oh, yes, 'As if you were whipping a soufflé.' What would she know about soufflés? She looks like she subsists on raw hamburger. OK, you've got it. Paper just a mite thinner than before, but if you don't make another mistake on this line, 'for all good' that's it, sweetie, keep going. Ten more minutes until break. Unbelievable. Ten more minutes of nonsense. They knew far more complicated exercises, but Miss Fargo made them practice this sentence once a week the way Sister Gregory used to make them repeat the commandments. Moira blew a strand of hair off her nose. She needed to keep things in perspective, to remember why she was here. Women were rising fast now. And if she didn't want to be Amelia Earhart, she wasn't going to be grounded by outdated expectations. Attitude, Moira remembered how Mother always said her attitude was wrong. Why Teddy was probably listening for minor chords and Ann would be figuring acrostics just to keep up her spirits. It was fun to share the misery of school with them at home each night.

Yes, the Stockton Street house did feel like home and it was much more convenient than commuting from Aunt Evie's place in Oakland. She would miss Aunt Evie, the most loquacious of Mother's fifteen sisters and brothers. Indeed, she had learned a lot about Mother staying with Aunt Evie, a lot of secrets. For instance, Grandma hadn't died in childbirth as Mother always told her, but rather of an abortion on the kitchen table of their Glasgow flat. While Mother had no idea just what Evie had revealed, but she sounded uncommonly relieved when Moira said she was moving in with a group of girls. 'Better to be with people your own age,' Mother had said.

Now, what could she do with this boring exercise? 'Country their of aid the to com. . . .' No, show a little imagination. Look at Wanda, fascinated by the clock – probably figuring out the internal mechanism while typing four sheets to my one. At this rate, I'll never get hired by MGM. I'll be an ancient crone before they discover me falling off the soda fountain stool. 'One more dose of Geritol, please, with hot fudge and almonds.' Uh, oh, there's Miss Fargo's buzzard eye. Back to work, Moira.

Wanda tried to extricate the ticking clock from her brain. She tried to ignore the way it syncopated against, 'All good men come to the aid of. . . .' The rote exercise was lined with potholes of tedium. Well, it was a little better than, 'qwertyuiop qwertyuiop qwertyuiop.' She smiled, remembering the first day of class last year. 'Now is the time for all good men to come to the aid of. . . .' Clip. Clip. Clip. Like shears against a hedge. Fastest in the class, Wanda grew weary of surpassing her own speed. Besides, Miss Fargo still found something wrong; she had inserted the paper a fraction of a second too early or the margin was one space off. When she became a journalist, she would report on racial prejudice, not only against Orientals, but against Negroes in the South. Meanwhile, she would write in her diary every night and find an office job to take her through college. Mama and Papa would be proud, once they stopped being mad.

She knew they would be upset about the house with the three *Hakujin*. They were mad enough last fall when she moved in with the Murakamis to make a little more money helping with the new twins. But Mrs Murakami didn't need her any more and living at Stockton Street was a logical choice. The rent was cheap and the house was close to school. She could study there with the others. It was safe. It was fun. And she deserved a little of that before she got married. '*Hakujin*,' Mama warned, but her voice was tinged with curiosity. Wanda understood she had been raised to be independent only within the limitations of her mother's imagination. Wanda treated Mama with a deference Teddy, Moira and Ann didn't have for their mothers. Still, in her generation, people mixed more. She had to admit feeling conspicuous as the 'Oriental girl' on the block.

Wanda sought out the impassive clock. She stared at the black minute hand and the red second hand revolving over the creamy face. She knew the typing exercise backwards, so she looked for the brand name, to see if she could read from this distance as well as from the front row. 'General Electric' was clear enough, but she could not make out the bottom word, the city of origin. 3.40 – five more minutes until coffee break.

'Now is the time' Ann tapped easily. It wasn't bad once you found a rhythm. You could think about anything you liked. She recalled the Latin from her library book. How did they conjugate *dono*? Perhaps she could work as a secretary at a university and sneak into courses on lunch hour. Papa would see his 'dark beauty' had a mind and a grave determination.

Meanwhile, she typed, 'for all good women'. Well, why not? Just see if Miss Fargo noticed, if Papa noticed. What was the point of coming to America if half your children didn't get a chance? Of course nothing was too good for her brother. When Daniel was granted partial scholarships at Stanford and San Francisco State, Papa decided, 'Stanford. We can afford it, if you work and I give something each month. We can make it.'

Family! Ann clenched her teeth. But of course there were plenty of happy memories, in New York and here. She remembered making a snowman in Washington Square with Mama and Daniel.

She remembered Papa showing them the giant dinosaur bones at the Museum of Natural History. She remembered those early, good Sabbaths at Synagogue, enveloped by the rich, sticky Hebrew words, cozy among her parents and their friends. Also the first sunny days in California were quite splendid.

Across the room, Ann caught a glimpse of Miss Fargo. Now there was a self-sufficient woman. Ann had warmed to her during the last twelve months, imagining what it must be like for a woman of that generation to have a career, to be a 'miss' at her age. Ann had no intention of letting her work obstruct her family. But she knew enough to get educated first. She had talked about it with the other girls.

Living with the others had been good for her. In the endless conversations with Teddy, Wanda and Moira, they all agreed you had to take from life when you were young. But the paradox was lurking. Despite their high expectations, they had each been raised by war women, whose memories and premonitions were shaped by rations of sugar and coffee and hope.

The buzzer sounded. Miss Fargo called on the same pitch, 'Break ladies.' Chairs screeched across the floor. 'Twenty minute break.'

Moira followed her three friends into the lounge. 'Old witch.' She tugged a curl, wishing her hair would grow faster. 'I'm sure she's going to flunk me.' She looked around the small table. Teddy was deep into an apple. Wanda sipped black tea with her eyes closed. Ann concentrated on her coffee. All of them represented Tracey Business School far better than she. How long could she stick it out? Would Miss Fargo pay her to quit so she wouldn't tarnish the school's reputation?

'They can't flunk you.' Ann was mildly exasperated. 'As Miss Fargo says, "It's just a question of finding the right spot for each girl."' She lit a cigarette and chuckled.

Wanda laughed with her.

Teddy added earnestly, 'True, Moi. I'm the typist; Wanda's the bookkeeper; Ann's the office manager. Don't you remember those aptitude tests?'

'But I've got no aptitude.' She pulled out a stick of gum and inched away from Ann's smoke.

'Sure you do, hon,' Teddy answered. 'What was it Miss Fargo said about you being a receptionist or something?'

'Receptionist! That's like being kicked out of choir for singing offkey and invited to collate the song sheets. Don't laugh; it happened to me in the seventh grade and it was humiliating. Being a receptionist isn't a real job; it's like being a mascot.'

Wanda raised her eyebrows at Ann. Ann stirred another sugar into her coffee. Wanda marvelled at Moira's capacity for self drama. Still, she enjoyed her quick wit.

'You're just too negative,' persisted Teddy. 'They need lively people like you in an office. Sharp, outgoing. . . .' Frankly, Teddy still thought business college was a peculiar way for Moira to break into movies.

The tea lady interrupted with a tray of gooey cakes. 'Sweets to make you that way.' Her sturdy hands claimed her hips as she shook her head in mock irritation at Teddy's apple and Ann's pack of Camels. Clearly Moira and Wanda were the only prospective customers at this table. All sophistication disintegrated as they selected their jelly donuts.

They were each attractive women, thought Moira, alike and different, with their hair held off their faces in various permanent waves. Wanda always looked the brightest and neatest. Today in her purple sweater and cultured pearls, she could have passed for a university coed. She knew all the styles from her cousin Keiko who attended Berkeley. Moira envied her friend's small, compact figure in comparison to her own loose, blowsy look. Perhaps the voluptuousness had a certain cinematic potential, but she admired Wanda's containment and felt that in comparison she was coming apart at the seams. Ann, on the other hand, usually dressed as if she had a secret, in dark greens and browns and the occasional tweed. At first Moira thought Ann ignored clothes but she was expressing herself, too, in a way Moira hadn't quite deciphered. Teddy, almost unconscious of fashion, wore the same navy sweater every day over a series of faded blouses handed down from her mother. She was used to being inconspicuous in a group. The shared house had been her brainchild.

Ann slowly exhaled smoke. Watching the ring reach her forehead, she said, 'So it's settled, the housewarming party? Friday the 11th? We get to invite five people each.'

Teddy wondered if Moira had ever noticed how Ann's deep, throaty voice was like Greta Garbo's.

'No, six people don't you think?' asked Wanda. 'Three guys and three girls. We don't want spare people mooning against the wall.'

'God knows, they might leave stains.' Ann massaged the back of her neck.

'But,' Moira burst in, 'if we invite an even number, then *we*'ll be spare.' She studied her fingernails, then licked powdered sugar from her donut.

'Good point.' Wanda tapped Moira's hand with her teaspoon.

Ann wondered whether Herb Cohen would come. She thought how Herb and her other friends from Synagogue who had formed the Forum discussion group were important to her. Herb brought dreadful tales each week about what they were doing to Jews in Germany. Papa, of course, would not believe it. He insisted that the problems in Germany were economic, not racial. He had got out. Anyone could come to America. Ann hadn't wanted to press him because she was getting one of her headaches; because she didn't want to give too many details about Herb Cohen and because the discussion had started to bother Mama. She took a puff and returned to the women's conversation. 'Moira's got her partner for the party all picked out, don'tcha?'

Moira's freckles receded in a bright blush. She continued licking the donut.

'You mean that mechanic down on Washington who whistles when we walk by?' Wanda asked disingenuously.

'When Moira walks by.' Teddy joined the banter reluctantly. She didn't know why, but this party made her jittery. Wasn't it enough that the four of them had each other? Why did they have to invite strangers to the house?

'Randy Girard,' nodded Wanda.

'Och,' exclaimed Moira, who carried some of her parents' Scottish brogue when she got flustered. She took a large bite of the donut and noticed too late that the purple jelly had shot out the end, staining the bow of her white blouse. 'Oh, damn.'

'What does it matter?' put in Teddy. She wanted to deflect attention from Moira's embarrassment, but her tense voice revealed more. 'Let's say five or six and make it a surprise party.'

Ann threw up her hands. Wanda wondered if Howard would bring his friend Roy Watanabe. The buzzer sounded. Moira yawned, and, remembering now that the bow was removable, she unbuttoned it from the back of her neck. 'Sure pal. Whatever you say.'

Miss Fargo stood at the classroom door, her arms across her chest.

Ann seated herself, swallowed and stared ahead. She tried to concentrate: *Dono. Donas.* The thought of university filled her with a still well-being. She would get through the afternoon fine. Breathing deeply, she savored the scent of smoke left in her nostrils.

As Teddy sat down, she noticed with disappointment that the sweater on the back of her chair was still damp from the morning rain.

•

Chapter Four

Spring 1939, San Francisco

ITALIANS INVADE ALBANIA

•

GERMANS CLAIM DANZIG

•

PAN AM BEGINS 'THE DIXIE CLIPPER' TO EUROPE

Randy Girard was late, Wanda noticed with relief and concern. She found Moira's friend a little loud, yet she knew if he didn't appear Moira would feel miserable. The party wasn't going the way she had expected. No one had arrived until an hour ago. Wanda stood at the door between the kitchen and the dining room watching young women and men mill around the food and inspect pictures on the wall, with the kind of nervous intensity people exhibit on Saturday night when they're wondering if they came to the wrong party. Wanda was dismayed that most of her *sushi* remained untouched on the serving dish. Perhaps she should have prepared something less exotic. However, Ann's potato salad and Moira's shortbread and Teddy's spare ribs and the rest of the menu were all waiting too.

Wanda caught sight of Moira opening the front door to her own brother Howard and his new friend Roy Watanabe. Roy was as handsome as Howard promised, tall and solid, with a wide, open face. Howard had told her so much about Roy that she was sure he would be a disappointment, but she was wrong. Had Howard given Roy as many details about her? Well, Howard's matchmaking had never worked before. Most of his friends were, like him, content with their jobs at the cannery and they found her a little ambitious.

Greeting the young men with firm handshakes, Moira tried to hide her disappointment at yet more guests who were not Randy Girard. She twirled around, displaying the full drama of Wanda's red jacket which she had borrowed to accent her svelte black dress. She had the two men joking and laughing as she eased them over to the drinks table.

Wanda joined them, offering glasses. Teddy was right, Moira had a talent for people. Wanda observed Roy more closely. Cute, a little tall, but very sweet. Moira stationed herself at the left of the table to keep watch on the front door.

Ann showed her friend Rachel their bedrooms on the second floor. 'This is mine.' She stood back self-consciously as Rachel looked around. 'I particularly like the morning sun. Sometimes I just sit up here with a cup of coffee before anyone else is awake. It's a good time to read or study.'

'Leave it to Ann, the purposeful employment of each moment.' Rachel smiled, backing out of the room. 'Some people just daydream in the mornings and in the afternoons for that matter.'

'You have to admit I've improved since high school. I used to read while I was walking to class.'

Rachel nodded tolerantly.

Ann smiled, thinking how she enjoyed her friendship with Rachel which had deepened over the years as they grew active in the Forum. They shared so many experiences and attitudes and the same ironic sense of humor. They were family in a way she could never be with her housemates. Was it the common values she appreciated the most? No, it was the humor.

'Are you sure you don't remember Wanda from Lowell?' Ann asked, opening a door.

'No.' Rachel shook her head. 'Is this her room?'

'Yes, how did you know?'

'It's so pretty – neat and colorful – like her. She's the only one of you to have framed pictures on the wall. And look at that quilt, I bet she made it herself, right? She has that kind of eye for detail.'

'Like you, my dear.' Ann closed the door and opened the next one. 'So tell me whose room this is?'

Rachel observed the clothes piled on a chair; shoes scattered on the floor; papers and bills spilling over the table. 'A Hurricane Moira if I ever saw one.'

'Right.' Ann laughed, noticing an edge of satisfaction. She was annoyed by Moira's sloppiness as much as she was charmed by her spontaneity. She probably also envied Moira's lack of inhibition. 'And this,' she opened the door to the room overlooking the small garden, 'is obviously Teddy's room.'

'Obviously,' Rachel nodded, 'with the spare, almost ascetic look. But what is that hideous picture in the corner?'

'Something her sister Patsy painted in school.' Ann smiled fondly.

'Anyway, the room's perfect for someone so indifferent to feminine things.'

'What do you mean?' Ann asked tentatively, her mind now switched downstairs, to the *kugel* in the oven. 'Say, come back to the kitchen with me.'

'Well,' Rachel whispered as they walked. 'She's kind of boyish the way she stands and with that straggling hair.'

Ann frowned, held the swinging kitchen door for Rachel and concentrated on her search for the sugar. Teddy wasn't boyish, just gangly. Women developed in different stages. Oh, why was she so tense? Just jitters about the party. Concentrate, Ann, sugar, where is the sugar?

'I envy you this house.' Rachel leaned against the icebox. 'It's a shame that most girls shuttle from their parents' home to their husband's without having a place of their own.'

'Teddy found the house, you know.' Ann sprinkled sugar on the crusty noodles and paused to enjoy the aroma. 'She still does cleaning for the family next door, who own the place. When it came up for rent, they wanted quiet people. Mr Minelli has a heart ailment. Also, they lost their daughter a while ago and liked the notion of four young women neighbors. *Mitzvah* all around.' She loved using Yiddish with Rachel. Usually the only time she could use these words was when she was alone with Mama. Sometimes they came in dreams.

'Sounds suspiciously communistic,' Rachel laughed, adding, in gruff imitation of Mr Rose, 'Pretty soon you'll be sharing boyfriends and eating out of a common dish.'

'Hardly,' Ann smiled, once again comforted by Rachel's familiarity – her teasing, her wonderful Jewish expressiveness. She never felt tongue-tied with Rachel as she sometimes did with Wanda. Well, their cultures were different. That was part of the adventure. 'Look at that table in there . . . all rather uncommon dishes prepared by uncommon dishes. Oh, well. . . .'

'Yes,' Rachel humored her friend. She glanced into the living room and noticed Teddy chatting in the corner with two dark women.

'We have a lot in common. We're all either the oldest girl or the only girl in the family,' Teddy was telling the Bertoli sisters. Sometimes it was hard to explain what had drawn them together, why they had decided to share a house. Angela and Rosa still lived above the family grocery on the corner. Teddy noticed with gratification that they both looked more comfortable now, halfway through their glasses of wine. Wanda had been skeptical about inviting them, about whether they would 'fit in', and was also smarting from their father's last crack about 'Chinks stealing the flower business from the Italians.' But Teddy knew the daughters were more neighborly than Mr Bertoli. Angela had offered to help carry some of the boxes and had stopped Teddy on the street once or twice to chat. She had a casualness that reminded Teddy of people back home in Oklahoma. Most Californians were too polite to drop in. It was natural to invite the Bertoli sisters. Besides, she didn't know any other friends who were suitable for the party.

'But all of you in one house, how do you stand it?' asked Angela, the older sister.

'Only four.' Teddy laughed easily. Angela was a big woman for whom space seemed an important consideration. 'How many do *you* live with?'

'Six brothers,' Rosa began, 'two sisters, Mama, Papa. See Angela, four isn't so many.'

When Angela flushed like this, Teddy noticed her brown eyes darkened. They invited curiosity and returned it. Teddy was filled with a sudden tranquility as she looked around the room at her friends and her friends' friends. She sank back into the old armchair Ann's father had loaned them. This corner was her favorite spot in the house. From here she could see into the dining room and kitchen and even upstairs to the second floor landing. Sometimes late at night, she liked to fix herself cocoa and sit in this frumpy chair, looking around.

'You come from a big family?' Angela asked.

'Yes,' nodded Teddy, wondering how long she had dropped out of the conversation. She reached over and patted Angela's hand and then looked steadily at Rosa. 'I'm used to noise. And company. I would be here except my older brother Hank got married and brought his bride home. They took over Jolene's and my room. Now Jolene's in with the other girls and there wasn't anywhere for me besides the tool shed. The folks didn't want me to go, we could have fixed something, but this house came up. Cleaning for the Minellis pays my share of the rent.'

'A suffragist.' Angela, recovered from her embarrassment, was eager to volley.

'Pardon?' Teddy took a gulp of wine, confused as she often was, when people changed the level of conversation to irony.

'For women's rights. A militant who believes women should live and work independently.'

Teddy noticed Angela said 'women' as if she spoke of an inferior species, which was strange since Angela was pretty self-confident, taking a job at the ceramic factory against her father's objections.

'Sure, why not?' Teddy answered finally. She didn't know these girls well enough to say she didn't ever plan to get married.

Teddy turned at a knock on the front door. Noticing that Moira had abandoned her post by the wine table, she excused herself from Angela and Rosa. Briskly walking to the door, Teddy hoped, for Moira's sake, that this was Randy Girard. But she also hoped that he had been run over by a large truck.

A persistent ringing of the bell followed the knock. Moira glanced up from her sherry, which she found more fortifying than wine. She checked the heavy wooden mantel clock Wanda's parents had presented as a housewarming present. 10.45, bloody late. Had he tried another party first? She paused, holding her breath, setting down the sherry glass and realizing how disappointed she would be if the caller were Ann's friend Herb or her brother Daniel or Wanda's cousin Keiko. There were only four guests who hadn't appeared. Moira thought that although she might not meet Miss Fargo's bookkeeping standards, she could calculate what was important to her – like any true Scot. Why was Teddy taking such a long time to reach the door, to open it. The ease in that girl would drive her crazy. The whole evening was playing in slow motion. As the door cracked, Moira strained to see, yes, blond curly hair; it must be him. She swivelled toward the bathroom, to wash her face.

The worst thing would be to give the impression that she had been waiting all evening for him. And of course, she hadn't. She had been enjoying her friends and, oh Christ, she hoped no one was in the bathroom because she was going to throw up.

Ann and Rachel were drawn into the front room by the sound of Benny Goodman's clarinet wowowowowing from their borrowed victrola. Wanda was swinging with Roy. Howard Nakatani had invited Rosa Bertoli. And there was Teddy dancing rather half-heartedly with Randy Girard. It was a new record.

Ann considered their second-hand furniture – the shabby elephant of a couch, the scarred mahogany table that Wanda had painted black, the ancient floor lamp which jiggled on and off to the Goodman beat, the thinning Persian rug which someone – must have been Teddy, who else would have thought to – had rolled against the fireplace. Surveying the room, Ann was alternately distracted by the dancers' electric sexuality and by the restful sensation that this was her home. For so many years the Roses had looked for home. First in the New York apartment and then in the one here in San Francisco where she and Daniel did most of their growing up. Their father was determined to make the homes American. Non-Jewish. Non-German. All the old things had been left behind. He had bought so many new American gadgets that they lived on the edge of poverty. Mama complained the soup was never right. She suspected the pans. She needed kitchen things from home. Papa would contradict. 'It is better in America [everything: the life, the soup], you just haven't learned the way yet.' And gradually Mama came to believe him. She tried and failed to learn the way, the language, the recipe, even the religion when he started to attend Episcopalian services. Just as gradually – or it was unconscious, no one was to blame – he transferred all his faith to the children. It would be different, better for them. Thus Ann had grown up among the furniture and books and music that frightened her mother, American artifacts upon which they were meant to build their family. How much better it would have been if they had had comfortable scraps like these here. Instead, their home was created with new American mines laid dangerously along the life of a woman who for years could speak only Yiddish before she stopped speaking completely. After all, Ann thought now, a couch, like this old elephant here, was to be sat upon, not exhibited. She sank down on the cushion next to Rachel, once more caught by the physical vitality of the dancers, particularly of Wanda and Roy.

Although Moira had brushed her hair in the bathroom, she was still twisting at a side curl as she walked toward the music. She moved as calmly as she could, her eyes everywhere but the dance floor. Who besides Randy would have brought such a new record? She had heard it once, on the radio this week. Randy was always up on the newest, from white-walled tires to Clark Gable wisecracks. What would he be wearing tonight? She could just imagine him in those new wide khaki slacks and the heliotrope shirt, leaning impatiently on the side of the couch jingling his coins. Well, let him wait. She spread some of Ann's cream cheese on a cracker. She hoped the chives would check the sourness in her mouth.

'Hey, Moi, come on and dance,' called Stephen, a husky long-shoreman who lived down the block.

She looked up, tickled at the thought and had almost joined him on the dance floor when she noticed Randy and Teddy. No, she hadn't 'noticed' them. More precisely Randy had noticed her and pulled her in with those green, green eyes. Sea green, she had decided this afternoon. Now they gleamed satanic green. Was she jealous? Jealous of Teddy for heaven's sake? Just look at the girl – nervous as a chicken skating on the Great Salt Lake. Look at Randy basking in his own self-confidence. Well, her silly feelings might be tender, but her head was tough and she knew the quickest way to lose Randy Girard was to mope. She smiled cheerfully, patted Teddy on the elbow and danced with her best Isadora Duncan abandon. Moira didn't know if she had had too much wine or too little as she swung with Stephen. As hard as she tried, she couldn't get into the mood. She had never liked this living room. She much preferred to sit in the kitchen with the others, cosy around the little table. The living room was at once too large and too confining. Now, she shook her head and tried to concentrate on Stephen's rugged jaw. Randy was putting on a new record, 'Jeepers Creepers'. Did he remember it was one of her favorites?

After an hour, the music grew slower and almost everyone rested on the sidelines. Randy and Teddy had given up several records before. Moira didn't want to encourage Stephen with too much cheek-to-cheek dancing, so she suggested they join the others in conversation. Looking around for a chair, Moira noticed that the only place was next to Randy on the love seat. What the hell, she sank down beside him. He smiled and returned to the argument among Ann, Rachel and Teddy.

Teddy was incredulous. 'But surely the Europeans won't let Hitler continue. He's only one man.' Why had she got into this discussion? She hated how war talk was everywhere nowadays – the radio, the newspapers, the bus. She sighed, remembering how many times she tried to get Pop to talk about something else over dinner. But this was taking over people's minds.

'He's driven,' Ann said, her neck aching. Should she get up and take an aspirin now? Yes, but she could not move. 'Hitler's not an ordinary man.' She wanted to tell them Herb's stories from the Forum, but they wouldn't believe her any more than Papa had.

'You just accept his propaganda if you take a defeatist attitude like that,' Teddy said, surprised by the conviction in her voice. Somtimes she believed they could stop the war with words.

Ann's headache was unequivocal now. 'His anti-Semitism?' she spluttered.

'Not that – I mean you couldn't accept that. You're a Jew. I mean, you're Jewish.' Teddy flushed. She had meant to talk with Ann about that. Mom said the term was 'Jewess', but she could no more say that than 'Negress'.

'There are anti-Semitic Jews,' Rachel said bluntly, 'but Ann's not one of them.'

'But, but,' Teddy twisted in her seat. 'I didn't mean . . . I didn't think. . . .'

Of course not,' Ann interrupted. 'No one does *think*. That's the problem. The "silly little hun" whom the newspapers joke about has power. The power of hate and lunacy. He'll march through half the continent before they stop laughing loud enough to see what's happening.'

Moira was alarmed by Ann's fear and anger. She wanted to do something to help, but nothing short of stopping Hitler counted. Everyone was talking like this lately. Was it selfish to want a rest on Saturday night?

'Roosevelt will save the day,' Moira interrupted, noticing the pitch of her voice rise as she lost their attention. 'Say,' she tried a different tone, 'did you hear the one about Eleanor and the rhinoceros?'

Wanda shook her head; she hated these cracks about Eleanor

Roosevelt's looks. From women too! She'd like to interview Mrs Roosevelt some day. She had been thinking a lot about writing tonight, because of the Willa Cather novels she had borrowed from the library. The author had started out as a journalist. She felt steadier and sipped her wine. 'You think there'll be a war here?'

Ann leaned forward. Before she could reply, Randy spoke. 'Sure. We've got so many damned treaties in Europe that the minute the next Lithuanian sneezes, we'll send 1,000 battleships across the Atlantic.'

'Or the Pacific,' said Howard.

'Because of China?' asked Randy. 'Nah, the Americans don't care about the Orient. Nothing personal, you understand.'

'How could we take it personally?' asked Wanda, avoiding her brother's critical glance. She thought she noticed a fleeting grin from Roy Watanabe. She wanted to tell everyone that Grandfather Nakatani opposed the Japanese invasion, but what did these people know of Manchuria? Fu Manchu probably. Someday she would go to the Orient and make that part of the world comprehensible to Westerners. She used to dream of her family returning to Japan for a holiday, as Emmy Yamamoto did. Now, she doubted they could afford it. But she would get an assignment. She would go alone.

'I only mean,' Randy stammered, 'that, that we're more likely to worry about Europe because that's where our people, Americans, oh, shoot, I get your point, Wanda. I'm sorry.'

Moira winced. How could they change this dreadful topic?

Wanda shrugged. 'You're right, of course, about the general bias.' At least he had apologized and Moira was fading by the second.

'Has anyone seen *Dawn Patrol*?' asked Moira.

Ann's jaw dropped, then she picked up the cue. People were too tired or too drunk or too angry or too scared. She was all four. 'The one with David Niven, Basil Rathbone and. . . .'

Moira laughed. 'How could you forget Errol Flynn?'

'Indeed.' Ann took a long drag on her cigarette.

'*Tail Spin* was the one I liked,' said Teddy, 'with Alice Faye, Constance Bennett and Nancy Kelly.'

Wanda turned to Roy. 'Teddy wants to be an aviatrix, like Jacqueline Cochran. She practically flew the entire Bendix Transcontinental Race with her last fall.'

'Not true.' Teddy glanced inadvertently at Angela who was

closely following the conversation. 'I just read the newspapers.'

'You practically ate the newspapers,' teased Moira. 'You couldn't breathe during the entire race.'

'Speaking of racing,' nodded Rachel, 'I'd better get home.'

'Honey!' exclaimed Moira, 'the party's just begun. I'm sure Randy has more records.'

Before she finished the sentence, Glenn Miller was swinging. Moira dragged everyone into a large circle on the dance floor.

Chapter Five

●

Spring 1941, San Francisco

GERMANS INVADE YUGOSLAVIA

●

JAPAN GETS HAIPHONG PORT PRIVILEGES FROM FRANCE

●

ITALIANS SURRENDER IN ETHIOPIA

●

VIET MINH CREATED BY HO CHI MINH

●

US SUPREME COURT BARS RACIAL DISCRIMINATION IN TRAIN ACCOMMODATION

'Smoke, smoke, smoke, god damn it, Ann, you're a regular loco-motive,' coughed Moira, waving away the cigarette trail. She pulled a dust rag from her old blue housecoat. 'Sometimes I wonder why I bother to clean the living room; it only ends up smelling like a Southern Pacific tunnel.'

Wanda sat on the couch reading a magazine. She tugged her pink chenille robe tighter. She felt that familiar 'middle' sensation – the middle child located between Howard's and Betty's needs, the understanding daughter caught between Mama's and Papa's temperaments. She also hated the smell of cigarettes, but Ann had a right to smoke in her own house.

Teddy stretched and walked toward the kitchen, humming 'You Are My Sunshine'. Slim, almost elegant in her new beige slacks, Teddy was the only one dressed this Saturday morning. She shook her head, wondering why Moira had started today's housekeeping so early.

Ann raised one eyebrow. Resisting Moira's tirade, she drew her legs into her nightgown and kept her eyes on the *Examiner* article about the Germans moving through Greece. 'Well, don't worry, honey, sometimes it doesn't look like you've been here at all.' Silly even to respond when Moira was in a mood. Ann had to admit she, herself, had been in a mood this week too – because of Mama's illness and because of Herb going off to Europe. She was going to miss him.

'What?' exclaimed Moira. OK, maybe she skipped an occasional spot. But she was damned if she was going to pin her heart on Mother's brand of fastidiousness. After twenty years of marriage, what did she have – a spotless house. Moira wanted a man easy about the state of the place – was this Randy? – somebody who understood her acting career, who loved her for her spirit and not for the speed of her mop. 'What are you getting at? I work hard around here.'

'Fighting, fighting in a house of women?' Wanda looked up from her *True Confessions*, pretending alarm.

'Well, we hardly see each other any more,' Moira said sadly.

'Come again?' asked Teddy, returning from the kitchen with an orange and a cup of coffee. Her back tightened as it always did with arguing in the house.

'Except on Saturday morning.' Moira hated herself for whining. 'I mean during the week Wanda and Ann creep out at some unearthly hour.'

'We're lucky to have wages.' Ann sat back, grateful yet again for her typing job at the college.

'You make us sound like burglars.' Wanda flapped the magazine down on the couch beside her. 'I can't help it that the cannery starts early.' She wanted to say that it was about the only place in town hiring Oriental bookkeepers. Of course the girls knew all about this. The point was to reach a broader audience with her articles. Lately she had felt too defeated to think much about writing.

'I'm not blaming anybody.' Moira opened her arms wide and flicked the dust cloth as if it were a lace handkerchief. 'It's just that I don't get home between the office and little theatre rehearsals. Teddy is never around between the Emporium and her family and the Bertolis.'

'So what are you getting at?' asked Ann, now thoroughly distracted from the newspaper. Her voice was harsher than she intended, but Moira was infuriating. 'We're not married to each other. We don't have any vows of forever and ever.'

Teddy stared at Ann. She was probably tied in knots about her mother being in that horrible hospital.

'All I'm trying to say is that if we can't see each other during the week, then everything will come out on Saturday mornings,' sighed Moira.

Teddy and Wanda frowned at each other and shrugged.

'I mean four people living together are bound to get on each other's nerves. We need to talk about what's bothering us.'

Wanda thought how her mother would cringe at Moira's intensity, how she had taught her daughter to show restraint, *uchiki na josei*.

'OK, honey, take a seat.' Ann closed down her cigarette against the green glass ashtray. 'What's on your mind?'

Moira slumped on the arm of the couch.

They waited.

Finally Teddy asked, 'What happened with that visit John Randolph made from LA? Didn't he come to Pan-O-Rama and wasn't he going to take you out to lunch and discover you?'

'Yes, I remember now,' said Wanda. 'It must have been yesterday. That's why you borrowed my scarlet hat with the veil. How did it go?' Despite her amazement at Moira's ego, she believed her friend had the talent and the will to succeed. Why hadn't she thought to ask yesterday? Wanda considered how Moira was the only one of them without a family in town. Maybe that's why she relied so heavily on the girls. Besides, it wasn't too much to expect friends to follow the most important thing in your life.

'Miserably.' Moira collapsed on the couch. 'I sat outside J.D.'s office all morning looking like Jean Harlow warmed over – answering phones, directing stuntmen to the back lot, doing my fabulous receptionist routine, wondering whether J.D. was going to introduce me to Randolph before lunch or whether he was going to pick me up on their way to Nikko's. Well, two hours of the damn conference passed and finally a buzz came over the intercom. I was

– 56 –

completely unnerved because how could I go in there when I had chewed off all my lipstick? I started to pick up Wanda's hat and then remembered I hadn't even answered the buzzer. It was J.D. all right and he said, hold all calls for the afternoon and could I send out for hamburgers – four rare hamburgers.'

'Oh, hon, I am sorry,' Ann said, reaching for her cigarettes and then drawing back abruptly.

'Maybe next time,' said Wanda, patting Moira's shoulder.

'But I've been waiting so long for this time! A whole year as Ever-Ready Receptionist at sleek and shoddy Pan-O-Rama Studios and I've never come close to that break J.D. promised me.'

'There's time yet,' said Teddy, sliding her coffee in front of Moira. At moments like this she was grateful not to have wild ambitions like the other girls. She enjoyed her job at the store, liked the people and the pace.

'That's what Randy said. He kept trying to reassure me last night.'

'Good,' smiled Ann.

'But, well, I'm not getting any younger.' Moira sipped the hot, black liquid, indifferent to their laughter. 'I'm almost twenty-two. For an actress every day counts.' She thought about her mother immigrating as a young bride in steerage at eighteen; bearing a child at nineteen; losing her husband at twenty; remarrying at twenty-one. What had she done with her own life?

'At least you're working in the right field,' said Wanda. 'What does keeping books in a cannery have to do with being a journalist?'

Moira nodded reluctantly. Wanda was right; she was fortunate in a way. But she was so frustrated. The other girls seemed to have natural stores of patience, but when she tried having faith and letting go of expectations, she felt as if she were drowning.

'The way I see it,' drawled Teddy, 'we're all lucky to have jobs. Look at what our parents went through.'

'Then look at what we're going to go through in the war,' Ann said abruptly.

Turning to Wanda's surprised look, Ann said, 'Oh, it's Mama again. They had to strap her down yesterday, like an animal.'

'No, Ann.' Moira stood and took her hand.

'She's been having these nightmares – visions she calls them – about the old country. All her brothers and sisters killed. It does no good to show her her Uncle Aaron's letter saying everyone is fine. "Dead," she lies there yelling with her eyes shut. "All dead." Then she screams the names of relatives I've never heard of.'

Wanda bowed her head in her hands.

'It must be so hard for you,' Teddy said.

'For Papa.' Ann fought back the tears. 'He sits there every day watching her, apologizing. "I should not have taken you away, Dvora." He thinks she's crazy.'

Wanda watched Ann's face. 'And you don't,' she said gently. You had to be careful with Ann. It was hard to tell which was more powerful, the love for her mother or the fear of her. 'You think she's some kind of prophet.'

Ann scrutinized her friend's face for doubt. Finding only concern, she answered, 'Who knows? Who in hell knows what is going on? Can you understand the reports from Germany? Seems to me there's a lot of censorship for a war America isn't fighting.'

Wanda was always taken aback by Ann's unmeasured cynicism about Roosevelt. For Oriental immigrants, who were unredeemably alien, who could not get citizenship, there was no room for public complaint.

Ann continued, 'I'd like to believe that Churchill will buffer England against the German assault. I'd like to believe that my Uncle Aaron is right about the family being safe, but. . . .'

'Yes.' Teddy stared at her empty cup, 'Everybody's got their blood up. My brothers are talking about enlisting. Even Hank with the baby and all. Mom's going nuts. And look at the newspapers and magazines. The covers of Ann's *Newsweek* have planes and tanks almost every week now.'

'Men,' muttered Wanda, unravelling the pink tassel on her sleeve. 'Wars are always designed by men and the results are mended by women.'

'What do you mean?' asked Moira, distressed because Wanda was usually on her side, defending men against Ann's fury and Teddy's indifference. 'Whatever happens will affect us all.'

'But not in the same way,' Wanda answered urgently. 'We're not chomping at the bit, like Teddy said about her brothers. Did you hear that talk between Howard and Randy last week – both of them dying to strut forth and gut the Krauts?'

'I think they're brave,' said Moira. 'It's not easy on them. Randy is scared and I'm sure Howard is – but they're going to fight to defend us.'

'Well, what do you think women will do if we have a war?' asked

Teddy. She imagined them all working together somehow, rolling bandages, knitting socks. Of course she could never voice this silly, sentimental notion and she dismissed the reassurance it provided.

Ann stared out the front window. 'Pick up the pieces.'

'We don't have to be passive,' said Wanda.

'I'm not talking about passivity,' answered Ann.

Moira interrupted. 'We'll do what our mothers did in the other war. Work in defense industries, support the troops.' She thought of how Mother said that despite the cold and hunger in Scotland, their sense of purpose made the war days some of the best in her life. Daddy never spoke about the war.

'Or we'll expose the lies.' Wanda was beginning to wonder if they had four soliloquies proceeding here. 'As a journalist I'd show who profits from these murders; it's not the ordinary people.'

'Don't be naive.' Ann lit another Camel. 'There are censors in this country, you know. Where do you think you can publish subversion anyway?'

'Where there's a will,' said Teddy.

'Oh, come on.' Moira shook her head at Teddy and backed away from the smoke.

'Well, there's one thing we don't have to worry about,' Wanda said. 'Women don't get drafted.'

•

Chapter Six

Summer 1941, San Francisco

GERMANS INVADE USSR

•

AMERICANS FREEZE JAPANESE ASSETS

•

ROOSEVELT AND CHURCHILL PROCLAIM ATLANTIC CHARTER

Teddy lay back on the couch drinking a beer and enjoying the warm Sunday afternoon. The house had lasted two years, she mused, no reason it would ever have to end. Hot and dry, she had spent the afternoon vacuuming and was content to deserve her beer, listening to the sounds of the three other women. Wanda's radio murmured 'Fibber McGee and Molly' through the floorboards. Ann sang in the kitchen, stopping in mid phrase, probably to check the lasagne ingredients and then resuming, 'I'm in the mood for. . . .', partial, still, to the Glenn Miller arrangements. From the yard below, Teddy could hear the irregular chomp-clip-chomp of the shears. She restrained herself from rushing aid to Moira who would prune her thumb as likely as the ivy.

Teddy stretched the length of the elephant couch and wondered if she had ever felt this happy. Maybe there had been times when she was very young in Fortun, before the depression dried their hopes into old bones, before Amanda got polio and Pop, spent in a craziness about how to manage bills, decided there was bound to be magic in San Francisco. Yes, they had some grand times in Fortun, like that blackberry summer when she thought she might turn into a pie or that autumn the whole family rode in the truck to Oklahoma City to celebrate Mom and Pop's twentieth anniversary. Mom still had a glow to her cheeks then. And Pop walked with a swagger, no hint of the flab of more recent years. But Teddy remembered that by the time she was thirteen the family was cracking from high debts and short tempers. San Francisco seemed the only direction – perhaps because it was on the edge.

Sometimes Teddy reckoned she could recall every hour of that long cross-country journey. She liked to run it through in sequence, like still photographs, like a prayer. She closed her eyes now and saw the dry, gold grass growing flat against wide, blue skies. As they drove west towards Texas, the soil became redder. Tumbleweed lazed across the road. She saw signs for 'Ho-Made Food' and 'Cheap Lodging', but the Fieldings camped out the whole way and what had begun as an adventure turned into hardship even for the younger children. There were more hills as you got to Texas. Hank wanted to visit Dallas and Houston, however they were slicing quickly across the panhandle, driving straight into the sunset every night. Teddy's favorite state was New Mexico, with its wide, open starkness. The colors were more gentle there and the contours more dramatic, mountains like points chiselled into the sky. Sante Fe was a pretty town built around a square where traders sold their goods. So high up, Teddy could hardly breathe sometimes. Mom was interested in the Navajos and Hopis, who seemed different from the Cherokees in Oklahoma. She even convinced her husband to stop at the Hubble Trading Post, but they couldn't afford any of the bright rugs or bracelets. Teddy made a resolution to take Mom back one day. In Arizona, Teddy imagined the green hills curling inward, like bears snuggling at night. Pop refused to take them to the Grand Canyon, but they met travellers who told stories about the huge natural carvings miles down into the earth. What Teddy remembered most about Arizona was the desert, the dry heat and the thousands of cacti poking through the dust. California was surprising at first. She had anticipated sun and ocean immediately; instead they drove for miles through a relentless fog until they spotted the orange groves and grape vines of the San Joaquin Valley. 'California,' Hank shouted, as if he were a gold panner. 'Eureka.'

Being an Okie in San Francisco was worse than being a sharecropper's daughter in Fortun. At least in Oklahoma *everyone* was eating dust and, if you had to swallow more than the neighbors, it wasn't your fault. In California, Okie meant parasite, meant vagabond tramp, meant funny accent and queer clothes. First it hit Pop's pride, then his nerve. He had no steady job for months. Had to watch Mom take in laundry and Hank and Arthur forget school for construction work. Compared to some, their family was blessed. When Pop's friend finally got him a spot in the shipyard, Pop was accustomed to days spent half time at the bar and half time in bed. Now Teddy wondered how he sobered up for shifts. But he did. What with all of them pitching in some way, there was enough to go around.

Teddy took another swig of beer, parched just remembering her housecleaning schedule after high school classes. But Mom insisted on school – almost pushed her – because one of her kids was going to graduate. Teddy had astonished both of them by winning the church scholarship. Now she felt she had used it well, really applying herself at Tracey and getting a decent job at the Emporium. She managed to send a little money home every week. Pop accepted it. 'Just for the meantime, just till I'm back on my feet.' Hank had barked, 'When Teddy has already filled your shoes?' Lucky for Hank, Pop was half way through his bottle because if he had been sober that would have been the last crack from the boy for a long while.

Teddy surveyed the living room and pondered just why she loved this house. It was more than a refuge from the crowd at home. She relished the evenness of life here, the way they were equally responsible for the rent and the cleaning and each other. Of course everyone had her little faults – Moira's temper, for instance, and Ann's sharpness – yet they seemed to balance each other, more than she had ever known in her family and more than she could imagine in a marriage. Marriage, she couldn't picture it – doing her 'partner's' housework. Lunatic arrangement.

'What are the choices, the alternatives?' Wanda asked. Angela Bertoli demanded. Ann sighed. Various options crossed Teddy's mind. Always she gave the same answer, 'This house is one choice, for now.'

Upstairs, Wanda tried to concentrate on her sewing and to follow the argument between Fibber and Molly, but all she could think about was Howard's story of the 'Yellow Peril' letter and her mother's notions of returning to Japan. Mama's parents were failing now, and she worried about the war growing in the Pacific. Besides, she knew how proud Americans were and she did not want to be an enemy stranded here. Wanda didn't want to believe in war, however, she knew her mother was right. They who were being treated like threats, were themselves being terrorized! Everyone knew about the arson at Fukahara's orchard in Fresno last month. And the FBI were investigating Buddhist priests because the temples received money for Japan. Now Howard, himself, had got an anonymous letter. 'We're watching you, Yellow Peril.' A warning? A joke? Howard shrugged it off, but Wanda was more cautious.

At the cannery, too, she felt strange. Orders had declined in the past two months. And last week a FBI agent phoned to say he would come for a 'routine check' of the accounts. Since then, Wanda had hardly been able to sleep. All right, it would be rough here, but Mama was mad to talk about Japan. She was so Americanized that it would be worse for her there. And what about her children? Betty and Howard and herself were neither Japanese nor American now. Would she leave her children in 'enemy hands'? Papa, predictably, would not consider leaving. Somehow his fierceness frightened Wanda more than her mother's determination. Rarely was there such a serious rift between her parents. Mama ruled the house while Papa supported them in his own idiosyncratic way. Wanda had never before seen them argue as they had last Sunday at supper.

'Miné, I cannot imagine. . . .'

'Of course you cannot imagine,' Mama had scolded him. 'Your imagination is spent on other things, like political injustice and talk of Emma Goldman. Workers' rights and birth control. See where it got her. Deported. Perhaps we'll be lucky enough to get deported.'

Papa nodded evenly.

Wanda wanted to jump in and defend Papa, for she knew it was Mama who had first told him about Emma Goldman and how she wrote to protest the execution of Kotoku in the Japanese Free Speech Trials of 1910. Perhaps as Papa's radical ideas had turned to idealism, Mama's had turned to cynicism. Wanda didn't know what to say. She found communication harder these days as she was forgetting her Japanese.

Wanda concentrated on the hem of the new blue print dress that she had bought to wear for Roy tonight. She enjoyed the simplicity of sewing and the direct reward of these even stitches. Mama had raised her to marry a good *Nisei* boy, to get a job and to make a contribution to the world. Not an easy mandate, but a mandate nonetheless, and for that she was grateful. Sometimes she felt she was walking a tightrope strung between conflicting interests. Well, she would try. The only times she was really nervous was when she turned around and saw Betty following on the tightrope, watching her closely.

Roy would like the navy shirtwaist. She thought the dress, with its white accents – like luminescent gulls sailing over a clear night sky – was the perfect combination of tailored and romantic. It highlighted her own contrasts, the shiny black hair and the warm, ivory complexion. I'm not vain, Wanda reflected, I just know my advantages. The question was, could Roy handle all this?

She pricked herself with the needle, and, sucking her finger, considered that another good question was did he want a wife? After all, he, himself, had big ideas of being a photographer, of travelling to Africa in search of animal faces. Deep down she believed that they would make a fine team, but he would have to discover that for himself. Lately she had seen more photographs by Dorothea Lange. That's what she wanted to do with journalism, tell social issues through people's lives. She would go to Mississippi and Alabama to interview the Negro people. And her special plan was that they would go back to Yokohama when things calmed down to do a story that would express the complexity of Japan. Last night in her diary, she had outlined their preparations. Language classes first, since neither of them spoke Japanese well enough. They would also study the geography and politics of the city. They would take gifts to Roy's grandparents and her own. They would . . . the diary had been crammed with plans lately. She used to chronicle the day's events, but work was so tense now that it was more relaxing to record plans. It seemed to help her sleep, too. Oh, there was lots of potential for her and Roy. That made the possibilities of failure all the more frightening. So she would play it day by day, stitch by stitch. She felt satisfied. Almost finished now. Yes, this dress would be perfect.

'I'm in the mood for . . . lasagne,' Ann laughed as she whipped the eggs. Lightly, as if you were whipping a soufflé, she remembered Miss Fargo's typing maxim. Why this ridiculous song? She liked Glenn Miller a thousand times better than Benny Goodman, so much more intelligent and subtle. But it would be more appropriate to sing 'Don't Fence Me In'. If there was one thing Ann was *not* in the mood for, it was romance. Lasagne, let's see now, she scanned the recipe in Angela's neat hand. All Catholic girls wrote so precisely. What did Angela call this way of writing? Yes, yes, the 'Palmer Method'. 'Tomato sauce, noodles, ricotta, eggs, salt, pepper, ground beef, mozzarella, Parmesan, pan 9 by 13 inches.' At least this was a practice run. It had been her own bright idea to invite the parents for dinner next week, *her* clever notion to serve an exotic dish that would be foreign to all of them. So it was only fair that she be elected cook. Staring at the cheese and egg mixture, she had grievous doubts that this would emerge as edible. She turned to shred the mozzarella; the long, even sheets of pale yellow reassured her. The lasagne was delicious when Angela cooked it. And she had been good at following directions since childhood. In fact, she was confident she, too, would have perfected the Palmer Method of Penmanship if she had been accepted at the Catholic school where her father tried to enroll her – over Mama's protests – because it was good on academic discipline. Yes, she would have learned the Palmer Method if she hadn't been Jewish and left-handed. They were sorry, said Sister Agatha, who could smell past the rose in her name, but there was no more room in the first grade.

Ann enjoyed grating the Parmesan, watching the soft flakes fill the bowl, savoring the sharp, hardrock aroma escrape from the grater. Very good at following directions . . . that's why she was flying through the Greek course. It was kind of Professor Watson to let her audit the classes, but she could see he was pleased to have a secretary who was interested in the curriculum. San Francisco State wasn't the most prestigious Greek faculty in the country, but she wasn't exactly ready for graduate work.

At least she was recovering from her jealousy of Daniel. For years her brother's courses at Stanford tormented her: history, English literature, calculus, French. She should never have taken him up on his invitation to visit the campus. It would have been easier to bear – him finishing college and going straight to law school – if she hadn't seen how elegant Stanford was. All those graceful Spanish buildings. The tall eucalyptus trees. The wonderful, large communal dining rooms. And his friends – boys from Long Island and Louisiana and Italy and Africa. Well, now she was making her own way, differently, more slowly. She would show Papa, who had dreamed she was going to business school so she could type in her brother's law office!

She hated this envy because she really loved Daniel. They had been natural allies – neutral in the war between their parents. Even though he was two years older, they often played together. They both hated leaving New York for California and they were buddies in this arid and overfragrant place, travelling to the zoo and the museums together on weekends. They also developed a mutual vigilance as Mama grew more quiet.

Papa said they were silly to miss New York. Who wouldn't prefer a nice, warm climate with beautiful palm trees and the Pacific Ocean. They were crazy. Soon they would forget the concrete land where people shoved and pushed and were always categorizing who you were and where you came from. California would be a new life for all of them. Mama would be happier. He promised they could move back to New York in five years if they still missed the damn place. When Ann and Daniel took him up on the bargain – Ann, aged fifteen and Daniel, seventeen – Papa said he was sorry they hadn't adjusted, but the family couldn't pull up its roots for such whim. Roots! Ann screamed. Papa thought they had roots here? Daniel tugged at her sleeve, come on, this is a waste of time. Ann wondered why she was the one who always got angry.

Now Ann shook her head and picked up another piece of the Parmesan Teddy had brought home from Bertolis'.

Teddy, faithful Teddy, encouraged her about college. Teddy would make the perfect mother – do what you want dear, whatever makes you happy. Yet there was something about her that made Ann feel Teddy would never have kids. Funny, the friends one chooses. Teddy was so different from anyone she or Carol ever talked to in high school. So slow and easy. They probably wouldn't have even noticed her. It still hurt to think about Carol, and Ann watched her mind return to a safer topic. This house would be a good place for studying Greek and Latin. After all, they helped each other survive Tracey Business School here. And she was close enough to Filbert Street to run home in an emergency, which, God knew, was likely.

Yes, she was getting a better perspective, like a palaeontologist predicting shifts in the surface of rock over time – the various layers of movement and possibility and resistance. She could not detach herself from her parents or their parents. They were all part of the same mountain.

Mountain was what this Parmesan was becoming. Well, fine, the extra cheese would keep in the icebox until next week for the real occasion. Meanwhile, the dry run was smelling more and more like lasagne.

Clip. Chomp. Clip. Moira manoeuvred the pruners gingerly, intent on avoiding her fingers as Teddy had warned. How did Teddy know just the right angle and pace? She was so like a man in her useful ways: fixing the sink, lighting the pilot of their water heater. It was nothing, Teddy insisted, she had learned on the trip West, helping Pop fix the truck that was always breaking down. Nothing, sniffed Moira, like typing was nothing. 'Now is the time. . . .' It gave her a neckache just remembering.

Actually, this looked halfway decent. She stood back, appreciating her handiwork. A little uneven by the porch there, but she could hide that with the potted geraniums. Mother would be so pleased to see them thriving since she had sent the seeds last winter. Moira was bloody amazed, never having potted anything besides herself before. So like Mother to send seeds rather than flowers. Seeds would renew the investment. Mother just assumed Moira could plant seeds and make them grow. She assumed Moira could do anything she put her head to. But since Moira had abandoned Los Angeles for San Francisco, nothing had gone according to plan except the geraniums. And they were flourishing only in comparison to the ivy.

Clip. Chomp. Clip. Funny how this part of the street was treeless. The Italian neighbors didn't want anything between them and the sun. Practical, thought Moira, none of those damn leaves to rake in the fall. Her parents would be startled. To them, America meant luscious trees and finely groomed lawns like the one they reverently tended in Los Angeles.

Of course she had been right about coming to San Francisco. If she had stayed in Los Angeles, she would have been required to parade daily along the intricately trimmed path through the Finlaysons' ideal lawn. She would never escape until she had won a husband and a contract. And living at home would make her fit for only one role – mad Lady MacBeth. Besides, J.D. had promised her an interview with Randolph next month.

What a funny conversation she had had with Wanda last night, Wanda asking why she wanted to be an actress. No one had questioned her motivations before. Because everyone wanted to be in the movies or because they dismissed her as a piece of fluff? But Wanda knew exactly why she was going to be a journalist. She would expose injustice and help people communicate. All Moira could say was that she liked being creative. 'But,' Wanda persisted, 'what do you want to *do* with acting?' Moira tried to shrug it off. However, when she went to bed last night, she reflected that her interest in acting came from the secrets.

Home had been padded with secrets. The more Mother protected her from the secrets, the more scared Moira felt. Now she wanted to tell the secrets, to have feelings and to shout them on a stage before thousands, millions of people. Moira didn't know when she first became aware of the secrets, probably when she began to compare her family with the families of her school friends. They all had brothers and sisters and cousins and aunts and uncles. Moira had distant relations spread throughout the Commonwealth whom Mother never mentioned unless Aunt Evie was in town. Moira still wondered if she would have learned about Daddy without Aunt Evie, who was as gregarious and irascible as Mother was reserved.

Although she was just seven at the time, Moira remembered almost every detail about that morning. Mother and Aunt Evie were sitting on the sofa. They must have been talking about Glasgow because their accents were noticeably thick. Moira liked it when Aunt Evie visited because she heard the music in Mother's voice that usually was so carefully subdued. Mother even tried to get Daddy to stop using 'Och now', and 'Aye'. Moira wasn't listening to the content of what they said so much as to their brogues; suddenly the room grew still.

'You've told her about Keith, of course.'

'No.' Mother lowered her voice. 'Not yet.'

'Well, when? The child is almost eight.'

'When she's ready.' Mother looked over at Moira with such a scowl that Moira threw a ball of yarn to their cat, awakening the animal on the other side of the room.

'She'll find out somehow. Surely Tim will want her to know.'

'Shhh, Evie, don't poke where you're not invited.' Mother stood and walked toward the kitchen. 'More tea?' Her voice was strained.

'No! You're bloody impossible. I'm going for a walk. That is if I can stand outside in this desert for more than five minutes without melting.'

Moira sat frozen. Even the cat seemed wary. Finally she found a voice. 'Shall I be your scout, Aunt Evie, like yesterday? I could show you the department stores.'

'You'll stay here, young lady. We have some talking to do.'

'Yes, Mother.' Moira curled up next to the bookcase to make herself smaller. She tried to understand what she had done. Eavesdropping was a sin, she knew that from Sister Robert. She hadn't done it intentionally and she had tried to close her ears when it sounded as if they were discussing important matters or at least when Mother had grown tense.

The front door slammed. It seemed like hours before Mother returned with a fresh cup of tea. 'Come here, Moira, come sit by me.'

Moira walked to the couch slowly, as if her pockets were weighted with 100 pounds of stolen chocolate. Mother had tears in her eyes. Since she had never seen her cry, Moira felt more guilty. What had she done to this poor woman who tried so hard? Suddenly Moira hated Aunt Evie's loud, brash ways.

'Not your fault,' Mother sobbed. 'Now come on, child, I have something important to tell you. There was another Daddy before Daddy. We came to America from Scotland together, but he died. . . .'

Although it had been a painful conversation, they seemed closer for the next week than they had in years. Aunt Evie left a day early. Moira didn't think much about her father – or fathers – at first because she felt so close to Mother. She understood now that it had been she and Mother alone, at first, against the world. As the weeks passed, she began to stare at Daddy in different ways, to observe how she resembled only her mother. She wondered what this other daddy, Keith, looked like. Would Mother have any pictures? Could she ask to see them? No, she would wait a while. Meanwhile, she savored being the girl with the biggest secret in the second grade.

But the intimacy didn't last. Mother always seemed nervous about something. Daddy – she tried calling him 'Daddy Tim' to herself, but it was too complicated – tried to cheer up Mother. He was always ready with a joke or a game. The more he laughed, the sterner Mother got. It was hard for the three of them to be together. Moira had great times with Daddy on her own, fishing and hiking. And she had some good days with Mother, mostly shopping. But with the three of them together, it always seemed awkward. Moira thought this was her fault. Without her, they would get along. She even worried that Daddy Keith had left because of her, but this was too crazy to talk about, so she didn't tell anyone about the worry. She just waited for the bad feelings to disappear, which they sometimes did. But other days she was depressed and listless. She would sit on the back step and brood until Mother caught her. 'Of course you have plenty to do. You have friends. You could help me inside the house.'

Turning to the ivy on the edge of the steps, Moira shook herself back to Sunday afternoon.

She spotted Angela Bertoli waddling down the street. No, that wasn't fair, she was a big woman, not obese, and Moira admired her solidity.

'Hiya?' called Angela.

'Fine,' said Moira, caught by the coolness in her own voice. 'Nice day.' But even this sounded more like, 'Leave me alone.'

'Yes,' said Angela, with her usual private smile.

Moira had a peculiar flash from the previous week – of Teddy and Angela walking off to see *Suez* together – two blocks ahead of herself and Randy who were going to another movie. She felt something like jealousy, which was ludicrous because she had her date with Randy. When they were a block behind the two women, Moira asked Randy once again if he had a friend for Teddy.

'I've tried, haven't I? With Jimmy last year, and Stan. She's not interested, I tell you,' he said nervously.

'Nonsense, she's only shy,' snapped Moira.

'Well, just see how shy she is with Ampela Bertoli.'

'What do you mean?' Moira spoke more slowly. 'Never mind. One more crack like that and we're through.'

'Listen, it's OK with me.' He tried to keep his voice light. 'So she doesn't like men. That's her choice. It's a free country.'

'You don't know what you're talking about.' She clasped her shaking hands over the strap of her black patent pocketbook.

'Like I said, it's fine as long as it's not contagious. You and me, we have a good time together, don't we?' He winked.

Thoroughly flustered now, by his remarks about Teddy and by his fingers creeping around her back to the edge of her breast, she was relieved to see the theatre marquee. By this time Teddy and Angela had turned the corner. Moira and Randy joined the long queue for *Drums*.

'Hey, this is packed for a re-run from '38.' Randy was just as anxious as Moira to switch to a friendly topic. 'Why the gigantic line?'

Moira pointed to a romantic poster of Raymond Massey, Valerie Hobson and Sabu. '"Brave men",' she read aloud, '"and the bravest women who follow".'

Angela was completely out of sight now and Moira returned to the ivy. Would her parents like Randy? Daddy would enjoy his spunk. Mother might find him charming. Really, he had a lot of good points – loyalty, intelligence, a hardworking nature. She just wished Teddy and Ann liked him more. Maybe they were jealous, no, not in the way Randy was insinuating, but because they didn't have boyfriends. She and Wanda had great laughs about Roy and Randy so maybe the others felt left out. Whatever her parents thought about Randy, they were bound to like this house. Unlike the other parents, who lived in San Francisco, the Finlaysons were reassured that their daughter was living safely with a group of friends in this strange city. Moira once heard Mother describe the house to Aunt Evie as 'a women's hotel, like the Barbizon'. Aunt Evie, who had learned some diplomacy, had kept her peace. The visit might prove a little problematic when they discovered Wanda really was Oriental and Ann was Jewish, because, after twenty-five years in the United States, the Finlaysons were surprised to meet anyone except the Daughters and Sons of the Revolution and, perhaps, a few Indians.

'Soup's on.' Ann opened the window wider and shouted. Garlic and tomato suffused the hot evening air. Moira would have to warn Ann to go slow on the garlic at the big dinner.

'Come on, Moi.' Teddy opened the front door. 'Supper's ready.'

'In a sec.' She waved the pruners. When Teddy closed the door, Moira stepped back. 'Well, yes, OK,' she spoke to herself. She moved the geraniums 4 inches to the left.

Chapter Seven

●

Fall 1941, San Francisco

AMERICANS SUSPEND OIL EXPORTS TO JAPAN

●

PANAMANIAN GOVERNMENT OVERTHROWN

●

US SUPREME COURT RULES CALIFORNIA'S 'ANTI-OKIE' LAWS UNCONSTITUTIONAL

The bus idled on a quiet street corner. 'Hold it please.' Teddy swooped up her belongings and shouted. 'This is my stop.'

'Lady, I ain't got all day.'

'Sorry.' She smiled, alighting from the bus with newfound grace. The lady secretary walked briskly past a yard of tentative fall flowers. Funny how you get used to mild weather. In Oklahoma the climate was harsh and hard. Here in California a day could turn to gold in January.

The Fieldings' house looked cramped and drab this afternoon. It was much smaller than the family place back home, but it was the tiny yard Teddy noticed most. Her eye caught the drainpipe hanging from the roof. Pop had promised to fix that two weeks ago. Not a good sign that he hadn't got around to it. Teddy held her arms across her chest, hoping that he wasn't drinking again. She could hear Patsy's music blaring from the radio, 'When You Wish Upon A Star'.

'Hi, Teddy.' Virgil looked up from his marble game with Jack.

'Hi there yourself.' She nodded fondly. 'Say, what are you two doing in here? Isn't this time for your chores in the yard?'

'No.' Virgil regarded her seriously. 'Mom told us to take the day off. Pop's out in the garden. You know he's. . . .' Virgil tipped an imaginary bottle.

'I see.' Teddy swallowed hard. 'Where's Jolene?'

'Sick in bed,' Jack answered. 'Bad cold.'

Teddy inhaled sharply. She smelled spaghetti from the kitchen. Nice that Mom was varying the menu a bit. She got tired of Pop's favourite Lima beans with hamhock and Jolene's white beans with ketchup. 'I think I'll see Mom. Let me know who wins at marbles and I'll take him on later.'

Patsy was doing her homework in the dining room, listening now to another song from last year, 'Oh, Johnny'. Teddy patted her sister's shoulder and thought how she used to read at this old oak table with its uneven legs. She was quite partial to the faded paisley rug. What would Wanda and the other girls think of this house? Would they be bothered by the noise and the clutter? Until Pop sobered up, she'd never be able to bring them home.

Mom was standing at the stove, staring out the window to the back yard. Teddy tried to guess her expression. Exasperation? Prayer? Teddy loved her mother's jet black hair and the high cheekbones and the dark skin that didn't seem to wrinkle. Sometimes the Cherokee was more visible, and she did look more than one-eighth Indian today. Mom turned and smiled, unflustered. Had she known her daughter was there all along? Mom had a shaman in her, which saw out the side of her head and understood things before they were said.

'Hello, dear.' Mom held out her arms. 'So how was work today?'

'Oh, fine, exciting, I mean.' Teddy wanted her mother to know how much she loved the Emporium. 'I've got a new boss, Mr Whitney. He's organized and calm and he. . . .' The exhilaration drained as she looked over her mother's shoulders to her father sitting in the garden squinting at the bright blue sky.

'But Mom, I could be contributing more.'

'Teresa Fielding, we've been around and around on this.' She wiped a dark hair off her face, back into the knot at her neck.

Teddy thought of Miss Fargo's bun and how different the two women were although they were about the same age. Mom's hair fell loosely at the back of her ears, with long strands wisping down to her shoulders. Her weight settled easily around the breasts and hips. Inadvertently she looked out to her husband.

Teddy knew Mom wouldn't complain. But she saw the anxiety in those competent hands, in the scratching of her middle nail on her thumb. Teddy watched her suck in her bottom lip. She held her back so tight she thought it might vibrate.

'So he's been at it since morning?' Teddy asked.

'Yes, you know he was planning some repairs today. He went down to the hardware store and they turned him down for credit.'

Teddy shook her head. 'I thought he wasn't going to buy any more till he had money.'

She turned back towards her husband. 'It's hard for him to sit still.'

Teddy shoved the bag of sugar and flour to the back of the counter, hoping Mom wouldn't notice it until she left tonight. 'Why couldn't he have fixed the drain pipe? That wouldn't have cost a nickel. Why couldn't he have used his head?'

'Teddy, what's got into you, judging your father?' Mom started cleaning the kitchen sink.

'Sorry, Mom, but it's so hard on you, all his drinking.'

'It's not like he can't stop when he wants to.' She scrubbed the white caulking between the blue tiles. 'Your father stays dry for weeks, sometimes months, at a time. Lots of men drink themselves to death. Look at your Uncle Leo.'

Teddy wanted to say, 'and he's just going to drink you to death.' Instead, she considered her mother's tired eyes. Mom wouldn't cry. When she felt helpless, she simply grew quieter. 'How're you doing?'

'A little weary, I guess. Amanda and Patsy have been helping out. But Jolene's sick.'

'So I heard.' Teddy nodded. She walked to the breadbox and cut a slice for herself.

'There's lard.'

'No thanks.' Teddy knew they had been running low on lard and with Pop off work they wouldn't be buying more for a while.

'Well, tell me about the store, the house, the other girls.' Mom leaned against the sink.

'Not much to tell.' Teddy sighed, unsatisfied with the bread, but unable to cut herself another slice. She looked out the window and, seeing Pop on the log, she looked back at the spotless sink. 'Mr Whitney praised my work twice this week.'

'You're not exactly bursting with joy.' Mom shook her head and held out her hand.

Teddy squeezed the hand and laughed. 'No, not yet, I guess I'm kind of nervous about having another boss.' How could she explain the new, unfounded fears to her mother who had always wanted to go to business college, who was contending with a drunken husband, an empty purse, ten children and a run on lard. 'Say, you need any help with supper?'

'No.' Her mother frowned at Teddy's abruptness.

'Then I may just say hi to Jolene.'

'That makes sense, hon.'

Sense, thought Teddy, how many times a day did her mother resort to the one unshakeable standard: common sense? It was sensible for Teddy to go to Tracey for it would pay off later. It wasn't sensible to worry about Pop, because what could you do?

Jolene was propped against two pillows reading *True Confessions*. She waved to Teddy.

'Hear you've been featherbedding.' Teddy grinned at her younger sister. How like Mom she was with her dark features. And like Pop in her flashing temper and quick wit. Teddy, in contrast, had inherited Pop's pale English blondness and Mom's even, laconic personality. Jolene was her favorite sister, although she was jealous of her inheritance.

'Not likely around here. Trying to nap in this house is like trying to sleep in the middle of Powell Street. Listen, if I was really featherbedding, I'd go to a park. Cheers.' She lifted a glass of water. 'What's the big news in the world of fashion?'

'You know, I haven't looked at the clothes for weeks. I just go straight on to the office.'

'And I was counting on you for the fall season.'

Teddy grinned and shrugged. 'Say, where's my sister-in-law?'

'Took the baby to visit her mother tonight. Knows when to duck outta this house.'

'Soup's on,' Mom's voice.

'Want me to bring you something?'

'No thanks.' Jolene pulled herself up. 'Been lying down all day. Think I'll just sit quietly at the table.'

'Everyone's bound to be quiet tonight,' Teddy sighed.

During grace, Pop sat silently, both hands on the edge of the table. The back door slammed; Hank stuck his head in the room.

'Sorry we're late, Mom. Arthur and I'll be right in, soon's we wash our hands.'

Teddy watched her mother's shoulders loosen.

Mom stood. 'I'll get their suppers from the oven.'

Pop was shaking his head. 'Can't they respect the family meal hour?'

'Probably got held up on the bus,' Teddy tried.

'Don't they know how long your mother worked on this supper. . . .'

Jolene interrupted, 'Yeah, she went out and shot every last piece of spaghetti. Slippery critters.'

Teddy cracked her knuckles.

'Don't sass your father, Miss,' Mom called from the kitchen.

'Hi there.' Hank sat with a thud. 'So how's everyone?' Avoiding his father's glance, he addressed Virgil. 'You get around to sweeping out the garage?'

Virgil nodded proudly.

Teddy wondered at the kindness in Hank's ways. He really was the perfect older brother, at least he had been since he decided to stay off the streets. She missed the old times with Hank and Arthur, the three of them. She had felt like one of the boys: the long, tall Fieldings going out bowling or for a beer.

'And Jolene,' Hank continued, 'you on your last legs or what?'

'Don't count your luck.' She grinned. 'I'll be up and around tomorrow.'

Mom brought in two plates of baked spaghetti for her eldest sons.

Teddy noticed her father scrutinizing the size of their helpings. She was sure Mom had given Pop as much, but lately he had been extra touchy about such things. As desperately as they needed the pay checks, the boys' income was a delicate affair.

'Teddy,' Arthur asked, 'how's the big downtown world?'

Teddy blushed. 'Fine, I've taken to strolling Market Street and that's fun.'

'Fun!' exploded her father.

'Oh, leave her alone, Pop,' said Jolene.

Teddy noticed Jolene was wearing her 'calm down' expression rather than her 'you jerk' expression and her father surveyed the table for something else to criticize.

'Helen,' he said, 'you're eating like a bird!'

'Now leave me, Dick. I've been nibbling as I cooked.'

'So what'd you do today?' Virgil asked Hank and Arthur.

Arthur chewed thoughtfully. 'We almost got our heads knocked off tearing down a building. Crane swiped by Hank, inch away.'

'But Arthur saved my life.' Hank spoke through a mouthful of spaghetti. 'I ducked and, well, here we are, all together again.'

Mom shook her head. 'That work's so dangerous.'

'Don't worry.' Arthur pushed forward his empty plate. 'Looks like we won't be there much longer.'

'What do you mean?' Pop demanded.

'They're laying people off at the end of the week.'

'Christ!' Pop threw his napkin on the floor and stood up. 'Whole country has gone to hell.'

'Dick,' Mom coaxed. 'Sit down and finish your supper. Remember what the doctor said about your health.'

'Health! None of us will have any health left if they keep draining blood from this family. Shoulda stayed in Oklahoma.'

'No, Pop, it's worse back there,' Teddy said. 'The depression's hard on everybody.'

'Everybody, don't tell me that.' His face reddened as he sat down. 'What this country needs is a good war and that's likely soon enough. That'll get us moving again.'

'Pop!' Jolene shouted and then lowered her voice. 'Don't even think like that. People get shot, people die in wars.'

'People die of starvation, too, missy. Don't speak where you don't know. War gets a nation moving, manufacturing, organizing. Happening already. It's either war or you all will have to learn German.' He sat back with his arms across his chest.

Teddy considered the cold spaghetti on her plate. She could no more eat it than eat the table. She hated Pop when he was like this. Hated him drawing them into fights. Over the years she had tried so many solutions – talking to Pop about the drinking, asking the doctor, praying, trying to ignore it. Nothing worked.

'So are we still going to Playland for Virgil's birthday?' Mom's voice was so light you could almost see through it, thought Teddy.

Virgil grinned. 'Yes, when are we going?'

'You think we have enough money for that kind of falderol when we're all being laid off? Sometimes you don't think, Helen.'

Jolene struck her fist on the table. 'Sometimes she's the only one who does think around here.' She stalked back to the bedroom.

Pop looked at his plate and flushed. 'I don't have to take this,' he shouted. 'Not from my own children.' He stomped into the kitchen and then outside, slamming the back door.

'One of those days?' Hank turned to his mother.

She nodded. 'But he's really a good father. He's just had a hard time.'

Hank and Arthur exchanged a skeptical glance. Teddy reached over for her mother's shoulder. 'You've had a hard time yourself.'

'Yes.' Mom pursed her lips. 'Now dessert. Can you dish up, Amanda? I'll just take a quiet cup of coffee in the kitchen.'

Amanda nodded. 'Yeah Mom, you have a nice rest.'

Teddy stared at her spaghetti and imagined an intestinal haemorrhage. She decided to wait ten minutes and then go into the kitchen. This would be the only time they'd have alone tonight, while the kids were doing their homework and Arthur and Hank were bathing.

As Teddy carried her coffee into the dark kitchen, her mother turned, catching the dining room light on her face. No sign of tears, no, Mom never cried, just grew more still. 'How're you doing?' Teddy tried.

'Fine,' Mom allowed. 'Come.' She patted the chair. 'Tell me more about your day.'

Teddy described her new typewriter and watched her mother's face soften.

'Teddy, I'm so proud of you.'

'Proud?'

'Yes, you're moving again, like we moved out here. It's going to be scarey, but you'll be fine.'

Hmmm, Teddy thought, just as the family had been fine after moving to California? How could you keep your hopes when so many other plans had failed? Then Teddy surprised herself. 'You could leave him, you know.'

'What?' Her mother sat straighter.

'You don't have to stay around. We'd all take care of you. Hank and Arthur and I would bring in enough. It's not like he adds to the family any more. He makes you upset and. . . .' Teddy bowed her head, regretting the words but unable to stop them. 'I heard about him hitting you the other night. Good thing Hank and Arthur were out. We can't stand for that, Mom, we really can't.'

Her mother's eyes were fierce and hard. 'Now you don't want to be talking that way. Pop is a good man, just down on his luck.'

'He's a drunk, Mom.'

'I don't want to hear this, you slandering your own father. He drinks when he's down. He'll change with the times.'

Unaccountably enraged with her mother, Teddy wanted to shake her. One thing her parents shared was their stubbornness. She just looked down at her lap and felt the tears welling.

'Now, there.' Mom put her arm around Teddy. 'You mean well, I know you don't want to hurt your father. I know you want what's best.'

Teddy sat there, breathing in her mother's familiar smell and tasting her own familiar surrender.

Wanda felt guilty eating the last of Teddy's apple pie, but Moira and Ann were digging in. Teddy had told them to finish it. Sometimes Wanda was bored by her endless compunctions.

'So, it looks like I may escape from Gilbert and Sullivan,' Moira said. 'They're auditioning for *Man and Superman* next week and I think I have a chance at a small part.'

'Terrific,' said Wanda, who wondered how Moira had time for work, Randy and her amateur theatre productions, but the girl didn't seem to need much sleep.

'We'll see.'

'Your parents will be pleased.' Ann sat back.

'Daddy, maybe.' Moira shrugged.

'But surely your mother will be impressed by Shaw,' Ann insisted.

'Mother will be impressed with a pay check!' she laughed.

'Oh, come on, she must see you have talent.' Wanda encouraged her.

'Listen, when I told Mother I was serious about acting, she hit the roof and she hasn't come down since. Did I ever tell you about that evening?'

'No,' said Ann, lighting up a cigarette. 'Tell us. We haven't talked about families in a long time.'

'Well.' Moira drained her coffee cup, drew herself into the roles and began.

'Mother's first remark was "Do you know how many advantages you have, young lady?"

'I stared at the stew congealing on my plate.

'"What kind of life is the stage?" she insisted.

'"I was thinking of the movies." I couldn't restrain a smile.

"'Don't be sarcastic with me,'" Mother said.

"'I'm serious, Mother. I have talent. Sister Lawrence said so.'"

"'Sister Lawrence, what does that old fool know, has she ever tried to support herself?'"

"'Jenny!' Daddy stepped in as he often did at the eleventh hour.

"'I'm sorry, Tim, but really, why is that teacher putting ideas into Moira's head? The girl has few enough practical bones.'"

"'Well, she may be right,' he tried. 'Moira does have a gift.'"

'I cringed, knowing what would come next, what always happened when Daddy tried to contradict Mother.

"'The two of you — sinking in the same leaky dreamboat. Well, it may be good enough for you that after twenty years of slogging in this country we're no better off than when we left Scotland, but I'm not going to watch my daughter treading in her own foolishness.'"

"'It's her life, Jenny.' He folded his napkin on the table and walked away.

'I looked past my fear long enough to see what he was doing. He couldn't stand up to her, but he could signal me a direction. I could leave. I could just get up from the table, away from the house and leave.

"'I'll not support you to do any fool thing like acting,'" Mother warned.

"'Yes, Mother,' I said, but with a new confidence. 'I'm going to get a secretarial job, make good money while I'm practicing my craft.' I don't know where I got the idea to be a secretary, to come to San Francisco, I was just in high school. But Mother, herself, was a powerful example of independence.'

Wanda was still staring at the pie. She was always amazed by how candid Moira was about her family. She could no more tell stories like that than turn blue.

No wonder she wanted to be an actress. Wanda was surprised by her reflex to change the topic. 'It's interesting to think how much of our characters was shaped already in high school.'

Moira nodded, somewhat deflated by Wanda's response, but still interested.

'For instance, did Ann ever tell you how she insisted on sharing the graduation podium with Howard?'

'Oh, Wanda.' Ann got up to clear the table.

'No, tell me,' Moira coaxed.

'Well, Ann beat him for Valedictorian by two points. And she told the teachers it was silly to compete that way. So they both spoke. Ann first, of course. But our family was so proud. I don't think I ever told you, Ann, how much I admired that.'

'It was nothing.' Ann blushed, but she noticed the pleasure welling inside her. 'It was actually Carol's idea, you know.'

'Carol.' Moira peered at Ann. 'That's your friend who died, isn't it?'

Wanda closed her eyes, what had she got them into? She still felt the pain in Ann's voice from the first day at Tracey when she told her about the suicide.

'You know,' Moira continued, 'I always wanted to know more about her, about your relationship. Will you tell us?'

Ann brought the coffee pot to the table and silently poured three cups. 'Yes,' she said with deliberation, 'I'd like to.'

'I still dream about her. We're walking in Washington Square or strolling along the wharf. Everything is fine. I say, "Don't go to New York" or "Wait and I'll come with you". But I never did that; I couldn't think of a way to warn her at the time. In the dreams I know something Carol doesn't know. Now she knows something I don't know.

'Once in high school Carol talked about suicide. I worried at first, but then Carol snapped out of her depression. She was always given to exaggeration, talking about Art as if it were something sacred which one climbed to and was received by. I told her things would be fine, that she had great ability, that she had to give it time. I encouraged her about the watercolors. The etchings were sinister – people with distorted bodies and magnified eyes. The oils were very bright, too bright. But the watercolors had fine clarity of feeling and a marvellous immediacy.'

Wanda remembered that's what her friend Sarah Murdoch had said, that Carol was a brilliant watercolor painter. Wanda watched Ann closely, remembering that, although high school seemed a universe away, it was only five years ago. How hard it must have been for her then, and now.

'Carol was my only friend to guess why I didn't invite people home. We were sitting at Wingman's Fountain sharing an ice-cream soda and Carol asked quietly, "It's your mother, isn't it? There's something wrong with your mother?"

'I flushed, relieved to hear someone speak this truth because Daniel and I always just said, "Mama's extra tired today" or "Mama looks better this afternoon." I asked Carol how she guessed.

'"Well," she snapped her gum thoughtfully, "you're always complaining about your father or talking about Daniel's college plans. But you never say anything about your mother. And I don't know, there's something in your eyes."

'"My eyes." I drew back, how could Carol know about the freckle in Mama's eye?

'"A sadness in your eyes," she said.

'"Yes," I admitted.

'"You don't have to tell me about it." Carol pulled out a pack of cigarettes.

'"No, I'd like to." But I was nervous so I said, "Mind if I have one of those?" I didn't have any friends who smoked.

'"Not at all." Carol's face almost concealed her smirk. "Camels are strong in case you haven't had this brand before."

'"Thanks." I had no trouble with the cigarette or with the next as I confided in Carol about Mama's receding presence.

'After that we became best friends, meeting every day after school and walking to my job. On Sunday evenings we went out for a soda and a smoke and a good long talk about the week ahead and the years ahead.

'I loved Carol's house. Both her parents were teachers and they took an interest in my languages. Sometimes I would sit in the kitchen with Mr and Mrs Sommers while Carol went to her room and drew. The ideal family, so educated, so liberal. Her parents doted on her, hung her pictures in the living room and agreed to pay for the best art school in the country. Oh, occasionally Mr and Mrs Sommers would worry about those episodes when Carol became talkative and loud and had a hard time sleeping, but they said Carol was much better than she had been as a child.

'We took beautiful graduation pictures: the Valedictorian and the Arts Award Winner. All summer we talked about Carol's trip to New York. I remembered things about Manhattan, things I hadn't thought about for years. Carol invited me to visit at Christmas and offered to pay the train fare. I said I couldn't possibly. Well, think on it, Carol said nonchalantly.

'I was still thinking on it at Thanksgiving when Carol's father phoned about the suicide.

'I couldn't move for a week. I couldn't eat for several more weeks. How to put it together? Had Carol been too depressed in New York? Would it have been different if I had been there to show her around? Had Carol decided she could never satisfy Art? Her parents were as bewildered as I and, understandably, didn't want to talk. In fact they didn't want to see me. After months of depression, I began to feel a strange anger, an anger in which it was hard to distinguish between Carol and Mama. And I understood I could either waste my life or I could continue living it. It was then, six months after Carol's death, that I decided to leave the house, to create my own life. No argument from Papa was strong enough. I had Carol's tenacity now. The first thing I did after moving into the rooming-house was to buy a pack of Camels. I went back to the room, lay on the bed and smoked three or four before falling asleep.'

Ann drew a deep breath and felt herself returning to the kitchen. Unable to bear the pained expressions of Wanda and Moira, she got up to pour herself another cup of coffee.

Moira stood and put her arm around Ann's shoulders. 'Oh, honey, I'm so sorry. It's so hard, so sad.'

Ann let herself relax under Moira's embrace. She was safe here, she reminded herself. She had grown up and she was safe.

Wanda stared at her uneaten slice of pie and then at the clock. 10.00. When was Teddy going to get home?

Chapter Eight

•

Fall 1941, San Francisco

TOJO FORMS CABINET IN JAPAN

•

GERMANS CAPTURE YALTA

•

BRITAIN DECLARES WAR ON FINLAND, RUMANIA AND HUNGARY

Wanda was not surprised to see that Roy was early for their picnic. She stood at the window watching him walk up Stockton Street carrying a brown bag. The sun glinted off his new wire-rimmed glasses. They did make him look more intellectual, as Moira said, almost middle-aged and distinguished. But everything else about him was that of a young man, like his long gait and touseled hair. Although he combed back the hair, it always parted in the middle and fell on to his high forehead. The broad shoulders and athletic legs belied his artistic intensity. There he was, rubbing his hands in that familiar gesture of nervousness. Wanda had been waiting for him although they had made no definite plans about time. She, too, had been awakened by the deep blue sky, more appropriate to June than December.

Wanda opened the front door before he could knock. 'Shhh,' she said softly as if blowing him a kiss. 'They're all asleep.'

He smiled, tiptoed into the living room and watched affectionately as Wanda hurried for her purse and jacket and a lap rug.

She savored the coincidence of timing. There had always been an intuition between them, as if they might have been twins separated at birth. Yes, she reflected, the larger questions were getting settled slowly. The South was a place he would like to visit, maybe before he went abroad. She had said nothing explicit about herself, but she assumed he understood. Taking a deep breath, she held her hands before her, admiring the manicure Moira had given her last night. The crimson shine matched her lipstick. The ringless hands would be elegant, if she could stop shaking.

When she returned to the living room, he was examining an iridescent orange bowl on the mantelpiece. Grinning curiously, he raised his eyebrows.

'A housewarming gift from Moira's parents,' she whispered and led him outside. The morning was warmer than she expected. Wanda closed her eyes and breathed deeply.

'Housewarming?' Roy persisted once they began walking toward Market Street. 'But you moved into this place ages ago.'

'The Finlaysons were slow to warm up,' she explained.

'Say, wasn't there some big shindig – all the parents for dinner recently?'

Wanda took a moment to answer as she considered how quickly time had passed since then. No, of course she wouldn't have felt safe enough with Roy to tell him the saga. He must have heard it from Howard who had got it from Mama and Papa – that was a version she shuddered to hear.

'Catastrophic?' He laughed, unnerved by her silence.

'Oh, no.' Her lips widened in an embarrassed smile. 'We all survived. Witness the amiable glass bowl. I'll tell you on the streetcar.' Boldly, she grabbed his hand. 'Let's run.'

They were still holding hands as they lurched toward an empty seat in the middle of the tram. An old Caucasian man across the aisle turned dramatically, squinted at them, then mumbling irritably, gathered his satchels and moved several seats further back.

'Afraid he'll get jaundice?' Roy joked anxiously.

'Hmmm,' she sighed and, unwilling to be consumed by anger, said, 'Back to the tale of the family repast!'

He nodded.

'There were four of us and six parents. Ann's mother was in the hospital and Teddy's father was "in the bottle" or that's how she put it.'

'Still, it must have felt like the League of Nations.'

'Yes.' She was conscious of her agitation, of her hand sweating profusely in his. Was she still upset by that obnoxious passenger or just nervous about being with Roy? She pulled back her hand and fiddled with several curls at the nape of her neck. Returning to the story, she folded her hands on the lap of her corduroy skirt.

'First of all, I guess they each had different expectations. Mrs Fielding seemed scared to death and kept virtually mute all evening. Mr Rose continually checked his watch and contemplated the appropriate time to call his wife at the hospital. Mr and Mrs Finlayson seemed genuinely taken aback that my parents were Oriental. And Mama, at one point – I still can't believe this – baffled by Mr Finlayson's Scottish accent asked him what his native tongue was!'

Roy burst out laughing.

'Well, that set the evening's tone. Ann's lasagne was delicious, but I almost spit it out when Mrs Fielding, in a brave stab at conversation, asked "Is it a Jewish dish, dear?"'

Roy clapped a hand over his mouth. 'What did Teddy say?'

'Oh, not much. She's pretty good at letting people make their own mistakes. She was the only one of us with any fingernails at the end of the evening.' Suddenly conscious of her own red nails, she curled her fingers into her palms. 'But Mr Rose intervened, explaining that the noodles were similar to those used in *kugel*.'

'Where did you go with *that* conversation?' Roy shook his head. Wanda noticed how the sun shone blue lights in his recently trimmed hair.

'Well, you'll never guess.' She smiled ruefully. 'Starch.'

'Pardon?'

'Starch! We did a twenty-minute interlude on international starches – with my mother and Mrs Finlayson swapping recipes for rice and potatoes.'

'At least you avoided explosive topics,' he sympathized, reaching toward her hand, then catching some unnamed fear in her eyes, pulling back.

'Oh, the war did arrive eventually, but not until the living room stage when Mama was safely engaged in conversation with Mrs Fielding about the tribulations of travelling with a family. The rest of them – Father, the Finlaysons and Mr Rose – all professed classic immigrant patriotism for the USA.'

Responding to the quaver in her voice, he inquired, 'Your

mother's not still talking about going back.'

Wanda shrugged, staring out at the street. 'She talks about it less. But you know my mother, Mrs Willpower.'

'So you survived the League of Nations,' he said with finality, reaching for their earlier tone.

'Yes.' She smiled. 'And in the end supper was far more helpful to us than to our parents. I mean I now know why Moira is such a drama girl. If I grew up with those straight laces, I'd be busting out all over. No wonder Ann is so sober with her mad mother and maddening father. And Teddy, her mom just exuded the same kind of modest good will. Maybe Teddy is a little more confident. I guess that's true of all of us. We feel like we have a right to be here. Oh, maybe the parents got something out of the evening. At least they know that their daughters aren't living with barbarians. Even if they don't understand why we are living together.'

'I'm not completely clear on that, myself,' he said tentatively.

She regarded him closely, scrutinizing the words behind his question – independent? strong-minded?

'I mean.' He adjusted his spectacles. 'It must take a lot of courage. It must be – I don't know – an adventure for girls to live alone and fix the lights and the sink and. . . .'

'Yes.' She nodded. 'Speaking of adventure – here's the park.' Looking back, she found the old man squinting at them again. 'Let's go out the front door; it's closer to the corner.'

They walked all the way to the ocean. Yesterday the plan had been cycling but this morning they were so caught in conversation that they were half-way to the beach before they missed the wheels. During the next hour, Roy talked about his admiration for Ansel Adams and Edward Weston and his pilgrimage to see their photographs in Carmel. Wanda related several recent incidents at the cannery: the Donner Stores closing their account and a new visit from the FBI. By mid-morning, they were walking hand in hand.

On the beach they stopped for lunch. Wanda unfurled their rug over the warm sand. She noticed how the waves reflected turquoise against the deep blue ceiling. Momentarily she wished she could simply sit here with Roy, close her eyes and float out to the middle of the ocean where there would be no government agents or squinting bus riders or fragile foreign grandparents. Perhaps that's where she belonged – on some mid-Pacific atoll. Japanese-American.

– 87 –

American-Japanese. Perhaps she could just rest on the hyphen.

'Apple?' he asked shyly.

She burst out laughing. 'Maybe Eve was *Nisei*, but I'd rather start with the cheese. What's this?' She pulled a plastic container from his sack. 'Coleslaw from Bertolis'. You think of everything. Forks, napkins.' She dug deeper. 'Plates?'

'Oh no.' He knocked his forehead with his right fist and his glasses wobbled comically.

Wanda laughed at the pained expression. She couldn't help herself. She threw back her head and laughed at the two of them sitting on the warm ledge of the Pacific. She laughed at the thought of her curls dissolving in the mist. She put her crimson fingertips to her red lips and looked at the apple and laughed.

Roy laughed, as if trying to catch her. Deep in the pleasure of her company, his eyes sought out the core of this lightness. Yet, because the spirit of the laugh was in her, he was the first to subside.

'Tell me,' he beckoned, cutting the cheddar with a pocket knife, 'about the importance of that house to you. I want to understand it.'

Wanda looked closely and saw only curiosity and affection in his eyes. Yet it was hard to respond. Where could she begin? How much should she reveal? Instead of answering, she thought about writing in her diary last night about recording the evening's conversation at Clooney's. She had asked them this same question, what made them friends?

'Because we don't need men to focus our lives,' said Ann.

'Maybe not to focus, but how about a little background music.' Moira drank the last of her lager and reached for the pitcher to pour refills.

Wanda put her hand over her glass and asked Ann what she meant.

'Only that we're interested in our own careers,' Ann said.

'That doesn't mean we can't have families,' Wanda answered quickly.

'No, just that we're not about to drop fruit yet,' winked Moira.

'I mean,' Ann's voice was calm, precise, 'that we're committed to working in the world as well as to having families – you with your journalism, Teddy at the Emporium, Moira in the movies.' Ann raised her glass. 'And me, knock wood, with Julius Caesar in Rome.'

'You're right there,' laughed Teddy. 'Some of the girls at Tracey said straight away that they were studying to be secretaries of the lawyers they were gonna marry.'

Well, Ann was right, Wanda decided in her diary. They did have a special perspective, wanting lives of their own.

Acknowledging this now, Wanda felt torn between Roy and the girls. Ridiculous notion. They had made no pact. They weren't a convent or a coven. However, she had never imagined she would lead the exodus. Moira had seemed most likely to wear the first white gown. Teddy, of course, would be the last to leave. She would be the most hurt and the most understanding about Wanda wanting to get married. Wanda shook herself out of the reverie. Why was she so bothered? This was completely unnatural. She should be ecstatic that she had found someone to love and all she could feel was guilty.

'Boy, that must be some cheese.' Roy's nervous voice roused her. 'What's it laced with? Opium?'

'Sorry,' she said, conscious again that she could not answer him. Looking at his long, masculine legs and staunch shoulders, she did feel 'sorry', as if she had landed on a strange planet. Who was this? A man. An other. How could they share lives? She would miss the common sensibility she had known with the girls. She had lived in a house of soft flesh and dulcet tones, save the occasional screech from Moira. She had grown accustomed to a light tread on the stairway and to the slight irony – or was it iron-like – odor of the bathroom during their monthly period, for it all came simultaneously from them, the discharge of unnecessary cargo from private wombs. She recollected the quiet swish of their nightgowns as they gathered in the kitchen on weekend mornings. She smelled their face cream and lipstick and perfume. She experienced all these sensations with a startling feeling of loss. What sounds and smells and textures would this 'other' being bring to her life? When you were married were you still a whole female or did you become half of a whole that was different, unrecognizable from your past and from your deepest visions of the future?

Wanda cleared her throat. 'No, not opium, just memories.'

'Better than hallucinations.' He smiled, too, trying for the light-heartedness of a few moments before.

Wanda watched the concern on his face. She wanted to protect him. She resisted an irrational anger about the need to translate.

Wouldn't another woman have understood? What did it matter? 'Memories of the house,' she said finally. 'Of how we met each other. It's still hard to piece together. Hard to take apart.'

'OK, OK, I was just wondering.' His eyes were shadowed now and she felt him moving away, perhaps toward doubt about her stiffness and distance.

She imagined herself a mermaid, longing after a shimmering fish as he moved from the sunny depths towards tangles of seaweed and faraway caves. Unwilling to leave the sweet air she breathed, unwilling to let him go too far into the ocean. Unwilling to lose him; unwilling to lose herself. Panicked at the impossibility of mutuality. Wanda broke the spell. 'Would you pass the coleslaw please?'

He laughed.

She laughed. Gradually, the acid in her stomach dissolved and she could feel lunch being digested. Roy talked about his admiration for Howard. Wanda agreed. 'Too generous for his own good.' They all loved him for it. Yet Wanda found herself, on this day of disloyalty, comparing Howard to Roy. As much as she agreed about her brother's qualities, she thought he lacked ambition. There he was, everyone's nice guy, the life of the party, with no direction of his own. In comparison, Roy had plans and, if they sometimes worried her, they also excited her. Howard had grown into all Papa was not – reliable, predictable and, for that, a little boring. Sometimes Wanda thought Roy was a cross between Papa's adventuresomeness and Howard's security. How much of this was Roy and how much was her fantasy?

Cool winds drew from nowhere, so they packed up the rest of lunch. She worried that she had been too distracted, but he seemed caught in his own thoughts now. Over the last few months, they had developed a companionable silence, as Teddy called it. Wanda noticed that only the red rind remained from the cheese, so they must have eaten quite a substantial meal.

Briskly, they walked back to the park entrance. The breeze haunted her with that chill which had crept between them on the shore. Just before the grove of eucalyptus, he took her hand. A flare coursed through her chest and stomach. The doubts faded. Jitters, of course she would have jitters about anything as serious as marriage. Surely she would miss her friends. That was normal. It was all very normal. Suddenly she became talkative.

They walked along purposefully and didn't even approach the

topic of marriage. Concerned that her chatter might be overwhelming, she became silent. He, too, remained silent. Then, fearing that she seemed aloof, she moved closer and took his arm. He drew near, seemingly content in the silence. When they reached the tram stop, her jaw was set. She was convinced that the time for proposals was past.

Climbing aboard the streetcar, Wanda was filled with disbelief and mortification. She sat down next to the window and stared blankly at the passing city. Had she imagined his attraction? Had vanity misled her? Did he lose his courage? Had she scared him when she became aphasic on the beach? Disoriented, as if a summer afternoon had just turned to snow, Wanda reconstructed her life. She would take the journalism course at night, finish the freelance article about abandoned children, stay in the house with her good friends. She and Roy could continue to date, but if nothing developed there were, as Uncle Fumio was fond of saying, 'plenty of fish in the sea'.

'Wanda?'

Startled, she focused on the scene outside the window. They were half-way home. Then, turning to Roy, she became aware of her right hand in his tight grasp.

'Something wrong?' he inquired gently.

'No, and with you?' she responded more brusquely than she intended.

'No.' He shrugged. But she saw the sweat beading along his temple.

'Do you think we could have dinner tonight?' He quickened his pace as if she might decline before he finished the sentence, 'because there's something important I want to ask you.'

His eyes were full. She was at once drenched in all the emotions from the park – fear, pleasure, panic, arousal, unqualified hope.

'Yes,' she said, willing him to hear the entirety of her meaning.

'Could you wear that blue and white dress?' He smiled at his own presumptuousness.

'Yes,' she said. 'Oh, yes.' She tried to sound calm. 'I'm glad you like that one.'

He left her at the door with a kiss on her cheek.

Wanda was shocked by the darkness of the living room. Adjusting to the light, she was further alarmed to find her three friends huddling around the radio, eyes transfixed by the dial as if it were a Ouija board. The jingle for Lux soap stung through the evening air. What was going on?

They all noticed her at once.

'Oh, Wanda,' Moira called mournfully.

'It's just terrible,' Ann apologized.

A score of emotions, thoughts, impressions avalanched against Wanda's lungs before she could breath a word of question. Was one of the family hurt? Could they see marriage written across her face? Had they lost the lease? What was going on?

Teddy was the first to recognize her confusion. She stood and put an arm around Wanda's shoulders. 'They bombed Pearl Harbor this morning.'

'Who . . .?' Wanda leaned back against the elephant couch.

'The Japanese,' said Moira, taking Wanda's hand, 'they bombed Pearl Harbor.'

'Didn't you hear?' asked Ann, walking towards her. 'This morning.'

Chapter Nine

●

Spring 1942, San Francisco

BURMA–CHINA ROUTE SEVERED

●

BRITISH TROOPS LAND IN MADAGASCAR

●

US SURRENDERS ON MINDANAO

●

RAF MASS BOMBING OF COLOGNE

Moira pulled her coat closer and tried to concentrate on her letter to Wanda. It seemed silly to write to her friend when she was interned only a few miles from home. But it was hard to visit the camp and she knew Wanda appreciated as much contact with the outside world as possible. Ridiculous, horrifying, enraging, she didn't know the right word. She still couldn't believe that the government had driven Mr Nakatani to suicide, that they had carted away the rest of the family, that so much had happened this winter and spring.

Here she was waiting for her mother in this drafty Oakland train station. Well, if the train were any later, she could post the letter from Oakland, that might lend it an exotic flavor. Four o'clock. The rosary for Uncle Willie was scheduled for five o'clock. What if they were late? Was everyone going out for a meal afterward? She should have asked Aunt Evie, but she didn't want to bother her with train schedules when her husband had just died. Well, Mother had no call to blame her.

Moira reread her letter to Wanda.

. . . . *So Uncle Willie died in an* RAF *crash. Poor Aunt Evie begged him not to enlist, told him that he was too old. But he had kept his British citizenship, well, you know this story because he enlisted shortly after we moved into the house together. When she got the telegram last week, Aunt Evie was calm and organized. But she fell apart the next day. And Mother is coming to see if she can set things in order. Aunt Flora and Uncle Benny are coming from Portland.*

It's so strange, how personally this war has affected me. I thought this was all history or politics or something abstract until you were dragged away. And now Uncle Willie dying. What's next? I'm petrified about Randy. Frankly, I think he's a little scared too because he hasn't made up his mind where to enlist. And Daniel is already on his way to Europe. Uncle Willie's crash made me worry about . . . .

'The train from Los Angeles has arrived at Track Six. The train from Los Angeles has arrived at Track Six.'

Moira stuffed Wanda's letter into her purse and snapped to her feet. She hurried over to the crowd of people waiting and was breathing almost normally by the time she spotted Mother's purple hat. Moira was filled with a longing for this striking woman. Tall, big bosomed, impeccably groomed. Moira had always hoped to grow into such elegant grace. She had enjoyed watching this face until it became set with disappointment. Moira knew she should shout and wave, but she wanted to watch for another moment.

'Dear!' Mother smiled. 'Over here!'

'Yes, Mother.' Moira held her voice from the quaver which would creep in soon enough. She waved the rose she had been carrying, hoping it hadn't wilted too much in the last two hours.

'Lovely, dear.' She accepted the flower and surveyed her daughter quickly.

'Let me take the bags. Randy's car is right out here. I got a great parking space.' Moira tried to relax, but she was afraid to stop talking.

'Sorry you had to wait so long, dear.' She smelled the rose and sighed with fatigue.

'Oh, it wasn't bad.' Moira was so relieved she lost her grip on the bags. 'I was writing a letter to Wanda.'

'Wanda. . . .' Mother began. 'Yes, Wanda.' She stared at the rose. 'A nice girl. Too bad about her people.'

Did Mother mean too bad her family was locked up or too bad the Japanese bombed Pearl Harbor? Or both? Well, now was not the time for political argument. No doubt opportunity would arise during the next few days.

The church was cold and musty, but the pews had been polished recently and the aisles were spotless. Moira peered through the dim light and found Aunt Evie kneeling near the aisle in the front pew. The prayers echoed Sodality Wednesdays, when Moira and her school friends recruited reluctant classmates from recess to pray the rosary. She also thought of her own private prayers to the Blessed Virgin. Now Moira encouraged her mother toward the front pew, but she insisted on remaining inconspicuously at the back. They joined the others murmuring the 'Our Father', 'Glory Be', and ten 'Hail Marys'.

It had been years since Moira said a rosary, yet it came back to her with amazing ease. She was fond of these familiar prayers, remembering the refuge they once had promised. Faith, hope and charity. The cross, the anchor and the heart. The greatest of these is love, He said. A good thing, too, Moira thought now, because she had lost the cross and the anchor. Blasphemy made her nervous with Mother kneeling nearby, so she tried to concentrate. '. . . Holy Mary, Mother of God, pray for us sinners now and at the hour of our death. Amen. Hail Mary, full of grace, blessed art thou. . . .' She could almost smell the starch of Sister Gregory's habit. How safe she felt as a child, enveloped by the odors of incense and stale holy water and Sister Gregory's very faint sweat. She never mentioned this last scent to anyone, but she found it reassuring that Sister Gregory had a body under the habit. It meant there was hope for Moira. One day she would find something to contain her, to make her appropriate in the sight of God.

'. . . the fruit of thy womb, Jesus,' Mother whispered.

Moira looked at her mother looking at Aunt Evie. Mother's face was creased with wary concern. How had the two of them survived sisterhood, Moira wondered. It must have been hard for Mother growing up with all those kids, under the helm of powerful Aunt Evie. Mother watched as Aunt Flora put an arm around Aunt Evie.

'. . . now and at the hour of our death. Hail Mary, full of grace, blessed is. . . .'

Moira had always thought of the rosary as a carousel she could get on at any moment. It didn't matter if you missed a couple of turns. It would always come around again.

'Glory be to the Father and to the Son and to the Holy Ghost. As it was in the beginning, is now, and ever shall be, world without end. Amen.'

World without end. Moira saw Aunt Evie compose herself and turn toward the aisle. Mother stood. Moira made the sign of the cross, as reflexively as saying good-bye at the end of a phone call. She stood as well. Aunt Evie was just a pew away before she caught sight of them.

'Jenny,' she gasped and reached for her sister. 'Wee Jenny, you made it.'

Moira watched the two tall women hug, watched Mother stiffen and then relax in her sister's arms, the sister she was supposed to be comforting. Wee Jenny, Moira thought, and started to cry for Uncle Willie and Aunt Evie and for wee Jenny and for Wanda and for Randy. She stood there, holding her mouth and crying until she heard someone clear her throat. It was tired and tense Mother, wee Jenny gone altogether.

Moira tried not to be anxious as she brought Mother home on Friday afternoon. After all, she could hardly stay alone now that Aunt Evie had gone up to Portland for a rest with Aunt Flora. And Mother had stayed an extra day in Northern California to spend time with Moira.

'The glass bowl. How nice to see it on the mantelpiece.' Mother spoke rapidly and Moira knew she was nervous. 'My, you've done well with this living room.'

'Your chamber's up this way, Mother. Let me get you settled and then we'll fix a cup of tea.'

'You do know how to treat a guest, Moira.'

Moira thought how Mother always turned formal when she was uncomfortable. She noticed her own comparative ease, showing Mother around *her* territory.

Ann entered from the kitchen. 'Welcome, Mrs Finlayson, how nice to see you again.'

'It's mutual, Ann. And haven't you changed quite a bit with your pretty new hair style.'

'Yes.' Ann flushed.

'So will you be joining us for dinner?'

'No thank you, Mrs Finlayson. I'm going to Shabbas – Synagogue – this evening.'

Mrs Finlayson looked at her closely. 'Oh, yes, you're Jewish, aren't you dear?'

'Yes, Mother,' Moira interrupted. 'Ann goes to Synagogue every week like you – we – go to Mass.'

'Of course.' She looked irritated, whether with her daughter, herself, or even Ann, Moira couldn't tell.

'I hope to see you in the morning?'

'Yes, Ann dear, I hope so too.'

Moira led Mother upstairs to her room, which she had been preparing all week. Just as they reached the landing, Teddy emerged.

'Hi there, Mrs Finlayson, how nice to have you visiting us.' She gave Moira's mother a hug. The woman held herself straight, so Teddy drew apart, still smiling. 'We've been looking forward to seeing you.'

'Thank you, dear,' Mrs Finlayson answered. 'I hope you'll be able to join us for dinner tonight. I'm taking Moira and her young man to what I understand is a very good restaurant.'

'Oh, no thanks, Ma'am. I'm going off to my family tonight. It's Jolene's – that's my younger sister – Jolene's birthday tonight.'

'How nice that you're in such close touch with your family. It must be a real comfort to your mother.'

'Yes, Ma'am.' Teddy considered Moira. 'Well, now, I reckon I'd better let you get settled.'

'Very nice to see you, Teddy.'

Moira clenched her teeth. What happened to wee Jenny?

Randy rang the bell with his usual flair and Moira rushed to greet him before Mother descended.

He was handsome in his new blue suit. His hair was a little on the longish side and she wondered what Mother would think. Then she stopped herself. She was twenty-two years old.

'Hi, sweetie, how're you doing with the old lady?'

'I'll do a lot better if you don't play Humphrey Bogart tonight.' She pecked his cheek.

He grabbed her by the waist, grinning.

'Not here, silly, she'll see.'

'OK, I'll be the perfect gentleman. Cary Grant. William Holden.

Whatever your heart desires.'

'Randy Girard is good enough, a sort of low-key Randy.'

'At your service.'

'Did I hear the doorbell, dear?' Mother came down the stairs in a new yellow dress, unlike any of the somber clothes she had worn for the last few days. In fact she looked dazzling and Moira was amused at her tinge of jealousy.

'Yes, Mother, you remember Randy.'

'Why of course. How nice to see you again.'

'Charmed.' He kissed her hand, causing both women to blush.

The next morning Moira borrowed Randy's car and drove her mother to Half Moon Bay. They reminisced about that long ago San Francisco vacation when Mother cut Moira's hair and told her the facts of life. Moira leaned back against the seat, feeling the great fondness between them.

Winds swept the beach with puffs of fog. Mrs Finlayson had warned Moira to bring a coat, but somehow, with all the last minute preparations, Moira had forgotten. So she grabbed a plaid blanket from the trunk and wore it Indian style. Did Indians really wear blankets? She would have to ask Teddy. Mother and daughter walked silently to the tideline.

Mother was reminiscing about Glasgow during the First World War and before that, when she and Aunt Evie were children. 'Evie was always going to marry Willie, you know. Ever since she met him at, oh, age nine or ten. And when he said he was going to strike it rich in America, she didn't even blink about following him. That was the start of all of us coming. They settled and then sponsored first Flora and then Nicolas and then myself and your father.'

Moira stared at the changing waves. The shore would crash with white foam and then the next wave would begin and the next would be wild and white. She concentrated on the water because she feared that, if she paid too much attention to Mother, the intimacy would dissolve. Had Uncle Willie's death opened some ruminating part of her? Moira was uneasy.

'Why did you come here, rather than Australia, like Aunt Nell? Or Canada like Uncle Charles?'

Moira waited, watching Mother's curls blow around her high forehead. She was a glamorous woman, with those high cheek bones and full lips. Her eyes were distant, as if looking for something she had left behind.

'I love the Pacific.' She smiled at her daughter's attentive face. 'I love to skim miles and miles of water and knowing that the Orient is on the other side. One of the things I hated about New York was that every time I went to the ocean, I was facing backwards, toward home. And here, well, one feels only a sense of possibility.'

'So you thought Australia or Canada would be too British. That America would be a new chance.'

'Something like that. Yes, that's a good way to put it.'

Moira started at her mother's praise. 'And has it been that for you? A new chance?'

She observed Moira closely. Her shoulders rose and fell. 'We're a lot better off here. We have enough to eat. We have a decent house. You had an education. And you chose to do what you wanted with it.'

Moira ignored the volley.

'It is important to have something like teaching to fall back on.' She looked back into the wind. 'As much as I love your father, if I had an education, I would have had different choices.'

'Yes,' Moira said, afraid that Mother would soon regret these confidences. 'I understand what you mean.'

'Do you? Sometimes I wonder,' Mother persisted, 'still working as a receptionist. It's not too late to take a night course.'

Moira's stomach tipped. Of course the real source of her irritation was that she had the same doubts about herself. Moira was furious at this implacable woman daring the Pacific wind. OK, so she wasn't practical. Mother had spent her entire life being practical and where had it got her – the rim of the New World, in a tidy house with a man she didn't respect and a daughter who wouldn't do her bidding. Could she understand how strongly Moira felt about acting? Moira knew she would be a great actress, given the chance. Not given. Nothing was given. Mother had taught that in her pragmatic way. One had to reach in and take. And she was going to claim her life.

Moira cleared her throat. 'We're walking south. In the direction of Wanda's camp. It's really a dreary place.'

Mother frowned and regarded her daughter's cold, red hands. 'Perhaps we should turn back now. You'll get a chill.'

'Yes.' Moira nodded. 'We don't want to go too far.'

The Chinese restaurant was warm and steamy. Moira considered

Randy through his cigarette smoke. He was talking about enlisting, about giving up his deferment, about something. But she couldn't concentrate. Ever since she had taken Mother to the train this afternoon, she had been nagged by guilt. Why hadn't she played the perfect daughter just once, just during the family crisis? As Moira watched Mother board the train, she felt as if she were seeing off a stranger. Waving good-bye, she had found herself crying.

'So I thought I'd join the French Foreign Legion,' Randy continued with an impatient grin. 'And fight lions and tigers in deepest Africa.'

Deaf to his words, Moira finally caught his sarcastic expression. She nibbled on an egg roll.

'Come in, Moira.' He reached for her hand. 'Or are you on the train to Los Angeles?'

'The train.' She smiled ruefully and then started to cry.

'Hey, hey.' He gripped her hand tighter. 'The Wicked Witch is gone now. You're all right.'

'She's not wicked,' Moira flared. 'She's, she's. . . .' She breathed deeply, amazed at the depth of her defense. 'She's had a hard life. Immigrating. Losing her husband. Raising me. And before that, her own mother died. She just wants what's best for me.' Moira was grateful to see the waiter bringing their cashew chicken and mixed vegetables. She felt uneasy, exposed. She took a long drink of cold tea and tried to focus on Randy.

He was eating with a fork, waiting her out. When he saw her looking at him looking at her, he said, 'Good grub. I've always liked this place.'

She picked up her chopsticks. 'Me too.' Her stomach seemed to be settling. Randy was right. She should leave her mother on the train to Los Angeles.

'But I'll take you to a real swell place when I win my baseball bet with Harry. He's a clown to back St Louis. I'll take you to a French restaurant downtown, hey, how about it?'

He found Moira in tears again.

'What's going on, honey? You know I just want to take care of you. Don't you know that?'

'Yes.' She nodded, wondering at how much she wanted him. He loved her. He would take care of her. He had promised to come back from the war. And before that, he would win the baseball bet and take her to a fancy meal. Loyalty. She had ached for devotion her whole life. And yet, even as she acknowledged this, her throat grew tight. How could she be Randy's wife and a serious actress? She hated choices.

'Hey, Moi.' He reached his long blunt fingers for her cold hand.

She noticed that he had finished. And although she had hardly touched the supper, she couldn't eat.

'Hey, Moi, how about a ride. Great stars tonight. And we can cuddle if it gets cold.'

This luscious feeling through her body was almost enough to make her forget Mother. Randy was right. She worried too much. They would take care of each other, for tonight.

Chapter Ten

•

Racetrack, California, Spring 1942

MEXICO DECLARES WAR ON GERMANY, ITALY AND JAPAN

•

JAPANESE LAND IN ALEUTIANS

•

RAF BOMBS COLOGNE

Wanda awoke to the baby's squalling. Confused at first, she then realized that there was no baby in their room; she was not a mother. Yet the noise was not a dream. The child screamed again. Wanda was fully awake now. She lay back on her scratchy straw mattress and remembered that she was living at a racetrack. There were 8,000 other Japanese Americans at this temporary resettlement camp.

The baby was three stalls down and he had started to teeth last week. Wanda looked at her watch: 5.30. Unlikely that she would get back to sleep. The stench was ripe already. No matter how often they had scrubbed the walls these last six weeks, the fragrance of horse manure lingered. Six weeks since they had been carted off from their lives, herded into this ridiculous race track, fed like livestock in a disease-ridden mess hall and then bedded down in stalls. At least they had removed the horses first. People said that over 100,000 Japanese Americans had been evacuated, two-thirds of them, like herself, native born Americans. Well, obviously some sacrifices had to be made for national security and American liberty.

Wanda rolled over. It was probably just this ironic voice which got her article rejected the last two times. That and the accurate statistics. She sighed, resolved to rewrite it again and send it out by the end of the week. Perhaps next time she shouldn't call herself 'a foreign correspondent'. A little more detachment and dispassion, the last editor had suggested. Well, she supposed she could tone it down a little. Wanda closed her eyes and tried to put the article from her mind. The baby had calmed down, momentarily. She might as well try for sleep. Howard's alarm would wake them early enough.

At 12.30, Wanda brought Mama's lunch on a mess hall tray. Mama refused to wait in the long commissary lines for food which was usually inedible and potentially contaminated. Today Wanda was pleased to see some fresh coleslaw along with the tinned beans and meat.

Mama picked through the food as if looking for land mines.

Wanda tried to feign appetite for Mama's sake. 'Coleslaw,' she enthused feebly, 'good for the digestion.'

'Mayonnaise seems rancid to me,' Mama murmured in Japanese. She had hardly spoken English since the evacuation. 'And since when did you love coleslaw?'

'Since we were stuck with all those canned vegetables, I guess. It's a relief to taste some fresh food.' Wanda remembered the coleslaw from Roy's picnic in the park. That felt like years rather than months ago.

'Now that they have a Japanese cook, why can't we get a little okazu? Rice is cheap.'

It was good to see Mama emerging from her silence. Wanda usually hated the wordless vigil during Mama's meals.

Mama inspected the coleslaw closely, lifting the individual strands of cabbage and carrot with the prongs of her fork as if searching for an answer.

Wanda reached for the rapport of a moment earlier. 'Maybe they're trying to Americanize us from the inside.' She knew that Mama hated to be drawn out. Any attempt to revive her would be resisted. Where did Mama go in her silence? Did she become numb? Did she visit Papa? Mama had aged and sagged since his death.

Was this the beautiful woman Wanda used to watch in the mirror each morning, the woman she was going to grow up and become? Now there were wrinkles Wanda could not have imagined last year, rivulets in the dry skin. Flocks of grey roosted, like mad birds, on either side of her head. Even as Mama sat, she stooped, her back weary, her neck down. So Wanda was grateful for the periods of fury, the anger reviving Mama's old self. But it was too late today. Mama was gone for the rest of the lunch. Quiet, still. The way she had looked next to Papa's urn.

Papa had planned it so well, Wanda considered. He was always organizing, always scheming for money he would make and holidays they would take. When the family returned from Sebastopol and saw policemen on the front step, Wanda guessed what had happened. She wanted to see his body right away, to say good-bye before his spirit had completely left, but the police had removed the corpse for an autopsy. Within two days, they had pieced together the story in a forensics laboratory. Then they forced all the grim details on Mama over the telephone. They had even threatened charging her with collusion, citing the Japanese tradition of marital suicide. But a lawyer from the American Friends Service Committee firmly halted proceedings. The family eventually retrieved the body for a funeral.

Wanda stopped pretending to eat for Mama's sake. She stared at the coleslaw and felt a horrible guilt. If she hadn't moved to Stockton Street, this wouldn't have happened. She had always been able to distract Papa from his crazy schemes. He had drawn away from her after she moved in with the *Hakujin no* girlfriends. If she had stayed home, or visited more often, maybe he would have talked to her . . . maybe. . . .

And this pain over Papa's death was why she had left Stockton Street so abruptly. Of course she had to take care of Mama, but she also needed to retreat, herself. Now she could see how the girls had been confused and appalled and saddened by Papa's death and by her own evacuation. Still, she was angry at their immunity. She was a citizen like them, born in America. Why was she the only one carted away? The point was *no one* should be carted away. But she was immobilized by her fury. She had even imagined their complicity in the evacuation. She recalled every intimation of insensitivity. Moira refusing to believe the rumors of deportation. Teddy coming home with tales of those few Causasians who had protected their Japanese neighbors. Always the Lone Ranger, Teddy. Ann too absorbed in stories about Europe to concentrate on what was happening in front of her face. Of course, of course, it wasn't their fault. But whose fault was it? Then she began to feel an irrational rage at Papa. For leaving them. For claiming the dramatic exit. For driving Mama mute. The more Wanda tried to understand, the more she felt confused and frightened.

She looked over to find her mother staring blankly. Should she remove the plate now? No, she would give Mama every chance. She would wait for the bell ending lunch. These last few months she had become a specialist at waiting.

She always intended to return to Stockton Street. But at first Mama needed her. Then Wanda grew afraid to go out. Afraid to get hit by a rock as Alan Murakami had been hit – five stitches' worth across the forehead. Afraid to be ignored in the shops, called names or spat upon. Daily the news of harassment filtered home. And she almost began to look forward to these 'havens of refuge' as the War Relocation Authority called them. Wanda's anger and depression spiralled in on her until she became lost in her own madness. It was mad, for instance, to be afraid of Teddy and Ann and Moira, but she was afraid at times. It was mad not to return to Stockton Street, mad. So the girls' trip to the bus had meant a lot. Still, she wondered why she hadn't stood up that morning and given Teddy a hug. All the way to the race track, she had sniffed Teddy's flower and felt hope, a new sensation. This serenity allowed her to begin separating the anger from the terror from the grief. She wasn't clear yet, but she was starting to see her way out. She just wished she could bring Mama with her.

The camp bell gonged one o'clock and Wanda shook herself. Mother sat with her eyes closed, the barely touched lunch congealing on a cold, white commissary plate. Wanda noticed little bubbles in the coleslaw and imagined the food boiling at room temperature. She collected both plates; recalling the stern warning that 'sick plates must be returned by the end of lunch hour'. What did they think she was going to do with them? Sell them on the black market as Japanese war souvenirs?

On movie night Wanda tried to forget everything. She had been looking forward to seeing *The Grapes of Wrath* since it appeared two years before. She remembered now with some embarrassment how she had tried to drag Teddy to the film and how her friend refused to go. As she walked into the big room with Roy, blankets over their arms, she could almost imagine they were back at the Palace or the Verdi Theatre in San Francisco. She closed her eyes and tried to conjure the cosy seats and the aroma of popcorn. But this place did have its advantages. Since it was drafty, you could cuddle as close as you liked under the blankets. As they picked their way through friends and strangers for a good location on the floor, Wanda inhaled Roy's Old Spice shaving cream. Sweet of him to shave tonight, even though the hot water was probably gone from the men's room by the time he got there. Would camp conditions ever improve, or would they just get used to cold showers, toilets without doors and sewage pipes bursting to stink up the entire camp? Mama said it reminded her of the lumber camps when she and Papa had first immigrated. Wanda cleared her throat, this was movie night; she was here to forget everything.

'Do you like Henry Fonda?' she heard herself asking Roy.

'I guess so.' He was distracted, searching for the perfect place. 'But I always think of the director when I go to films. I really admire John Ford. Oh, there, by the Mirikitanis; there's a good spot.'

As they settled beneath their blankets, she wondered again if they had been right to postpone the wedding. Many young couples were getting married earlier because of the uncertainties. Roy said he didn't want to marry until he had something to offer – a job and an apartment. Besides, her mother needed her 'home' now. Yes, he was right. One more thing to wait for.

In the movie, Oklahoma looked bleak, hot and dry, just as Teddy had described it. Wanda wondered whether this $75 truck was like the one the Fieldings had driven and pushed across the country. Never before had she stopped to think how crowded it must have been with Teddy's nine brothers and sisters.

Roy moved closer and put his arm around her back. Wanda leaned into his shoulder, pretending to herself that she was oblivious to the gossip. Everything you did and said – even in your sleep – was recorded at camp. Well, they were engaged; what did people expect? She tried to concentrate on the film.

'Red River Valley' – was this the tune Teddy hummed when she cooked supper? Wanda couldn't remember. It seemed like ages since she sat reading in the dining room while Teddy cooked and Ann worked in the garden. Could she bring their faces to mind? Of course, she had seen all the girls during visitors' days here at the camp, but it wasn't the same. They looked different now.

Maybe she simply looked at them differently, being surrounded by Japanese faces for months. Until recently, she had considered herself American. However these days, because of her exclusion and her inclusion, she was beginning to understand how Japanese she was – in her facial expressions, in her gestures, in her values. At first she had resisted this, recalling Papa's long lectures about their equality with Caucasians. Then she began to enjoy the Japanese characteristics, to relax into them. She was not, as Papa had promised, an average American. It was an odd sensation – to discover suddenly that you're not only not who you thought you were when growing up but that you're who you thought you weren't. She reached into her purse for a pen and made a couple of notes.

Yet people kept trying to deny that things had changed irrevocably. She considered the story Roy told about this *Nisei* friend at Berkeley who won the university medal, but who, because he was in camp, couldn't receive it. The university official simply announced that he had been called elsewhere by his country. Now what was that supposed to mean? Is this the way history got written? She resolved again to revise that article and get it published.

Roy took off his glasses and wiped them with his handkerchief. She looked more closely and saw that he was crying. Yes, it was a horrible story and, if she had been concentrating more, she would have been crying too. No wonder Teddy had not wanted to see the movie two years ago.

It was late afternoon and Wanda was huddled next to the radio, furiously making notes on a news report about the internment. Mama was sitting at the table, staring across the camp and Betty lay on the cot, reading. Wanda wanted to get down every word, to quote the blatant propaganda, to compare the news coverage about these 'havens' to the reality.

'It is essential that Americans learn to distinguish between our loyal Chinese friends and people of Japanese ancestry. Many Chinese merchants have alerted Americans with signs in their shop windows, declaring "Chinese" or "Born in Hong Kong". But there are subtle differences in appearance and demeanor between the two separate races. . . .'

Wanda turned the page, scribbling furiously. Yes, this would be perfect as the opening to her piece, to use their own words to hang them. To show how they develop a climate of hysteria among Caucasians – and how all sense of proportion got lost.

Wanda thought back to this morning's interview with Mrs Omi, who almost lost her son at the haphazard dispensary that passed for medical care at this place. If Mrs Omi hadn't been right there, complaining until her voice gave out, little James would have died. Wanda had much more documentation now than when she submitted the article before. They wouldn't be able to reject it again.

'Enough noise.'

Had Mama said noise or news? Wanda sighed. 'Just a few more minutes, please. It's really important.'

'Write, write.' The older woman closed her eyes. 'For what good?'

Wanda clenched her teeth. It was hard enough to be rejected by these magazine editors. But the very act of writing seemed like a form of lunacy or betrayal to her mother. Lunacy because writing took so long and brought no money. Betrayal because it meant embracing a language Mama hardly ever spoke. Never before had Wanda realized how much encouragement and support she had had from the girls on Stockton Street.

'Just a few more minutes, Mama.'

Wanda wrote faster now, trying to remember what the announcer said while Mama was talking. Yes, this would be the perfect indictment.

'Hey.' Howard walked in. 'Time for the ball scores. What are you listening to this stuff for?'

'Leave me alone.' Wanda lost her temper. 'Just leave me alone.' Her voice rose uncontrollably.

Mrs Nakatani stood, moved between them and switched off the radio. 'Enough. Enough for the whole night!'

'Oh, no,' wailed Betty, slamming her book shut. 'My show's on tonight. See what you've done, Wanda.'

Wanda hadn't expected a visitor, because the three girls had just come the previous week. But one afternoon, she got word that somebody was waiting for her at the grandstand.

Wanda noticed Moira sitting off on her own, surrounded by packages, filing her nails and watching the crowds.

'Boo.'

'Oh, hiya.' Moira stood up and hugged Wanda. 'This is some parade.' She hated her own false cheer.

'Yes.' Wanda smiled, glad to see that Mrs Nakamura's friend had made it up from Fresno. 'How are you? Was it a long wait today?'

'Two hours, not as bad as last time.' Moira shrugged. 'Teddy and Ann send their love and,' she pointed to the boxes, 'some supplies.'

'You shouldn't have.' Wanda shook her head, although she knew that Betty would be grateful for the candy and Mama would appreciate the fruit the girls always sent. 'Thanks.'

'This is completely ridiculous, locking you up like this. I swear, I almost baked a cake with a saw inside, except that you know my baking. . . .' She trailed off, ashamed at her pathetic attempt at humor. 'So how's it going? How's that article? Did you send it out again?'

'Yes.' Wanda's face was impassive. 'Got it back just this morning, with a big round coffee stain on page four, so I know that they at least read that far. This is the seventh rejection.'

'Oh, no, kid, I'm sorry. Sounds like me and Pan-O-Rama Studios. But this is crazy. It was a good article; we all thought so.' Actually, she thought Wanda was brave and crazy. Brave to say those things. Crazy to think any magazine would print them.

'Hmmm.' Wanda knew that she shouldn't take the rejection personally. She found it hard to talk about her journalism. Should she tell Moira that she had gone back to writing Haiku? No, she would ask to read the poems. 'What's happening at Pan-O-Rama?'

'Nothing much. Except I'm thinking about leaving.'

Wanda frowned.

'I'm thinking of getting one of those good paying jobs in the war plants.' Moira blushed and then spoke more rapidly. 'I don't know, I'm not doing anything useful, typing for second-rate movie producers. And I've never been much of an office girl, as you know. I kind of fancy working with my hands – do you think that sounds funny?'

'Nothing you do would surprise me.' Wanda smiled. 'But you're all nerves.'

'It's Randy. He doesn't like the idea. Doesn't say why. Usually, his talk just makes me mad. But I can tell he's serious about this and I feel torn.' Christ, her problems were nothing compared to Wanda's. How could she go on like this?

Wanda looked at her friend and considered that Moira was always trying to please someone. Even her acting seemed to be that, reaching out to an audience and winning appreciation. 'Well, if you really want to, Moi, I don't see why you shouldn't.'

Moira nodded. 'I'm not very independent sometimes. Oh, well, here I am talking about myself again. You have any idea when they're going to ship you out to a more permanent place?'

'September – that's the rumor. And people are talking about Utah or Arizona.' She thought about the Jodes riding their truck through the Southwest. She kept confusing Henry Fonda with Hank Fielding. 'But we're the last to be told.'

'Arizona!' Moira's eyes widened. 'That's pretty far.'

'Full of scorpions, I hear,' Wanda said and watched Moira shiver. She was ashamed for tormenting poor Moira, who had driven all the way down here and then waited in line for two hours. 'Say, did you bring anything we could share right now?'

'Well, I did take the precaution,' Moira regained her equilibrium, 'of bringing two bottles of Coca Cola.'

At four o'clock, Wanda accompanied Moira to the gate. She stood there, waving good-bye, as Moira walked off to Randy's car. Rearranging the packages in her arms, Wanda smiled at the thought of Moira wearing overalls and riveting. Yes, Moi would be the most popular girl in the factory. Dear, adventurous, yet sometimes too tentative Moira. But – Wanda's ankle twisted on a rock and she almost dropped one of the packages – but Moira would be making bombs.

Chapter Eleven

•

Summer 1942, San Francisco

FIRST AMERICAN AIR RAIDS AGAINST GERMANY

•

AMERICAN MARINES CAPTURE GUADALCANAL AIRFIELD

•

BRAZIL DECLARES WAR ON GERMANY

•

US NAVY *WAVES* ESTABLISHED

The fog hugged low all morning as Ann and Teddy worked in the garden. They hadn't exchanged more than five sentences. Like so many experiences with Teddy, thought Ann, this was a meditative exercise.

Ann sat back on her heels and observed the small garden with a breath of satisfaction. This summer, they had produced all their vegetables. She had to smile at the radio blaring from the kitchen where Moira was baking. Although she could do without the noise, Ann was glad it was just she and Teddy in the garden. Working quietly like this brought a degree of tranquility.

Gardening was a whole different experience when Moira joined them. She would interrupt every five minutes to describe a tomato hornworm or to scream when she had accidentally bisected a slug. Moira had bowed out of the morning's planting, saying that her two left hands were better put to use in the kitchen. Ann had nodded, to keep her agreement low key. Typically, Teddy had encouraged Moira, 'You'll never learn if you don't try.'

Ann looked at Teddy who was softly whistling a tune she presumed to be from Oklahoma. Teddy hummed or whistled it often and Ann never thought to ask. Teddy wasn't a person who invited asking, despite her attentions to other people. It was easy to be fooled by her simplicity, which had been finely honed from painful wisdom and a basic optimism about human nature. When Teddy did talk, Ann could still be surprised by her friend's intelligence, which was expressed with dry humor and caught you coming around the corner. It was far too easy to lose Teddy in the veils of her own modesty. She knew what was going on. She just wasn't showy about her ideas the way Ann knew she, herself, could be. Ann sometimes saw her mind as a shield against the world while she guessed that Teddy used hers as a source of pleasure.

Suddenly conscious of her long rest, Ann scooped through the damp, black earth with her trowel and carefully laid the lettuce plant in a hole. It had been Wanda's idea to sprout the seeds in containers outside their sunny kitchen window. Too bad she wasn't here to watch the lettuce thrive. Well, Ann resolved, she would write to Wanda and describe how well the plan worked. Wanda wasn't dead, Ann reminded herself, and it was more useful to think about visiting her in camp than to moon like this. Ann lifted another plant and dusted soil from the dangling web of roots. As she set it down, she wondered if it would be accepted or rejected by the earth. Teddy didn't seem bothered by such questions. Ann looked over at her friend, whose movements had a graceful consistency no matter where she worked. Of course Teddy wasn't a saint, Ann reminded herself, she never would have been able to tolerate that. At first her friend's bottomless generosity made Ann feel edgy. Teddy's attention to her family made Ann's own desperate attempts at independence seem childish. But then she began to see that Teddy's responsibility for the rest of the world derived from a panic about losing control. Ann was familiar with such compulsion from Papa. While no one could approach his hubris, Teddy certainly had big pride.

'How's the Victory Garden?' Angela Bertoli called over the fence. Her hair was set in a new style today, pinned on the sides and showing more of her dark, open face.

Teddy stopped whistling, as if she had been roused from a heavy sleep.

'Aren't you ever gonna learn any new tunes?'

Ann looked up and noticed how Angela enjoyed flustering Teddy and how Teddy seemed to like it. Moira was wrong – Angela didn't boss Teddy. She teased her.

'Last week the snails won the biggest victory,' said Teddy.

'Ann, Teddy,' Moira called from the kitchen. 'Soup's ready.'

Ann stood slowly, first straightening her knees, then, with a hand on the base of her spine, her back. Ridiculous behavior for someone her age.

Teddy was still listening to Angela. 'Well, I guess I don't need to worry about you driving Papa out of business with the garden.'

'And just what's wrong with our garden?' Teddy rose to her feet in one long, fluid movement.

'Nothing that a little Tuscan knowhow couldn't cure.'

'Ann, Teddy.' Moira's voice was louder. 'There's a letter from Wanda. And the soup's getting cold.'

Ann collected the trowels and forks and waved her gloves to Moira. 'Just a sec.'

'Well.' Teddy cleared her throat. 'Pride goeth before the fall and look what happened to Rome.'

'Wouldn't have happened to Tuscany,' laughed Angela.

Teddy was torn between Moira's increasingly urgent voice and her desire to pass time with Angela. She wanted to invite their neighbor to lunch as would come naturally in Oklahoma. But she knew this wasn't Moira's way.

'I don't mean to interrupt your family meal,' said Angela. 'Are we still set for the movies Friday? I got news, but it'll wait till then.'

'Yeah, sure.' Teddy was uneasy. What news. Why did she have to wait for Friday? Why was Angela always trailing little mysteries?

'Right then. Six o'clock, my house?'

Teddy turned to see Ann had already rinsed off the tools and coiled the hose neatly beneath the tap. She hurried into the kitchen, slapping dirt from her gloves, thinking how much simpler life had seemed last year.

Moira wasn't kidding about the soup, thought Ann. It was turning cold here on the table in these horrible white bowls. She stared grimly at the unimposing stack of sliced white bread and the mound of oleomargarine. Even Moira could serve a more tempting meal than this. She must be in a snit.

Moira sat down and began to eat the soup with gusto. Ann reminded herself that the Scots didn't put a premium on cooking. Ordinarily she didn't mind Campbell's soup, but Campbell's *chicken* soup was an affront. Compared to Mama's nurturing chicken soup with *lokschen*, this was salty, greasy water – all the more offensive when tepid.

Teddy was the last to sit. Aware of Moira's irritation at her lateness and Ann's disappointment in the lunch, she swivelled around in search of distraction. 'You haven't opened the letter.' She reached for the white envelope addressed, 'The Ladies'. 'Nice of you to wait, Moi.'

Moira arched a thin eyebrow so high that it disappeared beneath her curly bangs. 'The soup's getting cold.'

Teddy regarded the still, beige substance in the white porcelain bowl. Not a trace of steam. She averted her eyes from Ann, afraid they might burst out laughing.

'Right.' She lifted the spoon to her mouth. 'Mmmm, Campbell's Chicken, my favorite.' As happened often when she was telling the truth, she knew she was choosing between her two friends. Moira relaxed against the chair. Teddy watched her face soften and her eyes regain their humor. Moira was a pretty girl, all right, especially without all that make-up she wore to work. Teddy finished the soup and consumed three slices of bread and marg. She looked around to find the others waiting for her to finish. 'May I?' She picked up the letter and began to read.

> . . . Well, it gets a little less horrible day by day. I think of this place as a lunar outpost travelling too close to the sun. The heat, you wouldn't believe the heat some days. Then the fog turns it cold as Antarctica.
>
> For the young kids, it's not quite so bad, perhaps, with everything so rough and strange and dirty. But for Mama and the Nakashimas and Roy's parents, who pulled themselves out of poverty, it's a nightmare. The worst part, I suppose, was having to clean the filth out of these horse stalls. All those niggling fears I've ever had about American prejudice turned to neon.

Ann stretched her neck and then rose to fill the kettle. 'Three coffees?'

They nodded.

'It's right she's angry,' Ann flared. 'It's abominable what they're doing to her people.'

'Who's they?' asked Moira. 'You mean we, what we're doing.'

'Yes,' Ann agreed. 'Did you hear about those two old Japanese men from Los Angeles who were arrested on sedition charges for "avoidance of the English language"?'

'Shall I continue?' Teddy cleared her throat.

'Yes,' said Moira.

> But the humiliation. They act as if we're freeloaders, here to vacation at government expense. When Mr Watanabe complained about the food – there were maggots in the hamburger meat! – he was told, 'beggars can't be choosers.' Can you believe it?

Moira found it impossible to sit still. She cleared the table. 'Next thing we'll hear is that Miss Fargo has gone there to teach typing and soufflé-making.'

Ann poured the coffee. Once they were settled again, Teddy continued.

> Sometimes Roy and I walk to the edge of camp to watch the sunset. Usually, this is a peaceful, relatively private time, but last week, I started to see explosions in those colors. Red, orange, yellow fire from bombs. I try not to dwell on it. I try not to think about my grandparents in Yokohama. I try to remember that our sunset is their sunrise and I hope they will pass a peaceful day and a quiet night.
>
> No word yet on the article. Must say I'm getting a little discouraged. I'm thinking of doing some kind of teaching once we get to the permanent camp – permanent camp! – I can't believe I'm talking like this. The pay is a step higher than my canteen work, so I should be making $16 a month. Well, here I am going on about myself. How are all of you? Your Mama, Ann, I hope there's some improvement. And how's the Emporium, Teddy? Moira, what's happened with the factory or shipyard?

Teddy dropped the letter on the table. Both she and Ann stared at Moira who was sucking in her lower lip.

'I planned on telling you tonight or tomorrow. I never dreamed Wanda would write back so fast. I wanted to see it all settled before I made an announcement.'

'Where?' Teddy caught her breath. Why did she feel so betrayed? It was just a job.

'Why?' asked Ann.

'One at a time. I start Monday. General welding and flanging, in Richmond. And why? I wanted to do something. Sort of like Wanda getting out of the canteen, I guess. Besides, I felt like such a dope passing the war in a dinky film office when I could be contributing.'

'You don't mean to tell me you fell for that propaganda baloney,' Ann said. 'Businessmen are going to make millions in this war off the backs of people like you.' She started at the harshness in her voice. It came from a sour place she recognized as guilt. What was she doing? About Uncle Aaron? About Mama? At least Moira was trying. Moira was always trying. That was the marvellous and aggravating thing about her.

Teddy glanced from one friend to the other, desperate to provide a palliative, but she was overwhelmed by pure, selfish disappointment about Moira's job. She was beginning to hate things that reminded her of the fighting. War surrounded them now – bloody reports on the radio every night; black-outs; ration talk; billboards and posters supporting the patriotic effort. People said San Francisco was going to boom. A big port on the Pacific, it would make a name for itself, but she felt like they had already been occupied by the American navy. She knew it would get worse; the city would lose its soul. Hank and Arthur had enlisted and Virgil was talking about it. Pop was getting more and more sloshed every night since the army turned him down. Even at the Emporium, WAR was written over everyone's face. Teddy wondered why she wanted to ignore it when everyone else was patriotic. She knew Angela's news would be like Moira's – only worse. Angela had also been aching 'to contribute'.

'Well.' Moira poured herself another coffee. 'I didn't expect a champagne ball, but you two could pick your faces off the table.'

'Sounds interesting,' Teddy managed. 'What exactly will you be doing?'

Moira pulled a brochure from the front pocket of her housekeeping smock. 'See here. . . .'

'Hello, Mama.'

The small, round woman in the bed was silent. No, not round now. She must have lost 20 pounds in this – hospital? holding cell?

prison? Ann thought how the war had washed away definitions and boundaries. Not only the lines of security, but the borders of understanding which were, after all, the real security. Mama was proof of that. Ann lit a cigarette, although – perhaps because – it seemed inappropriate in a hospital.

'Hello, Mama. It's me, Anna.' This was a long distance call. Reality faded in and out.

The woman turned her head on the pillow, reached for Ann's hand, then inspected it as if searching for counterfeit veins.

Ann stared through the smoke. She wanted from Mama something besides wanting. Would she recognize her daughter today? Would she say anything except 'Anna'? And what would that mean?

The visit was silent. Three cigarettes. A long look out the window. A cautious search of Mama's face. A kiss on her forehead. Ann sat back on the chair and waited for time to pass. The hospital was so clean it set her teeth on edge. None of the family had ever been hospitalized and Ann had always imagined harried doctors rushing stretchers down crowded corridors. This place was unnervingly quiet, more like a greenhouse. That was it, Mama was just another vegetable in the greenhouse. Ann leaned forward, staring into Mama's open eyes.

When the nurse tapped on the screen, Ann was ready to leave. She imagined the intruder as a guard, as a gardener of these vegetables. She inspected the white uniform for traces of leaves and thorns. The nurse sniffed twice, waving away Ann's smoke. But she didn't scold Ann, which made her question if the woman actually were a nurse.

Ann walked across the ward and down the long hall ruminating about nurses and daughters and mothers. Her whole life she believed that if she could make things better, Mama would be OK. If she could teach Mama English. If she could translate Mama's needs to Papa. For a while Ann even wanted to be a doctor, not only to cure Mama of her frequent ailments, but to make enough money to take her back to Germany where she met Papa or maybe to Galicia where she was born. But by high school, Ann's mind turned from medicine (although Papa was wrong about girls not making good doctors) to saving her own life.

Ann who had always been good at tongues enjoyed the stability of classical languages. The grammar wouldn't change. The very world they described was contained and safe. Sometimes she fretted that studying Classics was socially useless. How could Mama ever understand? Well, she grew weary thinking about Mama's needs. How could she get angry at a sick woman? Bad. A woman all alone with no one to understand her except a daughter. The headaches were the only thing that distracted Ann from the guilt. Even Mama noticed when the headaches got bad enough and left her alone. Ann knew she had to leave home. She was not surprised that Mama deteriorated after she left. Bad. Two months in that rooming house and a man broke in. Punishment. She was ready to go back home when Teddy suggested Stockton Street. She jumped at the offer even though she wasn't much of a group person. It was a selfish decision, Papa told her. Mama needed her home. Until they removed Mama to the hospital.

Slowly, Ann walked to the streetcar. The heat wasn't anything like Wanda's stories, but she felt exhausted. Exhausted at six o'clock in the afternoon? On the streetcar home, she pulled out a copy of the *Jewish Chronicle* that Uncle Manny had sent from London and returned to that article about refugee children: 10,000 kids out of Germany and Austria and they were still placing them in British homes.

Ann could hear the Andrews Sisters singing 'Boogie Woogie Bugle Boy' from the sidewalk. Funny since it was Friday. Usually music night was only on Moira's shift to cook. It was never this loud. Mrs Minelli would have a fit. Why didn't Teddy tell her to turn it down?

The music blared as she opened the front door. Ann felt exhausted and the anger burst quickly. 'Moira, for god's sake. . . .'

Moira was nowhere in sight.

Teddy came out of the kitchen wiping her hands on a striped green dishtowel. 'Am I glad you're home!'

Ann stared around, confused. 'The music. Mr Minelli,' she began.

'You prefer opera?' inquired Moira, rising from her haunches in front of the liquor cabinet, raising a bottle of gin to the counter and leaning fast against the wall. 'You'd prefer something more cultured?'

'I'd prefer something quieter,' she said, irritated by her own paralysis, then walking over and switching off the Andrews Sisters.

'You've never liked Laverne, admit it,' said Moira, listing toward the couch.

Ann restrained a smile. 'What,' she asked slowly, 'is going on here?'

Teddy shrugged, put her capable hands on Moira's shoulders and led her to the couch. 'Randy,' she whispered.

'You've never liked my taste.' Moira spoke in a sing-song to Ann. 'A bit downscale, right?'

Mama, Ann thought, the opposite of Mama. This one talks when she is crazy.

'Well, then you should be delighted,' Moira continued, 'to hear that my callow lad has left me.'

Ann turned to Teddy for a translation. Had Randy enlisted?

'Sit.' Teddy now had her hands on Ann's shoulders. 'Randy apparently doesn't want a shipyard worker for a girlfriend. Moira disobeyed so he's left.' Teddy hoped she sounded sympathetic.

Ann sighed and regarded Moira hunched on the couch.

'It's not only that,' Moira sobbed. 'There have been so many pressures lately – deciding if he should give up his Kaiser job and join the service. We've been bickering every day. It's not his fault. I don't know.'

'Let me have that bottle,' Ann said abruptly.

'Thank God you're home.' Teddy rested against the wall. 'I've been trying to get her to stop all evening.'

'Who mentioned stopping?' asked Ann. 'I'm starting.'

Moira giggled.

'It's been one of those days.' Ann walked over to the sideboard for a glass and toasted Moira. 'Listen, there's no other way out.'

'You two!' Teddy shook her head. 'If there's one thing I should have learned from Mom trying to stop Pop drinking all my life, it's that you can't step between a person and the bottle. Supper's gonna be served in 20 minutes, that is if you two souses are still awake.'

'What's got into her?' asked Moira, reaching over for a handful of the nuts Teddy had set out.

'Got me,' Ann said. She moved to the couch. A hand on her friend's arm, she said, 'Hey, tell me the story.'

'Not much to say.' Moira sipped the gin. She was relieved to be talking with Ann because as much as Teddy worried about her, she knew she didn't care for Randy. She missed Wanda today. She could always talk boyfriends with Wanda. Still, Ann was concerned. 'It's been hard for a couple of months now.' Moira took a long breath. 'You know what Daniel went through deciding on the service. Randy can't decide about whether to give up his work deferment and, well, choices come twice as hard for Randy as for anyone else.'

'You think he's mad at you for making a big decision before he knows his plans.'

'Doesn't make sense, but I guess so.'

'He'll recover.' Ann was distracted.

'I don't know.' Moira shook her head numbly. 'So strange, losing Randy means not just losing my past, but also losing my future. We didn't have plans exactly, but hopes. . . .'

'Yes.' Ann took her hand. She could feel the difference from Mama's hand. Moira's was firmer, more present.

Moira wondered how Ann could say yes. What did she know about it? How could either she or Teddy understand? Sometimes both friends reminded Moira of the strong, determined nuns who taught her. Moira had learned a lot from the sisters: passion and dedication and even an appreciation for her own talents. But she had never been able to develop that autonomy. 'Be independent of all except God,' Sister Lawrence had written in her high school yearbook. How did you do that?

'Hello,' called Teddy. 'Supper's ready. Anyone mobile in there?'

Teddy tried several topics of conversation – Moira's job, Ann's mother, the sweltering weather. Finally Ann lifted a thread of energy.

'I called the registrar at college today.'

Moira regarded her blankly, decided she was too drunk to concentrate and furtively ate two slices of bread for ballast.

'Yes?' Teddy asked eagerly.

'I'd be eligible to enroll in the fall, but I'd have to do it soon.'

'So what's stopping you?'

'How could I balance hours with work? Maybe I should just continue auditing classes.'

Teddy drew her brows together. 'You're stalling, aren't you?'

Ann shrugged. 'Well, sometimes it does seem like a frivolous pursuit.'

'Frivolous, shmivolous,' laughed Teddy.

'Yah,' agreed Moira. 'I could coach you from what I learned at Mass. *Agnus Dei, qui tollis peccata mundi. . . .*'

'Have some more communion bread, honey.' Teddy passed the

plate. 'Ann, I'm glad you've started to look into this.'

'What about Wanda's supply box?' Ann switched the topic.

'All set,' said Moira. 'I finally got those Milky Way bars for her sister. Teddy's going to take it down to them tomorrow.'

Teddy checked her watch. 'No time for coffee,' she said, 'Angela will be here any minute.'

'What movie?' asked Moira, trying for once to be conciliatory about Angela.

'Don't remember.' Teddy felt a little dizzy and stupid. 'I'm late. Gotta run.'

They walked past the Palace Theatre without acknowledging it. 'Lots to talk about,' as Angela had said last Saturday over the fence. They could go to a movie any time. Knots of people gathered on the sidewalks to cool off. Angela nodded to some men gathered in a circle. The Italian men were always out on summer nights like this, talking or playing *bocci* in the park. Teddy thought it was a nice custom. They worked hard all day and now they were as relaxed as if they were back in Calabria or Abruzzi. The women stayed home, cleaning after the evening meal and putting the kids to bed. They also worked long hours in the garment houses or, like Mrs Bertoli, in the shops. The only times they seemed to meet were over work, at church, in the laundry or on the bus. Moira complained they talked too loudly on the bus, but Teddy thought you noticed their voices because the language was different. And maybe sometimes they were a little over-excited about seeing each other.

Angela seemed twitchy tonight. She always walked fast, but now she was striding ahead. She almost knocked into Mr and Mrs Minelli as they strolled around the corner.

'Evening girls,' said Mr Minelli. He was a short, slight, bald man and he looked up at Teddy and Angela skeptically, as if nature had played mischief giving them such height.

'Evening folks,' Teddy smiled.

Angela nodded.

'A musicale this afternoon?' Mrs Minelli rubbed her thin hands.

'Oh, yes, sorry about that.' Teddy lowered her head. 'Guess we got a little carried away with the victrola.'

'Don't mind "Sonny Boy" and "Ich Ein Bein", but when they start in with those polkas my blood pressure skips a few notches,' laughed Mr Minelli.

Teddy grinned bashfully, then noticing Mrs Minelli's tight jaw, she said, 'It won't happen again. I assure you.'

'Very well, very well,' he waved them on.

'What's that all about?' asked Angela. 'You bailing out Moira again?'

Teddy related the afternoon drama.

'War seems so easy to understand in one way,' said Angela, as if she were responding to Moira's predicament. 'I mean Japan attacks us and we fight back.'

'Ann says Roosevelt probably knew Pearl Harbor was coming and did nothing to stop it.'

'Yeah, let me finish. Anyway, it seems like a thing between countries, where people follow their leaders regardless. Honor. Patriotism. Self-defense. Whatever. Yet in another way, it has nothing to do with those big notions. It's all about people changing and leaving and. . . .'

'But Moira isn't going anywhere. Randy is just being a jerk.'

Angela stopped with her arms across her large bosom and waited for Teddy to return to the point. Teddy finally admitting the hopelessness of her diversion said, 'OK, Angela, what's your news?'

'That's it.' Angela rested her arm over Teddy's shoulder and Teddy felt a flush from the bottom of her stomach. Angela cleared her throat, steered her off the sidewalk and across the street.

'The WAFs.'

'The WACs?' Teddy continued because she had half-expected this all week. 'You mean you're going off "to support our boys in uniform, to be a right hand to the men who bring home victory"?'

'I see you have some ideas about the subject even if they're not exactly on target. Not the WACs, the WAF, the Women's Auxiliary Flying Corps.

'Just in the States – taking supplies back and forth. Of course, who knows if we'll be able to go abroad. I figure it's only a question of time.'

Teddy shook her head and was suddenly furious. 'You're excited about this, aren't you?'

'Why not?' Angela walked straighter and faster. 'What's wrong with it, taking advantage of a change to learn something interesting, to do something useful?'

'I hate this war. Maybe the Germans and the Japanese started it, but the Americans are joining with gusto. It's such a waste. Not just the deaths.' Teddy realized she was blabbering, but so what, this needed to be said, some of it. 'Like you say, all the friendships torn apart, for what?'

'Hey, hang on lady. I didn't start the war. I'm just going to lug some cargo around in a tin box.'

'Just don't talk about it like such a great adventure.'

'I don't know about adventure.' Angela stopped and gazed at her directly. 'I think it's going to be pretty lonely.'

Teddy saw Angela's eyes were wet. She preferred being angry to this weak sensation in her stomach. 'Chocolate,' she said and she hoped not too abruptly, but then the craving for chocolate took a person by surprise. 'Let's go find a chocolate sundae.'

August 1942.

Ann listened to Moira as her friend packed Wanda's supply box. She sat by the open door, to let out the smoke. They had a truce: Ann would blow her smoke outside if Moira would refrain from cracking gum. Occasionally Ann wondered if they had cultivated these habits to underscore their differences or just to nettle each other. Moira was such a fanatic about health – exercise, diet, sleep – still, it fitted into the general narcissism of acting. But how could you worry about a little tobacco when the world was full of speeding cars and fires and guns and tanks? Why was she, herself, in turn, so critical of Moira's gum chewing? She was just as silly.

'I hope the canned peaches are OK,' Moira said. 'I couldn't get Del Monte like Mrs Nakatani wanted. What do you think, Ann?'

Ann stood and walked to the window over the sink, wondering if she should open it or whether that would just admit more heat.

Sometimes Moira felt intimidated by Ann's silence. She imagined getting lost in the dark, cavernous spaces. She enjoyed Ann's mind when she wasn't worrying about their differences. She admired her friend's certitude. She liked to ask questions about politics and history because 90 percent of the time Ann had answers. Yet she had a tendency to brood, to hold on to the cold side of an experience. Sometimes Moira just wanted to cradle Ann and say, 'It's OK. You're fine. You didn't do anything wrong.'

Gradually aware of the silence, unusual in a room with Moira, Ann surfaced. 'What, oh, peaches. Yes I'm sure they'll be satisfactory. They know supplies are short, even out here.'

'So you're feeling excited about college?' Moira sealed the box and draped brown paper over it. 'About your acceptance and all?'

'Yes, September.' Ann took a long drag on her cigarette. 'I guess that's next month.'

'Excuse me,' Moira affected a laconic Katharine Hepburn, 'but aren't we talking about your dreams of becoming a Classics scholar and rewriting *The Odyssey*?'

Ann laughed shortly. 'First of all, taking classes part-time while doing a full shift at the typewriter every day is hardly being a Classics scholar.'

'OK.' Moira sipped her coffee and stared across the table at her friend. 'What's up?'

'Papa.' Ann shook her head in exasperation. Exasperation with him, with Mama's illness, with her whole twenty-four-year-old life which seemed tied in knots. 'He wants me to move back and take care of him.'

Moira sighed, unsure what she would do in the same situation.

'Sometimes it seems the only choice. I could visit Mama every day on the way home from work. Then I could fix his supper and clean.'

'Wouldn't leave much time for *dono* and *donas*,' Moira said.

'No.' Ann was half listening. 'For a while, I thought Daniel and I could split the duty.'

Moira shrugged. 'It's so hard, you spend your whole childhood desperately waiting for choices and then when you grow up the choices are like spiked wheels.'

'Some of your Catholic symbolism is quite apt.' Ann laughed and then turned sober, butting out her cigarette. 'But I think if I went back to that house, I would catch it.'

'Catch what?' Moira was alarmed by Ann's sudden pale mask.

'Mama's sickness. I think I could go raving just like that.' She snapped her fingers.

Moira noticed the deep sores around Ann's cuticles were worse than usual.

'Oh, Ann, you can't catch that kind of thing. And you're different from your mother – I don't know, stronger.'

Ann shut her eyes. 'I hope so.' She marched over to the coffee pot to pour the dregs in a cup. 'Phew.' She set the cup on the linoleum counter. 'How can you drink this bilge, Moira?'

'I had kind of a rocky night, a few too many cups of gin. It's been over a month now and I keep thinking Randy will disappear from my mind with one more drink.'

'Moira, you've got to watch that stuff.'

Moira nodded. Ann could see she didn't need any advice and she wasn't particularly looking for sympathy. Ann checked her watch. 'Hey, shall we listen to the news?' Before Moira could answer, she walked into the living room and turned on the radio.

Moira was always amazed at Ann's capacity for distraction. She, herself, liked a proper ending to conversations. As the static simmered down, she asked, 'So you have some time to decide about school?'

'Yes.' Ann flopped on the elephant couch. 'A couple of weeks. Shh, here's H.J. Kaltenborn.'

'The meeting of Averell Harriman, Winston Churchill and Joseph Stalin in Moscow. . . .'

Teddy sat at Clooney's waiting for Dawn to bring their pitcher. She thought about how she had met the woman, in the cafeteria line after having watched her working around the Emporium for weeks. Dawn was a short, strong-looking person with deep mahogany skin. She usually wore dark dresses and no make-up. She had a habit of peering through her glasses as if they were a microscope. Teddy liked her a lot. They were both different from the other employees in obvious but also inexplicable ways. As farm people they moved differently. Dawn had a familiar easiness with her shoulders and busyness with her hands. Teddy particularly enjoyed her quick, pungent laugh. Since the first lunch when they got to talking about coming North – both of them had pictured California as North – Teddy wanted Dawn for a friend. This wasn't hard to accomplish once she set her mind on it. Dawn always sat alone at lunch and, although she first behaved indifferently to Teddy's company, after a while she seemed to look forward to it.

Tonight at Clooney's, Teddy watched her short friend carrying the pitcher and wondered at their Mutt and Jeff appearance. Initially she felt odd bringing Dawn to this bar, almost as if she were being unfaithful to her housemates. They often talked about returning to Clooney's for a nostalgic drink, but they never did, what with Ann rushing off to see her Mama and Moira's late shifts at the shipyards. They all knew it wouldn't be the same without Wanda.

Teddy pulled out a chair for Dawn. Interesting how different this friendship was – at once more formal, because they had only known each other three months, and easier, perhaps because of their attitudes about the North. Teddy listened to the Benny Goodman music.

'OK.' Dawn filled their glasses. She circled her fingers as if tuning in a radio. 'And now for the latest episode in "The House on Stockton Street". Ta ta.'

Teddy shook her head and sipped the beer. 'Some day soon you're gonna meet them. Come for supper on a weekend. Ann makes terrific lasagne.'

'Lasagne?'

'It's a long story. Anyway, why don't we set it up now? Next Saturday?'

'I have a friend who comes down from Martinez on weekends,' she said tersely.

'Bring her – or him.' Teddy blushed. Why didn't she think about Dawn having a boyfriend – most women did. Dawn was quiet about her social life. Mostly they discussed the other people at work, their own large families and, as Dawn liked to put it, 'The House on Stockton Street'.

'Her.' Dawn yawned. 'Yeah, maybe some time.'

'OK.' Teddy was unsure whether she had insulted Dawn or simply surprised her. Suddenly feeling conspicuous sitting at a table alone with another woman, Teddy looked around and noticed that half the tables in the bar were occupied by groups of women. Of course, with the men enlisting and more women out working they would go to public places together. Why did it always take her months to notice the world around her?

'I'd think it more likely that Angela would make the lasagne.'

'Oh.' Teddy was disappointed that Dawn didn't remember. 'Angela doesn't live in the house with us.'

'I know that dear,' grinned Dawn. 'Not yet anyhow.'

Teddy took the comment a step further. 'Angela's moving away from Stockton Street altogether.'

'Yeah?' Dawn pulled out a pack of cigarettes. 'Did she enlist?'

Teddy winced. 'She joined the WAFs.'

Dawn was intrigued. 'I almost did that myself.' She smiled sadly. 'You're going to miss her, huh?'

'We had good times together.'

'You still have Ann and Moira.'

'Still have,' Teddy mused. 'It sounds like there's a plague.'

Dawn took a long drink. 'But Angela is different from the others, special?'

'Each of them is special in her own way.' Teddy could tell she wasn't fooling Dawn a bit. 'I guess Angela is different.'

'Tell me how?'

Teddy returned Dawn's steady glance and felt safe in the feelings she had been hiding from. Her affection for Angela was more physical. Unnatural? It didn't seem so, still she couldn't talk about it at home. She hadn't even mentioned it to Angela although she knew, somehow, that Angela had the same feelings for her. Teddy didn't allow herself to rest too long in the safety because she was afraid to lose her courage. 'I don't rightly know. There's a way I am with her, easier, but also more nervous.' Teddy found her eyes fixed on the table. She turned to Dawn's attentive face. 'Easier in the sense of knowing we have common interests. A closeness like family. Things don't need to be said out loud. They're just understood. Sometimes when we sit together it's like one body.' Teddy felt her temperature rise, but if she stopped now she might never talk about this for a year. 'You know, when you sit with someone over dinner – or drinks like tonight – you're always careful not to touch, not to intrude too close. But with Angela, we never notice.'

'Never notice?' Dawn raised her thick eyebrows.

'Well, she doesn't seem to be bothered.' Teddy picked up her glass. Maybe this conversation should stop here.

'Bothered's one thing; noticing's another.' Dawn peered through the microscope.

'All I'm saying is we feel easy together. We like being with each other.' Teddy heard her voice was tight like Moira's when she was protesting a misunderstanding with Ann. Teddy strained to hear Benny Goodman, but the music had stopped.

'Great,' Dawn said finally. 'That's a fine feeling and I can surely see why you're going to miss her.'

Teddy felt relieved. 'Maybe we can discuss Angela another time. It's hard to talk about her at home. Moira has taken a dislike to her and Ann, well, Ann seems to ignore her. I don't know, maybe it's easier with a stranger. Not that you're a stranger to me, but a stranger to Angela.' Teddy despaired at her backtracking cowardice. 'Maybe we can talk again?'

'Any time.' Dawn finished her beer.

'And think about dinner, will you? Ask your Martinez friend?'

'She's not big on crowds. Maybe we could go out to dinner – with you and Angela.'

'Yes.' Teddy smiled. 'That's a possibility.'

Chapter Twelve

●

Fall 1942–Winter 1943, Lion's Head, Arizona

BRITISH AND AMERICANS LAND IN ALGERIA AND MOROCCO

●

JAPANESE NAVY DEFEATED AT GUADALCANAL

●

GERMANS START TO ENCIRCLE STALINGRAD

●

US CIVILIAN COFFEE RATIONING ORDERED

Sand without ocean. Miles of it all around. An endless beach robbed of shoreline. Maybe this was a bad dream after all. Autumn, with the temperature still striking 90 degrees. Sun so hot, so few buildings for shade that you sometimes felt you were going to melt into your shadow. Wanda never imagined herself a city person, but, for the first few weeks here in Arizona, the barrenness of the desert exhausted her before noon. Sometimes she even missed that damned race track. She spent hours looking, as if for an answer, at the wasteland surrounding the camp. To the north was a hillside filled with boulders, so densely layered that she imagined it an apartment complex. The only way she could accept anything was through urban metaphors – the clouds speeding like cars, the coyotes calling like sirens, the sky as blue as those pastel houses down on the Marina, the sun as hot as a foundry. When the heat calmed down, Wanda recovered from her delirium. She looked around and agreed this was not the surface of Mars. She knew there would be a difference between summer and autumn. There were gradations of color. She observed that the cactus came in different sizes. As did the rattlesnakes.

Washing clothes this hot morning – sweltering at 9 a.m. – she reflected that the most remarkable aspect of their internment was not the location, but the camp itself. She looked up at the sentry box towering inside one corner of the barbed wire fence. The guard walked back and forth. Was it cooler up there? Could you catch a breeze that far above it all? What was he thinking? Did he pretend he was a cavalry man guarding government land from Indians? She had taken to reading about Indians in that section of the mess hall which the Authority called a library. A couple of dozen mystery novels and an old encyclopedia. They promised more books. The encyclopedia did offer a lot of details about Comanches and Sioux. Wanda began to realize that this inland internment was not a new practice. Had they put barbed-wire around the reservations too? These precautions were such a farce. Did they expect the Japanese to run away to the nearest town and mingle inconspicuously? Or were these camps, as the press reported, built equally to protect the *Nihonjin* from outsiders? Did they expect vigilantes from town to come riding in with lynch ropes? She had been ranting with these questions all last evening. 'Quiet,' Howard had admonished her, 'there's nothing we can do about it. You'll only upset Mama.' Now Wanda concentrated her fury on the laundry tubs, pounding the clothes against coarse concrete.

At least her article was coming out, she reassured herself, at least one magazine was willing to publish the truth about these camps. So what if the *American Mind* wasn't *Colliers*, at least they had serious readers who might be able to do something. At least, she shook her head at her own modesty. She should just absorb the good feeling of getting an acceptance. Her first professional article. Roy had brought flowers and told her she was on her way.

''morning, Wanda. Enjoying your day off from the office?'

It was Carolyn Sasaki with an armload of sacks headed to the post office. Carolyn liked her job and had got it easily – perhaps because she had a year of college and her father, an accomplished musician, knew people in important positions. Although Wanda hated her own temporary clerical work, she didn't begrudge Carolyn the job. She knew she should apply for a paid position on the camp newspaper – or at least for the job assisting the new grade school teacher who was coming from Chicago.

'My, you're industrious, washing so early in the day.' When Carolyn smiled, her eyes were almost lost behind her plump cheeks. She was a pretty girl. Wanda admired her gracefulness.

'Not really.' Wanda wiped the hair from her face with a dry forearm. She hadn't permed her hair since the evacuation order, so it was harder to control. 'This is the coolest pursuit in camp, unless they install the Olympic swimming pool.'

Carolyn laughed. 'I thought it was going to be an ice rink, dedicated by Sonja Henie.'

'Maybe you're right, what's a Haven of Refuge without an ice rink? Did you manage to get down the breakfast?'

'No, just the coffee-looking liquid.' Carolyn shook her head.
'Were you brave enough for the cereal?'

'Had to eat something. I checked for maggots. The dark lumps were raisins. Morning's the only time I can eat. Then it's too hot until sundown. If I don't eat what they call breakfast, I get sick. You know, I've lost 10 pounds in this place.'

'I know.' Carolyn shook her head warily. 'Part of that's from overwork. You do too much, Wanda.'

'That or go looney.' Wanda waved her away. Not wanting to seem unfriendly, she said, 'You have a nice time with Howard on Saturday?'

Carolyn was bashful, yet eager to talk. 'You noticed?'

'Well, quarters are a little intimate not to notice when my brother slips out before the rest of the family for the evening movie, sits in the back with my good friend and then walks her home to the next block.'

'Yeah, it was fun.' Carolyn blushed. 'Of course the movie was dumb and the hall too hot and crowded. So what's new? But Howard's got a great sense of humor.'

Wanda nodded, weighing her own possessive feelings about Howard. If they married, would all his allegiance go to Carolyn? She reminded herself that they would be part of one big family. Still, would he be closer to his wife than to his own sister who had known him for almost a quarter of a century? Would he be more Carolyn's husband than her brother? What peculiar thoughts. One day she would have her own husband. It was hard to believe they had been engaged for over five months now. Mama kept asking about the wedding date. Wanda had grown thankful that Roy didn't want to rush into it. All the young wives here seemed to be getting pregnant. What would that do to their grand expedition plans?

'Yes, Carolyn, Howard can be hilarious. Why don't you come over some afternoon for tea? So you and Mama can talk.' Wanda reflected how most women in camp wouldn't have to make appointments to meet, because you saw everyone in the canteen or the mess hall or the baths, but Mama had been sick so much.

'Thanks.' Carolyn smiled broadly.

Wanda could see what Howard valued about Carolyn. Bright and cheerful, she was a respite from all the greyness of the Nakatani household. Yes, they made a good couple.

'So long for now.' Wanda waved. She watched the young woman walk briskly toward the little post office which was dwarfed beside the flagpole. Wanda found Carolyn kind and warm; in fact she was her closest friend in camp. But she wasn't Moira or Teddy or Ann. She wasn't, well, tough enough in certain ways. Maybe this was unfair. She hadn't known Carolyn very long. After all, she had lived on Stockton Street for three years. They had been through a lot together. They had built a friendship in that house. She knew her resentment about losing Moira, Ann and Teddy stood between her and her new friends. She missed Stockton Street horribly, all the more when she got a letter. Sometimes she wished they wouldn't write. But this was selfish because they missed *her*, too. The last letter from Moira was miserable. Nervous in her new job and pining for Randy. Well, even if he was a bit of a heel, he was awfully cute and quite in love with Moira. He just had a little growing up to do. Moira would learn. Men had such pride. How different was Roy? Of course he was different. He understood her ambitions. He shared them. Look how pleased he was about the magazine article. Look how he encouraged her to apply to the camp paper. She mustn't let the sun get her down.

Wanda dug deeper into the water, the suds up to her elbows now. Seep. Stream. Creek. The water was so scarce here people didn't use words like lake, let alone sea or ocean. She had been thinking a lot about marine biology lately. Maybe she would give up journalism to write about creatures in the sea. She imagined herself settling into a bathysphere for months, all alone in the water, studying colorful fish and delicate seaweed and comical octopuses. Peaceful. Cool. Wet. The encyclopedia had a large section on marine life. Unfortunately she had let her imagination lead her to 'R', 'Rattlesnake'. 'The rattle, long the subject of myth and fanciful story, tends to frighten or warn creatures that might harm the snake. The sound is produced by transverse vibrations of the tail; the speed of vibration varies with the temperature, but averages about 48 cycles per second.' She used to think that memory was one of her assets.

She scrubbed in the hard, cool water. Think positive, Wanda; maybe Mr Omi will write today and say you've been accepted on the camp paper. The idea was enough to carry her through the rest of the laundry.

Walking down the gravelled path through camp, she could see the post office was crowded. She should come back later. It would be considerate since this was her day off and most of these people wouldn't have another chance to check. But she couldn't restrain herself. As she continued, a rock skipped into her sandal and lodged between her toes, slicing the tender web of skin.

Wanda knew she couldn't count on the mail. But it had become a kind of addiction. The promise of mail often hit her during a particularly tough time with Mama or on a very tedious typing job. Maybe there would be a letter, an escape. Maybe she would hear from Stockton Street. And then she grew fixed on the delivery truck's arrival at 11.00. If she were at the office, she would stare out the window, sometimes contriving an excuse to step outside and crane her neck. Often she felt as if she had powered that truck all the way from town. Just seeing it lightened her morning. So by the end of lunch, it was impossible to keep away, even on days like today when it would be more sensible – and courteous – to check the mail later in the afternoon.

The line was orderly and quiet. Several people had brought books to read. Roy stood two people ahead of her. She wanted him to turn around. But it would be rude to reach past Mrs Nakashima and Mr Hata. Besides, she liked watching him when he wasn't aware of her. She admired the broad, straight back. The dark, rich, shiny hair. The glint of gold from his spectacles around his ears. The nervous thumb tapping on his thigh. He would be late for work if this line didn't speed up. Howard was probably already back on the construction site. Her brother would never be so impractical as to wait for mail in the lunch hour even if he couldn't count on his sister's compulsion to check the family file every day. Wanda considered how she liked Roy's impractical side. But who was he writing to?

His room-mates at Berkeley? Did men get as attached to their friends as women did? Of course, why not? Roy had all sorts of close buddies. Including girls. Was he waiting for a letter from one of those pretty blond sorority sisters Howard had teased him about? Wanda distracted herself, checking her wallet for stamp money, recalling with irritation that she had forgotten to bring the Sears catalogue bill. Sometimes that thing lay around the table for weeks. Mama refused to order herself a new nightgown because she felt confined by the meager selection. Everyone else would be wearing the same thing, she complained. Who would know? Wanda had asked, but Mother just sniffed and fell silent. Wanda made a note to order her another nightie before this one went to shreds.

'Waiting for something special?'

Roy beamed down at her, a packet of letters and a parcel under his arm. He did look strangely cheerful for this time in a sweltering day with four hours of heavy labor ahead.

'No, nothing special,' she murmured, regretting the boring reply immediately and imagining how Moira would play coy. 'Maybe a letter from one of my room-mates. And you?'

'Ha. The guys at college never write. My little sister's the one who gets mail in our family.' He showed Wanda the letters. 'She hears from four or five pen pals every week.'

'Yes.' Wanda answered stupidly, still wondering at the source of his pleasure. The package might be a care parcel from Miss College Coed. She didn't expect to know all his comings and goings even if they were engaged. She wasn't jealous, she told herself, only curious. There was a difference. 'So what have you got there? Did you win the Cream O' Wheat jingle contest?'

'Nothing that exciting.' He blushed. 'Just a photography book. I ordered it months – maybe a year – ago, but what with our – social mobility – it didn't catch up with me till now.'

'Oh,' she said, not wanting to appear reassured. 'It's great that you're still studying. I don't know if I'd have the discipline.' Of course she did keep her diary, but that didn't seem like real writing. And she'd only managed to write one article – albeit over and over again – in six months. She noticed the last shades of red in his cheeks and felt grateful for his shyness. Sometimes she imagined him as virtuous, stalwart, rigorous – completely out of reach.

'Don't know about discipline.' He smoothed back his hair. 'I like the stuff. I miss it. I mean all this camp exercise may be invigorating, but. . . .'

'Maybe you could lend it to me when you're finished? Are these from Africa?'

'No, Dorothea Lange, you know those photos. You told me about them. And I thought we might look at them together some night this week.'

'Yes,' she said, confused that she could be so flustered. Sunstroke, yes, it was getting to her. 'I. . . .'

'Next,' called the clerk. Wanda could feel the eyes of a dozen impatient people. 'Yes, maybe tomorrow,' she said to Roy quickly. 'See you later.'

'Nakatani.' The woman thumbed through her file.

Wanda was surprised that the brusque Caucasian clerk recognized her. Yesterday she had heard one of the whites telling another, 'They all look alike.'

She spotted Teddy's spidery scrawl. And two letters for Betty, who, like Roy's sister, had cultivated pen pals through a Quaker group. Wanda questioned this practice – it made the camp seem like an exotic outpost. She reminded herself the kids had little enough pleasure. It couldn't be a bad thing to make genuine communication with other people. She walked to the door, checking through the letters. Another Sears, Roebuck bill. Boy, they kept track of their customers. And a baseball catalogue for Howard. Nothing from Mr Omi about her newspaper job.

Since there was no mail for Mama, Wanda stopped by the canteen to buy her some Lifesavers. And since the canteen was right next to Mr Omi's office, she decided to drop by and ask when she could expect a decision about the job.

Mr Omi sat at the far end of a long office, his back to the door and his head bent beneath a brass lamp which illuminated his crowded desk. He hardly needed the light at this hour, Wanda thought, and wondered if this was one of his ways of protesting the government budget restrictions. Mr Omi, an older *Nisei*, was a complicated man. Intense, smart, very practical. He frightened her a little with his cool reason. Perhaps this wasn't the right time. Perhaps she should just be patient. Wanda started to turn and dropped Howard's catalogue on the floor.

'What's that?' Mr Omi was startled. 'Oh, Wanda. Come in. I was just thinking about you.'

'You were?' She picked up the catalogue and struggled to hold all the mail in her arms while looking like a competent journalist. 'I mean, yes sir, I was in the neighborhood and thought I would check to see if. . . .'

'Yes, yes.' He sounded more awake now. 'Sit here young lady and let's talk about this job.'

Wanda tried to relax, pretended she were Teddy, who would know the most sensible way to behave in a situation like this.

'You had excellent writing samples. And congratulations on getting your article into *American Mind*.'

'Thank you, sir.' She felt better now; she could feel her body cooling down.

'And you can type splendidly.'

Wanda nodded, listening to his tone. She imagined him a doctor advising, Yes, it's a healthy baby, with just one or two birth defects. 'But,' she said.

He smiled. 'Women's intuition. Yes, but. It's an embarrassment of riches. We had four people apply for that paid position. The decision came down to John Takata or you.'

'And John won.' Her eyes were fixed on the Sears bill.

'That's about the size of it.' He shook his head sympathetically. 'You see, as a young man, he's more likely to use the experience when he gets out in the world.'

Wanda couldn't help the tears. She kept her eyes down so Mr Omi wouldn't notice.

'And a pretty girl like you, already engaged as I understand, will be raising a family soon.'

'It's not fair,' she heard herself protest.

'Fair?' Mr Omi looked more closely. 'No, I suppose not, Wanda.' He stared out his window toward the sentry tower. 'No one said life was "fair". The choice, shall we say, was practical.'

'Yes, sir.' Wanda blinked back the tears. She tried to remember Mr Omi's kindness after Papa's death. He was an old family friend. He liked her.

'So you'll apply for that position at the school?'

'Yes, that seems most likely.' She couldn't chase the bitterness from her voice. Oh, she wished she were going home to the girls tonight.

'You'll be good at that, Wanda. You have a natural talent with people, like your father.'

'Yes, sir.' She stood. 'I'll let you get back to work now.'
'Give my regards to your mother.'
'Yes, thank you. Good-bye Mr Omi.'

It was 4 p.m. before she got home, finished her chores and had a chance to read Teddy's letter. The promise of this letter had carried her through the afternoon. Now if Mama would only continue napping until Betty got home. Betty would be excited by her mail too. It pleased Wanda how like her sister she was. In a time when difference meant social hardship, similarity was reassuring. It would be fun to share their letters when Betty got home. Had Betty come to think of this horrible place as home? Well, she wasn't blind. She could see the barbed wire. She could see the guns. Sometimes it was the hypocrisy of camp that oppressed Wanda as much as the restrictions – the pretense of leading a normal American life in this abandoned crater.

Tea prepared, Wanda sank down at the kitchen table, which Howard had contrived from spare lumber. Luckily they had been given some old chairs by a committee at the nearby Hopi reservation. She put her feet up and pulled out Teddy's letter.

Dear Wanda,

How are you? I hope the heat has calmed down. We're moving through Indian summer now – temperatures pretty high outside. But inside the house we're all doing OK.

Ann is really enjoying the scholarship. She impressed her professor so much that she's skipped a class. Real brain. Still, I fret about her. She's been awfully caught up with her mother who, sadly, isn't any better. Ann seems to think Mama's waiting for her daughter to rescue her. I go to the hospital with Ann every couple of weeks and, believe me, it's enough to chill your heart. I reckon the important thing is that Ann loves this book work. She and Moira joke in Church Latin over supper. I don't follow, but this is better than the bickering.

Wanda shook her head. She had to talk Teddy out of her constant self-effacement. Of all the girls, Teddy possessed the most common sense. She just didn't credit that as intelligence.

Moira is also a little happier, although I don't count on it lasting. She ran into a pal of Randy's at a party who said Randy was missing her a lot. Who knows? I'm sure I was never fair to the fellow, but I can't help thinking Moira is better off without him. She's doing great stuff at the shipyard. Won some kind of morale-booster award. She has a couple of new friends. One of them – Vivian – has been over to the house a couple of times. A livewire. Hep, I guess. A lot of fun, anyway.

We're still pulling cucumbers in from the garden. It's been a great salad season, but then I guess I shouldn't mention it since you've been getting such lousy rations. Let us know if you need anything new in the next parcel.

Wanda was still embarrassed by the parcels. Not that she was too proud for welfare. No, she was over that. With the tight supplies here at camp, they all hoped for shipments from outside friends. And it wasn't as if she had asked for a ticket to this desert wonderland. But she worried about Teddy, Moira and Ann doing it so often. They didn't make much money. They all had family obligations too.

Now, no objections. I can just hear your worrying. We all love to do this. Like Christmas. Anyway, Moira found some of that chili for Howard. Is there anything special your mother wants? How's she doing anyway?

I got a letter from Angela yesterday. She loves the flying lessons. It sounds pretty exciting. The WAFs still say all her work will be in the US, that it's too dangerous for women to fly across the ocean. Baloney, but I'm glad she's staying Stateside.

I've been thinking a lot about how dumb it is for me to be typing sales reports while there's a war going on. And as much as I'd like to go off flying like Angela, I kind of think I'm needed here with my family (Pop is having a tough time with the drink again) and with Stockton Street. But I got to talking with this woman, Dawn. Have I mentioned her before? She suggested that I ask to help with the War Bonds Campaign – The Emporium has a booth on the street floor now, did you know that? Anyway, they said yes, so that's what I do part-time – sit on the street floor with those forms. Plan a bulletin board. I even got interviewed by two reporters from the *Examiner* last week. What a lark.

Otherwise, nothing much is happening. Dawn and her friend Sandra, who works in the Martinez shipyard, took me to Baker Beach Sunday. That was fun – like being a kid – at least the sand was familiar from my girlhood. Sometimes it is possible to forget about the war. For us, here, anyway. I'm sure it's not true for you. . . .

Wanda wondered about that. She sometimes forgot this place was an internment camp and imagined it as hell. When the sewage stench got ripe and the crowds of people blocked out any shred of privacy, she was sure she was inside one of Moira's Catholic torture legends. At other times, walking with Roy on a rare, cool evening, she imagined Lion's Head as a Japanese ranch. But usually the war was hard to forget. She remembered Mr Omi's shrug when she called him unfair. She was beginning to realize how much she had wanted that silly job on the camp newspaper. Well, what could she do? She glanced around at the makeshift table and the skimpy decorations and Mama sleeping fitfully on the cot against the wall. Wanda closed her eyes in exhaustion.

'Hi, Wanda.' A greeting from the doorway. High-pitched, precise. She resisted the voice, resisted identification. This was her day off.

'Anybody home?'

'Shhh, you'll wake Mama.' Wanda opened one eye.

Betty was standing by the door, hands on her tiny hips, eight years old and already the châtelaine. Betty was a pretty child, taller than Wanda had been at her age, and more outspoken. Wanda found herself staring at the girl's short, straight black hair. Mama didn't bother with all the falderal she had done to Wanda's hair as a child. Betty seemed grateful for this; she said she liked to feel the wind on her head.

'No, I won't.' Betty hesitated, with amusement or confusion, Wanda couldn't tell. For of course she was correct. Mama could sleep through their voices during the day. Only the dark silence robbed her of sleep. Mama was generally quiet in her suffering. But in the middle of the night, Wanda could hear her groaning and rolling over and over.

Stretching her arms back now, Wanda yawned. 'How was your day, old pal?'

Betty smiled, sat down, her hands clasped around her knees. 'Mr Sasaki is going to start giving piano lessons. And he said I could do it, if Mama approves.'

'Piano.' Wanda felt a twinge. She had always wanted to learn piano when she was little. But Papa said there wasn't enough money yet. And besides, Mama reminded her, they could never fit one of those big horses into the house.

'Yes, you know that instrument with the black and white teeth that makes music.'

Wanda regarded Betty closely. This was one of those horrible moments when she felt like Betty's mother. Wanda didn't enjoy the responsibility of knowing more, of having to restrain her feelings. Yes, she was jealous of Betty. Jealous of her youthful insensitivity. Jealous that Betty had two mothers where she, herself, only had one who hardly spoke English. Jealous that Betty would learn the piano. Wanda considered that she was jealous of a childhood in jail and she felt ashamed.

'So what do you think?' Betty was on her feet now, clearing off the table, impatient with Wanda's distraction.

'I think it's a good idea,' she said. 'And very generous of Mr Sasaki.' She watched the grin spread across Betty's face. Wanda would have to remember that Betty was a child. She could not compensate Wanda for the lost voices of Stockton Street. Wanda would have to rely on letters.

Winter 1943.

Howard came home late from work and hurriedly changed clothes for supper. Mama, as usual, shook her head; she could not make it to the mess hall. She sat silently on the bed, her brow tight and her jaw set. Betty offered to bring home her meal. The three of them set out across the camp together.

'News from the city?' Howard asked.

Wanda smiled, thinking how he, too, had grown accustomed to the regular dispatches from Stockton Street.

'Moira's job is fine. Looks like she may get back together with Randy.'

'Oh, good,' Betty said firmly.

Howard and Wanda laughed.

'Teddy is spending more time with Dawn. And her father is on the wagon.'

'How about Ann's classes?' Howard asked.

Wanda realized that she had left this news for last because she was hiding something. Just that ridiculous idea Mrs Nakashima had about her going to college. She was one of the few older women who wasn't pressuring gently about her wedding date. Apparently the government was allowing some young people from most camps to attend colleges in the East and Midwest. Mrs Nakashima had put down Wanda's name. You had to go where they sent you – Nebraska, Missouri, Colorado, Ohio. No, no, she had told Mrs Nakashima, she had too many obligations and no money. That's exactly why you must go, said Mrs Nakashima. Too many responsibilities for a girl your age and don't worry about the funds. They have scholarships. How could she leave Mama? And Roy? Would he think she had deserted him? No, it was a selfish idea and impractical.

'Ann's doing very well with the advanced courses. And managing to visit her parents a lot too.' She was trying to convince herself of something.

The dinner line stretched three yards out the front entrance. Chicken pot pie, the unappetizing word had passed down to them. Betty told Howard about the day's piano lesson. Wanda noticed that he seemed distracted. He didn't even notice Carolyn until she waved in his face. But then this kind of vagueness was part of Howard's personality. Sometimes it felt like he left the planet for hours at a time. The gentle absentmindedness was charming, really. Why did she have to criticize his lack of ambition?

Inside the mess hall, Wanda thought how she had described the place in her last letter, 'spare and utilitarian'. She had explained that people tended to eat quickly – out of courtesy for those waiting in line and out of resistance to the cold atmosphere. Wanda felt like she was being fed rather than that she was eating. The real culinary rituals occurred during afternoon tea or at the occasional small party. They came to the mess hall for sustenance, not for nourishment. Often conversation was minimal like tonight and Wanda regretted this. She wanted distraction from Mrs Nakashima's far-flung ideas. She looked around at the faces – counting the friends she had made in the last month. The Morozumis sat in the corner. She wasn't sure, but she thought Betty had a crush on Tommy Morozumi. Carolyn Sasaki was helping old Mr Hata to a bench. Morton Shimasaki stood by the door to the dining hall, looking for his family. He was an excellent dentist and they were lucky to have him in camp. Funny the things she never thought about being grateful for.

'Hello, Wanda.' Howard's voice. Betty was giggling. Wanda

looked at her brother and sister and then down at their empty plates. Embarrassed, she turned to the chilly chicken and ate as fast as she could, trying not to think of prunes when the fowl slithered down her throat.

As they cleared their plates, she looked again for Roy because they always met after supper for a walk to the edge of camp. Howard caught her glance and said, 'Roy's gonna meet you later. I told him I needed to discuss something with you.'

'Oh.' Wanda looked at him curiously. Although he was head of the house now, he never made decisions for them. Whatever his concern was, it must be serious. Did he want to ask her advice about Carolyn? 'Sure,' she answered finally. 'Shall we go for a walk?'

They waved to Betty, who was collecting a sick tray for Mama.

After supper, camp was as noisy as it ever got. People chatted in front of the barracks. Friends strolled in the cool air, the only time of day comfortable for socializing. The old men sat in groups, playing *goh* and *shoji*. Wanda nodded to Katherine and Jean, the two middle-aged sisters who worked in the infirmary. They were laying a fence around their bonzai garden. Mr Sukamoto was painting his window frame a deep blue. Odd how your expectations scaled down here, how you became houseproud about two dingy rooms in a barracks. Dingy – very few of them were dingy any more thought Wanda. If they had stayed at the racetrack Katherine and Jean would probably have transformed their horsestall into an elegant mews studio.

Howard was silent until they reached the edge of camp. He headed directly for the bench Roy had built. Wanda felt odd sitting here with Howard. Sharing it with someone other than Roy violated the spirit of the place. Still, she was touched that Howard needed her advice. When they were little, the year between them was painful to Wanda. She tried a hundred ways to get her brother to notice her but she remained, always, his insignificant kid sister, the burden he had to walk home from school, the female he refused to play catch with, the girl who couldn't be interested in serious endeavors like stamp collecting and marble shooting. When he did deign to play with her, it was on sufferance. Mama promised this would change with adolescence and she was right. Soon after his first date, he began to perceive Wanda's special kind of wisdom. And she was only too happy to advise about Mary and Julia. Later, he was delighted to return the favor by introducing her to Roy.

'So,' Howard said, just as in his early dating days, as if making a statement, as if implying she had summoned him.

'So.' Her familiar volley.

'I wanted to ask some advice.'

'I guessed that.'

'Have you heard of the 442nd Regimental Combat Team?'

'No,' she answered. 'A film?' She felt a cool breeze along her neck; this was nothing as easy as a film.

'It's an all Japanese–American division of the army.' He paused.

She stared at length, trying to detour her imagination. 'But I heard they put all the *Nisei* soldiers in clerical posts, unfit for service.'

'Well, this is relatively new. They're thinking about drafting us too.'

'You've got to be joking?'

'No, Mr Watson knows all this stuff because his brother's in Washington.' Howard frowned.

'They're keeping us in prison and drafting us from here?' Her voice was strangled.

'Not the women.' He was momentarily confused. 'Anyway, I want to enlist.'

'You what?'

'They're never going to believe our loyalty until we're on the line. I want to show them this is *our* country.' He was pacing in front of the fence.

'It's a fairly one-sided relationship.'

'Wanda, be reasonable. I knew Mama would be upset, but I was counting on your support.'

Head in her hands now, she felt like a buckling wall. Everyone was leaning on her – Mama, Betty, Howard, Roy, Carolyn. She was everyone's confidante. And suddenly she recognized another implication of Howard's decision. University was out of the question. Betty and Mama could hardly cope alone. And would he die too? Where would it end? What were the borders of anguish and loss? She felt her tears and then his hand on her shoulder.

'Don't cry,' he said. 'I'll be OK.'

The tears were for herself and she was snagged between fury and guilt. Of course she should be worried about him. She must stop the madness. 'No, Howard, you can't go.' She spoke from an ineffable moral authority. 'If you don't believe me, talk with your friends. Talk to Roy, surely. . . .'

His long face stopped her.

'Oh, no,' she railed. 'No!'

'He wants to talk with you, himself.'

'What's the point in that? What's the point in this? You don't want to talk; you want to tell. You don't want advice; you want support. Well, I'm not a filling station.' She knew she would regret the meanness, but her heart pounded with the fever of relentless desert mornings. 'You've made up your minds. I'm not going to tell you you're right, because you're wrong.' She stood up. 'Wrong!'

Wanda marched back to the barracks like a mad woman, her face set against the evening wind, refusing to see neighbors, pretending not to hear their greetings, averting her eyes from the tall figure waving to her from beneath the flagpole. She looked straight ahead to the security of their rooms. As she opened the door to find Betty clearing up after Mama's barely eaten meal, she felt part of herself turn to stone. Glancing in the mirror over the trunk, she noticed the tight set of her own brow and the firmness of her jaw.

———————— • ————————

Chapter Thirteen

Winter 1942–3, San Francisco

SOVIETS LAUNCH UKRAINE OFFENSIVE

———————— • ————————

JAPANESE EVACUATE GUADALCANAL

———————— • ————————

NORWEGIANS DESTROY HEAVY WATER FACTORY AT VEMORK

———————— • ————————

CAROLE LOMBARD DIES IN PLANE CRASH

———————— • ————————

JOE LOUIS KNOCKS OUT BUDDY BAER

Ann glanced into the tall mirror above the sideboard as she sorted the cutlery from Sunday lunch. Moira had forgotten to dry several forks and as Ann picked them up she noticed water stains on the oak counter. So like Moira, well intentioned, but a little lacking on follow-through. Ann tried to catch her face in the mirror like this before she had a chance to set it in a pose of indifference or objective scrutiny from which she could perceive nothing. Here for a second, she saw a slightly lowered right eyelid, a winter pale complexion, a general fatigue which concealed something – defeat, fear? Displeased with the image, she looked in the mirror over her own shoulder to Teddy stretched long on the parlor couch, staring at the ceiling and listening to the radio. 'Japanese troops secured four more islands yesterday. . . .' The announcers had become part of the family, soothsaying uncles. Ann thought how she used to hate the radio because of the inane music and comedy programs. Now she hated it because of the news. She felt guilty if she wasn't listening to Edward R. Murrow or Walter Winchell, but the very sound of their voices removed her to a different, dangerous reality. Still, she stared at Teddy, who seemed to be listening as if they were announcing horse races. Not that Teddy was callous, she was simply more fatalistic. Suddenly Teddy glanced into the mirror, catching Ann's stare quizzically; she was not defensive as Ann, herself, might have been.

'How're you doing?' Teddy inquired softly.

'OK.' Ann sighed. 'Just grateful for a quiet afternoon.'

'You can say that again. What with work and family and all I don't expect I properly relax until Friday night. Can you imagine if we had kids too?'

Ann shook her head, thinking about the surprise and sincerity in Teddy's voice. At times like this Teddy reminded Ann of her brother Daniel's ingenuousness. He was always set on making the world a better place. Who would have guessed he would wind up marching through Europe? It had been weeks since she had heard from him. It did no good to worry. She walked over and shut off the radio.

Teddy looked up, surprised.

'Oh, sorry,' Ann said, distracted. 'You were listening.' She bent down.

'No don't bother. I'd rather talk to you.'

Ann leaned against the armchair, buoyed with appreciation for her friend, for their house, for the refuge – however temporary it might be. 'I've got an idea.' She startled herself with her own enthusiasm. 'Let's have a little party, nothing elaborate, just a few friends. To dispel headaches and heartaches and to revive our old spirit. This place has turned into a rest home.'

'Well.' Teddy paused, pulled her legs around and sat straighter. 'Sounds OK to me.' Her hesitation came from some vague sense of betrayal to Wanda. Then she reckoned that Wanda would hardly mind; she would enjoy the party gossip. 'Sure, why not? Might get Moira out of herself. She could find a new boyfriend.'

'Speaking of which,' Ann lit a cigarette, 'did you hear she's going to have a "civilized drink" with Randy? She ran into him at the movies last night.'

'Oh.' Teddy tried to ignore the turmoil in her stomach. Of course it made sense for Moira to be talking to him again since they lived in the same neighborhood.

'How about two weeks from Saturday?' Ann marvelled again at her initiative. She felt revived already and was tempted to inspect herself in the mirror.

'Can't.' Teddy knew Ann would be surprised that she had prior plans. 'I agreed to go out that night with Dawn and her friend Sandra. It would be hard to change because Sandra is only down from Martinez on weekends.'

'Oh, I think you told me about her.' Ann waited for Teddy to elaborate. She didn't want to push, although she was curious. Teddy never went out with anyone except her family or with Moira and herself.

'Did I?' Teddy was flustered. Since she was always self-conscious talking about Dawn, it was possible she had forgotten.

'Three weeks then?'

'Sure,' said Teddy, running a hand through her hair. She fiddled with the bobbypin behind her ear, wondering why she was so reluctant. In the past, she had been the one who wanted to get the girls together, to hold them together. Something about this party didn't seem quite right. But, Ann was like Moira, when she set her mind on a plan, there was no changing.

'Speaking of how people are,' Ann shut the kitchen door and moved closer to Teddy, 'you seemed quiet over lunch. Something happening at home again?'

'Home,' mused Teddy, 'guess I do think of that place as home still. Can you have two homes?'

'All of us do. Maybe until we get married.'

Teddy closed her eyes. 'Mom said something to me last week. "Remember this will always be your home." I said "yes", and nodded gratefully, but how could I go back to that tiny, crowded little house? I look around at the doilies and the curtains and the popcorn bedspreads we brought from Oklahoma and the table Virgil made and I think, yes, this is where I came from. Part of me hasn't left. But I wouldn't fit in now, not with Hank's kids. I don't think I could cope any more with Pop's drinking in a daily way. And my notions have outgrown that place. I wanted to turn back to Mom and say, "You've got a home with me whenever you want it".'

'I know what you mean.' Ann sat down at the end of the couch, leaving plenty of room in case Teddy wanted to stretch again. She loved to see Teddy claim the length of her long body. She imagined that she was living with a particularly large and friendly cat.

'But the fact is I couldn't pull her away from Pop. Despite his drinking – because of it – I don't know. Anyway, they're kind of one person in a way. I just don't think there's a thing I can do.'

Ann studied Teddy's bewilderment, appreciating her opening up like this. You couldn't call Teddy a cold person. In fact she was often so concerned with others, so intent on filling the house with cheer or settling the differences between herself and Moira that she became almost disembodied.

'I think you're right.' Ann patted Teddy's ankle. 'It's like visiting Mama. I know it's important just to make an appearance.'

'But the worst thing,' Teddy shook her head to keep from crying, 'is that I don't know if it's for me I'm appearing or for them.'

'Probably both.' Ann put her hand on Teddy's shoulder. She wanted to tell her it was all right to cry, but frankly she wasn't sure. What would she do with this giant woman rolling over Niagara Falls? Could she put the pieces back together? She remembered this sharp, anxious feeling from her childhood.

'When am I gonna figure out what they need? I'm already twenty-five.'

'Maybe the point is to figure out what *you* need.'

'I have what I need.' Teddy looked surprised when Ann didn't nod as she expected her to. She pressed on urgently. 'I have my friends, this home, you know, my job. No, I don't think I need to be wondering more about myself.'

Ann waited. There was so much she didn't understand about Teddy. Was she really happy being a secretary in a department store? Maybe she, herself, was the odd one for wanting to be a teacher. In many ways, Teddy was the model of realism.

'Anyway, the party.' Teddy sat straighter. 'It'll be great. Let's draw up a list tonight. Moira will be thrilled.'

Right, Ann nodded, resigned to Teddy's implacable shyness.

Teddy stood in front of the bathroom mirror, moving her head like a frantic prairie dog over the collars of two dresses – one a navy shirtwaist and the other a brown tweed suit. Ridiculous is what this was. She never worried about clothes. She always thought Wanda's and Moira's preoccupation with wardrobe was a quaint feminine custom that bordered too close to frivolous when they stayed overlong in the bathroom. But she felt some special charge about tonight. When Dawn said she and Sandra wanted to take her to a 'club', she felt stripped. Maybe people were obsessed with costume because they needed to hide. Clothes provided a means of fitting in or standing out in a 'role' you had developed to cover yourself. Interesting as this speculating was, it didn't make the choice between brown and navy any easier. She could hardly ask Ann's or Moira's advice. They would just start in with questions about where she was going.

She hadn't said anything to Dawn about her feelings for Angela. Nor had Dawn been forthcoming about Sandra, although she had been unable to suppress a smile when showing her picture. Still, Teddy knew Dawn was a homosexual and she suspected Dawn knew she was. But was she truly? No, she was just in love with Angela Bertoli. Simply thinking this made her blanch. When was the girl going to write back? Noticing her chalky face in the mirror, she remembered it was rude to monopolize the bathroom on Saturday night. Besides if she didn't get moving, Ann and Moira would start in with those questions.

Back in her room, Terry decided on – or became reconciled to – the brown suit. It was more comfortable, less showy. If she could only find something to make her invisible. If she was so nervous, why was she going? Well, she felt a certain loneliness. Although she didn't really figure herself a homosexual, she liked being able to talk to Dawn about Angela. Besides, she was curious about this club, no two ways about it.

'Bye, Teddy,' Ann called on her way out the front door.

'See you later, hon,' shouted Moira.

'Right,' she called back. 'Enjoy the movie.' She wished she was going to see *For Whom The Bell Tolls* with them. 'Catch you tonight, or maybe tomorrow morning. Don't worry if I'm late.' She babbled on. What were they going to think? For sure she'd get the third degree at lunch tomorrow.

'OK, we won't,' Moira called.

Teddy decided not to interpret Moira's tone of voice.

She scrambled for her shoes. She was going to be late for supper at the Glass Boat, another place she had never heard of – around the corner from the Quiet Cat Club. Sounded like a chapter from *Dr Doolittle*. As she buttoned her coat at the front door, Teddy wondered if she had this figured all wrong. Maybe, she felt a shade of disappointment, this was just going to be a sedate evening with two friends.

In the dark alley outside the Quiet Cat, Teddy shifted from one foot to another. It was ten o'clock by the time they arrived at the door of the bar. Dawn kept fussing that it was still too early for any life, but Sandra had rushed them to the club because this was Teddy's first night. Teddy had blinked, since this implied that she would be invited again.

Dawn leaned on the bell and Sandra stood on her toes peering, impatiently, into the tiny window. It was a blustery evening and Teddy rubbed her hands to keep warm. She thought how much she enjoyed Sandra, who made Dawn laugh and feel embarrassed in a way that opened up a whole new person. They even seemed to fit together like puzzle pieces. Sandra was thin, almost stringy, while Dawn was stocky. Both were 8 or 9 inches shorter than herself, Teddy reckoned. Despite Sandra's frail appearance, she was highly animated, a refreshing counterpoint to the laconic Dawn. For the first part of the evening, Teddy felt self-conscious about socializing with two colored women. She hadn't spent any time with Negroes since Oklahoma, where, much to her parents' dismay, she made friends with Anita Green and liked to hang out at the Greens' in the evening, laughing and eating their spicy foods. There was a separateness to the races in Fortun, Oklahoma, but nothing like in California. Although Mom and Pop objected to her friendship with Anita, they often ran into Negroes on the streets and passed courtesies. Certainly the blacks and whites wound up on the same road west once the dust hit. When they got to California, one of the most noticeable things was that all the folks in the stores where they shopped were white. It wasn't until she finished high school that she began to comprehend 'Northern' segregation.

Both Sandra and Dawn had their backs to her now. She could turn and disappear around the corner. They would understand her nervousness. They would forget about her in half an hour and start having a fine time with their friends. Teddy smiled and shook her head at her own cowardice. She thought how much she wanted to tell Dawn and Sandra about Anita, but she feared they might find it odd. They might take offense. She didn't want to sound over-eager for their friendship. An easiness had grown between them during dinner. Funny that she hadn't thought about Anita for years, not even after months of lunches with Dawn. They tended to talk mostly about the Emporium or about Stockton Street or, more recently, about Angela and Sandra. There was something about Sandra that evoked childhood days and old feelings.

'She's coming.' Sandra's voice was high-pitched, almost like Gracie Allen, when she got excited.

'About time.' Dawn scolded someone through the wrought iron grille.

Teddy felt as if she were at a 1920s speakeasy. She couldn't decide whether the gurgling in her stomach was excitement or fear.

Slowly, they adjusted their eyes to the light. Teddy coughed several times, from the thickness of the smoke and the tart, sour smell of liquor. A few delicate men sat at the far end. But most of the people in the bar appeared to be women.

'New one with you?' A tough blond woman with red earrings greeted Dawn.

'Yeah, a friend,' Dawn responded brusquely. 'Come on girls, let's requisition a table before the hordes invade.'

Sandra pointed to a place half-way down the room, against a wall.

As they settled themselves on rickety wooden chairs, Dawn turned to Teddy. 'I woulda introduced you to Gretta, but I didn't know how public you wanted to be.'

Teddy felt an ache in her chest. Was it the smoke, was it the explosive 'South American Way' blaring from the jukebox or was it this slim warning about being visible as one of 'those girls'? It had never occurred to her that she would be 'caught' here. This seemed so separate from home and work, as if she had gone to Mars for the evening. Why did it matter to other people? Mr Whitney caroused at the Steer Inn bar with the guys after work. Why couldn't she go out on Saturday with Sandra and Dawn? She wondered what Moira and Ann and Wanda would think of Gretta. She found herself looking down at the table and breathing rapidly.

'Dawn, look what you've done to the girl, thrown her into a tizzy and we only just got here. Don't make it sound deadly. It's not like Gretta has a direct line to the cop shop.' She patted Teddy's hand. 'You just relax and don't let our darkest Dawn fuss you none, understand?'

Before Teddy had a chance to reply, two women hurried over to their table.

'Mary Ellen and Hannah!' whooped Sandra. Teddy tried to

ignore the implications of their previous conversation – police, loyalty, subterfuge – by concentrating on the two new girls. Mary Ellen was a pretty Negro with elegant curls shining down her back. Her luminous round face was further brightened by a smear of carmine lipstick. Hannah was almost unidentifiable as female – a tall, white woman with close-cropped hair, she wore slacks and a pin-striped shirt. The four women seemed close friends. Teddy remembered something Dawn had said over lunch about the Quiet Cat being one of the few places where it was safe to go with racially mixed groups. Apparently the city had all types of bars, like Wallace's Spot for upper-class women; there was some talk that when the spinster princess from Argentina was in town, she spent several nights at Wallace's Spot. The Carousel was patronized by white working women. Anyway, the Quiet Cat had always been mixed. When Teddy asked why, Dawn shrugged as if she couldn't take the time to figure it out. And there was the Whispering Well, which was mostly colored women. Dawn and Sandra split their weekends between the Quiet Cat and the Whispering Well, plainly tailoring tonight's venue to Teddy.

'OK, girls.' Gretta sasayed over and wiped a grey rag in front of them as if cleaning the table. Teddy noticed that she barely skimmed the damp cloth over the various spots and scars on the wooden surface. 'Let's have less gasps and more gulps. What'll it be?'

'Beer?' Dawn asked.

'Yes,' said Teddy.

Sandra nodded.

'Pitcher, please,' Dawn ordered.

'So don't we get an introduction?' asked the white woman, now leaning against the wall, with one arm around her friend's shoulder.

'Oh, Teddy Fielding,' Sandra laughed. 'This is Hannah Kelly and Mary Ellen Moore.'

'Hi, Teddy.' Hannah had a surprisingly sweet voice.

'Charmed, I'm sure.' Mary Ellen gave her a meticulously manicured hand and a broad smile.

'Mind if we join you?' Hannah asked Dawn.

Dawn looked at Teddy protectively.

'Oh, we won't eat her for God's sake,' Hannah laughed.

Teddy tried to smile. She wanted to reassure Dawn that she could fend for herself. While she was touched by Dawn's concern, she was also troubled about being a burden. After all, this was Saturday night.

'Make yourself at home.' Teddy invoked her easiest Oklahoma welcome. 'Sorry we can't offer more cosy accommodation.'

Mary Ellen laughed, sat down beside Sandra and immediately began whispering and giggling. Dawn kept a close watch on Hannah as she sat beside Teddy.

'That's the spirit, girl,' Hannah grinned. 'A little hospitality goes a long way in this cold world.'

Within twenty minutes the bar was bustling like Market Street at noon. The small room grew smokier; the conversations and the Andrews Sisters were tuned up.

> Shrimps and Rice, won't you hold tight?
> Hold tight. Hold tight. Hold tight.

The four friends obviously had a lot to talk about and Teddy was relieved to sit back, soaking in the atmosphere. She watched the single women at the bar ordering drink after drink, working up the courage to converse. The graceful men in the far corner laughed quietly. It took her fifteen minutes to turn her head and watch the people on the dance floor.

A dozen girls were swinging under yellow lights.

> Mother, may I go out dancing? Mother, may I go romancing?
> Must I keep on dancing? . . . yes, my darling daughter.

Teddy tried to forget her mother. Suddenly, she fell into a deep hollowness. Could she write to Angela about the Quiet Cat? Were there Quiet Cats in Texas? Was Angela right now dancing to 'One Night When The Moon Was So Mellow' with some yellow rose? Did Angela go for the cowgirl types? Teddy looked back to the bar, above the tapping fingers and the stiff necks, to the mirror which caught all the sources of light and spent them back through bottles of whisky and gin. Phew, this place did smell like a tavern. She recalled those terrifying Saturday nights when they couldn't find Pop and she and Hank and Arthur had to comb the bars until they spotted him huddled at the back of Joe's Hut or the Dry Stick or one of a dozen Okie watering holes.

Teddy was conscious of her stomach ache easing. She heard a loud buzzing in her ear. The beer. How had she gone through three glasses already? It was the same for everyone at the table. Dawn could usually handle only one glass after work. This place wasn't at all what she had expected. Better in some ways. Far more women than she had imagined. And the variety! Integrated couldn't describe it. Not only had she seen Negroes, Orientals, whites and even a woman who looked like an East Indian – was she the Argentine princess in disguise? – but they were wearing all sorts of outfits – butch and femme and some, like herself, in between. Teddy was surprised at how familiar this place was, at all the terms she knew, from her reading . . . from her imagination? She thought how Moira was always teasing her about not being observant with what she wore. It was true, on Saturday morning she could be found with two different colored socks. And worse, occasionally she arrived at work to find a hem falling from her dress. Sometimes she felt that Moira was her mother, the way she groomed her. Anyway, here she was, suddenly fascinated with the clothes people wore in this new, yet comfortable territory. What a relief to be in a room almost empty of men. One layer of tension was replaced by another because of the way the women scrutinized you.

'How about a dance?' Hannah asked.

Teddy let in the music again.

> Oh, beat me Daddy eight to the bar . . . he plays the
> boogie . . . he plays eight to the bar!

'What's the matter?' Hannah persisted. 'Don't they dance in Oklahoma?'

'Oh.' Teddy's jaw locked. Inadvertently, she glanced at Mary Ellen who was busy whispering to Sandra. She caught Dawn's eye. Her friend seemed to be saying, do what you like, but watch it.

Hannah observed the exchange. 'Unless your chaperone objects.'

'You know, Hannah,' Dawn wiped her glasses, 'sometimes you're a pain in the ass.'

Teddy was glad their teasing gave her a chance to pull herself together. What was Dawn so worried about? 'Sure,' she answered. 'We dance up a storm in Oklahoma.' Now where did that confident voice come from? She remembered her last dance – with Randy at the house party while Angela and Moira looked on. If she could handle that, she could do 'Beat Me Daddy' with Hannah Kelly.

'So you're new to the scene?' Hannah inquired, drawing closer to Teddy.

> Yes, my darling daughter. . . .

Teddy tried to shut out the jukebox. These girls did have a thing for the Andrews Sisters. Then, abruptly conscious of Hannah's question – actually the warmth of Hannah's body pressed against her own, she said, 'No, I've lived in San Francisco for about ten years.' She knew this was the wrong answer. She felt like she had to continue immediately or she would explode. 'And you?'

'Born in the city.' Hannah pulled back, frowning. 'I mean,' she drew close again and spoke more slowly, 'you new to this bar scene?'

Teddy thought Hannah's question was more challenge than inquiry. If she said yes, did that mean she was a lesbian? Was she a lesbian? Was she like the women in the frilly dresses or the ones masquerading as men? She must admit that this evening had released fantasies she never had allowed herself to consider with the lights on. If she wasn't a lesbian, what was she doing here? She was so nervous she didn't know what she felt. And why was Hannah asking? She was with Mary Ellen, wasn't she?

'I've never been here before, if that's what you're asking.' Clarity emerged from somewhere.

'That satisfies part of the question.'

I'll be with you in apple blossom time. . . .

Teddy tried to remember the words from Moira's record. She had played this song over and over and over after Randy left.

'You known Dawn and Sandra long?'

'I work with Dawn at . . . downtown,' Teddy said carefully, for she had developed a wariness during the last hour. Of course Hannah wouldn't tell anyone at the Emporium, of course she was a lesbian herself. She knew Dawn worked there, didn't she? How much did these people know about each other? Ridiculous, they were all people. Could Hannah see how nervous she was?

A couple bumped into them and Teddy was relieved to encounter a real, physical obstacle. She let out a long sigh, releasing 5 minutes of breath.

'What the hell?' Hannah screeched. 'Oh, Lucille, do me a favor, will you stay off the floor when you're soused? Liquor and polkas do not mix.'

Teddy detected a shade of concern in Hannah's rebuke.

'Come on, Kay, take Lucille back to the table. She's in no condition.'

Maybe Hannah's interview was just another tough role. Maybe she was trying to be welcoming to Teddy.

Hannah leaned closer. 'Dawn and I have been pals for a long time now. How come she never mentioned you?'

'Don't know.' Teddy concentrated on breathing. 'She never mentioned you either. Dawn can be close-mouthed when she likes.'

> Then add a boogie woogie and look what they got. Rum Boogie. Rum boogie woogie. . . .

She was enjoying the dancing more now. Hannah nodded to the beat of the music. Teddy imagined them travelling to Cuba.

> Then throw your body a way back in. . . .

Teddy looked around, wondering if she would ever return to this place. Her mind raced with excitement, fear, irritation, confusion. She didn't much like the sensation of being lost. But she did like this new feeling of letting go. How come she could feel this good in a room full of strangers? She stretched her head back and noticed a mirror in the ceiling. There below her, beside her, around her were women dressed as women, women dressed as men. Women looking for something in each other and looking at each other in the mirror and ultimately releasing themselves for the evening. What would Moira think of all this? Why did she think of Moi? Maybe she felt Moi would understand this world better than Wanda or Ann. She was more daring, herself. Someday she would tell Moi all about this. The thought startled her so that she fell straight back into Hannah's curious gaze. Was this woman cold, challenging, amused? The music had stopped. Two couples near the wall hung on each other, whether from passion or booze, Teddy couldn't tell.

'You OK?'

'Yes,' Teddy said evenly. She played back Hannah's voice. She had a rough concern, a veiled irony like Angela. Teddy pictured Angela hanging over the fence, tossing sarcasms about her Victory Garden. Her edge came from shyness. The evening started to spin again. Dawn-Moira-Angela-Teddy-Hannah-Mary Ellen-Gretta-Sandra. Was she a lesbian? Did she have the flu? Could she give Hannah an answer?

'Sure, I'm fine. But I wouldn't mind sitting out the next one.'

'No choice.' Hannah smiled. 'They break the music every hour – to encourage trade at the bar.'

Hour, thought Teddy, no wonder she was tired. She barely felt Hannah's hand at the back of her elbow. Her cheeks were burning as they approached the small table. Dawn observed closely. Hannah stared back in bluff defiance. Satisfied that Teddy was safe, Dawn returned to her drink. As she sat down, Dawn pushed a glass of beer to her. 'You're not a bad dancer.' This was one aspect of the carnival that Teddy had overlooked, the business of being on display. Had Dawn really admired the way she danced? Why would Dawn watch her? She was with Sandra, wasn't she? Were they all together? How did they come apart? How many parts were there? Was she playing a part now?

'What do you think of "South American Way",' Sandra asked Hannah. 'Don't you think they're better with the fast music?'

'No.' Hannah shook her head and defended her favorite Andrews Sisters songs in intricate detail. Teddy could barely follow the conversation, but she didn't mind. She wanted to sit back and rest and let the parts reassemble. She was just a little worried that they would never find the old pattern again. Just a little worried.

'Teddy, don't sulk.' Moira sat across from her unusually snappish friend in the living room. 'You know I want to have this party too. I just need to make sure things are a little smoother with Randy before I do.'

'I'm not sulking,' answered Teddy, who didn't know how she was behaving. She had been in a state for weeks now, as if her period were always due the next day. Her one certainty was that she wasn't upset about the party. She was upset about the Quiet Cat. And excited. She was upset about Randy. But why? Moira had a right to her own life. 'It's fine with me to postpone the party. It will be easier next month.' By then, she might be clearer whether she should invite Dawn and Sandra. She had considered Hannah and Mary Ellen, in a mad moment.

'Leave her alone, Moi.' Ann lifted her eyes from the magazine she had been trying to read. 'You're just feeling confused about Randy and taking it out on her. I'm the one who's going to start sulking. The party was my idea.' She returned to the article about Jewish refugee children in England. They had placed a lot of them in homes now, but they held the others in hostels. It reminded her of the SPCA. She often wondered whether Uncle Aaron's kids – her own cousins – were among them. She couldn't postpone it any more. She would start inquiring what she could do. She thought about how much closer she felt to Rachel and her other friends in the Forum every month. They had been right to ask why she was studying Latin. As the war 'progressed' and the world fell apart, she became less and less certain of why she was learning a dead language.

Moira kept her eyes on Teddy. 'Then why are you acting so odd lately? What have I done? Are you mad at me for something?'

The phone rang. Ann jumped, more eager than she realized to escape the tension.

Teddy and Moira watched her walk into the kitchen and waited silently.

'Yes,' she said loudly, obviously talking to a long distance operator.

Teddy and Moira looked at each other.

Moira thought how they had grown to distrust long distance calls. Was something wrong with Wanda? Or with Hank, perhaps. They hadn't heard from him in months. She hoped it wasn't her mother calling.

'Teddy,' Ann called, 'it's for you.'

Teddy rushed into the kitchen. 'Hello, hello?' She could hear her own drawl at times of excitement. 'Oh, Angela. Where are you?'

Ann sat down on the couch across from Moira, not ready to return to the article, immensely relieved that it was just Angela. She worried every hour about Daniel.

'Where are you?' Teddy's voice trailed into the living room. 'Why are you calling? Of course I'm glad to hear your voice, but it's awfully expensive. OK. OK.'

Ann tried not to listen. She turned to Moira. 'So things are better with Randy?'

'Truth is they're just fine.' Moira reluctantly turned away from the kitchen. 'Don't know why I'm being so cautious about the damn party.'

'You're back, um, together?' Ann was surprised and then aggravated with herself for being so dense. She needed to pay more attention to Moira.

'Until he enlists.' Moira shook her head.

Ann waited.

'It's selfish, I know. I worry about what will happen to us. There's a world war going on.'

'Most people do worry about personal losses.'

'But you, you're all caught up in those stories about kids in England, sending money and writing letters.' She looked at the dark swatches under Ann's eyes. She noticed the hand at the back of her neck.

Ann fell silent, thinking about the stories she had read this week. Two brothers, five and nine, from Vienna were separated in the Midlands and London. A fourteen-year-old girl never found a home because she was too old. There were hundreds of kids, thousands. And then all the adults in camps. What could be done about them? Moira was right to worry about Randy. Maybe she couldn't do anything about him, but she could at least comprehend him.

'But that's personal, too.' Ann spoke. 'I read for me. For Mama. Because I can't do anything else.' She closed her eyes.

The two women fell silent, hearing Teddy's excited voice from the kitchen.

'We've talked about marriage,' Moira said tentatively. What she really wanted to talk about was the sex. Had Ann ever done it? Would Ann think she was cheap or horrible? It seemed OK if you were engaged. Her friend at work, Vivian, said Moira was silly to worry about an outdated custom like virginity. Moira agreed, but somehow wanted an OK from Ann. She could never tell Teddy. She wanted something from Ann.

'Oh, yes?' Ann wondered if it were important to contain her surprise. She considered the different lines of communication – how Moira would tell her this rather than Teddy; how she and Teddy liked to garden together; how she and Wanda talked about politics. When she moved into the house three-and-a-half years ago, it had been for convenience and company. Little did she expect to find new relationships as complex as a family.

'I mean everybody is getting married – Vivian, Dorothy – but we've decided to wait for more stable times.' Moira would postpone her lovemaking talk. Ann wasn't in one of her open moods. 'I mean it's not as if we could move into the rose-covered cottage right now.'

Ann nodded. She wanted to ask about sex, to talk about the times with Herb, but since she wasn't seeing anyone now, it didn't seem appropriate. These conversations required a fair exchange.

'And after this last fight, as much as I love him, I can't imagine a wedding yet. Still, it seems crazy to be so calculated about it.'

'Not crazy.'

'I guess you're right.' Moira sniffed back the tears. No time for self-pity. Compared to Ann, she did feel terribly naive and romantic.

'How are the classes?' she heard herself ask. 'What are you studying now?'

'We're reading Caesar and I must say the second semester is easier than the first.' Ann was a little perplexed and vaguely amused that Moira would steer so abruptly away from feelings. She supposed Moira was better at displaying emotions than at analyzing them. Teddy and Wanda weren't partial to doing either.

'Do you think I could come to campus with you sometime?'

'Sure,' Ann said neutrally.

'A delayed New Year's resolution. I was thinking about taking a drama class.' She wished she could find more common ground. It was just a question of personality. Moira knew her pyrotechnic temper bothered Ann. And Ann's weary resignation annoyed her. But Moira thought if they could share something outside the house they would understand each other more. School seemed the safest interest to explore. Ann was always prickly about politics. Her family weighed her down. And her increasing interest in her Jewishness made Moira feel excluded. Maybe she was just jealous about that, wishing she could feel passionate about a heritage. She once asked Ann if she could go to Synagogue and the idea seemed to embarrass her friend so much that Moira never brought it up again.

'But you're already at the shipyard and with rehearsals for the USO show and Randy. Don't you have enough on your plate?' Ann hated that expression, the heavy Puritan criticism of self-indulgence. Looking at Moira's long face, she realized that she had said the wrong thing.

'Forgive me, hon. I'd love to show you around school. And they do some decent student theatre. Bring Randy. Pardon my bristly mood; it's been a hard week with Mama, school and my job. Sure, tell me when you want to go out to the college. Any time.'

'Right,' said Moira, unwrapping a piece of gum and then, remembering how it irritated her friend, who had refrained from smoking for the last hour, rewrapped it.

Teddy returned to the room. Suddenly conscious of her broad grin, she composed her face.

'That was Angela,' she said. Everything in the living room seemed too familiar. She was even a little disappointed to see Moira and Ann sitting there in the same places.

'I told you she'd "write",' laughed Moira. She stretched on the floor, thinking that one of the benefits of the shipyard was that she had developed a taste and a flair for these comfortable slacks.

Ann looked from one woman to the other, conscious that she had been missing something these last couple of months. She, who was so proud of perceiving psychological nuance, had been completely oblivious. There were parts of Teddy's story she'd prefer to ignore.

'She only called to say hi.' Help, thought Teddy. She was getting herself in deeper with each word.

'Nice!' Moira said, interested that she didn't feel any of the old jealousy about Angela. Well, the girl was 1,500 miles away. 'It's nice some people are spontaneous, that they don't consider the telephone an instrument of doom.'

'Yeah and generous,' Teddy said in spite of herself. She heard her voice rattling on about Angela's flight with cargo to Andover, Maine; the other girls in their squadron; her new friend Mabel; the weather in Texas. Teddy thought how unlike her this talkativeness was. She knew the others noticed and she didn't care. Talking about Angela kept her more alive, kept the telephone conversation from ending. Oh, she was glad that all those letters hadn't been wasted. She was glad Angela had got them and read them over and over again. She was glad Angela had called. She would tell Dawn on Monday. Dawn said the others would notice nothing, that they would see what they wanted to see. All straight people were like that. Teddy didn't appreciate Dawn's cynicism, especially when it applied to friends. She did feel cautious, herself, but she would not get anxious. It would be all right. Everything would be all right now that Angela was on her side. Angela was on her side, wasn't she? She hadn't said much on the telephone. 'How's your puny little garden?' 'I miss you sometimes.' But what could you say from a pay phone?

Teddy looked at them waiting for her to continue. She took a deep breath and thought about their party discussion. 'Have you set a date?'

Moira and Ann blinked.

Eventually Moira picked it up. 'Oh, the party. How about the 14th? Is that fine with you?'

'Fine,' laughed Teddy, 'oh, fine.'

Chapter Fourteen

———————————————— • ————————————————

Spring 1943, San Francisco

POLIO EPIDEMIC SPREADS IN USA

———————————————— • ————————————————

DANISH VOTERS REJECT NATIONAL SOCIALISM

———————————————— • ————————————————

DE GAULLE AND GIRAUD HEAD FRENCH COMMITTEE OF NATIONAL LIBERATION

Moira glanced at Randy's ruddy face and then down at their hands as they walked from the theatre. Here they were holding hands as if nothing had happened, as if they had never separated into terrible months of silence. No, that wasn't true. They had discussed the fight and it had brought them closer. She knew that despite the differences, because they were able to overcome them, she loved Randy more. She cherished his impetuousness, his temper and his willingness to put both in tow to his passion for her. Where that came from, she didn't quite understand. Oh, she knew she was pretty and bright, but Randy Girard could have any girl in San Francisco. And he had chosen her.

'Go for a ride?' he invited. 'Gorgeous night.'

She looked down at her feet. Really, they should get back home. It was crazy to stay out late during the week like this. She needed to be alert at the shipyard in the morning. But he was right. The almost summery night was heavy with the fragrance of almond and cherry blossoms. And who knew how much time they had left.

'You there, Moira?'

She smiled at his urgency. Maybe she loved him because he was the only person in the world more impatient than she. Why was she so defensive about their love tonight? It was that critical remark from Teddy. A comment that Teddy, herself, might say, 'didn't bear thinking about.'

'Yes,' she nodded shyly and then with more certainty. 'Just a ride.'

'Sure.' He squeezed closer.

They walked silently to the car, past groups of people chatting on the sidewalk. Moira noticed several clutches of sailors. San Francisco had been invaded by the American navy these past months. The city would never be the same again. Of course they were good for the economy. And Moira felt a surprising safety in their presence. She was also conscious of the bad humor in which they put Randy.

He opened the car door and she couldn't help thinking about that time last spring when she borrowed this car to see Wanda off. Now she knew they had done the right thing; Wanda had told her so. But she had been consumed with doubt all the way down to the bus depot. Lately, a vague uneasiness haunted all her decisions. Would nothing ever be certain again? Was this because of the war or because she was growing up?

Randy was lost in a cold fury as he manoeuvred through the knotted traffic on Market Street. As he attempted a left turn, a Buick full of sailors slashed out in front of their car. 'Fuckers, god damned show-offs.' He leaned on the horn.

Moira reached over and stroked his elbow, feeling the arm grow more rigid. She sat back.

'Sorry, Moi.' He shook his head once he was through the intersection.

'Your brother decided?'

'Yup, army.'

She waited, knowing his job deferment was bothering him a lot this week.

'It's not that I don't want to go. I'm no yellow belly. It's just that, I don't know, this god damned war comes along right when I think I'm getting on my feet.' He concentrated on the traffic.

'I know,' she said quietly.

'And who knows what this does to us, to our plans.'

Hold on, she wanted to say, what plans?

'What a time. You grow up in this Depression where your dad can't find work. You pull out of that, barely into manhood and the government calls you away to fight. Don't get me wrong. We have to fight this war. I just wish we were born at another time.'

'Like our parents? Remember the First World War? Or maybe before that – the Civil War? Or how about the War of 1812?'

He couldn't help smiling. 'You've been spending too much time around Ann and her intellectual friends.'

Her stomach sank. Did he think she was stupid? No, they were both on edge tonight.

He pulled from the main road into a gravelled drive. The tires rolled over the tiny rocks sounding like water coming to boil. She held her hands tightly together, promising herself that after a talk and a couple of kisses, they would drive home. She would get to bed early tonight.

He seemed to be continuing a conversation from earlier in the day, perhaps his talk with Boyd. 'In the army I would see more direct action. I'd feel I was really doing something. On the other hand, Dad was in the navy and I know he'd like one of us at sea. There's something scarier about all that water, about sailing into the unknown, sort of like going to the stars. But someone has to do it.' Suddenly his voice grew less reflective. 'You don't think I'm a chicken, taking so long to decide, do you, Moi?'

'No, Randy, of course not. But,' she spoke in spite of herself, 'I'm just not sure the decision is going to get any easier. It's not like there's a right choice and a wrong choice.'

'You think I should just flip a coin and jump in?' He stared into the dark night.

'No.' She drew closer and rubbed his arm which had lost all its tightness. 'No, I want you to stay here as long as possible.' She thought about Uncle Willie careening to earth in his RAF plane. And Angela flying between Maine and Texas. Last night she had dreamed about Angela. Moira was grateful Randy wasn't talking about the Air Force.

'Well, I've got to do something.'

'Sometimes I imagine we'll wake up and hear Gabriel Heater announcing that we've won, that it's all over.'

'Allied virtue rewarded?'

She looked at him closely, but he was not making fun.

'Sort of.' She shrugged. Often during the last year she realized how she had taken the nuns too literally. Good versus Evil. It was such a safe world then. How did Sister Lawrence teach her morality nowadays? She felt a tired irritation with Sister, who had promised her a great deal, who had once seemed so wise and now seemed so simple.

'It does make you appreciate the "now" more.' He put his arms around her.

'Yes.' She rested her head on his chest. She was lucky to have him. His quickness. His love. Now.

He lifted her chin with his hand. 'I love you, Moira.'

'Yes, I . . .' She kissed him.

The heartbeats struck faster, louder and she couldn't tell whose heart it was. She drew closer along an invisible thread, closer and closer, aching to enter his skin. She knew she shouldn't allow this, that it was the girl who had to hold the line, that she needed to get up early tomorrow morning, but his tongue was in her mouth now. And now was all there was. Who knew about tomorrow morning? She sucked on his tongue and felt her breasts rise with sweet fullness. He reached inside her dress and stroked her neck with his thumb, then moved his fingers down further, exploring and stroking and stirring the sweetness higher. When he touched her nipples, she sighed unconsciously, waking herself to obligation.

'Darling.' She tried to pull away gently. 'I think we should stop before.'

'All we know is before,' Randy whispered. 'We can't count on after, Moira honey.'

'Mmmm.' She felt herself submerge, with sadness and hunger and complete surrender. Next time she would refuse a ride in the car. But now she inhaled his warm breath and said, 'Yes'.

Lying on the back seat with him, she shivered. 'Let's close the windows.'

'Don't worry, we'll take care of the cold in a minute.' He bit her ear and unbuttoned her blouse. Sometimes she thought she liked this part the best, the anticipation. He was so hungry for her, and this wanting awoke a hunger of her own. She reached down and stroked his stomach, his waist, his hardness. She imagined him entering her and she closed her eyes.

'Ya know, you've really got to talk to those girls. It'd be much more comfortable in the house.'

'Shhh.' She kissed his lips. He unzipped his pants and pulled a condom from his pocket. Had he been sure of her agreement? Or did he always carry sheaths with him? Even on Sunday morning when he went to Mass? Shh, she told herself. At least he was responsible. Lie back and enjoy him while you have him. The sadness mingled with the hunger again and she could hardly hold back the tears.

He kissed her hairline, licked her nose, nibbled at her lips and proceeded down her neck to her full, ripe breasts. Her body relaxed and she drew apart her legs. Soon he was in her, stirring deeper and deeper until she climaxed. Swiftly, he followed.

Lying next to him now, she stroked his sweaty face and licked the salt from his chest.

'You know what one of those French sailors told me about sex?'

'Oh, don't Randy, you'll spoil it. Save your dirty jokes for Boyd.'

'No, no joke, really. Just that the word for "to climax" in French is *"finir"*. You know, "to finish".'

'So?' She did not want to be part of this conversation.

'So I don't know. We say "to come". They say "to finish". Kind of sad. Don't know; it makes me sort of. . . .'

'Melancholy? Well, I guess it wasn't that good for you tonight.' She frowned and sat up, buttoning her blouse.

'Moi, it's got nothing to do with tonight – which was great – I guess I've just been thinking odd things lately.' He dressed and helped her into the front seat.

'I'm sorry,' she said.

'There you go apologizing again. Always apologizing.'

'I'm sorry, I didn't mean to. . . .' She laughed.

'I love you.'

'Why?'

'Why?' He sighed and humored her although he had explained a hundred times. 'Because you're spontaneous. Because you're willing to try things. Like acting. Like typing all those silly letters for a chance at a movie part. Like leaving Los Angeles on your own. I love the fact that you take chances. I admire it.'

'Admire?'

'Yes, you goose.' He pulled her close. 'I think you'd be surprised how many people admire you.'

'What for?'

'Well, among other things, for taking that crazy job at the shipyard. Even though I acted like a jackass. You persisted. A lot of girls wouldn't have done that.'

Teddy lay on her bed, exhausted. She had been fighting fatigue since she got home from visiting her family. But 9 o'clock was far too early for sleeping. Maybe if she just lay here for a few moments, she would revive and then she could go scrub the bathroom or clean the linen closet. You could get little things like this done at night and feel better for them in the morning. Besides, she had to stay awake to talk with Moira and Ann about the party. If they didn't get organized, they would have to cancel it again. Moira should be home by 10. She said before she left she would make Randy bring her back on time tonight. And Ann, yes, she was off at the Forum with Rachel, so she wouldn't be too late. She had to stay awake.

Teddy held her head, thinking about Pop. He seemed to get worse after the doctor warned him about his liver. It was almost as if he had more of a thirst for defiance than for whisky. Mom was growing quieter by the day. And Jolene looked like she was about to explode. Either that or marry too early and escape the house. Teddy knew there was nothing she could do except to visit, to show them she loved them and to be available when disaster struck. Had it struck already?

Teddy opened the drawer of her bedside table and pulled out the picture Angela had sent from Texas. There she was, all 6 foot 1 inch of her standing proud next to her airplane. She looked even taller than usual in the uniform. It was such a rich face, round and swarthy, supported by firm brows, broad cheekbones and a handsome nose. Angela joked about the nose, but Teddy thought it gave her face character. And she saw how the same nose on Mrs Bertoli lent dignity with the years. Yes, Angela was a fine looking woman; Teddy wished she thought the same about the airplane. It seemed a little rickety compared to what some people were flying. . . . The only way to stop worrying, she reminded herself, was to practice and to change the subject.

Dawn had admired the picture. 'She's in the life, OK. You can tell by the way she stands. By the way she's looking at you, Teddy.'

Teddy poured them each a glass of Clooney's beer. 'Looking at me, that's silly. It's a picture.'

'It's a picture she sent *you*. And what does it say on the other side?'

Teddy read silently. '"To Teddy. Love, Angela." Well, that could mean anything.'

Dawn removed her glasses and slowly wiped the lenses with a napkin. 'Girl, you do have a dose of jitters.'

Teddy flipped over the picture now. 'Love, Angela.' Love Angela. She did love Angela. She loved her warmth and her drive. She loved her smartness – a practical savvy about the world – that was different from Ann's intellect or Wanda's writing talent or Moira's creativity. Well, she was a little like Moira in her brazenness. Angela would try anything.

Would she try the Quiet Cat? Of course, of course, Dawn kept reassuring her. But Teddy knew she couldn't write about such things in letters. Maybe Angela in her boldness would let something slip about a girls' bar in Texas. No, Teddy shivered, if Angela was going to girls' bars, she didn't want to know about it.

Teddy studied the picture. She loved her individuality, her irreverence. She loved what Moira called Angela's 'surliness', which was actually a powerful independence.

'Love, Angela,' she read again. Of course Dawn was right, for Angela hated to write letters and didn't Teddy have not only a letter but a picture? Love.

Teddy imagined Angela coming home and surprising her in the garden. No one else would be around. Angela would just walk in through the gate and throw her arms around her. Teddy would say, 'Oh, not here, Angela'. Angela would take her by the hand into the kitchen where she would hold Teddy tight and smother her with . . . No, no, Angela would pretend to sulk and Teddy would lead Angela into the house. Maybe she would take her upstairs. Yes, that was it. She would take Angela up to see how she had painted her room. Angela's picture would be by the bed. Angela would be overcome with emotion and . . . No, no, she couldn't have Angela's picture by the bed because the other girls would notice. She could have it displayed with pictures of her family, but that would spoil the effect. Maybe she would lead Angela directly over to the bed – for there was no other place to sit comfortably in the room – and leaning on the pillow, she would inch it to one side, revealing underneath a photo of a handsome woman with her flying machine. Once on the bed, of course. . . .

Teddy woke to a slamming of the door. She listened to Moira's dainty footsteps stomping up the stairs.

'Shhh.' Ann walked into the hall. 'I think she's asleep. I knocked softly on the door and she didn't answer.'

'Oh, sorry,' Moira whispered. 'It is late.'

'No, not too late,' Teddy called. 'Come on in.' Sitting up, she tucked Angela's letter and picture beneath her pillow.

Chapter Fifteen

———————————— • ————————————

Spring 1943, San Francisco, Arizona, England

BRITISH AND US FORCES LINK IN TUNISIA

———————————— • ————————————

UPRISING IN WARSAW GHETTO

———————————— • ————————————

SHOE RATIONING BEGINS IN US

———————————— • ————————————

FUNDING OF UN RELIEF AND REHABILITATION ADMINISTRATION

'Why do you do this, Ann? To torment me?' Papa sat at the green kitchen table staring past his treacherous daughter to the silent living room of the family flat.

Ann perceived her father as the impeccable creation of his own will. A man almost sixty who looked forty-five. A foreigner who moved with the confidence of an American. A father who would always be a boy living out the world's promises. He rotated a gear on the stainless steel can opener which he bought just before his wife was hospitalized. Such a clean, sleek instrument. Ann watched, nervous that he might slice the tip of his thumb.

'Why are you doing this to your father?'

The previous day, when the documents arrived, she began to really dread telling Papa. She was so worried about his reaction to the trip that she was half-way down the library steps before she noticed the rain. Then, suddenly, there were walls of wet. She rubbed her left shoulder under her coat and observed that she was not tense. She could even feel the ping-ping through the cloth. Rain, damn rain. She slipped the prized papers into her briefcase. For months she had sought these documents and now if she were any more foolish, crucial dates and signatures would be lost to the storm.

She was heading straight for the storm in Europe. First the gale on Filbert Street. Papa would explode when he heard it was settled. Why? he kept asking her since she concocted this crazy scheme to work with refugee children in London. Why? Why was the Forum subsidizing her trip? Why did she want to go? Ann knew that none of her answers would satisfy him. She could never respond quickly enough, logically enough. Papa always had plenty of answers, of all dimensions, until Mama had been hospitalized. Still, even these days, Papa tried to maintain his dead certainty – about the quick resolution of the war, about Daniel's safety, about Mama's recovery. So Ann knew Papa would lecture her again that she was wrong to go to Europe.

Ann did not set her umbrella against the sky. She wanted to feel the raindrops on her cheeks and eyelids. She would not hide. This is what Mama did in her madness and Papa did in his sureness. She thought of the papers in her briefcase, the official letter from Professor Rothman's friend inviting her to work in London and the travel documents which only a magician like Rothman could have procured so swiftly. The rain eased as she walked through the plaza. Students emerged speculatively from doorways, their umbrellas raised in anxious defense against the next shower. But Ann knew this shower was over. Already, she could smell the oils of laurel and eucalyptus. Mischievously, she sloshed through puddles in her shiny black galoshes.

Mr Foster went to Gloucester in a shower of rain.
He stepped in a puddle right up to his middle and never was seen again.

How far was it from London to Gloucester? London, she would be in London in two months. She would be leaving college. Tears came at this. What the hell, she needed to cry at losing this campus, the only ground she had ever claimed for herself. Ann shot her umbrella into the sunny sky and wept as she rushed for a bus to take her home.

Now in the kitchen on Filbert Street, she stared back at Papa and a flash of anger struck her shoulder. Shifting her weight on the chair, she reminded herself to calm down. She could release these claws digging into her skull. She imitated Teddy's cool, slow and guiltless voice, consciously avoiding her friend's drawl. 'I'm not doing anything to you,' she said.

He glanced balefully at his cup of black coffee.

'Really, Papa, we've been around and around on this.' She pushed away her coffee. 'I have to do something. Those children are ours. They could be my own cousins. We still don't know about Uncle Aaron's family or your Aunt Judith.' She held her breath because he hadn't mentioned the family in a month.

'Aaron and Judith are intelligent people. They will be fine, I'm sure.'

Ann shook her head. She could not press him on this. 'I want to find out, to help. Papa, what about all those little Jewish children, their parents in concentration camp?'

He stiffened. 'What about me? Here I am, all alone. Your Mama in a crazy ward. Daniel in the army. And you, the only family left, you traipsing off to *England*. Who cares about Papa? Who's left to take care of Papa?'

'Papa can take care of himself,' she said hastily. Then more softly, 'You're well, Papa. You have your job and your friends at the factory.' She stood, packing herself a sandwich to eat on the way to the library.

'We understand each other, Ann.' He sighed. For a moment he fell silent, surveying the spotless kitchen – lined with appliances and gadgets he had worked so hard to accumulate because the kitchen was the heart of family life and he so desperately wanted an American family. 'We wilful ones understand each other. Daniel and your Mama, they are idealists. But you and I are pioneers. Yes, and I have been exploring longer, so let me give you one piece of advice. Europe is over. I have labored all these years to save you from disintegration and decay. . . . America is the future.'

The mustard? Ann searched. Worked to save me, she sniffed. Uneasily she reached for her shoulder. She should sympathize with him. This was his way of coping, pretending to take care of her when he needed her to take care of him. Not needed, wanted.

'The mustard is in the icebox,' he offered. 'It lasts longer that way. You don't learn such things living in a house of girls?'

'No time.' She wrapped the meatloaf in wax paper. She had no more time to argue with him. 'I'm gonna be late.'

– 172 –

He winced at her enunciation.

'We'll talk soon.' She pecked him on the cheek. 'I'll drop by Saturday so we can visit Mama together. OK, Papa?'

'Gee, Ann, I'm sorry we can't see you off. It doesn't seem right, you going away to war in a taxi.' Teddy poured Ann a fourth cup of coffee.

Moira pulled her bathrobe close and sneezed. 'With me sick and you going to work in twenty minutes, there isn't much choice.' She coughed painfully. 'Stop being a basset hound and enjoy the farewells.' Damn bronchitis. She thought she was used to the six day week and the heavy work. More than anything she was suffering from frayed dignity.

'Besides.' Ann paused, counting her bags one last time. 'I'm not going to war in a taxi. Professor Rothman's nephew is taking me to the bus which I'm riding to Wanda's camp. Then it's a train to New York. Then a ship to London. I wish I were travelling all the way in a taxi.'

'Did you pack the chocolates and socks for Wanda?' Teddy spread oleomargarine over her cold toast. 'And Vicks for yourself? I've read about how damp and foggy it gets in London.'

'Yes, Teddy, I packed everything except you.' Ann had come to admire Teddy's equilibrium, a core of spiritual stability, she, herself, would never find. And in the last few months, Ann considered, she had also grown much closer to Moira. Since Randy had returned, Moira was calmer, older somehow.

Teddy shook her head in embarrassment and regarded her toast bleakly.

'She takes care of everything, all right, except herself,' said Moira. 'What a week: I catch a cold that turns into consumption, you leave for the end of the earth and Teddy runs herself ragged with her family.'

'Right,' nodded Ann. 'No sleep last night?'

'Pop hit Jolene pretty bad yesterday.' Teddy noticed that she was talking with that Oklahoma accent, which emerged when she was with her family or when she was overtired. 'Mom tried to stop him. You know Mom is a small little nothing compared to Pop. It's only when he gets drinking that this anger takes over. He's had it real rough, you know, first the crops going, then driving way out here to be unemployed.' Teddy repeated the familiar saga to quell her fury with him. 'Then just when we get back on our feet, war comes and takes the boys. It's been rough on Pop.'

'What about your mother?' Moira knew they should be talking about something else at Ann's last breakfast. But she couldn't help herself. Teddy's father was ruining the entire family. Besides, in the back of Moira's mind was the notion that if they avoided ceremony, this wouldn't be Ann's last breakfast. She would come back to them. 'Your mother's the one who gets knocked around.'

'Yeah, sure,' Teddy answered reluctantly. 'That's why I went over last night. But Pop is complicated. He's got big pride.' She knew she could let go and cry. She had told them before how desperate she felt. But the more out of hand Pop got, the harder it was to talk. The more worried she became, the bigger her own pride grew.

'I know what you mean.' Ann recalled Papa's stiff, formal farewell yesterday. 'Family, it's hard to see one member separately from one another.'

'You'll write to us,' Teddy said.

'Let us know when you've made each leg of the journey – Wanda, New York, London?' Moira coughed to conceal the quaver in her voice and then wished she hadn't because of the blade slitting through her chest. So this is what Mother called 'Scottish lungs', the family inheritance. 'We'll write back as soon as we hear.'

Ann nodded.

'You just might run into Randy in London.' Moira forced a brightness in her voice. 'He's thinking about the army now and could get stationed there.'

Teddy raised an eyebrow. She was trying to like Randy more these days. She still thought he played loose with Moira's feelings. But Ann said she was too critical, that he was simply a pressured young man, dissociated by the war. And Randy had been particularly nice to her since he and Moira had reconciled. He often asked after her brothers. Maybe Ann was right. She would miss Ann's good sense.

'At Trafalgar Square,' Moira continued. 'Or Piccadilly Circus. They're right downtown, Randy says, and full of pigeons.'

Ann smiled at the notion of meeting Moira's boyfriend in a crowd of greycoated Londoners who mumbled and swallowed their words. She could hear Randy's loud cheer now. 'That would be fun.' Already she felt lonely, and grateful for Randy's familiar face. 'We'll go to a pub and toast your health.'

'Make sure that's all you do!' Moira felt herself getting weepy, so she coughed again, wiped her mouth with a napkin and averted her eyes from Teddy to avoid being ordered back to bed.

'Funny,' remarked Moira, 'you going off to war in England like this. And us getting food limits and blackouts. Sometimes the war hits home and seems more real than ever. Look at Angela in the WAFs!'

'I'm hardly "going off to war",' Ann said. Although she wasn't a pacifist and she could see no way to stop Hitler without guns, she couldn't imagine herself fighting. Moira would disagree; she would say if she could work in the shipyards, she could handle a gun. They had had this argument before. And since her friend was a bit of a mind-reader, Ann tried to concentrate on something else. Looking around the table at the half-eaten eggs and potatocakes and the rack of cold toast, she felt sorry for Teddy who had fussed to fix a nourishing breakfast. Because of this and because of the journey ahead, she forced herself to eat.

The others returned to their meals. Knives and forks scratched and rang across the plates. Coffee was consumed in loud gulps. When the door bell rang, they all sat frozen.

As Ann drove away with Professor Rothman's nephew, Teddy and Moira stood at the door holding on to each other and waving. When the car turned the corner, Moira looked at Teddy. 'Never thought I'd say this, but, Jesus, I wish we could go back to those simple old Fargod days.'

'Shhh.' Teddy moved her index finger to Moira's lips. Moira flushed, then shivered. 'Up to bed with you. When you start missing Miss Fargo, you're truly sick.'

Teddy cleared the table. In the kitchen, she checked her watch. She'd be late for work if she didn't step on it. Just as well; no use pining. They were all good women, but what was this in the face of history? The war was pulling apart their friendship and their individual lives. It didn't bear thinking about. Teddy checked her watch again and hurried out the door.

After the old man with the Irish setters got off, Ann was the only passenger on the country bus rattling towards Lion's Head. Spring in this high desert was a glory of beaming red, orange and gold.

Mountains shot into the blue ceiling like fingers impulsively raised at an auction. One, two, three sudden bids for space in the vast flatness and then miles before another contour. The bus driver made several attempts at conversation, but Ann passed them off politely, preferring to linger with memories from the train which had been crowded with soldiers and their families. She learned more about the war on that train ride than she had during a whole year of reading the raging headlines in the *Examiner*. Funny country, she thought, so rough and untried in places. Her eyes stretched over the miles of dry earth punctuated with occasional touches of scrub. How far was she seeing?

'Lion's Head comin' up,' called the driver. Ann thought she could spot a group of low buildings in the distance. She wondered if Wanda really wanted to see her. Oh, she had said yes in a letter. But there was a tightness in the language, a vague embarrassment. Ann recalled that spring morning last year when they had seen Wanda off to camp. Moira was right then, Wanda could be so private. Was she blundering into Wanda's world now? Would she be just another burden?

'You a teacher?' he asked, swerving the bus left.

'No,' she said and opened the book on her lap. Why was she being so unfriendly? He was probably just bored and lonely. She was going to encounter a lot of her own loneliness on this trip.

'You with the Authority then?'

'Pardon me?' She tried to perk up, searching his face in the rearview mirror. Fifty maybe, with greying straw hair and a tired face, except for electric blue eyes. 'What's "The Authority"?'

'Oh.' His voice fell. It was his turn at the rearview mirror and he scrutinized her before answering. 'The War Relocation Authority,' he said more loudly.

'No,' she repeated, staring at the barbed wire encircling a settlement of plain, makeshift quarters. High in his sentry box, about 2 yards from the gate, a soldier paced with a rifle.

Wanda and her sister Betty waved from the opposite side of the fence. Ann smiled and waved back. Wanda looked pretty much the same, though thinner. Betty was a completely different person, 3 inches taller, more of a young lady now, as Papa would say. What a place to grow up, Ann thought, then pushed the idea to the back of her mind.

The bus stopped abruptly, reminding Ann this was not a movie.

She was meant to get off. The visit began here. Now. She climbed down to the desert.

'Paying a social call?' inquired the driver as he hauled out her bags from beneath the bus.

Ann made sure she had all her luggage. She faced him squarely and saw that he was both curious and hostile, but more of the former. 'Visiting old friends,' she said. He nodded, perhaps satisfied.

A guard helped her drag the cases inside the gate. Ann worried the bags might rip. They had a long way to go. And so did she, she reminded herself, focusing on her old friend, who approached shyly. They were both reserved women and Ann had a sudden longing for Teddy and Moira, who could start the hugging without self-consciousness. She closed her eyes and put her arms around Wanda, shocked at the bony embrace.

'How are you?'

Wanda's voice, Ann registered. Had the desert done something to her? She had felt disembodied all morning. 'Fine, fine, and you?' The voice sounded vacant and, remembering it was her own voice, she reached for Betty and drew her into a hug. 'How is my young friend?'

'Fine,' the girl answered. 'Welcome.'

Ann and Wanda regarded each other. They smiled – at the absurdity of being welcomed to prison, at the comfort of finding each other again – at what, they didn't know – but it was good to be together.

Mrs Nakatani was pouring water into the tea pot when they arrived at the barracks. Wanda and Betty bustled Ann's bags behind a partition, then set out cups and plates. Highly sensitive about intruding in this cramped space, Ann could not look at her friends. Instead, she walked over to the door and considered the grim camp. She watched two women walk by slowly, carrying heavy baskets of laundry. All the women seemed to be wearing slacks. A man was sawing wood near the flagpole. Her eyes shimmied up the pole, over the roofs, above the armed sentry, beyond the lift of distant hills and into the wide spring sky. An American flag hung limp in the still air.

'Sit, sit.' Mrs Nakatani seemed to remember her.

Ann was struck by how this last year had brought her together with people in sudden intimacies and strange constellations. Who would she meet in England? Would she wind up sleeping with strangers in the subways if the Germans started bombing London again?

'Good heavens, yes, Annie.' Wanda returned to the common room. 'You must be exhausted after that journey. Sit down and let's have some of Mama's special tea.'

They all conspired to pass the following days as if Ann were a cousin visiting country relatives. The tea parties were particularly festive. Aside from a few wry comments about 'The Authority', their time was spent catching up with gossip from Stockton Street and dealing with the daily routines of Lion's Head. Ann met Howard's fiancée, Carolyn Sasaki, and the three girls talked excitedly about next month's wedding. Wanda apologized for the cramped conditions, for Ann's bed being separated by a thin curtain from the common room where she slept with her mother and Betty. Ann, in turn, apologized for evicting Howard to the Watanabes' place in the next barracks. Soon she understood how much the Nakatanis were protecting her, embarrassed by what her people had done to them and nervous about her presence.

The second night, as Ann tried to fall asleep, she was trailed by the number 99899 which the Nakatanis had put on everything of value, the family number, the code by which the government identified them. All over again, she saw how thin Wanda had become and heard her friend's protests that she would eat when she had grown used to the food and the climate. But you've been here for months, Ann had retorted. Wanda had replied that there were more serious worries, like Mama. Now Ann could hear Mrs Nakatani coughing in the dark – a deep, hollow cough that she associated with people who were being eaten alive by tuberculosis. In between the spells of coughing, Ann recalled old radio broadcasts. Roosevelt and MacArthur predicting American victories. Walter Lippman demanding the internment of the dangerous Japanese. Gabriel Heater making his 'good news' reports. Jack Benny cheering up Papa.

The evening before Ann left, Wanda took her to the far side of camp to watch the sunset.

'You'll like this, being an old romantic.' Wanda smiled. She watched doubt play over Ann's mouth. 'Don't you think you're idealistic? I mean of the four of us, you've always had the greatest ambitions.'

Ann kicked a stone down the dirt road. 'What about Moira? Wanting to be Jean Harlow is a lot more romantic than learning Latin.'

'But what's she doing now? Making ships – wearing a hard hat and overalls to work every day.'

'The war detours people,' Ann said sharply. Then, looking around the barracks, 'Oh, I'm sorry. . . .'

'Forget it. Listen, you're going off to Europe to help kids. What's that if not romantic?'

'Desperate, perhaps. And according to Papa, selfish. Maybe reckless, stupid.' Ann was distracted now by a dramatic mountain range in the distance – 10 miles, 50 miles – she had lost all sense of perspective. Ann had always pictured deserts as voluptuous, white, sandy places. But here the desert was pocked with bleak shrubs and tufts of grass and malevolent cactus. Here the desert spelled emptiness.

'Here we are.' With her walking stick, Wanda pointed to a bench fashioned from two logs.

Ann nodded approvingly and sat down. What a relief to be alone with Wanda for a few minutes, away from the rest of the people in camp. It was such a schizophrenic experience – being isolated in this wasteland, packed together with people so closely that you almost lost track of your own smell.

Everything was impromptu here, from the furniture to the entertainment. Wanda had told her about the hobby show and the sumo wrestling and the talent evenings and how eager people were for these diversions from the grim reality of this 'temporary refuge'. Ann couldn't believe the government was still using language like that. She wondered how 'temporary' it was. For even after the war, how many people could return to their former lives? Already there was talk about their farms disappearing. What would happen to Wanda's family?

'Beautiful,' Wanda sighed. 'I love that mountain.'

For a moment Ann was lost again in the view. Then her eyes caught the barbed wire. She could see nothing beyond the rusty coils and the tiny, mean spikes. She imagined the spikes piercing the blue sky, with blood dribbling at their feet.

'We call it "Central Park West". Roy made the bench. We come here as often as we can.'

'I can see why.' Ann was back on the mountain range now, inconsolably saddened by the closing sky.

'They've joined up, you know.'

'Who?' Ann didn't want to talk. But they must. This would be their last private time for God knew how many years. She moved down the mountain, across the desert, through the barbed wire. She heard a sudden rustle. 'What's that?'

'Lizard. She's been watching us for 10 minutes,' said Wanda. 'Don't worry.' She touched Ann's wrist. 'The rattlers don't usually come into camp.'

Ann, who hadn't thought about rattlers since her sixth grade science class, regarded Wanda with new respect. 'Who's joining what?'

'Howard and Roy. The army.'

Ann's jaw dropped.

'Well, this is yet another opportunity for "the Japs" to prove their allegiance. Send their boys off to fight the Germans and the Italians.'

'While you stay behind,' she pointed to the spikes, 'barbed wire!' Ann watched Wanda's cold, set face. No wonder the girl was harder than when she left San Francisco. Suddenly Ann felt another sliver of Wanda's resentment. Maybe she shouldn't have come. Of course Wanda would never say this.

'Yes, while they keep the rest of us safely locked up.' Wanda twisted her walking stick into the dirt. She had lied about the rattlers. Someone was struck just two weeks before. She always carried a large stick when she came to the edge of camp.

Ann slept in a pub near the docks her first night in England. She had intended to go straight to London and write Moira an aerogram from Piccadilly Circus. But by the time she passed through customs, the sky was dark. So she followed the purser's suggestion and found her way to the Opera Box, a small pub on the edge of town.

The public bar was noisy, crowded and thick with smoke. Thirty seconds passed before she understood she was the only woman in the room and that most of the flushed, stubble-jawed men were staring at her. An old man seated alone with his newspaper rose to take her elbow. 'This way, luv, the ladies' saloon is this way.'

'Ah, old John's got himself a girl.'

'Hey, Johnny boy, where are you two going?'

'Hang about John.'

'Don't mind 'em, Miss,' the old man said, picking up two of her cases. 'Where are you from?'

'Oh, don't please,' she said, trying to pull back her bags.

'A Yank.' He was surprised and then glanced over to the silhouette of the new ship in port. 'Brave of you to join the party. Mind if I ask why?'

'I've come to work with Jewish refugee children,' she said and stopped at the blind lowering over his blue eyes.

'Here you go, Miss.' His tone was more formal now – or was he perhaps just straining over the din? This bar was as noisy as the other, but the pitch of voices was higher since it was filled with women.

'Got a customer for you, Mae, from America!' He patted Ann's shoulder. 'Best of luck, now.'

Mae, a broad, competent woman, directed her to a bedroom downstairs in the rear. Despite noise from both saloons, she fell asleep within minutes. Her weary, seasick body was in England; her uneasy dreams visited Papa and Wanda and Moira and Teddy. How was the garden on Stockton Street? Would the beans be up yet? Fragments of conversation with Mama came and went, for even in her sleep Ann found it hard to let her thoughts rest on Mama. Back in the kitchen, arguing with Papa about the trip, about going to business school, about . . . when the bell sounded. A raid! She sat up. They had told her there was a shelter 500 yards to the rear. The bell again. Bell, not siren.

'Mornin', Miss.' A hardy woman's voice came through the door. 'You up and about now?'

'Yes,' Ann called, sounding to herself like a six year old.

'You did ask for an early call, Miss?'

'Yes, yes, thank you.' She was more awake now, but still scared. Everything seemed strange and she was filled with wariness about rockets and rattlers.

'Breakfast in the saloon bar, soon's you're up for it.'

'I'll be right there.' Finally she recognized the voice of the big woman who had greeted her so warmly last night.

'No hurry, luv, take your time.'

But she was in a hurry, to shake this panic, to get to London and to start being useful after all these wasted weeks of travel. Besides, she thought she felt a little hungry. She hadn't eaten since the second day of the voyage. After that she had only been able to ingest rubber cheese and stale crackers and seltzer water. From the looseness of her skirts, she guessed she had lost 5 pounds. Ann thought about her bony hug from Wanda and her last visit with Mama, wasting away in the hospital.

Seated in the corner of the pub, Ann regarded an egg floating in fat, a shrivelled lump of black pudding and fried bread. She tried to mask her disappointment.

'Best we can offer. With the rations and all, this was a bit of a fuss,' said Mae.

'Looks good.' Ann stared at the plate, speculating where to begin. What had she got herself into? Why wasn't she home on Stockton Street? What lay ahead of her among these English people with their strange accents and pale skin? She thought of Daniel and Mama and Wanda and cut off a corner of the bread.

'Take milk in your tea, luv?'

'Coff. . . .' Ann began, quickly recognizing that the only pot in the room contained tea. 'Yes, please, with milk, thank you very much.'

By the time Mae returned with the milk, Ann managed an experimental nibble of egg and had finished the bread.

The Englishwoman poured the stewed tea. 'That's it. Eat up, luv. You'll need your strength.'

Chapter Sixteen

•

Fall 1943, San Francisco

ALLIES LAND IN NAPLES

•

ITALIANS DECLARE WAR ON GERMANY

•

JAPANESE DECLARE FILIPINO INDEPENDENCE

•

CHIANG KAI-SHEK, ROOSEVELT AND CHURCHILL MEET IN CAIRO

Moira felt the house was getting larger and larger, swollen, yet cramped. She watched Teddy writing another letter to Wanda or Ann. It would be to Wanda because Teddy had mailed a letter with airmail stripes yesterday. Teddy was completely absorbed, her fair brows knitted tightly as she chewed her pen. Moira considered that, although her friend was slow with words, she persisted. Persistence was one of her talents.

'Less than two weeks after the Allies entered Naples,' Moira listened to the radio half-heartedly, 'Italy has declared war on the Nazis.'

Moira tried to concentrate, to find security in the deep, authoritative voice, but she was levitated by ghosts. Wanda and Ann had left their traces throughout the house, particularly in the living room and dining room. Alternately, Moira wanted to remove the traces – like the tablecloth Ann's mother had embroidered and the clock

Wanda had presented to the girls the day she moved in – or she wanted to meditate on these relics. Yes, she should do something constructive like writing letters rather than wallow in her loneliness and grief. It wasn't as if they were dead. She hadn't lost anyone in this war, not her father who was too old to fight; not Randy, who was safe, knock wood, in the Pacific. Wanda and Ann wouldn't be in danger. Well, Ann should be careful, but by now the only German business in Britain was reconnaissance flights to check out military installations. It looked as if the war were approaching a new stage with the Allies growing more aggressive. Still, she wasn't counting on anything.

Teddy glanced from the letter and caught Moira's expression. 'You OK?'

'Yeah, just missing people.'

'Me too.'

Moira smiled. Teddy would never admonish her, never say, get off your duff and do something. Sometimes she wished Teddy were a little more critical. After years of her own exhortative mother, Moira never thought that she would ask anyone for criticism, but occasionally Teddy was too accommodating.

Teddy returned to her writing and Moira considered how quiet the house had been since their friends left. She knew she should get out more – do another USO show or volunteer at Oak Knoll Hospital. Her excuse was the shipyard. She thought of how exhausted she had been coming home yesterday. She sat in the back seat with her hard hat over her face to block out the sounds of the other people in her carpool who were so cheerful that it was Saturday. She felt more than fatigue; she was horribly depressed. Teddy was busy with her family and the extra war bonds work and the evenings with Dawn and Sandra. At the very least Moira knew she should be checking for new room-mate possibilities at the yard. Mr Minelli had told them to forget Wanda's rent; he was so ashamed of the internment, saving her room was the least he could do. But now without Ann's monthly cheque, it was hard on him. Mr Minelli expected a replacement soon. Moira knew this task was up to her – and why not, Teddy did a lot of other things for the house. She switched off the radio. She promised herself not to disturb Teddy's serenity.

'You writing to Wanda?' Moira asked suddenly.

'Yes.' Teddy emerged with reluctance.

'Well, how's she doing?'

Teddy looked at her curiously. 'You read her letter to me over supper last night.'

'Sorry. I guess I've been kind of distracted about work. Do you think I should try to get transferred from the plate shop? There are other jobs I can do with welding experience. At first I liked it there because it was easy to cut and mark the plates and assemble them. But an outdoor job would probably be healthier. After a while, the smoke and squeal of the machines gets to you. Sometimes it's hard to hear properly until after supper.'

'That's not what's bothering you.' Teddy set down her pen and pad on the coffee table.

'To tell the truth, I've been fretting about Randy.' Moira shrugged. 'I tell myself he's going to be OK. But I still fret.'

'Do you do anything about it?'

Now that Teddy was beginning to sound like Mother, Moira was irritated. 'You're saying I should write more.'

'What do you think?'

'Well, it's hard to write when you don't know if a letter will get torn to shreds by the censors or lost on the way.'

'But you know who you're writing to and that's what matters.' Teddy tried to sound convincing. She picked up her tea and glanced around the living room. The house got messier with just the two of them, maybe because they weren't so polite with each other. She liked the ease with which they circled one another's lives. Although she missed Wanda and Ann the house felt quite full.

'You're right, Teddy, I'm just lazy.'

'And a little scared.'

'And a lot scared.' Moira nodded. She joined Teddy on the couch. Clapping her hands, she said, 'Hey, we never did have that party before Ann left. Let's have a celebration in mem . . . in honor of Ann. We can write and tell her all about it.'

Teddy was relieved by the vitality in Moira's eyes, but afraid to ask the next question. 'Who do we invite?'

'Well, let's make it a hen party. Let's ask Vivian and Dorothy from the yard and – yes, let's keep it small. Now how about your friends Dawn and Sandra?'

'I, I just don't know,' Teddy shook her head.

'Social jitters?'

'Hardly,' said Teddy. 'You seem to forget that crack Dorothy made last week about "colored girls."

'Oh, yes, right, drop the party.' Moira was defeated, angry at her own insensitivity and then angry at being so disappointed. What was wrong with her? In the last six months, she had lost all patience, savvy, toughness. She missed Randy terribly. And the war had done strange things to her sense of timing. Some days flew by because of overwork and obligations. Other days seemed to crawl. She was all too aware that the drama was happening elsewhere. She wasn't imprisoned in Arizona. She wasn't treading through a Pacific swamp. She wasn't stepping around bomb craters in London. She was staying behind, hardly holding together the home front when she couldn't hold together herself.

Teddy offered, 'OK, let's have a little supper party. Several. Let's start with your friends. Just the four of us, that should be fine.'

'But not just *my* friends.' Moira grew more distraught. 'I want to fill the house with life, with our lives.'

'It isn't full?'

'You know what I mean, with talk and music and laughter.'

Teddy smiled at the thought of Dawn and Sandra. Snickers and chuckles and irony, maybe, but musical laughter was unlikely. Sometimes she realized that she was a little more wordly than Moira. 'How about if I ask Jolene and Mom and Amanda some evening?'

Moira didn't like to think she was jealous of Teddy's family, but she couldn't understand the weekly visits and daily telephone conversations.

'Moira?' Teddy smiled.

'Yes, oh, yes, that would be nice.'

'Your acting is better than that. I've seen you do Desdemona and Ophelia, not to mention Lady Macbeth.' Her smile receded. 'Do you mean you don't want to have the family? They can fray a person's nerves.'

'Oh, it's not that,' Moira was remorseful. 'I'm just a little distracted. I was thinking how different you are with your family than I am with mine.'

'You take everything too seriously. But if you don't want them. . . .'

'No, I get a kick out of all of you together. I especially like Jolene. So let's do it.'

'How about Friday for Vivian and Dorothy and then Sunday the following week for Mama and Jolene and Amanda – after church –

say around ten o'clock?'

Moira considered her quizzically. 'You wouldn't care to switch that to eleven, would you? Sunday morning does arrive after Saturday night.'

'Fine.'

Already Moira felt renewed.

Teddy sat at the piano, picking out a tune she had heard earlier that day. She hated waiting for Moira when she worked overtime at the shipyard. No telling when she would return, but more than that Teddy worried about her. Moira said she was careful and that women at the yard had less accidents than men. But Teddy had heard terrible stories about women being scalped when their hair got caught in machinery.

She swivelled to the coffee table where she had placed Wanda's letter. They hadn't heard from Wanda in weeks and she was dying to open it. But that didn't feel right, since it was addressed to both of them. Moira would probably open it, but Teddy thought these letters from Wanda and Ann were like meals, more enjoyable when you shared them. Maybe that was why Moira called her romantic. Teddy reddened; that must be it.

Teddy turned back to the piano, but it was a silly tune and she was getting hungry. She walked into the kitchen, pulled out the hamburger meat and plopped it in a pan. Then she turned on the water to boil for spaghetti. Teddy had to admit one of the pleasurable things about being left with Moira was that they each had simple, complementary appetites. The sizzling and smell of the hamburger brought back camp trips with Hank and Arthur. Out in the woods, they'd camp for days at a time, tracking each other, pretending to be old-time Cherokees. Exhausted at night, they would lie around the campfire telling ghost stories and cooking beans. The world was full of peace away from Pop's drinking and Mom's worrying. Now she opened the Del Monte tomato sauce and rinsed the container, thinking they wouldn't have these tins much longer. She would have to plant a very serious garden this spring. How could she do that without Ann's devotion and Angela's kibbutzing? Stirring the red sauce into the beef, she breathed deeply. The savory aroma conjured feelings of one evening when she had fixed this dish for Angela.

Dawn kept reassuring her that Angela cared despite the absence of letters. She reminded her that poor women didn't telephone from Texas if they weren't making an investment. Teddy hoped Dawn was right. She wished she had more people to talk to about Angela. Maybe she would feel less critical of good old Randy if she could talk to Moira about her own heart. How would Moira take it? Either she would be completely blasé or she would become Zazu Pitts, flinging her arms and screaming. The front door slammed.

'Hello, anybody home?' Moira was obviously in a good mood.

Teddy thought she would postpone the romance discussion a while longer.

'Fabulous.' Moira burst into the kitchen. 'Baked spaghetti, my favorite. Good thing we don't have to deal with those two old fogies. You and me, kid, and our baked spaghetti. Hey.' She held up the letter she had found in the living room. 'Waiting for me, eh?'

'Well, yes.' Teddy spoke hesitantly, unclear if she were being criticized or praised.

'The soul of honor, kid.' Moira put her hand on Teddy's shoulder.

'Open the letter.' Teddy laughed.

'OK, OK, just a second. I always need a couple of breaths before a new reading, to check my wind and center my mind.' She sat down at the table, putting her hard hat on a chair.

Teddy stared at the battered white hat with the big 'Moira' painted on the front. After all these months, it was still odd to think of Moira in a hard hat.

Moira cleared her throat and began.

Dear Moira and Teddy,

How are you? I'm doing a little better. Things are pretty much the same, but different. Having a sister-in-law, for instance. Ever since Howard and Carolyn's wedding, I've been telling myself that I have a sister-in-law. Gradually, I have come to believe it. Actually, during the last month, Carolyn and I have become very good friends.

Teaching is going well. Mrs W. and I seem to have reached an understanding. I work with the older kids and she sticks with the younger ones. I hate to admit how much I enjoy teaching. I keep telling myself, over and over, like a refrain, that I am a writer, writer, writer, writer. But I must admit there are a lot of immediate rewards in teaching and few enough rewards in writing about the dreary conditions of this weatherbeaten camp for magazines that are going to reject my article. Maybe I should stick to letters because I do get answers.

The landscape here seems to rob your senses. The terrain is dry and bleak and grey and beige. The weather is still relentlessly hot. The night sounds are eerie. I feel like I've lost the impulse to see and touch and taste and hear. I worry about losing my other sense, too, my 'good sense' as you would call it, Teddy. I feel like I'm experiencing everything second hand, either because I'm too dulled to feel it directly or because I'm too frightened. This is all a lot of ranting and raving, the last thing you need. I understand you have your own problems, with the rationing and blackouts and longer hours at work. It's just good to get it off my chest, you know.

'I think she's even more apologetic than us.' Moira turned to Teddy who was stirring spaghetti into the meat sauce.

Teddy sprinkled cheese on top and lowered the casserole into the oven. Carefully she turned toward the window so Moira wouldn't see the tears. Lord, she wished she could do something for Wanda. She was both looking forward to and dreading her visit to Arizona. Maybe she could still talk Moira into going with her.

The family is OK. What's left of it. Mama seems to be coming around a bit. Betty loves the piano lessons. One thing about this camp experience is that we've become closer sisters. I feel like I've been granted another childhood. It's fun to see things through her optimistic eyes. And she has such a bright, wry spirit that she sometimes reminds me of you, Moira.

I hear from Roy once a month or so. I guess you hear from Howard as much as we do, Teddy. He says he is really enjoying your letters, keeping him in touch with San Francisco happenings.

Moira frowned at Teddy. 'So that's why you've been reading the newspaper so thoroughly. You're really something.'

Teddy concentrated on sponging off the sink.

Moira continued.

I try not to worry about them. At least they have each other. The regiment has lost lots of men, you know. I still think they were crazy to enlist. Who are they fighting for when their own people are locked up? Probably part of my resentment is that I wish I also had been able to leave Arizona. I mean, it still hurts when I think about losing the scholarship. Plenty of girls wind up taking care of their families. Why am I so selfish?

Speaking of families, how are yours? Your brothers and sisters, Teddy? Hope your Mom and Pop are fine too. Do tell me about work. And the acting, Moira, do you have any parts? I got a letter from Ann the other day. I'm sure you know, she's moving along with her usual determination. The kids seem to love her. Odd how she keeps repeating that she doesn't plan to be a mother. I think she'd be terrific. So much more patient than I'd be.

Do write when you can. And thanks for the pioneer parcels. I don't know what Betty would do without that gum. It's one of her biggest trumps in the popularity game here. Mama really appreciated the soap. And the fudge was divine. But remember to use your sugar rations for yourselves. I promise to be in a better mood when I next write. Meanwhile, lots of love, Wanda.

Teddy set the casserole in the center of the yellow table. She watched the hot bubbles spitting along the edge. Pouring them each a glass of water, she noticed that Moira was re-reading Wanda's letter to herself.

'Hi there,' Moira said finally. 'Sorry I'm fading tonight. But I had some good news. Vivian and Dorothy said they are looking forward to dinner.'

Teddy's face went blank.

'This Friday,' continued Moira. 'Don't you remember, our campaign to brighten up Stockton Street?'

Teddy dug into the spaghetti. Why couldn't Moira have waited until after supper? No, she was being ridiculous.

'You're losing nerve.'

'Oh, just a little shy.'

'You'll love Dorothy. And you've already met Vivian. They both have a great sense of humor. We decided on pot-luck. Viv's bringing salad. Dorothy's bringing wine. And I said 7.30. Is that OK with you?'

'Pot-luck?' Teddy asked, betraying her uneasiness. She could hardly believe she had agreed to the evening. Would they all talk and laugh above her head? Both Vivian and Dorothy came from New York and she understood from Ann that those people could be pretty snooty.

'Yes.' Moira twirled spaghetti on to her fork. 'Great supper. Let's fix this for them.'

'Baked spaghetti?' Teddy winced.

'We're not inviting the King and Queen of Persia.'

'Well, I don't know what's wrong with making them a real supper – I mean with pork chops and potatoes and vegetables. I can be clever with the ration coupons. Why make them bring something; this isn't a church charity bazaar.'

'No, it just makes it easier on us. Moneywise. Timewise. It's a modern custom. Everybody does it.'

'Everybody.' Teddy curbed the hurt in her voice. Why was she so scared about a little supper? She was afraid of losing Moira, that was it. When Moira saw them all together, she would choose her sophisticated, married friends over her. In the last few months, with the others gone, Teddy had felt a special pressure about the house. Sometimes she was a little girl again. Once or twice she had cried when Moira left in the morning. Just a bit. Silly, but she missed her already. The slightest crease in their life petrified her. Of course Moira would get married some day. Teddy had no illusions about competing with a man, but that wouldn't happen until the end of the war. And as much as she hated the war, as much as she mourned the loss of Ann and Wanda, she cherished her refuge with Moira. What would happen now with vivacious Vivian and mysterious Dorothy? Would Moira suggest they move into the house? Teddy noticed Moira waiting for an answer.

'Well.' Teddy blinked. 'I don't care what everyone does. I would have been happier to offer a decent meal.'

'Decent, indecent, Teddy sometimes you kill me. Actually, you remind me of my proper Mother. Listen, they're just friends. They'll love your cooking. And I know they'll love you. Vivian already does. She thinks you're cute.'

Teddy stared at her.

'Don't look shocked.' Moira wondered at Teddy's lack of confidence. Maybe she didn't tell her often enough how much she appreciated her.

Teddy twirled and untwirled the spaghetti. 'OK, OK, I'm sure it will be a fine dinner, uh, I mean pot-luck.'

Moira sipped her water thoughtfully. 'Dorothy's husband is in the navy too. She has the same kind of worries. We had a great talk over lunch today.'

'Good,' Teddy nodded, taken aback by her own jealousy.

'Have you heard anything from Virgil?' Moira tried to rouse her friend. 'Didn't you say he was going to enlist this week?'

'Yes.' Teddy nodded. She could barely hold back the tears. 'He got his papers today. Should be leaving on the weekend.' Finally she put down her fork and fell to weeping.

Moira stood behind her, hugging Teddy's thin, stiff shoulders. As they quivered and heaved, Moira realized that Teddy had been upset all night. She breathed in Teddy's dark sweat through the lavender talcum powder. Of course, this had been a strain on her too. Of course she was worried about her brothers and Ann and Wanda and Angela. They hadn't talked about Angela in ages. Maybe something had gone wrong there, too. Teddy was sobbing now.

Moira held her a moment longer, then, keeping one hand on Teddy's shoulder, sat next to her friend and tried to make eye contact. She stared at the strings of blond hair dangling in Teddy's face. Never had she seen her this unwound. In some senses it was a relief. Moira's eyes wandered to the spaghetti hardening in the tomato sauce. Poor Teddy. Dear Teddy. Gradually, long breaths replaced the sobs.

Teddy looked up at Moira. Suddenly she felt as if she were seven years old again, having her tonsils out. Throughout the operation, she was held together by fear. She tried to hear the nurse's soothing words as she fitted the foul smelling ether mask. But she couldn't so she simply continued to count backwards. She thought about her mother, who had been refused entry to the operating room.

'Oh, my.' Teddy withheld an apologetic laugh. She remembered how much she liked taking care of Moira and assumed the instinct was mutual. 'It's just that Virgil is Mom's favorite and I don't know what she'll do with him away. He's been pretty good now at keeping Pop in check. You know he could kid round with anyone. Truth is, *I*'ll miss the boy. Even though he's nine years younger, he's really my favorite. Got a sweet temperament, you know.'

'Do I know,' laughed Moira. 'If he were a few years older, I'd drop Randy for him. Remember when he delivered the jams from your mother? He found me fiddling with the leaky pipe and scooted me away as if I were the Duchess of Windsor. He lay on the floor, fixing the pipe and telling me one joke after another in between commenting on my green-green eyes and admiring my red-red hair. He practically had me running off to Mexico with him. Quite a charmer, your brother. That must be the Celtic side of the Fieldings.'

'We've always thought it had more to do with the Cherokee, even if we are only one-sixteenth Indian.' Teddy grinned. 'You know there's a fey spirit in Indians too.' Her face grew longer. 'It's selfish, I just don't want him, of all people, to be taken. Taken, I don't mean taken. I'm sure he'll be OK. I mean I pray to God he'll be safe. But you know when they drafted Arthur and Hank, it seemed more fitting. Virgil hated being the baby. . . .' Teddy trailed off. She picked up her fork and fiddled with the cold spaghetti. 'It's not my life. It's his right. Who knows what's right in all this mess. I'm just being selfish.'

'And human.' Moira remembered Ann comforting her about Randy. 'Cry, it's good for you. To be honest, it's good for me, too.'

'Well, just look at the two of us.' Teddy shook her head. 'We need a party.'

Teddy was a little more relaxed by Saturday night. She dusted the mantelpiece, reviewing the worst possibilities. She might not be able to follow the pace of their conversation. She might appear too cold or too shy. She might not be able to control the jealousy she felt about Moira and Vivian. They might ask her about her 'man in the war' and what could she say? As she considered each possibility in excruciating detail, she realized she would survive.

The next dilemma had been clothes. Both Vivian and Dorothy were very chic. Moira complained of feeling like a slouch in comparison. Teddy had dug out the black dress she had worn to Mr Nakatani's funeral. She didn't trust any of her country prints or bright blouses. At least she would look dignified, tailored, maybe even invisible. Teddy had to get rid of this chip she carried on her shoulder from Oklahoma. These people weren't Roosevelts. Vivian, according to Moira, was from a poor neighborhood in the Bronx. Dorothy lost her father when she was five and her mother when she was fifteen. Lord, she hoped they wouldn't be wearing slacks.

Moira called from the top of the stairs, 'You seen my red belt?'

Teddy was pleased to see Moira in her grey-striped shirtwaist and red pumps. Yes, it was right to dress up for your women friends. Why not? She had always dressed up for Angela. All week she had been aching to tell Moira about Angela.

'Hello, Teddy,' Moira called again. 'have you seen my. . . .'

'Oh, sorry, did you check my room? I think you dropped it the other night when you came in from the party. Try the chair.' Teddy considered how she enjoyed it when Moira dropped things in her room.

'Thanks.' Moira came bounding down the stairs. 'Hey, country girl, you OK tonight?'

'Do me a favor,' Teddy sighed. 'Don't call me "country girl" this evening.'

'Hey, friend,' Moira grinned, 'what's wrong? You still nervous?'

'I want it to be a nice party.'

'Listen, honey, with all the hors d'oeuvres and flowers you've laid in, it'll be a nice weekend.' Moira stopped, seeing that she was upsetting Teddy more. 'They're just my friends. Riveters in the shipyard. You'll love them. They'll love you.'

Teddy stretched her neck back.

'How's Virg?' Moira inquired tentatively.

'He's fine. It's Mom. We're all going down to see him off tomorrow. Mom will be OK. I just wish it were over. I mean, I wish the damn war were over.'

'I know, honey. Look, can I come along tomorrow?'

Teddy was taken aback.

'I mean, would your family mind? Would I be in the way?' Moira knew she had a knack for butting in. She remembered when Mr Minelli broke his arm, tripping on the sidewalk, how she had run around for the doctor and the ambulance as if she handled emergencies every day. Grateful Mrs Minelli had just sat there on the pavement with her husband, paralyzed, and amazed that their scatty young neighbor could be taking charge. Butting in was OK that time. But Moira also remembered inviting herself to Ann's class and how Ann never brought it up again. 'I mean,' Moira continued more slowly, 'if it's a family thing, I don't want to impose.'

'Oh, no, they wouldn't mind. And it'd make me feel real good. It's not necessary, though. Weren't you going to the matinée tomorrow? Listen, don't change your plans for me.'

'Who else would I change them for? You're my best friend.'

Teddy took her hand. She would remember that tonight.

'By the way, you look real swish in that outfit.'

Teddy frowned, but decided that Moira was telling the truth.

Vivian and Dorothy arrived together, twenty minutes late. Fashionably late, Teddy realized dismally, conscious of how hungry she was.

Dorothy was wearing a kelly green print dress, like the one Teddy's Mother had made her last Christmas. And Vivian really did look like she had walked out of the *Ladies Home Journal*. Still Teddy noticed that underneath all the shine and style, she seemed jittery.

'Great house,' Vivian said, walking swiftly around the living room.

Teddy remembered their first party when she nervously entertained Angela and Rosa and wound up trying to dance with Randy. She felt grateful for the calm she felt now. Compared to Vivian, she was in slow motion. Did Vivian remember she had made this same remark when she dropped by last month?

'The piano,' Vivian exclaimed. 'Who plays the piano? Not you, Moira lass, with the tin ear. Oh, that's right, you mentioned Teddy plays, doesn't she?'

'Yes,' Moira said proudly. 'Maybe we can talk her into a concert later.'

'What do you play?' asked Dorothy in a light, friendly voice.

Ridiculous to have feared these women, Teddy thought. Moira interjected before she could answer.

'Oh, just about anything. Rag. Swing. Blues. Even some classical.'

Teddy ushered them to the couch, hoping to change the topic.

'Where did you learn?' Dorothy persisted.

'Oh, I didn't. I just picked it up. You know, by listening.' Teddy noticed with approval that all her words had emerged in order.

'I wish I was creative!' Vivian sighed.

'But you are.' Teddy spoke without hesitation. 'The way you dress!' She hoped she hadn't embarrassed the woman. 'I mean. . . .'

'Listen, honey, it's OK. I love comments on my outfits. And you're right. It's a different kind of talent, but not as entertaining as playing piano.'

Moira laughed with Dorothy. Teddy regarded both of them and smiled uneasily.

The hors d'oeuvres course progressed quickly. In fact, it was Moira who said, 'Shouldn't we serve supper? I'm starving.' She led them into the dining room.

'What is it?' asked Dorothy as Teddy set down the covered dish. 'Smells terrific.'

'Baked spaghetti,' said Moira, trying to conceal her tension. 'A speciality of the house.'

'I thought that was lasagne. Is this another Italian dish?' asked Vivian. 'Delicious, bet you made it though, Teddy.'

Teddy shrugged. There was something seductive about Vivian. On the other hand, Teddy didn't appreciate these cracks about Moira. Still, Moira seemed to be taking it pretty well.

Moira nodded. 'Yeah, Teddy's the cook and the gardener around here. I'm better at the scullery maid stuff. And the décor. Very femme minus a few standard talents.'

Teddy gulped; she hadn't heard the word 'femme' outside the bars. Moira changed the subject, 'So what do you think of *So Proudly We Hail?*'

'Best movie all year,' sighed Vivian.

'You think so?' Dorothy frowned. 'Those nurses on Bataan had it tough all right. I admired them. But it wasn't much of a woman's film. You know, I liked *Mrs Miniver*. No one can beat Greer Garson.'

'That was last year.' Vivian shook her head. 'Anyway, it was too gushy for my taste.'

'I liked Ann Southern in *Swing Shift Maisie*,' Teddy said.

'Yeah,' Moira agreed. 'That aircraft plant reminded me of the shipyard.' She hoped Vivian and Dorothy might recount some of the funny incidents from work about Sergeant Tom or Mrs Leaman. Instead they got tangled in gripes about payroll. Vivian went on a long tirade scolding Moira to leave the plateshop for some open air. It was time for dessert before they left the topic of the shipyard. Teddy seemed to be faring OK, paying her quiet attention to each guest.

Over the cake, Vivian asked Teddy about her job. Teddy said that the Emporium, like many department stores, had been getting complaints about shoddy clothes, ripped seams and shrinking. Standards had gone down since the war started. But they were handling it. She talked enthusiastically about the War Bond Drive.

Moira was surprised to hear Teddy being so forthcoming, so relaxed. She felt ashamed to consider how little she, herself, knew about Teddy's job. For instance, she didn't know that Teddy had started a Red Cross campaign at the store. Vivian was quite adept at drawing people out.

'So our "navy wives" meeting is all set?' Dorothy put in.

'Right.' Moira nodded.

'Do you have anybody in the service?' Dorothy asked Teddy.

'Brother who just joined in the army. And two others. And a friend in the WAFs.'

'The WAFs.' Vivian frowned, as if grasping a thought that had been eluding her all evening.

Teddy recognized her mistake. The only way out was to proceed naturally. 'The Women's Auxiliary Flying Corps'; they bring arms and equipment to bases across the country. The friend is our neighbor, Angela.'

'The lasagne lady, I bet.' Vivian laughed.

'Yeah,' smiled Teddy. She would have to talk to Moira soon. There was something about Vivian that recalled Dawn's toughness and Angela's sarcasm.

After coffee, Dorothy looked at her watch and made moving noises. Before they left the table, Vivian turned to Teddy. 'This has been great. Let's do it again. Why don't you come over to my roominghouse in a couple of weeks? We've got a piano in the common room. I'd love to hear you. And I'll treat you to *my* mother's *pièce de résistance*, Meatloaf à la Swenson.'

'A deal.' Teddy offered her hand.

Teddy cleared the table as Moira washed dishes.

'Well, you certainly came out.' Moira glanced over her shoulder.

Teddy paused in the doorway.

'I mean you were a social butterfly.'

'You think I talked too much?'

'No, no, I'm happy you got on with them is all. Vivian took a shine to you.'

Teddy blushed. 'Was it OK that I agreed to go to Vivian's house?'

'I'm delighted. I was afraid you wouldn't like Vivian.'

'So was I. Just shows I judge people too quickly.'

'You too?' Moira wiped the hair off her face with her forearm. 'Teddy isn't the kindest person in the world? Where will you find a new character to play, my dear?'

'Enough.' Teddy felt bold and high because the evening had gone much better than she had reckoned. 'Enough,' she repeated, pleased by the sass in her voice, 'or I won't share our special dessert.'

'Wasn't the cake enough?'

'I saved Ann's letter. We got it this afternoon. I thought it would be fun to read when everybody left. Something to relax with.'

Teddy sat down at the table as Moira put the last dish in the rack. Pouring the remainder of the tea into their cups, Moira nodded to Teddy.

> Dear Moira and Teddy,
>
> How are you? Thanks so much for the last package. It arrived intact, with surprise after surprise.
>
> The work has become more clear to me lately. How can one be clear in chaos? Believe me, you have to be thinking six things at once here. How are you going to find something to eat tonight? What will happen if there's another air raid? How many kids will be returned to the hostels? What's happening in the camps with their parents? So many practical crises as well as broad international tangles. I don't know how Esther and Sheila have been able to go it alone all these months.
>
> The kids are the bright side – with their eager faces – scared, but always brave. I feel so privileged in comparison. Can you imagine being uprooted and sent to a country where they don't speak your language? Can you imagine not knowing if you'll ever see your parents again? Yet their courage renews my faith in human endurance.
>
> I've thought a lot about having kids since I came over. There's something about the eradication that makes you think about reproducing. I don't know if I would have the patience to raise a kid. And it would interfere with scholarly work. But I don't know how important all that is any more. Coming face-to-face with daily misery diminishes the urgency of Latin conjugations.
>
> I know Moira, you're saying this war will be over one day and that I shouldn't throw away my ambitions. Teddy, I know you'll be worrying that I'm taking all this too seriously, that I'm running myself down.

Teddy set aside the letter and took a sip of tea. Moira patted her arm.

'Who needs letters when you can read minds?' Teddy sniffed, but she *was* concerned about Ann. The girl had a way of living in her head, following her will to the extreme. This was the source of her headaches, Teddy was convinced.

But really, my ambitions are shifting – getting larger. I think more and more about changing the world rather than understanding it. I don't know. Could I just have the DT's?

One of the best parts of working here has been the girls in the office. Esther and Sheila are bricks. They are completely reliable in the face of thunder. There's also a man named Reuben. I like him – quiet and reliable. Sometimes a little moody, but generally a steadying influence around here. He asked me to go to the movies next week. As much as I loathe British films with all that hectic, slapstick humor, I'm looking forward to the evening. We'll see.

Thanks for keeping tabs on my parents. I've really appreciated the letters from each of you. I know Mama is grateful for the company, even if she doesn't respond. Papa wrote and told me you invited him to supper. He was very pleased to have two young women doting on him. For my part, it's such a relief to be away for a while. Daniel writes occasionally, but by the time I get his letters it's so late I often wonder if he's still alive. You can't endure with thoughts like that. You have to stop worrying sometimes. But . . . I'm rambling. Whatever happened to the fine art of letter writing Papa taught me? Concentrate on the pleasant topics, ask about your friend, be positive and make sure each paragraph is a clear statement. Clear statement – I'd be delighted if I could find one in this entire day.

So tell me about YOUR days. I know you must be having it tough with the rations and the confusing news. (At least *I* know for sure whether London was bombed last night.) Sometimes I think it would be harder to be back there, knowing even less than I do here.

Tell me everything. What's happening with Virgil, Teddy, has he enlisted yet? And your work? And Angela? And you, Moi, I'm sure you're worried about Randy. How's the job? Are you able to keep up with the acting. I think you should. Despite all my equivocating on the previous page, I must admit I'm considering a night course. Living is not just enduring. It's being whole and unless I'm whole I can't do this job.

Heard from Wanda last week. She seems to be doing better. I think it's great you're going to visit her, Teddy. Who would have imagined when we sat in typing class that we'd be scattered like this, writing letters across the world?

I promise the next letter will be less jumpy. I guess I just needed to use this as a diary tonight. Let me finish by saying I think I'm doing 'something' here. And there are personal gains. Despite their ridiculous humor, I've come to love the British, for their resolve. Moira, you'll be pleased to know that the Scots are some of the toughest. Persistent and no nonsense. You should see how people recover after these blasts. They're selling goods from bombed-out hovels and living in the most precarious buildings because they don't want to leave their homes. Often I think of Stockton Street before I go to sleep. I imagine the four of us sitting in the living room sharing war stories. I do believe this will happen. My only worry is when. How much more devastation will we have to face first? Remember you're in my thoughts. Keep well and take care of each other. All my love, Ann.

'Well, she's in a pensive mood.' Moira smiled.

'Yes, it's nice to see her being so personal. I shouldn't criticize since I'm a terrible letter writer, but the other letters worried me, so dry and factual. Anyway, she seems OK.'

'Yeah, I know what she means about being happy apart from her family. It's the only way to survive.'

Teddy felt sad for Moira. She was grateful that her own family, despite all the troubles, was a source of comfort to her.

'What she says about Daniel and the letters,' Moira straightened her collar, 'it's just what I was explaining about Randy. It's hard not knowing. He's so god damned cheerful in his letters that it's even worse when he does write.'

Teddy nodded.

'But I've already worn out that topic for tonight. The stuff about the Scots is interesting. We do have a stubborn streak I guess.'

'Guess so.' Teddy raised her eyes affectionately. She sipped her tea, thinking about Reuben. They would have already gone to the film. Who knows what would happen with them.

'I wonder about that Reuben guy,' Moira said. 'Sounds temperamental. I just hope she's careful.'

'What's wrong with a little romance?' Teddy teased.

Moira searched her friend's face. 'Now you're the funny one. I thought you were always worrying about us going off and marrying and leaving you.'

Teddy pulled back, unable to focus for a moment.

'Don't worry, honey. I'm not saying you've blocked the church door. Just that you've been concerned. Look, I'm not complaining.' She held Teddy's arm. 'We've all enjoyed the attention. And we all knew it wasn't anything serious – that you weren't our possessive stepmother or anything.'

'Well, I guess I did have dreams about us living here a few more years.' Now she was on the verge of crying. How stupid.

'Hey, hey. Here we've had a lovely evening with friends. We've just read a great letter from Ann. And we're talking about romance. What could be the matter?'

Teddy stared down at her lap. Did she want to confess about Angela? To brag? To instruct? Was it safe to talk now?

'We haven't examined your heart in a long time,' Moira smiled, 'not since that talk about your old flame, Dexter what's-his-name in high school.'

Teddy remained silent, amazed that she had ever breathed a word about Dexter. She couldn't remember thinking about him in the last 10 years. But when Moira got her chatting she could hardly stop herself. Now she was conscious of a great stillness. Everything in the room seemed frozen except for her thumping heart. She inhaled deeply and opened her mouth although she didn't know what she would say.

Moira, who was uncomfortable with silence, spoke first. Deciding she had embarrassed Teddy long enough for one evening, she changed the topic. 'So when is Dawn coming to dinner?'

Moira watched a funny flicker in Teddy's eyes and grew nervous about intruding.

Astonished by her friend's prescience, Teddy regarded Moira closely. She saw a girl she had trusted for years and she reckoned there was something of a witch in Moira.

'I'd like to invite Dawn and Sandra here next weekend.' Teddy couldn't believe the words. 'But there's something you should know about them before they come.'

Moira's eyes widened in sudden clarity. She was at once shocked and relieved. Smiling at Teddy, she said, 'I think I get it. They're homosexuals, aren't they?'

'How did you figure it out?'

'Oh, something about those bars they took you to.'

'So you know.' Teddy could hardly believe her ears.

Moira watched with caution. Yes, she nodded, she believed she did know, now.

'That I'm a homosexual too.' Once it was out of her mouth, it sounded like a medical diagnosis, rather than her magnificent secret. 'I mean I'm in love with a woman.'

'With Angela,' Moira said.

Teddy noticed Moira was talking as if she were asking Ann about Reuben. Had she been hiding unnecessarily all this time? What would Ann and Wanda say? 'Yes. How did you know?'

'Well, there were all those movies you two went to.' Moira tried to remain calm. Still fairly shocked at the accuracy of her half guess, she considered that Randy was right all along. Had she known too? She recalled two lesbian actresses she met last year. She had liked them well enough so what was the big deal? But Teddy didn't behave like them. 'And the letters from Texas. The phone calls. There was something in the way you looked at each other.'

'So how long have you known?' Teddy leaned forward, then sat back nervously.

'Oh, for the last five minutes,' Moira grinned. She stood and put her arms around Teddy. 'You know how you know something and then light dawns and you really know it? Dawn it was. When I mentioned her and you looked back so meaningfully, it all became clear.'

'You don't mind?' Teddy faced her friend squarely. She was feeling easier. Still, she needed to be completely sure.

'Yeah, it's OK. I guess it's a little odd. But if it makes you happy, it's all right with me. I don't mean odd; I mean different, oh hell, I'm not sure what I mean. But I know one thing – I'm glad you have someone who loves you and who you love. It makes me feel easier about you.'

Teddy hugged her.

'And selfishly,' Moira continued, 'this is good news because it means I can talk more about Randy. I know he's not your favorite topic. But we could swap stories about our sweethearts in the war!' Was it OK to speak like this, oh, she had a lot to think about.

Teddy had to laugh at Moira's quick resolution. She knew this talk was just one step. She would need to tell other people. But she would settle for this, for now.

They looked at each other and laughed.

Chapter Seventeen

———————— • ————————

Mid-winter 1944, London

DE GAULLE AND CHURCHILL MEET AT MARRAKESH

———————— • ————————

BRITISH AND AMERICAN FORCES LAND AT ANZIO

———————— • ————————

LIBERIA DECLARES WAR ON JAPAN AND GERMANY

———————— • ————————

AMERICANS LAND IN MARSHALL ISLANDS

Ann walked from the Finsbury Park tube station, along Seven Sisters Road, trying not to feel oppressed by the early darkness of British winter. She supposed this gloom was a fair trade for long June nights. But she had a hard time recalling the glories of summer evenings during a rainy, dark 4 p.m. in January. Besides, there was a special ominous quality about night during war. The land was more vulnerable. And London was getting the heaviest air raids since 1941. Some people were calling this the 'Little Blitz'. The bomb craters brought back Mr Minelli's tales of the 1906 earthquake in San Francisco – buildings there one minute and gone the next. She was never scared during the day. However a darkness that might connote peace or reassurance in another era frightened her now. Coughing and sniffing, she trudged ahead.

Lorries pounded down the road, roaring defiantly, spewing

exhaust. The grass in the park was sleek and fragrant. Should she walk home through the park or stay on the sidewalk, the pavement as they called it here, next to the blaring traffic? Ann felt now, as she often felt on dim English afternoons, that she was treading on the edge of a nightmare. Which was real, the park or the roadway? Was she mad? Looking around at the people marching briskly past, loaded with shopping, she wondered if the real problem was her flu. Normally, she hustled along as preoccupied as the others.

The walk home took ten minutes. Every Saturday morning she came to Finsbury Park to write letters. Reuben teased her about it, but she felt too confined writing inside. The park was a neutral zone, a place where she could pretend. She might be in San Francisco. It was easier to reach out when you didn't feel so far away. Besides the park was one of the few touches of beauty in her life. She loved to stroll around the pond and the flower plots. Last June she had been delighted when the gardeners had offered the last tulips and bulbs to passers-by. So this spring she would have her own tulips, if the window box got enough light. When would the light come, when would spring come, when would this darkness end? She felt drops of rain on her shoulders, then on her head. Soon it was raining steadily and she walked faster, dodging cars across Queen's Drive and then beginning her last leg up Chester Court.

Everyone at work asked why she didn't live closer to the hostel. But the truth was, when she originally moved to London, she was attracted to the very English names in this section of Hackney – Seven Sisters Road, Blackstock Road, Portland Rise. And then Mrs MacDonald enchanted her with those grey, Scottish eyes. Mrs Mac reminded her of Moira's mother – a shorter, warmer version. Mrs Mac's house was cheap, as bedsitters went. And Ann got along tolerantly with the other tenants, except for that American journalist who had the big room downstairs. She had looked for weeks for a place and now she could never imagine moving. However, today she felt particularly cold and tired. She prayed there would be enough coal in her room to take her through tomorrow, when the fever was sure to be gone.

Chester Court – when she had first read the ad, she dreamed of a stately road with Georgian houses set in quaint gardens, well back from the pavement. The reality was just as quaint, but less stately. The street, now lined with tattered, Victorian bedsitters, was formerly a neighborhood of one-family residences set apart from the bustle of central London. The block between Queen's Drive and Seven Sisters Road did give the illusion of community. At first she hoped to get a room at the top of the house with a view of the park, but then she realized she would also have a view of Seven Sisters highway and she needed to retain some of her illusions. Also, she knew those rooms in the upper reaches would be the coldest in the house. The top floor was now inhabited by two Dutch women who worked for the Red Cross. She kept meaning to chat with them, but their schedules conflicted with hers. And they seemed to go away at weekends. So she remained cordial strangers with most of the tenants – Ginny, the nurse on the first floor, and Henry, the librarian on the ground floor, and Mrs MacDonald. They were all as busy as she was. Amiable enough – except for that American – but very preoccupied.

Ann unlatched the heavy front door, a sturdy, solid British door. She breathed in the acrid-sweet smell of coal. Someone was home. Maybe Mrs MacDonald had finished her volunteer tasks for the day. She felt a sudden rush of comfort, imagining Mrs MacDonald tending her with tea and toast. No, she reminded herself, she was twenty-five years old, long past coddling. And Mrs MacDonald had better uses for her time. Just a little rest was all she needed and she was perfectly capable of fixing her own tea.

She shut the door quietly, careful not to disturb anyone, for people slept at odd hours here. On the small table by the stairwell, she saw two airletters. They were either for her or for the journalist. Maybe that's why she resented him so much. Maybe she was just angry that he stole letters from her. Rather, she imagined he did. How often had she come home and found American post on this table, assumed it was hers, only to be disappointed to see it addressed to Mr Mark Speidel as she took the first step up to her room. She thought of making a little set of mailboxes to avoid this confusion. But Mrs MacDonald had her ways, not to be altered for the whims of a lonely tenant.

Ann hung her wet coat on the hook at the end of the dark wooden rack. Small pearls of rain ran down the front and made her shiver. Rubbing her hands together for warmth, she approached the table and glanced down with determined indifference to find that both letters were for her. One was from Papa, which she had half expected since he was so reliable. And one from Wanda. It had been a long time since she had heard from Wanda. She was very busy teaching and taking care of the family now that Howard was in Europe. Ann had pieced together fragments of Wanda's life from Moira's and Teddy's letters, but there was nothing like direct communication. Well, this would surpass Mrs MacDonald's ministrations. She would have tea with Wanda and save Papa for after dinner.

The house smelled especially damp today and Ann couldn't help noticing the wallpaper next to the stair lamp had unpeeled another ½ inch. She was alternately fascinated and beleaguered by life in this cold, musty house. The most exotic aspect was leaving your cosy room in the middle of the evening for the lav and finding yourself breathing fog in the hallway. The British prized their ability to survive. London Pride they called that flower which grew like weeds from bomb craters. Suffering was a test of virtue. Why was she in this ratty mood today? Must be the flu.

Tucking the letters into her purse, she climbed to her room. The door was latched with yarn on the outside, to keep out Mrs Mac's five cats. Unhooking the yarn, she entered the room, switching on the light. Suddenly she was overcome with sentimentality for her nest of London treasures: the lace curtains from Petticoat Lane; the Indian rug from Portobello Road; the framed broadsheet of 'A Valediction Forbidding Mourning' she had found in St Martin's Lane. She sat down on the small, hard bed and felt a rush of affection for the city she had inhabited this last nine months. The notion of deserting London at some point in the future filled her with a dull dread. Of course she would have to leave; she never intended to stay. So why the tension? She would leave when the war was over. If the war was ever over. Deserting London, is that what bothered her, or was it deserting Reuben? Reuben and that child, Leah.

Enough. She needed a cup of tea. And a biscuit. God, she was even feeling weepy about these digestive biscuits. She could get herself to bed immediately. Ann set her kettle on the hot plate, put out the pot, pulled down the tea canister and opened the condensed milk. Somehow she had grown accustomed to this gruesome imitation milk. What had happened to her voracious appetite for rich, black coffee and bittersweet chocolate? Well, the rations had cured that, with only 12 ounces of sweets allowed per month. The war got to you on all levels. Now, as she stood waiting for the water to boil on the hot plate, she felt fine. Maybe she didn't have the flu after all. Had she left Esther with all those files on account of a little cold? Or was she simply more comfortable now that she was home?

Home, she considered the empty hearth and decided to start a small fire. A bit extravagant this early in the day, but she was sick. Yes, as she listed across the room she knew she was quite ill. Oh, dear. She grabbed a bedpost for support. Bending down to fill the grate, she suddenly felt nauseated by the oily coal. She reached forward, arranging the chunks evenly, struck a match and sat back on her haunches, savoring the first rays of warmth.

All her life she had this problem of not knowing if she were really sick until she had a high fever and grew dizzy. She knew Papa would be disappointed in her because she was stronger than Daniel. And there was no more room for illness at home. Ann and Daniel conspired to survive, to be well, to do well. When she had her appendix removed at age seven, he believed she had defected. She couldn't wait to leave the hospital, to prove that she was all right, that they would be all right. Even now as an adult, she felt uneasy about her illness, as if she had done something to warrant it or as if it were an attention-getting ruse.

Ann sat down at the blue wooden table by the window, watching steam rise from the tea. Down on the street three school girls – she recognized the little one from two doors along – shouted and pulled at each other. So many of the London kids had been removed to the country. These English girls were different from the kids at the shelter, who played at a much quieter pitch. They took so long to emerge from their shells and, when they did, often became little adults – responsible and guarded. Ann looked down again. She couldn't hear the words. How did she know they were English? It was something about their bearing, a confidence in their childishness. Kids at the hostel were accessible only through their darkened eyes at the rare moments when they returned your look directly. The tea had cooled. And yes, she did feel better with the first sip. The biscuit loomed too large and sweet. Resting her head on the table, she was overcome with exhaustion.

Startled by a knock on the door, Ann found herself in bed. The ceiling lamp still burned and she checked her watch. 7.30. She looked down to discover that she was fully clothed. Then she responded automatically. 'Come in.'

A stab of memory warned her too late. The man who broke into her room on Turk Street. He came back to her at odd moments. Usually in dreams. But she wasn't dreaming, even though she was in bed, was she? 'Never open your door to strangers,' Papa had warned. Well, she hadn't opened the door – any door – he had come through the window. This one was coming through the door. Who?

'Mark Speidel.' He spoke shyly from the doorframe. He was taller than she remembered. And blonder. His hair was curly, receding around the forehead. His eyes were a cerulean blue, but slightly too close together. Then he grew more embarrassed, taking in her wrinkled clothes, watching her rise shakily from the bed, 'Sorry, I didn't mean to disturb you. But it's fairly early. I didn't mean. . . .'

'Yes,' she said in what she noticed was a reassuring tone. 'It's fine. I'm fine.' Then she swayed, holding on to the wall.

'You don't look fine.' He took her arm and led her back to bed. 'Can I get you something? A doctor maybe? What's wrong?'

'Doctor, no. It's just the flu. Thank you very much.'

'Hey, calm down. I didn't say you had typhoid fever. Doctors are pretty benign characters, you know. My dad is a doctor in Englewood, New Jersey.'

She knew he was trying to be kind, but she simply wished he would leave. She sat tall on the bed. Then she saw the airletter in his hand. Her letter probably.

'The letter.' He smiled and his great white teeth were an advertizement for suburban dentistry. 'Almost forgot. I took this by mistake. You get so eager for news from home. I saw the stamps so I grabbed it on the way out. Came yesterday, but I was gone last night and all day on a story.' He stopped, suddenly aware of her distraught expression. 'It's OK, isn't it? I mean you weren't expecting a legacy? Or a passionate love letter?' He inspected the handwriting before giving it to her. 'Nope, looks like it's from a woman.'

She couldn't tell whether or not she hated his cheerful confidence. After all, he hadn't stolen the letter intentionally. Accepting it now, she read the address and answered, wondering in the middle of her sentence whether she was foolish to be so forthcoming. 'No, my girl friends in San Francisco. People I used to share a house with.'

'Like this?' he asked. 'Folks were more friendly there, I guess. Can't imagine corresponding with Mrs MacDonald or the nurse next door.'

'No,' she answered too quickly to catch his drift. 'We shared the house – you know: the rent, the living room, the garden.'

'Ah, you were friends. All girls. Hey, that's nice. Independent. Sounds more cosy than this place.'

She caught his glance and, in spite of herself, she laughed.

He laughed too, a deep, ironic laugh. 'Well, you can't be dying if you've still got a sense of humor. Anyway, Dad would recommend bland foods and lots of liquids, especially fruit juice. Grant you, fruit is fairly exotic for London under siege. Might as well be prescribing heroin. But I've got some rice down in my room. Why don't you let me make you a bowl of rice? I can even concoct another pot of that foul tea,' he glanced at the pot by the window.

'That's very kind of you,' she said, groping for words to free her from his sunny American presence. She had found herself avoiding Americans in recent months. He looked like an athlete, relaxed after a long race. She couldn't help but admire the breadth of his shoulders, yet there was something off-putting about his perfect posture. The poor man had offered to do her a favor and she was turning him into a monster. She desperately wished to be alone with her letters. What on earth could she do to make him leave?

She sat straighter. 'I'm kind of tired tonight. Perhaps tomorrow? Perhaps I could impose on you another time?'

'Impose.' He was taken aback, then amused. 'You've been in this country too long. But I get the point. I'll leave you alone now. And check back tomorrow.'

'Bye, thanks for the letter,' she replied. 'And for your kindness.' He seemed somewhat smaller now.

'It was nothing.' He sounded disappointed, or was it concerned? He closed the door gently.

Ann switched on the lamp next to her bed, then rose to turn off the ceiling light. As she passed her face in the mirror, she was struck by the dark lines beneath her eyes. No wonder Mark seemed worried. She looked a 'proper wreck', as Esther said. She suspected this was as much from overwork as from flu. She felt she should eat or drink something, but she was too tired and too weak to think what to fix. Should she have accepted his offer? Why was she always defensive? She leaned back on the bed and picked up Wanda's letter.

Dear Ann,

We've been so worried with all the news of these raids on London. Are you all right? Do they come near where you work and live? Please write soon, even if it's just a note, to let me know you're OK.

And tell me more about this man Reuben. He sounds
fascinating with his education and his travels. I've always been
curious about Vienna. He seems like he would be good company, and stimulating. . . .

Ann closed her eyes in fright. How much had she told Wanda about
Reuben? She must have written ages ago. Had she been that
interested in him then?

Life here is pretty much the same. The teaching is fun,
although I have to tiptoe around Mrs W. sometimes. We don't
hear much from Howard and Roy. Do you hear from Daniel? I
continue to write the diary; often I think it's the only thing that
keeps me from going nuts – that and the letters. Writing is my
only link with the past – with old friends, but just as important,
with old goals. Sometimes I can pretend that this place doesn't
even exist, that I'm back on Stockton Street. And then other
times I like to write about this place because it's a way of
containing it. I have learned a lot about geography and while
I'm not too keen on the extremes of temperature and the barren
vistas, I have come to perceive another layer of the world – tiny
changes in the desert flowers, for instance. So far I've seen a lot
of Milkwort and Soapberry. I feel like renaming some of these
beautiful things because they were so obviously identified by
harsh Anglo-Saxons. Some of the names are OK, though, like
Jojoba.

I'm really looking forward to Teddy's visit. Her Pop seems
better so she can leave now. Wish Moira could come too. It will
be so good to catch up on the news, but I'm mainly looking
forward to seeing that familiar face and hearing her drawl. . . .

Ann put the letter on the bedside table. Falling straight asleep, she
dreamt of Leah. Leah curled outside her bedroom window meowing
like a cat. Such a beautiful child, with golden hair and deep brown
eyes. Familiar in an eerie way. Shivering from cold or fear. How
could Ann resist her? Yet what could she do *for* her? She could do
everything. No, Leah would be better off in a proper home. Was she
dreaming? Wasn't this the same stream of feelings that tormented
her when she was awake?

She turned on the light. 4.00. She slipped off her dress and
crawled beneath the covers. Had she been sleeping? This was the

common pattern – worrying about being sick and being sick from the worry. Ann reached for the aspirins on her bedside table and a glass of stale water. She took three pills, enough to quell a headache, enough to put her to sleep. Sleep of a sort. The child was still there, behind the window, crawling her way up now, wanting in, demanding something from Ann. Why Ann? Better that she chose parents in the safer countryside. Leah didn't realize how lucky she was, a young healthy girl. She could have a good life, grow up in a professional family, safe until her own parents could reclaim her. Ann knew she was supposed to be realistic about this: *if* her own parents could claim her. It was so hard to be realistic. The child's tail was wagging now – a great fluffy, yellow tail – yes, this must be a dream – she still wanted to come into the room. Ann turned over into blessed darkness, away from the window.

The knock was loud and persistent. Ann recalled Mae, the pub maid at the Opera Box. 'Yes,' her own voice. She struggled from sleep, thinking of Mark Speidel. And the rice. 11 a.m. Too early for rice. The knock continued. 'Yes,' she said louder, 'I'll be right there.' She gathered her robe from the chair and answered the door, vaguely expecting a meow from the other side.

'Phone, dear,' Mrs MacDonald said, nervously plucking at her grey hairnet. The ample woman frowned closely. 'Oh, hen, whatever is the matter with you?'

'Just a touch of flu,' Ann murmured, interested in her own resistance to Mrs MacDonald's sympathy.

'Well, perhaps I should have the party ring back. I don't know that it's wise for you to traipse around the hallway when you look so peelywally.'

Ann smiled. 'No, I'm fine. I can answer the phone. It may be something important about work.'

'Aye, those poor children.' Mrs Mac sucked in her breath, seeming to forget Ann altogether.

Ann tied the robe and scrambled for her slippers. The phone was downstairs, just outside Mark Speidel's room. She would be careful to keep her voice low. If she were lucky, he would be away working.

'Hello, Ann?'

Esther. Ann was relieved that it wasn't Reuben.

'Yes, yes, kind of you to call. But I do think I'm back on my feet again.' She looked down at her slippers, amused how two toes stuck out. The tabby and the black cat sniffed curiously at the hem of her bathrobe. She did feel better. If she rested all morning, she might be able to do some paper work this afternoon.

'Good, good.' Esther's voice was shaking. 'Because you'll need your strength. Reuben was quite put out you hadn't told him about being ill. I got the impression he's planning a visit today.'

'Thanks, Esther.' Ann leaned against the wall. 'Don't worry, you couldn't have done a thing to forestall him. It will be fine. Probably do him good to see me off that uncomfortable pedestal. Thanks for ringing. And don't worry about me. I'll be in Monday.'

She walked away from the phone, noticing her breath fog in front of her. It was kind of him to worry. Really, he was a decent fellow. But how could he just walk into her house without ringing? They were hardly intimate; they had always had such formal dates. Or had she been too thick to perceive his affection? Oh, she didn't know. She was too tired to think about it. Why was she irascible with people who just wanted to do her a kindness? Climbing back up to her room, she felt the damp creep through her robe. She thought of the warm house on Stockton Street and Teddy's hot chocolate. She missed the very smells of that house – the fragrant gardenias in early summer; Moira's lemon talc in the bathroom; Teddy's ever present lavender cologne. All she ever smelled in this place was the damp, musty scent of things falling apart: rotting upholstery, peeling wallpaper, molding tea leaves. And there wasn't much visual relief. Mrs Mac was as frugal with her money as she was with her time. A few pictures wouldn't break her. The single hall window stared out onto the brick wall of the neighboring house. Ann climbed wearily.

At the top of the stairs, Mrs MacDonald waited by her door. 'Is there anything I can do for you, hen, before I run along? Some tea, or a wee bit of toast?'

'No,' Ann said, completely relinquishing yesterday's fantasies of being pampered.

'I'll have a look in this evening. Stay wrapped up. You have enough coal now?'

'Oh, yes, yes. It's very kind of you to inquire. Don't bother about me at all.' Mark was right; she sounded perfectly British.

The fire was cold. She walked steadily to the grate and again was overcome by nausea. Maybe she would just let the fire go while she napped. If Reuben were coming she should apply a little rouge, but that would look ridiculous when she was still in a dressing gown. If he wanted to tend the sick, he might as well see how she felt. Why was she angry with him? What was going on with her today?

She rested fitfully in bed for half an hour. Then she reached for Wanda's letter.

> Betty's piano lessons are going well. Mama has refused to listen to her practice, though. Betty's turning into quite an accomplished young lady. Sometimes it does amaze me how life seems to go on here 'as usual', how much we have forgotten about 'usual' life.
>
> The war feels upside down sometimes. Our friends turn into enemies – like Italy – and our enemies – like Russia – turn into friends. I can hardly believe the daily reports of heroic Russian troops we get in the newspapers here. You too? It makes you wonder what war is really about and who we'll be fighting next.

The rap on her door was louder this time, more forceful. Immediately Ann regretted the state of her hair and face.

'Come in,' she said, feeling exposed on her bed. But this was more dignified than stumbling to the door and collapsing in Reuben's arms.

'OK.' She heard him set something on the floor – probably flowers; that was sweet of him – and slide the door ajar. She saw his boot push open the door and was flabbergasted to find Mark Speidel carrying a tray of food.

'So how's the patient?' he began and, before she responded, he continued, 'I heard you were awake half an hour ago. On the phone. So I thought you might have a little appetite.'

She coughed, further astonished that he was right; she was famished. The rice looked quite inviting. And somewhere – oh, glorious – he had found a fruit cordial. Before she could speak, he was down on his knees fussing with the fire.

'You'll never recover in this environment. Sounds like you've got it bad in the chest.' He eyed her cigarette papers and packet of tobacco. 'You need to stay as warm as possible. Say, where did you learn not to take care of yourself?'

'That's a long story.' She laughed, at herself or him, she didn't know.

Downstairs the bell rang. Ann heard someone – was it Ginny, the nurse? – greet the caller. Well, it served Reuben right, coming unannounced, to find another man in her bedroom. She tried to feel amused, but she began to cough fitfully.

He walked in empty-handed – his broad palms extended, his face all a worry. What a tall man he was. Ten times bigger than Mark who was kneeling at her fire.

'So why didn't you tell me? Why did I have to hear from Esther that you are sick?'

Not hello, may I come in, how are you, but an accusation right away. This had a familiar ring.

'It was sudden, Reuben.' Then, composing herself, she added, 'Would you like to come in?'

'I am in.' He was aggrieved. 'And,' he finally noticed Mark, who was now gaping at him, 'apparently I'm not the only one.'

'Let me introduce you to my kind neighbor, Mark Speidel.' She was surprised at the warmth in her own voice. She realized again how American Mark really was. By avoiding Americans she had tried to guard against homesickness and to preserve an illusory sense of life here. Mark brought her down to earth in a way that was both comfortable and unsettling.

'Glad to meet you.' Mark extended his one clean hand.

Reuben advanced grudgingly. 'The same,' he nodded shyly. Ann noticed how reticent he was meeting English or American people. Once he got used to you, he could talk your ear off. But at first he was testing the sensitivity of his listener and the comprehensibility of his accent. He was a proud man and also a considerate one, alternately afraid of mortifying himself and of imposing.

'Mark's father is a doctor and he prescribed this boiled rice.'

'I see.' Reuben said.

Ann was caught, enjoying this attention, worrying about Reuben and feeling embarrassed for Mark. After all, it wasn't every girl who had men flitting around her room with food and good cheer. Why, just yesterday she thought she was all alone in London and here she was, surrounded by international chivalry.

'Reuben works at the hostel with us.' Ann turned to Mark, certain he would be more civil.

'Oh, yes, very important work.' Mark nodded. 'What country are you from originally?'

'Austria.' Reuben spoke warily. 'Vienna. Do you know it?'

'I reported there before the war. Beautiful city. I remember many fine weekends in the hills.'

'Well, let's hope the hills still exist and that we'll all survive to walk there again,' Reuben answered thoughtfully.

Ann could tell Reuben was trying now. She looked at Mark who also seemed conscious of Reuben's effort. As he was wiping his big hands on the towel near the grate, Ann watched the blond hairs glimmer from the fire. She reflected on the ease of his movements and the directness of his speech. He was so unEnglish, right down to this enormous portion of rice. She must eat before it turned cold. 'Please sit down,' she said to Reuben. He perched on the edge of a wooden chair; she could have predicted he would avoid the comfortable arm chair.

'I'd better get going.' Mark waved.

Ann nodded, her mouth full. She regretted his departure as much as she was relieved to be left alone with Reuben. He had made her realize just how lonely she was for the States. 'Thanks for everything,' she finally managed to say. 'Are you sure you won't stay?'

'Sure.' Mark smiled. 'Nice to meet you.' He clapped Reuben on the shoulder. Reuben smiled, considerably more relaxed.

'So how are you?' Reuben became more himself, his dark eyes waiting for an answer.

'Oh, I'll be OK. You know how illness spreads around the hostel.'

'And I think you are worn out. How late did you work every night last week? This and your visits to Mrs Fineman and Mr Herscher. And that class at the university. How long can this go on? You're going to be your own casualty.'

Ann leaned back into her pillow, remembering how Papa could also be conciliatory and scolding at the same time. On first glance, the men seemed completely distinct, but their resemblance was becoming unmistakable.

'I know you mean well, but life here is different.' He butted his head forward. 'You can't expect to accomplish the same amount you did in the States, in California, for God's sake. Conditions just aren't the same. Things take three times as long in Europe. And with a war on!' He stared dubiously at the rice. 'This is good?'

They both laughed.

'We had two more placed yesterday.' Reuben spoke with quiet anticipation. He could go into theatre this man, as a suspense artist.

'After I left? So quickly? When? Who?' She was taken aback by her own alarm.

'David and Anna Friedman. That family in Carshalton. I think it will be good. I have to drive them this afternoon.' He sighed, revealing weeks of fatigue.

No doubt he was as exhausted as she. Possibly he had the flu too. You could never tell about Reuben. He was fine at taking care of others and terrible at looking after himself.

'You thought it was Leah, didn't you?' he asked.

She nodded, deliberately filling her mouth with the rice which now tasted like gold glue.

'We have to talk about that girl.' He shook his head.

She tried to read his expression and was lost in admiration for his face: deep-set eyes; large, proud nose; wide, sensuous lips; dark hair curling around the periphery. She was particularly fond of his eyebrows, so thickly knitted and firm.

She felt a sudden shiver of fear. They had hardly mentioned the child before this, at least they had said nothing particular about her. What did he know of her affection ? Ann understood she must let go of Leah. In fact, she wasn't certain how she was holding on to her.

'She needs a home.' His voice was low, almost stoic, the way it often got after a long day. 'She is too little for the hostel. She has many chances for placement.'

'I know.' Ann was defensive.

'But we both know she'll never go.'

Her stomach sank. 'What do you mean?'

'She's found her mother. She wants to be with you, Anna.'

'That's impossible.' She sat straighter. 'Look at this room; look at my hours. What do I know about raising a child?'

'It's not what you know,' he smiled. 'It's what you feel.'

She stared at the rice, incapable of another bite.

'I have responsibilities elsewhere,' she began.

'Anna, dear Anna, I don't think there's anywhere on earth you don't have responsibilities.'

'No, I mean Papa.' Her voice was more determined. 'Let me read you his letter!'

> Dear Ann,
> How are you all the way over in London? I read about these air raids and worry every day. Things here are quiet. Work goes along well. I hear from Daniel every week, a little more regularly than I get letters from London. Isn't it strange, don't you think the post should be better from England?

Mama is the same. I visit her every evening. The nurse says she has never seen such a devoted husband. But sometimes it is hard to believe this is really my wife. She is so different from the woman I married. I talk to her, although I don't know how much she hears. Sometimes she moans. Occasionally she nods. Yesterday she said, 'wasser'.

I read her the letters from Daniel and you. She seems peaceful at such times. Or am I imagining? Yesterday she cried during your letter. Since we don't hear from you so often, I read them over again. She sleeps a lot. The nurses say this is a good sign. Perhaps she is dreaming away the sadness. I keep thinking that some day I will walk in there and she will be waiting for me with a ribbon in her hair. That my Dvora will talk to me about our children and plans for our house. Oh, Ann, if you only knew how good it was once. We had everything – hope, health, ambition. I know it is my fault. I know I brought her to the wrong climate, that she could not endure here. But how was I to understand, then?

Reuben sniffed. 'If he had to do it all over again, he would have stayed in Germany and you would all be in concentration camps. A big responsibility your father takes. It helps me to understand his daughter's burden. And her eloquence. He writes fine English for an immigrant.'

Ann nodded, surprised to be compared to her father.

The ramblings of an old man. It is hard to be in this big flat with no one to talk to. Tell me if you have clearer plans for returning. I know your work there is important. But we have refugees here too. You could do so much. And then, not in the least, is your Mama. She misses you, my love. You don't need to worry about me. I have even come to like cooking. I can get around. I have all the physical comforts. Physical. But it would be a blessing to have my daughter back.

I hear from Teddy and Moira every few weeks. Teddy brought over a lovely apple pie. Neither of the girls is married yet, which surprises me. There is a rash of weddings. I am not so surprised about Teddy. But that Moira is a pretty one.

Well, this paper is running out. And Jack Benny is coming on the radio. One of the few bits of company in a week. I send the best from Mama and me. Love, Papa.

She lay back, spent.

Reuben reached over and carefully retrieved the letter.

She could not open her eyes. She didn't want him to see the tears. She rolled over and wiped her face on the pillow case. But she could not stop crying. So she remained on her side, thankful he didn't reach over to touch her. She needed to release the anger and frustration of Papa. Finally, she turned back to Reuben, almost unashamed.

'You see why the decision about Leah is so hard.'

He nodded. 'Somewhat.'

'I've started to tell you about Papa several times. But he is so much more revealing in his own words.'

'Most people are.' He took her hand.

She wept again.

'All right,' he whispered. 'Nothing to be embarrassed about. Cry. It is cleansing.'

'It's the flu,' she began.

'It's the family.'

'Yes,' she admitted. Tears streamed down her cheeks. Finally, when she opened her eyes, he was still there. 'I feel so selfish,' she said. 'I mean this is nothing compared to your family.'

'You have much pain,' he murmured.

'I don't know what will hapen to Leah, if she keeps hanging on like this. I mean we could just send her to a family. We could tell her it's for her own good.'

'We tried that with the Rosen children. You remember. No, we want her to want to go. We have some time. She will be young a while longer. And today is not the day for decisions.'

She nodded, holding open her eyes with great effort.

'In fact,' he pulled away and regarded her seriously, 'today is the day for you to sleep. I don't know what I am thinking – coming to the sick with problems.' He shook his head and stood, filling the room with a powerful vitality. 'You have enough . . . nourishment,' he considered the rice less critically now and she imagined he was happy she could eat at all. 'I will ring tomorrow.'

'I'll see you at work on Monday.'

'No, you won't. You're going to sleep here until Tuesday and maybe Wednesday if necessary. Your Papa is right about one thing; you worry too much about too many people and not enough about your home – yourself. Now I will ring, and you must tell me if you need anything.'

'Yes,' she agreed, raising herself and regarding him with affection.

'Farewell.' He bent to kiss her forehead.

'See you Tuesday,' she said with determination.

London hadn't changed much in the last week, Ann considered as she rushed to the tube. Seven Sisters Road was still dark and clamorous. She had an even harder time inhaling the soot because she had grown used to the relatively clean air of her room. But she was eager to return to work. Just thinking about the files on Esther's desk created knots in her stomach. She was looking forward to catching up on Esther's news and to seeing Reuben. He had kept his promise, ringing every day, but not returning. What an endearing mixture of formal reserve and insistent intimacy. Quiet man on the brink of explosion.

Ann was the first one at the office, as she had hoped. Setting out the biscuits she had brought to surprise Esther, she started the kettle. She surveyed the empty room and was struck by its dinginess. No one had washed the outside windows for years. They seemed to be streaked a permanent grey, intensifying the wintry landscape. British people didn't find heat or light essential. On mornings like this, Ann longed for the daily presumptions of California. She could almost taste a nectarine. Never mind that Californians didn't eat nectarines in winter. What she tasted was a life she missed more than she ever predicted. Waiting for the water to boil, she sorted through the post on her desk. At the bottom of the pile was a piece of lined yellow paper, folded in four. She opened it to find a child's drawing: a woman holding the arm of a little girl. Ann's hand shook. It was too early to think about Leah. She shoved the picture in her top drawer, grateful for the high pitched distraction of the kettle's whistle.

'I might have expected this,' Esther said, shaking her curly head and removing her overcoat. 'Not only do you return to work too soon, but you arrive early. I'm surprised you're not scrubbing the floor.'

'Hi there.' Ann was glad to see her friend, aware how much she admired Esther's bright sarcasm. She reminded her of Moira in her liveliness, with a touch of Teddy in her maternal qualities. She looked a little like the early pictures of Mama – round face and sturdy body, rich, red-black hair, high color in her cheeks. 'Don't worry, I'm just fine. Needed a little vacation from this place I guess.'

'From what Reuben reported, you needed two weeks in hospital. He was worried.' She paused and, apparently deciding Ann didn't want to talk about him, continued, 'We all were.'

Ann set a steaming cup on Esther's desk.

'Thanks.'

Ann smiled, pondering the ease she felt with Esther. Was it simply the consequence of being Jewish in an overly polite country which didn't even pretend to be courteous about its anti-Semitism? Americans were bigoted, all right, but she had never felt so alien there, perhaps because there were so many other kinds of aliens. At first Ann thought her strangeness here came from being American, but gradually she understood that it was often her Americanness that saved her from being too Jewish in the eyes of many English people. She loved Esther's expressive hands and her passionate responses to everyone around her. Ann cleared her throat and listened carefully, lest her friend think she were still dozy from the flu.

'Is it still OK for me to go up to the meeting at Birmingham next week?'

'Sure, sure,' Ann answered. 'I should have this cleared away by then. Any new developments?'

'No. Got a nice letter from the Cohen kids. They're fine. And Mrs Goldman rang yesterday. She thought she could take another. She inquired about the six year old she met.'

Ann stared at her hands. 'Leah?'

Esther nodded. 'By the way, Leah's been asking for you every day.'

'How do you think she would do at the Goldmans'? Is the house large enough? Would she get along with little Sarah?'

Esther stared at her. There was something of Teddy in the way she looked straight through you.

'Sure these are the appropriate questions?'

'Oh, Leah and I. Esther, that's crazy. We both know it. Aside from anything else, it's very unprofessional.' She swivelled in her chair and stared out the dirty grey windows across the dirty grey city and wondered whether, in fact, she was well enough to be at work today.

'Professional? No, love isn't professional.' Esther's scrutiny was softer now, but equally intense. She sipped her tea and waited.

'How do we know that child loves me? Maybe she just identifies with me.' She was breathing too fast.

'I wasn't talking about her love.'

'Oh.' Ann blushed and took another draught of tea. 'Yes, I adore her. But I don't trust that. A person gets lonely far away from her family and friends. Of course I have you and Sheila and Judith, but most of my roots are back home.'

'Yes.' Esther nodded patiently.

'How do I know what I feel for her, this little child, isn't some kind of personal need?'

'Don't most people come to each other out of need?'

'Yes, but when they're adults that's all right. When one of them is twenty years younger than the other, it's not very equal.'

'Equal or not, you have a date with her this morning.' Esther evaded Ann's eyes. 'I couldn't help it. Every day she asked after you. I promised you would say hello on your first morning back.'

Ann swept her hand across the stacks of reports and papers on her desk.

'She's counting on you, Ann, fifteen minutes won't hurt.'

'You've missed your calling, Esther. You would have made a brilliant *schochkin*.'

'I come from a long line of matchmakers.'

The hostel felt particularly chilly this morning. They had been saving money by heating only the rooms where the children were playing or sleeping. Now with all of them in the recreation room, the little dormitory was cold and damp. She considered the beds, so neatly made, in almost military precision, yet touched with personal mementoes – a teddy bear here, a picture taped to the bedpost, a special pillow case. They had each made their own beds private territories, claiming what individuality they could. What would it be like to sleep with these other bodies each night? Did you hear the others tossing and coughing? Or did the even breathing of the bodies help you sleep? How long did the kids whisper after lights out? Ann used to dream of being sent away to summer camp, where everyone slept together, where kids told ghost stories and played pranks with each other. She had heard marvellous tales from Daniel about Boy Scouts. But Mama would never let her go away. There was so much that Mama felt Ann couldn't handle until Mama became unable to handle anything herself. Was this why Ann took on so much responsibility nowadays? She looked around again. Yes, her concern for these children in their impersonal dormitory was mixed with a little envy from her own missed adventures. She shivered and walked faster toward the recreation room.

The kids were scattered around the room playing games neither she nor they had heard of before landing in England. Ann loved to run the names through her head – rounders, tig, whip and loop, ludo, snap. In the corner a group of girls stood singing. This was a game Mrs Weinstein had taught them and Ann always smiled to hear their perfect English sentences. Esther had told her Mrs Weinstein had cleaned up the jingle a little.

> Jolly old sailor took a notion,
> For to sail across the sea.
> There he met his dearest Susie
> Wishing you to marry me.
> Weep no more my dearest Susie
> Take the dolly on your knee.
> I'll be back six months later,
> Wishing you to marry me.

Arthur and Robert stood watching the girls, poking each other and laughing. Ann felt a pang, remembering how the boys had been sent back after six months with their family in Penge because both mother and father had contracted tuberculosis. What must it feel like to be abandoned by two sets of parents? Well, as Esther had pointed out, at least they had each other. Standing against the wall, she tried to divine whether these kids felt happy or at least safe. Did they lose themselves in the games and the Saturday movies of *Hop Along Cassidy* and *Gene Autrey*? As Ann watched two girls giggling in the game, she was surprised by a tug on her skirt.

'Anna, Anna!'

She looked down at the curly head which caught light in a half-dozen shades of gold. Leah's brown eyes were set in an expression of wide watchfulness. As she smiled at Ann, the eyes disappeared and her cheeks grew pinker giving her a grave vibrance.

'Honey.' Ann patted her head. 'How are you doing today?'

'Better? Is Anna ill?'

Ann considered that Leah had more of an English accent than a German one, but then she had been here for four years. And, like Arthur and Robert, she had spent time with an English family before they had to return her to the hostel. Would Leah recognize her German mother, if she ever saw her again? No matter where these kids grew up it would be tough.

'No, I'm fine now. Just fine. And how are you?'

'Good now. You're here! Pick me up! Pick me up!'

Ann bent down, studying the child with concern. She saw such affectionate expectation that she was caught between delight and fear.

'So we play now? Go for a walk?'

'No, I just got back to work. I came to say hello because Esther said, well, because I missed you too.' She regretted the acknowledgement immediately. She wanted to ask Leah if she remembered Sarah, if she would like to live with her and Mrs Goldman in a nice house with a garden. But she couldn't trust herself this morning.

'Tomorrow? Tomorrow?' Her dark eyes were filling. 'You'll come back tomorrow?'

For a six year old, Leah had a remarkable memory. Maybe not; maybe all children were like this, Ann didn't know. But of course tomorrow was Wednesday and she always taught history on Wednesday. Afterwards she and Leah usually went for a walk around the neighborhood.

'Yes, tomorrow, honey, I'll see you tomorrow.' She set the child down.

But Leah held on to her skirt. 'You're not still ill?'

'No, Leah, I promise. I'm better. All better. Now, go play with the others.'

She waved to Mrs Weinstein and turned quickly without glancing back at Leah. Wiping her eyes, she hurried through the dormitory. Maybe Esther was right. Maybe they did belong together. Yes, she did feel love for the child. Clearly it was returned. How could they manage? Well, she could bring her back here every day. And if Mrs MacDonald objected – no, she doubted that would be a problem – but if she did they could find another place to live. Still, was it good for a child to be brought up by a single woman? And what would this do to her own plans of returning to the States and studying and teaching? The questions raised more questions, like scratching after poison oak. Whatever the answers, she knew she could not cope now.

The next morning as she arrived at work, she was startled to see light coming from under the door. Since she had made a special effort to get here early, she was concerned as well as curious.

Reuben stood looking perplexed with the tea pot in his hands. Rarely did she see Reuben out of control. She burst out laughing.

'The tea strainer,' he muttered. 'Damn thing broke open when I poured. English devices! Never trust them. What a mess.'

'Easily mended,' she said, relieving him of the pot and dumping the mess in the sink. 'What are you doing here so early? I thought you were down in Eastbourne until late last night.'

'Couldn't sleep,' he said. 'I wanted to talk with you. Didn't want to wake up dear Mrs MacDonald, or gallant Mr Speidel, for that matter. So I knew I could catch you here before Esther came.'

'Something wrong?'

'I've been thinking about Leah,' he said.

'Yes,' she answered slowly. 'What about her?'

'She needs a home,' he shuffled over to the window and studied the street below. 'She's too young for that hostel. Can you imagine the nightmares it will give her when she is older?'

'Yes, I know. I know.'

'She needs you.' He spoke quickly. 'You need someone else to take care of both of you.'

She could think of nothing to say, so she focused on making tea. Each small task required her whole concentration. She understood what he was saying. Yes, she would have to respond, but she was silenced by people from home. Mama in that damn bed in the warm, white room. Teddy, crouched down in the garden. Wanda, peering through the barbed wire. Moira dancing wildly with herself on the living room floor. He knew who she was now, but he did not know where she came from or where she was going. It was far too soon to talk of things like this. She wanted to be rational and explain that she wouldn't really be 'adopting' Leah, that she couldn't do that until they had official word from the girl's family. But he knew that. He was talking about a foster home. Yes, she needed to make a decision. Leah had made *her* decision. Reuben had made his decision. Now it was up to her.

She held the pot in both hands, feeling the warmth from Reuben's failed tea. Warm and empty. She set the pot on the edge of her desk. She was old enough to make decisions. Despite all her friends, despite the love she felt from Reuben and Leah, she had to make these decisions alone.

Chapter Eighteen

———————————— • ————————————

Summer 1944, San Francisco

GENERAL STRIKE IN DENMARK

———————————— • ————————————

US FORCES LAND ON GUAM

———————————— • ————————————

DE GAULLE ENTERS PARIS

———————————— • ————————————

ALLIES MOVE TO GERMANY

Moira woke at dawn with a heaviness throughout her body. She felt as if she were being pushed through layers of sleep. Much too early for breakfast. Breakfast, that did it. She was at the toilet in a flash, throwing up the remains of the previous night's fish stew.

She wiped her face with a warm cloth. Then she sprinkled Dr Lion's toothpowder on her brush and scoured her mouth, but she could not erase the sour taste. Her watch read 6 a.m. There was still an hour of sleep left, if she could catch it.

Moira tossed on the bed. 6.08. It would still be night in the Pacific. Randy would be asleep in his tent or, God forbid, in some freezing damp trench. Moira would have preferred Europe. She could imagine France or Italy or Germany. But who could imagine anything as huge as 'The Pacific?' She pulled the blanket closer, as if protecting both of them, and whispered, 'Be safe. Be warm. I'm waiting.' She remembered his bravado their last night dancing at Pluto's before he shipped out from his recent leave. Out where? Every time she heard about sea casualties, she shuddered. He was in the middle of the blue, on one of a thousand secret islands in the ceaseless ocean. She knew she could communicate better if she were told his location. And if he wrote more. It felt like ages since she had had a letter. 'Be safe,' she whispered. 'Keep warm. I'm waiting.' She lay there conjuring his face, a strong face that had grown in character over the years. He still had those teasing eyes, but he had become much more mature, much kinder too. The sort of guy she sometimes supposed her own father was, her real father. Oh, she loved Daddy; but her real father wouldn't have waited twenty-four years to stand up to Mother. Randy had a confidence to him, yet a softness.

Her stomach somersaulted again. 6.14. Must have been that fish Teddy cooked last night. No telling what Bertoli's was selling nowadays. She listened to the stillness. Teddy wasn't sick; she would have heard her moving about. 6.20. No use lying around comparing digestive tracts, she decided, but she got up too quickly, felt dizzy, then nauseated and headed straight for the bathroom. She heaved into the toilet once, twice, then leaned against the bathroom wall.

The lav. She recalled one of Ann's letters. Ann said she was sick like this every day of the voyage to Britain.

'You OK?' Teddy called groggily.

'Yes,' said Moira. 'Go back to sleep.'

'Sure, but what's wrong?'

'Oh, just the fish. It didn't agree with me.' Moira considered the maddening thing about Teddy was that she *would* go back to sleep.

'We didn't have fish last night. It was eggs.'

'Yes, yes,' said Moira. 'Now go back to sleep.'

Must be losing my marbles as well, Moira thought. And no wonder, worrying about Randy in the middle of the ocean – why *had* it been so long since the last letter – and Ann in devastated London and Wanda fighting coyotes in the desert. The war had become so real she was afraid to read the papers. When she wasn't worrying, she was feeling guilty.

Of course you didn't have to be far away to suffer. Poor Mrs Minelli had died in a flash last month when her four nephews were lost in Europe. Heart attack, explained Mr Minelli, who was supposed to be the sick one. Eggs, sure, Mr Minelli had brought them a carton of eggs from his sister's farm in Petaluma.

Well, she would get up and walk to Vivian's. One less stop for the carpool and the air would do her good.

Moira peered out the window through the fog as she pulled on her overalls. Couldn't see more than 3 feet this morning. Stubborn fastener. She held the pants tighter and accomplished the task. Downstairs she brewed a half pot of precious, rationed coffee. A cup for herself and enough for Teddy. She would skip breakfast. As she left, she grabbed an apple from the sideboard.

Teddy woke again with the slamming of the front door. Moira needed more practice playing elf. Yet, even in her irritation, she felt fond of the girl. Although Teddy missed Wanda and Ann terribly, she was never lonely. Moira filled the house with a great vitality. What was it going to be like when Mr Minelli's niece from Cleveland arrived? If she arrived. Mr Minelli had asked them to save the room months ago. Of course, it was him losing out on the rent, but sometimes Teddy felt guilty rattling around a big house when there was a housing shortage in San Francisco. She was also enjoying the time alone with Moira.

Teddy could smell the coffee as she reached the first floor. Sweet of Moira to make her some. No dish in the sink. Had she skipped breakfast again? The kid was going to get sick. Not that she looked skinny. The picture of health, Mom would say, all that color in her cheeks and the halo of red vibrating from her hennaed hair. Teddy smiled now, recalling her distress when Moira confessed she colored her hair. She hadn't exactly confessed. Teddy had found the plastic gloves, stained red, in the bathroom sink and didn't know what to imagine. Moira had laughed at her horror-stricken face and stood with her back to the window, the low winter sun blazing through her curls. Teddy had to wonder at the difference between them – Moira always one step to adventure and herself standing back, surveying the ground, or the sink or the stove. Moira laced the house with surprise. And Teddy looked forward to coming home, especially with Randy gone. He had been perfectly civil to her during his leave in May. Moira was right – he had grown up in recent months. Still, his presence nettled her. This was probably her fault. It was a terrible thought, wishing the war on someone and in fact she hadn't wished anything except that he leave the premises. Moira seemed half-missing when he was around – more ladylike, more cautious.

Teddy wiped up the coffee grounds, poured milk over a bowl of Rice Krispies and sat down at the table. She was glad they had cancelled the morning paper because it always made her reluctant to leave the house. She pulled Wanda's letter from the bread basket, although she had memorized it along with the letters from Virgil and Ann and Angela.

> We have better quarters for visitors than when Ann came through. The whole camp is more settled. I still waver every day between believing we'll be leaving tomorrow and planning life here as an old woman.

Teddy promised herself she wouldn't cancel the Arizona trip again unless Pop's new tests in the hospital proved serious. She wished Moira would come with her. Moira was always better at social situations. And they would have a lark riding the bus together. But Moi insisted on staying home, in case she missed a letter from Randy. Anyway, it was better to have someone here to keep an eye on Mr Minelli and Mr Rose. Teddy checked her watch, then washed her breakfast dishes with Moira's coffee cup.

The rain poured as Moira trudged uphill to the doctor's office. One of those freak summer storms, spoiling the well-being of July. Of course she had no raincoat or umbrella. Unprepared. How can you be prepared for an assault? She thought of Randy, shellfire bursting from behind tropical bushes. 'Hail Mary, full of grace, blessed is the fruit of thy womb, Jesus. . . .' she dredged up the old prayers for him, distracting herself from the hill. Moira could feel herself sweating; sweating in the rain. Just as Daddy complained: San Francisco seemed built on a 90° angle. She was overcome with claustrophobia, queasy and tired. Maybe Teddy could warm up some chicken soup. If she had the flu, this rain would not help. Brushing wet hair from her forehead, she slopped on. For a week now, she had been postponing this visit. A nurse was closing the door as she approached. Moira delivered one of her best Loretta Young entreaties. The woman waved her into the office.

'Some afternoon,' commiserated the grey-haired nurse. Moira noticed how clean her white coat was, except for some blue scratches by the pocket where she kept her pen.

'Yes,' said Moira shaking rain from her hair and then thinking better of it.

The woman sat behind a desk. She looked so much like Sister Lawrence. Moira twisted her ring, moving the birthstone toward the palm and summoned confidence. 'The test.' She tried to forget

Sister Lawrence. 'I came for the result of the test I-I-I took last week.'

'Yes,' the woman's face softened. 'And the name? Mrs. . . .?'

'Girard,' Moira said to the doctor ten minutes later. 'Girard,' she was aware of the hard, abrupt edges of that name compared to the music of *Fin*layson. Fin*lays*on. Finlay*son*.

'Yes,' he said.

'Girard,' Moira raised her voice, irritated with herself for mumbling.

'I mean,' the doctor spoke carefully, 'the answer is "yes".' He pointed to a box on the blue form. 'You're going to have a baby, my dear.'

Moira's face was flushed and wet. 'Damn rain,' she said.

'Would you like to lie down?'

'No,' Moira looked at him as if he were mad. 'No time. Thank you.' She made her way to the door, breathing deeply to keep from collapsing.

'Good-bye, then.'

When Moira walked outside, it was July again, warm and sunny, her favorite month. Two thoughts collided as she hiked down to the bus stop: this explains the french fries; and it isn't fair. He was wearing a sheath. She had watched him peel it off each time. She had suspected something for a month, not because of her period. That was never regular. But because of the french fries. Lately, she was eating massive amounts of french fries doused in vinegar. She used to hate how Mother and Daddy poured disgusting malt vinegar on their chips. Yet for weeks now, she had not been able to sate her appetite for the concoction.

The bus stop was crowded. Vaguely, she recalled Mother's stories of being pregnant and having to stand on the bus – almost fainting from the smell of someone's perfume. Until now, she had suspected such stories were manufactured to induce guilt. Overcome with exhaustion, she leaned on a telephone pole. A young Chinese woman, younger than she, held the hand of a little boy. Next to them, an old Italian couple stood solidly with, yet apart from, each other. To the left, a blond woman, in overalls like herself, held a squirming infant. Moira forced her eyes away from the woman's ring finger. Several more people arrived at the bus top. Christ, this was different from the orderly queues Ann described in London.

Here people milled restlessly. Would she get a seat? What was the priority – old people? Women with children? Inside or outside the belly? She was a woman with a child. It wasn't possible. It was entirely possible.

The bus wheezed to a stop in front of them, packed to the gills. Did babies have gills? How did they breathe inside your stomach? People squeezed aboard the bus. They all stood, save for the little boy who charmed his way on to a woman's lap. Moira found herself between the old couple. She offered to change places, so they might stand together, but they both shook their heads resolutely. Were they Russian, she reconsidered. Ann said the buses in London were always crowded – when they came. The little boy was sucking a dried fig. Would it be a boy – lively and tough like Randy? The bus jolted. Tighter, she gripped the handrail. God, she was glad it was Teddy's turn to cook supper tonight. How could she have mistaken her eggs for Teddy's fish? What would she fix this evening? What on earth would she say about this . . . well, she didn't have to tell Teddy quite yet. She still had Vivian's contingency plan.

The aroma of pigs' feet slapped Moira in the face as she opened the front door. That's right, Teddy, trying to be inventive with the rations, had promised a real down-home meal tonight. She hung up her sweater, wondering what to do. The very smell made her reach for the arm of the couch. She heard Teddy's voice from the kitchen.

'That you, Moi?'

Closer, 'Moira?'

Alarmed, 'Hey, Moi, you OK?'

Suddenly she felt Teddy lifting her to the couch.

'That's it; easy girl.'

What had happened? Moira yawned. Had she fainted? Not hardy Moira. Crazy. Crazy. She had imagined the entire afternoon. She wasn't carrying a baby. She was a baby. A crazy baby. Teddy's face swam in and out of focus. She wondered again about the gills.

'I warned you that you've been running yourself ragged. I said you'd get sick.'

Mother's words. Teddy's voice. Ragged. Tramp. Was she a tramp? Did the woman in the bus line have a ring?

'I'll bring tea.' Teddy gently settled Moira back against the couch.

She had tried to get up. Tried to face the pigs' feet. It was the trying that counted. A sin is a knowing offense. She had tried not to get pregnant. Did trying not to count as much as trying to? Probably not.

'So what's up?' Teddy was sitting on the floor beside the couch, her long legs folded to the side of her slim, upright frame. She had set Moira's tea on the coffee table.

'I'm just a little woozy. Maybe a touch of flu.' Moira considered Teddy closely. What did she know? She needed to talk with Vivian. As soon as possible.

'Heard you heaving this morning. You shouldn'ta gone to the shipyard.'

'I think it's a walking flu,' said Moira, blanching. 'Only hits at odd hours.' What would Mother say?

'Odd, I'll say odd.' Teddy regarded her quizzically. 'It's a pity, just when I'm about to serve "Porcine Supreme".'

Moira held her mouth shut.

'Oh, sorry, hon.' Teddy's face grew still. 'I'll bring you some toast – and maybe a little cottage cheese?'

Moira nodded gratefully.

'Here, this should cheer you up.' Teddy tossed a letter on Moira's lap. Moira kept her eyes on Teddy. 'Post card from Angela and a letter from Ann. Came this morning.'

She waited until Teddy had closed the kitchen door against the horrible odor. She skimmed the card about Angela and her friend Mabel doing the town. Then she pulled out Ann's letter which Teddy had replaced fastidiously in the envelope. At least she no longer waited ceremoniously for them to open the mail together.

Dear Ladies,

I'm on my yearly 'holiday' as they say here. One day in the country. Gloriously sunny, reminding me of legends about California and of you. Thanks for your. . . .

Moira skipped ahead to the news.

Spirits are still remarkably high. Reuben is certain Germany will be crushed in six months. Papa keeps trying to pull me home. But since the end is so near. . . .

Moira winced, remembering that she hadn't called Mr Rose for two weeks. She was staring at the telephone when Teddy entered with a pretty tray of toast and cheese.

'So what do you think of the letter?' Teddy stood stiffly.

'She sounds worn out, but OK.'

'And about him?' Teddy settled on the floor beside Moira.

'Like she says,' Moira shrugged, biting into the toast and pleased with her appetite, 'she'll come back to him at the end of the war. He's had a tough time, but. . . .'

'Not Papa,' Teddy interrupted. 'The man. Reuben. Do you think she's in love?'

Moira was puzzled. 'Reuben?'

Teddy grew aware of the urgency in her voice. She glanced through the front curtains and shrugged. She remembered Angela sitting in the window seat and laughing at Teddy's sentimentality.

'Hey, why the long face?' Moira lifted Teddy's chin with her thumb. 'I'm sure she won't make any rash decisions.'

Teddy got to her feet, shaking away her agitation. 'More for m'lady?'

'No thanks, hon. I think I'll go up and rest now.'

Teddy watched her wobble to the stairs. What could have hit her so violently? She watched until Moira reached the top and turned into her room. Teddy hoped she would recover in the next couple of days. Otherwise, it wouldn't be right to leave on that visit to Wanda. She bent down, to collect the tray – and Ann's letter which Moira had left scattered around the couch.

About 10 o'clock that night, Teddy checked on Moira to find her snoring loudly, the light burning by her bed. She tiptoed into the room, switched off the lamp and closed the door quietly. She went to her own room, crawled into bed with her mystery and was suddenly startled by a brilliant glare from the far window. Japanese planes – that was her first thought. But when the fiery light was not followed by sirens or other unusual sounds, Teddy returned to her book and wondered if she had simply imagined the glare.

The next morning they learned that an ammunitions ship had blown up in Port Chicago, 35 miles away, killing hundreds of men, most of them Negroes. Sandra, Teddy remembered, Sandra worked not far from Port Chicago.

Moira came home to dark silence the following night. Frightened to be alone, she switched on the lights as she walked from the living room to the dining room to the kitchen. It took a minute to remember Teddy was visiting her father in the hospital. Ever the dutiful daughter. Moira's own parents would love almost everything about Teddy.

'Moira,' read the note on the yellow table. 'Dawn finally got through to Sandra. She's fine. But a lot of people died, over 300. See you later tonight. Love, Teddy.'

Sandra, Moira remonstrated with herself, she had completely forgotten about Sandra this horrible day. Well, at least she was safe. Safer than herself at this point. Moira looked vaguely around the kitchen. No, she wasn't hungry. She had come here for the Scotch, the 'national beverage' as Daddy called it. Despite the warm day, she was chilly and she knew this would ease her into the evening. She thought back to her talk with Vivian in the locker room.

'How far along?' Vivian seemed irritated and sympathetic. Maybe, as usual, just resigned.

'Don't know. My periods are never predictable.' Moira looked around for the third time to ensure they were alone. The narrow, dingy room was as vacant as a block of convent cells at rosary hour. She and Vivian sat alone amid the lockers which held the spirits of women they worked with, the lipstick and perfume and scarves and earrings which they abandoned for the serviceable gear of the shipyard. She often felt jailed when she heard the heavy clank of her locker and the quick click of the padlock.

'Well, like I told you, this stuff worked for the last two times.' Vivian dug into her purse. 'Just take the bottle tonight and. . . .'

'The whole thing?' Moira's eyes widened.

'It ain't for cocktail hour, you know.'

Moira was petrified. Had her grandmother tried something like this before they laid her out on the kitchen table? She felt a terrible longing to phone Mother, but of course she couldn't. She would have to go back so far, untangle so many lies. You can't summon trust in emergencies.

'Listen, if you don't want the stuff, I'm not forcing it on you.' Vivian began to sound nervous.

'No, I didn't say that.' Moira figured she could accept the bottle now and decide later.

'I'll give you a call about 10 p.m. Hey, you're not going to be alone tonight? Your room-mate's going to be in?'

'Yes,' Moira lied. She had no intention of burdening Teddy with this. 'You say it, it just comes out in the toilet?' Quivering, she held on to her locker.

'You'll be fine.' Vivian put an arm around her shoulders. 'I'm not giving you anything I wouldn't take myself.'

The door swung open, followed by a roar of voices.

Settling in her bedroom, Moira put out the bottle of Scotch, a glass and Vivian's bottle. She couldn't possibly have a baby now. Lying on the bed, she ran through the argument once more before touching the Scotch. Yes, she wanted a baby – babies, yes, three or four – some day after the war. She rolled over and thought about making love with Randy the last time, at the end of his leave.

Teddy was out dancing with Dawn and Sandra. The house was quiet that night, peaceful rather than empty. Randy was tender and slow and then so passionate. Afterward they lay together and talked about getting married after the war, about the garage he wanted to buy, about the way he would take care of her. The navy had done a lot for him, he said, although she thought the love of a good woman was worth more than military training. She remembered watching him doze off that last night and wishing he could stay until morning.

Moira stared at the Scotch again. She wanted a home and a father for the children. Her mother would be horrified at the abortion. MURDER. But she would also be horrified to be a grandmother out of wedlock. Of course maybe Randy would get back in time to marry. No, that was ridiculous. Besides, was he the father she wanted for her children? A little late to ask. He was the father of . . . of . . . what was growing inside her. She had gone over this again and again since the results. She just didn't know. She just . . . needed to relax. Horrible to think of anything living from her body when she herself was not a complete person. Was this thing in her belly a person? That's what the Church said. It would be a mortal sin to . . . but she didn't *feel* that way. It had been the same with sex. She *knew* it was a mortal sin, but her conscience didn't bother her. Making love with Randy seemed the most natural thing in the world. And having a baby didn't seem natural at all. It seemed impossible.

Pouring Scotch into the glass, she smelled its tart richness and wondered if she liked the aroma itself or the release it promised. Before she touched the drink, she ran everything through her mind again. How could she take care of a baby now? She had not lived her

– 235 –

own life. Whatever it was that rocked in her belly would not be born. She would take Vivian's medicine first. And then the Scotch. That was her decision. It was clear. For the moment it was clear. The medicine had a bitter flavor and Moira finished the last of it with her eyes closed. Inside her lids were mother and child. 'Take all of it, dear. That's it, lick the last off the spoon.' The Scotch was tasteless against the sharp medicine. So she poured another, bigger measure.

Vivian would call at 10 p.m. What would she do for three hours? Sleep perhaps. Surely the phone would wake her. She opened the door to her room so she could hear it, and as she turned back toward the bed her foot caught on the rug. Just one more, she thought. One more won't hurt.

'Moira?' Teddy tried to contain her fear. But it was so unlike Moira to leave the lights blazing. 10.30. Teddy checked her watch. She said she would be home straight after work. 'Moira. Moira.' She saw a glass on the stairs and bounded up, almost knocking Moira, sprawled on the landing in front of her room. 'Moira!'

'Hello, Vivian?' Moira noticed her nose was pressed into the carpet. She turned her head sideways and saw Teddy's shoes. She began to weep.

Teddy gathered Moira in her arms, surprised by the stink of whisky.

'Moira, hon, you OK?'

'It didn't work. Vivian didn't call.' She looked puzzled. 'Or maybe she did. Maybe I fell on the way back . . . oh. . . . ' She passed out.

Teddy carried Moira to bed and tried to revive her. The phone was ringing. Don't die, Moira, she wanted to say, but of course that was too dramatic. She had probably just collapsed from exhaustion. And drink. Vinegar, she remembered Mom's cure from Jolene's fainting spells. Dashing down to the kitchen she became conscious that the damn phone was still ringing. Irritably, she answered it. 'Yes?'

'Moira, this is Vivian, where the hell . . .?'

Four hours later Teddy was admitted to the patient's ward.

Moira's eyes were red sores against a bleached white face. 'Pissholes in the snow.' Teddy remembered Arthur's ugly joke about the dark eyes of her fourth grade friend Sharon.

'Oh, Teddy,' she was crying.

Teddy stroked Moira's shoulder. 'You're gonna be OK.'

'Yes,' Moira murmured.

'Both of ya.' Teddy regarded her tentatively. 'The doctor is a sympathetic sort. And he says that potion you took was harmless enough. Not very effective in any way.'

Moira closed her eyes.

'They say you're over three months gone.' She shook her head and tried to smile. 'Too late for anything but being a Mama.'

Moira covered her face with her hands.

'It'll be fine. We've got lots of room. This baby is going to have a great home if her godmother has anything to say about it.'

Moira raised her head. Her eyes were curious, searching, as if meeting Teddy's for the first time.

Chapter Nineteen

———————— • ————————

Fall 1944, Lion's Head

BLACKOUT RESTRICTIONS RELAXED IN BRITAIN
———————— • ————————
US TAKES AACHEN
———————— • ————————
JAPANESE DEFEATED AT LEYTE
———————— • ————————
ST LOUIS VERSUS ST LOUIS IN WORLD SERIES BASEBALL

Letters. Wanda envisioned herself living in a post office. The real world happened where the letters originated. In London where Ann was dodging missiles and falling in love with Reuben. In Wisconsin, where her cousin Keiko was finishing college. In Italy where Howard and Roy were liberating villages. In San Francisco where Moira was having a baby! Of course Teddy would need to help Moira now. Of course that was more important than a social visit to Arizona. Still, Wanda couldn't get over her resentment at Moira for stealing Teddy, at both of them for abandoning her. Here she was, stuck during the war, but not in it. Dead letter office. She was exiled to a desert wasteland. Wasting time. No, teaching school was not a waste of time. Betty and her friends needed to learn. And certainly the government wasn't going to pay enough for another real teacher. She must stop diminishing herself. She was a real teacher. Although she was going to be a writer. Glancing at her watch, she realized that she had better get moving or she would be unemployed on this frozen, windy day.

She had never pictured the desert as cold, yet she now knew she had never understood cold until she came here. The wind roamed recklessly for miles without obstacle and struck through you with a bitter chill. She thought about the ratany and hibiscus and other new flowers. Did they have as many names for the wind? At night, writing in her diary, she pretended she was an anthropologist, cataloguing details of their external life. It was easier to believe this extraordinary place if she didn't see herself as part of the story. Yesterday evening she had described the different insects she found in the latrines. A year ago she was frightened of those spiders and beetles, but now she inspected them curiously because she planned to write about them.

Hurrying across camp to 'The Little Red Quonset Hut', as Mrs Wright quaintly called it, Wanda counted the ravages of last night's wind. Mr Matsumoto's bonsai trees were swept of leaves. Several plants were uprooted. Two awnings were knocked off their hinges at the latrines. Sometimes she imagined the wind as Papa, furious at the government for jailing them here. Furious at them for complying. Yes, uprooting the plants would be just like Papa. No matter how one tried to make peace here, one failed. Right now she would settle for an end to the hostility among her neighbors.

Passing the Nakashimas' window, she wondered how Mrs Nakashima was bearing up. Her husband's terrible death this month had spread deep panic through the camp. The stockade had never been used until Henry Nakashima rekindled debate about the treatment of those who had been sent to Tule Lake the previous year for refusing to sign the Loyalty Oath. People warned him that he was overdoing it with public speeches under the flagpole. They told him it was too late. But he persisted. The arrest was swift and brutal. No one could explain exactly what had passed in jail. Henry was an old man, the guards said later; he suffered a heart attack. But the bruises on his back raised heavy doubts. Wanda had a terrible time relating the story to Howard. Her brother had been especially close to Mr Nakashima since Papa's death. She didn't know if her letter would pass the censors. Ever since the 'incident' as the officials called it, Wanda was more conscious of the barbed wire. Frequently, she could hardly see the mountains at all.

What frightened her most was the wrath splintering through the camp since Mr Nakashima's funeral. 'Only *Issei* would make such trouble,' complained one *Nisei* who founded the *Nisei* Community League. '*Deru kugi utareru,* the nail which sticks out longest takes the most pounding.'

'We must remember the homeland,' said the *Issei* men who met every Wednesday night 'to maintain Japanese ethics and culture.' The anger between generations festered in the disappointment that even in this camp, surrounded by Japanese faces, they were unsafe. Wanda made a note to visit Mrs Nakashima that afternoon.

Opening the classroom door, she was overcome by sour fumes from the coal furnace. She hated the smell until Ann wrote so lovingly about the romantic coal fires. Now she associated the odor with her friend sitting in a dimly lit pub after a long day at work. Five minutes to class. Half the students were present; the other half would dash in as they heard the bell. Yes, there it was. Would these kids ever feel nostalgic for the screech of that bell when they were older? What would they remember from this period of their lives? It was a period, wasn't it? Of course. The end was coming already. But because it was impossible to imagine what would happen after the end, after they returned to 'normal', Wanda occasionally imagined Lion's Head as a life sentence.

Mrs Wright cleared her throat as she arranged papers on her large oak desk. Wanda regarded the teacher carefully, sorting out her impressions. The tall, almost gaunt woman was between fifty and sixty. It was hard to tell because everything she wore heightened her blandness. Beige blouses and brown sweaters and olive skirts. Hazel eyes were her most distinct characteristic – especially in the later afternoon during story hour. At other times, her tough Midwestern accent and her extraordinary straight back reminded Wanda of Miss Fargo. But Mrs Wright was at once softer and less wry than the typing teacher. While Miss Fargo prized efficiency, kindness was Mrs W's premium. Wanda, who never thought she could miss typing exercises, would gladly trade this teacher's complicated charity for Miss Fargo's impersonal discipline.

Still, Wanda reminded herself as she sat in the back row by the door, Mrs W. was a decent person. She loved children and she worked hard. The woman didn't have to teach at Lion's Head. However, while Reverend Wright was ministering to the troops in Europe, she chose to leave her cherished Chicago home and do her 'part' in Arizona.

Wanda just wished her own position in the class were clear. Mrs W. was reluctant to relinquish control, yet she wanted to make use of Wanda. Thus she created two classes – which met together in the morning and then separated. For the rest of the day, Wanda was the teacher in grades four through eight. However, at the beginning of school, she was teacher's aide, attendance monitor, parent-school liaison or what Mrs W. called her 'right arm'. Most often, Wanda felt like an unexpected daughter-in-law. Their amiability was growing less forced.

Now the teacher drew her pale lips into a formal welcome and nodded at Wanda to shut the door. Automatically the children stood to pledge allegiance. When they sat down, hands folded in front of them, Mrs W. announced, 'Papers arrived today from Los Angeles and San Francisco.' They all knew what this meant and sat straighter at their desks.

'Today we'll commence with current affairs.' She adjusted her glasses and read, 'Jap Fleet Defeated at Leyte,' 'Japs Destroy West Side of. . . .' The children stared ahead – some of them listening, some daydreaming. Wanda, who thought she had grown used to this, closed her eyes against angry tears.

'And now to the European theatre. . . .'

Perhaps it was a stage to her, thought Wanda, simply a historical drama. She ran through all the nicknames for FDR: Hoodini, Squire of Hyde Park, The Sphinx, Batman in the White House. Could Mrs W. feel her blasphemy?

'My father is an ally,' said Alan Morozumi and, ignoring Mrs W.'s irritated frown, he persisted, 'The 442nd Regimental Combat Team is the bravest in Europe. We got a letter from our Daddy.'

'Yes,' Mrs W. answered instructively. 'It has sustained the highest casualty rate.'

'What's a casualty rate?' Tommy Morozumi whispered to Wanda.

'Shh, I'll explain later.' She stared at the teacher, amazed at her insensitivity, or was it sadism? No, probably insensitivity. She carried this patronizing attitude outside the classroom, too. Wanda had seen her talk to Mr and Mrs Takata last week as if they were students, speaking slowly, using simple language. Did she know that Mrs Takata had worked for the city of Oakland as a stenographer and that Mr Takata had a Master's degree from Stanford? Would it have mattered? This was the trouble developing friendly feelings for the Caucasians, it just raised uncomfortable questions.

'Are there any more questions – or comments?' Mrs W. addressed the class.

'Nothing? Fine then, Miss Nakatani, will you take the older girls and boys to the back room to work on essays. And the rest of us,' she winked at the smaller children in the front rows, 'also will find something interesting to do.'

'OK, gang,' Wanda said, once they were separated. Then she warned herself against appearing flippant. 'Who wants to read the first paper?' No one responded. 'You know, Mrs Wright's assignments about "Adventures in Lion's Head".'

Alan's hand shot in the air. He read three paragraphs about a vulture cleaning out the carcass of a coyote. Other papers followed the same theme – city kids exploring the desert. Although Wanda was usually annoyed by Mrs W's Pollyanna assignments, she was surprised by how much she learned from them – how different was her experience of camp from theirs. While she was bored or aggravated or even suffocated, they were stimulated by their own inventiveness. Her nightmares were their explorations. Today Wanda was very moved by Betty's paper.

> My adventure at Lion's Head has been in notes and chords. On the old piano in the rec hall I have learned to make tunes. Every day I go practice with Mr Sasaki. He listens to my terrible noises and promises that they will turn into music. He is right. I now play Chopin, Beethoven, Liszt. I am practicing for the big recital in February. One day I want to perform on stage as a piano player.

'Pianist,' Wanda mumbled out of the storm in her chest. She could hardly believe her jealousy. After all, she didn't want to play the piano; she wanted to write and nothing was keeping her from that. She could do more freelance work. That was better than reporting for Mr Omi's silly camp paper.

'Pardon me?' asked Betty, still glowing from her public reading and now suddenly distressed by her sister's expression.

Two boys in the corner were smirking and whispering 'pianist' to each other.

'Stanley and Ricky,' said Wanda, straining for Mrs W.'s authority, 'your papers are next.' She was amused with herself for everything – the sentimentality, the sternness, the embarrassment. Mrs W. was wrong, she would not 'make a very good teacher'. Even now, half her mind was on the letters she wanted to write Teddy and Roy this evening. Before that, she would have to find time to explain 'casualty rate' to Tommy and to visit Mrs Nakashima. As she was juggling these obligations, the noon bell clanged.

The wind had died down. She was grateful because it was exhausting enough to race to the post office, the mess hall, serve Mama lunch and make it back to class on time. Lately, Wanda was continuously tired. Nerves. She knew she had to conserve her spirit. Standing in line now, she didn't turn around, lest she encounter someone who needed something. This was selfish. She was a young woman in good health. But with Papa dead and Howard gone, there were so many demands. Everything in camp was a trial. Was Lion's Head actually a scientific experiment in cultural deprivation? Wanda sighed, remembering that she had promised to do some translation for the Yamaguchis this week. In addition to these personal demands they all made on each other, there were pressures from the Authority – blood drives and bond campaigns. How you could lock people up and then squeeze their blood and money in defense of democracy, she didn't know, but she had given up being amazed months ago. She was just frightened.

She was as frightened as Mama was enraged. During the last six months, Mama had wavered between illness and uncontrollable fury. She kept saying she would return to Japan after the war. She cried that she never should have left. She worried about her parents. The Watanabes warned her to keep quiet because they were still sending subversives to that horrible camp in Tule Lake. 'Horrible camp,' Mama had shouted. 'Do you think this is Shangri-La?' But she did tone down her public anger. Many of the *Nisei* shunned Mama, and even Betty and herself, as dangerous elements. When Howard enlisted, the family status improved slightly. And Mama's condition got worse. She mourned for Howard every day and seemed surprised when they received a letter from him.

In the post office Wanda saw a young woman with a baby carriage. Then another girl, carrying a child. Then three toddlers trailing after Mrs Takata, her grandchildren. Come to think of it, had Carolyn put on weight lately? The increasing birthrate was creating a whole new generation, tiny creatures who experienced life on a different scale. These children lived so much closer to the ground, playing in the rock gardens and sand piles. What was their perspective of this desert world? Did it seem strange to them? How could it if they were born here? She shuddered at the thought that Lion's Head was accepted as a natural habitat by any human being.

The letter from Roy was on top. The one from Ann. Then a bill from Sears and a flyer from a Baptist organization. Wanda stuffed the mail in her pocket. How comfortable these baggy slacks were. She had lost all vanity in her dress. Everyone had. You just couldn't wear a skirt in this climate. Sometimes she was grateful Roy couldn't see her. She checked her watch: just enough time to get Mama's food and return to class. She wasn't feeling very hungry, herself.

Pea soup today, Wanda sniffed as she approached the vats. All the more trouble with Mama who still carried heavy suspicions about mess hall food. She insisted on being able to distinguish ingredients – a little fish on boiled rice was her favorite – and grew jittery about murky soups and casseroles.

Sure enough, Mama was in one of her ranting moods this afternoon. She took one look at the soup and pushed the slop away. Nibbling on the bread, she was full of stories from the morning visit with Mrs Hara. 'Did you know they were taking Japanese girls and boys to translate against the Imperial forces?' she demanded as Wanda perched on the edge of her chair.

'Yes,' Wanda nodded. She didn't have time for a long discussion. 'Not too many Caucasians know Japanese.'

'But the horror of it,' she continued in Japanese and English. 'Most of us have enough trouble talking to our children in our own language. Some of us can't communicate at all. And those few who know Japanese are, well, to be passing on the language for such a purpose. . . . It is worse than fighting in their army.'

'It *is* fighting in their army. The OSS is a branch of the service.'

'Oh, I don't understand. Your father could explain these things to me. I miss Papa.' She looked over at his pictures, where she had set fresh daisies today.

Wanda held up her mother's frail hand and nodded. Of course it would take a long time to get used to his passing. But Wanda had gradually learnt how much Mama had relied on Papa. She had always seen her mother as the more responsible parent, leaning on common sense when Papa would embark on one of his travels or schemes for making quick money. Now Wanda could see that Mama was leaning on her love for Papa, that they had held the house together with a mutual spirit and now that one of them was gone the force had disappeared. Sometimes Wanda felt as if her family had disintegrated into sand.

'Go daughter, I know you have your job.'

Nervous throughout the arithmetic lesson, Wanda kept brushing her hand against the bulge in her sweater pocket. This kind of distraction was exactly why she never collected the mail until after school. Yet concentrate she must because Mrs Wright would shoot her if the fourth graders failed another long division exam. She reminded herself that she had been Uncle Fumio's star bookkeeper. She loved math. Surely she could make this interesting.

'Now remember we're dividing the treasure Alice found behind the guard shed.' They were paying attention. Were they caught up in the story or simply amused by her foolish acting? So many theatres to this war. By 2.15, she was depleted from the math, the worries about Mrs W. and the hunger gnawing in her stomach. She assigned them a quiet reading period and pulled out the letter from Ann.

> I really don't know what to do about this girl, Leah. She's such a sweetheart with those big brown eyes.

Wanda imagined Ann and herself walking together through Green Park. She looked up to find her class quietly reading. Ricky and Stanley, whispering at the back, caught her critical glance and returned to their books.

> Reuben thinks it's a great idea. But what would I do with a kid? I go back and forth, back and forth on this.

The bell rang.

'School dismissed.'

Stale classroom air lightened as the children rustled papers into their bags. Wanda caught sight of Tommy Morozumi dashing out the door, punching Bobby on the arm. Just as she was about to call him, Betty walked up.

'Can you tell Mama I'm at piano?'

'Weren't you supposed to sit with her this afternoon?' Wanda sighed.

'Yes, but Mr Sasaki says I really need to practice the Beethoven.'

Wanda wanted to say no. She needed time alone. There were letters to read and write. However she was feeling guilty about the 'pianist' slip. She nodded. 'Yeah, sure, I'll spell you this afternoon, after I visit Mrs Nakashima.'

'Swell,' smiled Betty. 'You know you're not bad for a sister – or for a teacher either.'

The afternoon sky was made of cold pink and the wind had started to whine. Well, if there weren't proper names for the winds, she could name them herself. Siren, she could call this one. She stood by the laundry room, composing herself to call on Mrs Nakashima, when she saw a Western Union car driving toward the gate.

Wanda felt a terrible pang, as if the chill of the day was coming from within her. Telegrams brought bad news. A stranger delivered the verdict in an official envelope. It was up to the family to break down in private or to open the wound at the door. It was between you and this piece of paper. Or between you and the messenger. Forget the Congress. Forget the guns. Forget the bodies. Death was one of the efficiencies of war; the government didn't have to wait for everyone to grow old and disintegrate. Death came in neat columns of statistics. It was expected. It was honored. The taking was a given. The real news was survival. That arrived in letters, not telegrams. Wanda tried not to think about Roy or Howard. She tried to remember the other young men who had enlisted. She imagined different reasons for a Western Union car to be driving through the gate. A lucky lottery winner. A message from Washington to the Authority.

Mrs Nakashima waved from her window. Wanda nodded, smiled and held up her index finger. She would be there in one minute. First she would hold her ground and follow the path of the Western Union car.

The driver was slowing down near her barracks. He looked confused, checking the numbers against the envelope in his hand. Of course he was lost; he was meant to be on the other side or. . . . No, he had stopped now. Wanda could see Mama move the curtain and peer out. Her own feet were stuck to the ground. She must stop this. She must intervene and point him in the right direction. But her legs were made of bricks. The tall, thin man was climbing out the car, cautiously, awkwardly.

Now she was standing between him and the door. Her teeth were clenched so hard her jaw hurt. He didn't seem to notice her, as if he were still getting his bearings.

'Hello,' she said, to take charge, to show him who was in control.

'Afternoon, Mam,' he said shyly. 'This number forty-four?'

'No,' she answered. 'No!'

He looked around her to the number 44 on the doorframe.

'Number forty-four, Mam?' he asked again.

Wanda searched his milky blue eyes and felt there was nothing solid in the world.

He looked down and shuffled his feet.

She reached out, taking the telegram from his hand.

He glanced up.

'You can go now,' she said.

'You don't want me to stay.'

'No,' she managed.

'Yes, Mam.' He tipped his hat and folded himself back into the car.

Wanda turned from him, and saw Mama close the curtains, moving back into the room. Wanda took a breath and looked away from the ugly envelope. She needed time. She needed room to breathe. She wanted to be somewhere else right now, in a movie, reading a book, but this telegram was not part of her imagination. No hoping or praying or rewriting could change this. This was real. She smelled the ink from the telegram. She would have to tell Mama, but she needed some strength first. If only she could take this foul paper off and read it alone. She thought about the bench at the edge of camp. There she could pull herself together. There she could . . . no, Mama had seen the car. She needed to know. Now, now, NOW, NOW!!!

Wanda ripped open the envelope. Mama appeared at the window again.

Wanda's eyes skimmed across the salutation to read, '. . . Howard Nakatani is missing in action in the service of his country. . . .'

Missing. Not dead. And weren't they all missing in some way? Not dead. Missing. Howard was missing. She looked up and caught Mama's dark eyes. The woman with the missing son.

●

Chapter Twenty

Fall 1944, San Francisco

CALAIS LIBERATED

●

INDIAN AND BRITISH TROOPS TAKE TIDDIM, BURMA

●

ROOSEVELT RUNS FOR FOURTH TERM

●

CHURCHILL, STALIN AND HARRIMAN MEET IN MOSCOW

It was Moira's birthday and she felt particularly hot and pregnant. She thought of her own mother, carrying and delivering her in this heat. How close she had felt during the last few months to the confused girl of years ago, if not to the irascible forty-seven-year-old mother who still refused to believe a daughter of hers would get pregnant out of wedlock. Moira stared at the table of pork chops and fried potatoes and apple sauce Teddy had prepared to celebrate her birthday. She was exhausted at the thought of another bite. She watched Teddy walk back into the dining room with a new pitcher of water and wondered why her friend was so silent.

Teddy smiled at Moira as she sat down. So if the girl didn't want to talk much; it was her choice. Frankly, she was feeling a little low-spirited herself. She couldn't shake that last postcard from Angela declaring she and her 'girlfriend' Mabel were having the time of their lives on the Gulf of Mexico. Fine thing to write after months of nothing. Of course Teddy hadn't expected much since the note this summer when Angela mentioned Mabel. Angela said she knew Teddy would understand, that it was a long war and Texas was years apart from California. Teddy understood, all right. She had even suspected for a while. What could she say? They had no agreement. God knows, they had been too shy to express their feelings the whole time they knew each other. It was decent of Angela to write, Teddy kept insisting. But she found herself thinking about how Mabel might disappear or die, painlessly and instantly, in a crash landing.

Moira endured the meal with lethargic cheer, trying hard to enjoy Teddy's good cooking. She couldn't help wonder why birth caused such fanfare.

Each woman made several attempts at conversation and returned to silence.

'Some celebration,' said Teddy, 'both of us still mooning about our long, lost loves.'

'Yeah,' Moira shrugged. 'I'm getting over it. I mean I only cried once this month. But I still feel so humiliated. To get a "Dear Jane" letter. And I used to wonder if he were the right person for me. After all the breaking up and patching up! I guess it's just as well he wrote before I had a chance to tell him I was pregnant. I wouldn't want him out of pity. I just have to stop thinking about it, that's all. Don't know why I brought it up again.'

Teddy waited.

'I still can't bring myself to tell Mother. She'll see him as another one of my failures.'

'You know that's silly.' Teddy sighed, thinking how grateful she was that she hadn't told her own mother about Angela.

'Can't imagine Randy spending the rest of his life on a Pacific Island.' Moira forced the sarcasm. 'How will he keep supplied with records and clothes?' Then she surprised herself by laughing.

'Yes,' Teddy said, trying to keep up with her friend.

Moira fell silent again.

Teddy served her special sugarless cake made from Mom's ration cookbook. It looked pretty enough, but you could tell something was missing.

All evening they tried to lift each other's spirits. Only when it came to opening the presents did Moira revive. She held up Teddy's gift –

a trim dress – and danced around the room in a listing polka. 'You think I'll ever squeeze into this? You really think I'll take a size 10 again?'

'Why not, honey?' Teddy sat back on the couch and beamed. 'Pregnancy is a short-term project.'

'Oh, Teddy, this is wonderful. I am tired of "accentuating the positive".' She patted her heavy stomach. 'You always know what I need to cheer me up.'

Moira waddled over to the couch and threw her arms around Teddy. Each of them turned scarlet. Moira kissed her friend on the mouth and pulled back. She was still so excited about the dress and her salvaged birthday that she apparently didn't notice Teddy was gulping for breath.

'Oh, what would I do without you, Teddy? For all I know, I might be dead, lying at the top of the stairs, if you hadn't come home and found me.'

'Vivian would have checked.' Teddy tried to cool down. 'Besides, you wouldn't have died. You would have come to with a doosy of a hangover.'

'You can't tolerate gratitude.' Moira's lower lip extended.

Helpless now, Teddy shrugged. 'I didn't mean a thing. I mean. . . .'

'Oh, hush.' Moira turned and ran her hand along Teddy's cheek. 'It's OK, I didn't mean to get you "riled up".'

Teddy drew back slowly. She knew Moira was touching her in a family way, yearning for a sister. And Teddy would do well not to confuse that yearning with anything else.

But Moira continued to stare at her, through her. 'Really Teddy, I feel so much for you, so much gratitude and so much, well, so much love.'

Teddy blushed.

'Look at the color on you!' Moira laughed gently. She reached for Teddy's hand and stared silently at her friend. Silent perhaps because she didn't know what to expect, what to want. Lately she had come to feel more than an affection for Teddy; it was almost a physical longing. No, more than almost, she would lie in bed and yearn for Teddy's arms. But why? She wasn't a lesbian. She wasn't even sure what lesbians did. All she knew was that she wanted this closeness to ripen. Yet how? She didn't want to lead Teddy on. Who was to know that Teddy was 'interested' in her? She didn't even know if you used the same terms for 'women-women' affairs. All she knew was that she wanted to be tucked into Teddy's arms right now. But where to begin? She was so used to Randy taking the lead. And something told her she would have to lead tonight.

Teddy inhaled sharply, willing the blush to disappear. Confused at first, she thought how she was never shy of physical contact. She was always putting her arms around Moira, punching her on the shoulder, kissing her head. But lately, Moira had been extra sensitive to the touch. Teddy had put that down to her pregnancy. She couldn't explain it exactly, but Moira seemed to respond more. Didn't women get tender at times like this? She often had to close her mind to daydreams of her and Moira in bed – the thoughts never went very far, just holding and hugging – because she knew it was a sure way to lose her most important friendship. But what was the girl saying with this look now? Maybe women became a little mad with pregnancy. Yes, she remembered how weepy Mom had got with the last two.

Moira's eyes held Teddy's face steadily as she picked up her hand and kissed the fingers. 'You know,' she spoke fast to outdistance her nervousness. 'I have a very deep affection for you.'

Teddy nodded.

'Do you think you could move a little closer?'

Teddy nodded again, but sat still. She knew that once she moved, her whole life would be transformed. As much as she wanted to accommodate Moira, as much as she didn't want to embarrass her, she couldn't move. Although she desperately desired to touch Moira, she needed to sit still and cherish this moment. She took a long breath and returned to reality, suddenly noticing the sweat on her upper lip and the beads of wetness between her breasts. 'Just a moment, hon,' she managed in her old voice – now how had she summoned that? – 'I need to go to the bathroom for a sec to wash my face.'

Refreshed and more composed, Teddy returned slowly from the bathroom. There was Moira sitting on the couch, staring at the floor, her hands cradling her belly. She had never seen Moira more beautiful. The pregnancy brought a glow to her cheeks and forced her to rest so that the lines around her eyes softened. She was much more of a woman now, with a kind of self-acceptance Teddy could never have imagined. In comparison, she, herself, felt like a gawky teenager. She sat down, watching the woman carefully.

Moira moved over and put her hand on Teddy's shoulder. This affectionate, asexual gesture made Teddy's stomach sink.

'You're not making this any easier, old pal,' Moira teased, turning Teddy's worried face towards hers. Was she doing the wrong thing? Was she going too fast? Too late to turn back. She moved closer, brushing Teddy's lips with her own. Now this could not be mistaken as sisterly. Teddy would have to take the next step.

Moira wasn't prepared for the surge of passion in Teddy, who drew them together so tightly that they could hardly breathe. She smelled lavender and beneath that Teddy's musky scent. When she kissed Teddy again, her attention shifted to her own body. A strong current flowed as Teddy touched her nipples. She could feel her groin loosening and moistening.

Teddy kept comparing this to her fantasies and it was much more elaborate. She had considered kissing and touching another woman, but she had never known what would happen inside her. Her appetite heightened with each touch. Briefly she thought of Angela, who was so much taller than Moira. When she had imagined sex, it had always been with a large-boned woman. Moira felt like a figurine. Despite and because of her pregnancy, Moira was so delicate.

'Shall we go upstairs?' Moira asked.

Teddy grew scared. Had Moira had enough? Was this the end? Perhaps she had only wanted a little cuddling. Teddy drew back, still within the curve of Moira's arms, but stiff and tense.

'I mean,' Moira spoke carefully, 'we're bound to be more cosy in bed.' She found herself reddening, but if she didn't take the lead they would be here all night.

'Yes, sure,' said Teddy. 'Let's go to your bed. It's bigger.' Did that sound too crude? Teddy forgave herself; no matter what she said would be awkward. She was pleased to note that this was English coming out of her mouth.

They climbed the stairs, shyly holding hands. Moira didn't know if she wanted to forget or to remember that Teddy was the woman with whom she had lived during the last five years. This made her feel at once more embarrassed and more comfortable. She pushed open the door to her room and wished she had picked up her clothes this week. The floor was piled with overalls and dirty stockings and fading nightgowns. She even noticed the blue belt she had been looking for all month. The room felt hot and confining. But Teddy didn't seem to bother. She was sitting on the bed, holding out her arms.

Moira sat down and kissed Teddy's ear. Teddy sighed and closed her eyes. Then she pulled Moira back on the bed so their legs dangled over the side. They snuggled for several minutes until Teddy said, 'You sure this is all right with you?'

'Mmmm,' Moira said.

'Well, in that case,' Teddy smiled to herself and then at Moira, 'I must confess I don't know the next step.'

Moira bit her lip, remembering again how Teddy was still a virgin. She had only gone to the movies with Angela and maybe done some serious imagining. She, herself, was more practiced. Moira decided to be light-hearted. 'Guess,' she grinned.

'I'd say it has something to do with removing these clothes and getting under the covers.' Teddy sat forward, pulling Moira flat on the bed. She started to unbutton her own blouse.

Moira interrupted, 'Oh, no, let me.'

Teddy looked down at the floor, nervous about her nervousness.

'Unless you think it's silly,' Moira offered.

'No, no,' Teddy's voice slurred, 'not silly.'

> Mother, may I go out dancing
> Mother, may I go romancing?
> Must I keep on dancing. . . .

Moira unbuttoned the blouse cautiously as if opening a secret between them. Teddy, always irritated by her own large breasts, was amazed by Moira's appreciation. Moira unsnapped Teddy's bra, ran her finger along the contour and began to suck greedily on the nipple. Teddy considered this pregnant woman sipping at her breast and she closed her eyes for what seemed like an hour, floating above the bed. Then she turned her face fully on Moira and unzipped her top. Moira seemed to be floating with her – happier, freer than she had looked in months. When Teddy's fingers drew away from Moira's bra, she glanced down and pulled back in surprise at the ripeness of Moira's breasts. They had seen each other naked a hundred times before – in the bath or as they dressed to go out for the evening – but Teddy, at least, had never dared a real look. Moira's breasts were full and freckled and pink at the tips, where her own were a burnt amber. Carefully, Teddy rested her

– 253 –

head on this softness. She stroked and licked and touched as Moira moaned and then, somehow, she was over on her back and Moira was undoing her skirt, unhooking her stockings. The swish of nylon and the rustle of taffeta distracted Teddy from her self-consciousness and allowed her to savor the sensations.

For the longest time, Moira couldn't get enough stroking. Her vagina throbbed to be touched, but her eyes and her fingertips were hungry for the feel of Teddy's athletic, graceful body.

'Graceful?' Teddy turned on the pillow. 'Long, yes, but graceful I'm not.'

'I've often coveted these legs, you know, so lithe. I feel like a clunk in comparison.'

Teddy couldn't believe that Moira had been watching in the same way. No, it was hardly the same way. Moira's interest was much bolder. '"Clunk," what do you mean by "clunk?" You're beautiful, Moira, more beautiful than anyone I know.'

Moira tried to stop – but failed – hearing Randy's voice. But his words had been different. He had meant beautiful in the sense of measurements and complexion and turned-up nose. She felt more deeply scrutinized by Teddy's appreciation. She returned to the present, reaching down to Teddy's belly and below.

Teddy stretched back and waited, hungrily. She watched Moira's intent fingers, hoping they would slide lower, go deeper between her legs, and enter her. Yes, yes, this was the way Moira was moving. Brushing Teddy's pubic hair with the palms of her hands, gently parting her legs and stroking the soft skin on the inside of her thighs, tentatively outlining the vulva until she looked up, locking Teddy with her eyes, asking 'OK?'

'Yes,' Teddy nodded, no wind left for speech, so she nodded again, yes, yes.

As Moira explored her private place, Teddy wavered between experiencing the physical pleasure and rejoicing: this is Moira; this is Moira. She imagined her body as a star, glowing fuller and fuller, about to catch fire. She saw Moira's face over the dinner table; she watched Moira walk across the living room. She opened her eyes and there was Moira right here, holding her, looking back passionately. Overwhelmed by this intensity, she closed her eyes until finally, oh, it wasn't long, it was soon, too soon, she burst into flame and heard a scream from across the room, an echo, her voice, 'Oh, Moira, Moira, Moira. Yes, yes.'

Taut between exhaustion from her own journey and hunger for Moira, Teddy lay back on the bed and listened to the waves lapping through her body. Then she turned to kiss this friend, this new partner, who suddenly opened her mouth and drew Teddy into a warm, wet, cavernous caress. At first Teddy felt cautious about Moira's pregnancy. She didn't want to disturb anything.

But Moira's appetite was clear. Slowly, Teddy moved from Moira's mouth, kissing down her chest, across her stomach and lower. The smell of Moira's sex drew saliva in her mouth, but she felt too shy, too fearful of Moira's shock to lick the skin below. Instead, she unfolded the petals with her fingers, delighted by the glistening softness. Then, with her thumb, she stroked Moira's clitoris, inhaling the tart scent, until Moira's breaths came more rapidly. Then Teddy was too excited for anything except stroking and watching Moira's flushed face, her red, red mouth wide, drinking in the heavy air, her eyes closed, but concentrating, the sweat pearling down her hairline to her moist neck.

•

Chapter Twenty-One

Fall 1944, London

BOULOGNE LIBERATED

•

TITO TAKES BELGRADE

•

SOVIET TROOPS CROSS DANUBE

The tube was packed. Ann realized how long she had spent musing in the park. She would have to stand. She wanted a smoke, but she couldn't balance a briefcase, a book and a cigarette. Damn. Squeezing near a man who was buried in the *Daily Mail*, she held tight to the overhead strap. He raised his eyes, evaluating her brown wool suit. Self-conscious, she considered she never would have worn anything this tailored at home. But the British women were more conservative and the climate was so much damper. How she hated feeling physically crowded like this, backed against her own anxieties. She had planned to read that book that everyone was raving about, *The Horse's Mouth*. It was a birthday present from Esther, part of her campaign to 'Anglicize Ann'. She would have her drinking shandy any day now.

There was no way to stand steady and hold the book. So she fell back to thoughts about Leah. Motherhood. Moira would tell her to take the child. Her friend's last letter was full of a new excitement about the pregnancy. Well, being a mother was less complicated for Moira. Besides, she had already made a decision. Today was the day she would have to explain to Leah about going to the Goldmans. It had all been arranged. They were the perfect family – a built-in sister with Sarah, her own room, Kosher kitchen. She was lucky. She would be loved and cared for. Ann could visit her. Anerley Park was not that far by rail. Yes, it would be OK, she kept telling herself. She had made the decision last night. Which is why she couldn't sleep. Which is why this headache was nagging at her neck. Well, she would talk to Leah first thing. That was the only way.

The dormitory seemed the safest, most private place to meet. Ann arrived ten minutes early, paced the length of the cots twice, then sat on Leah's bed. She knew it by the teddy bear Reuben had given her last month. Ann begged Reuben not to treat the child specially, not to give her false hopes. She stared blankly at the bedraggled animal. How could it get this ragged in one month? Still, it was Leah's only reliable family, her daily confidant and companion.

Ann really did not understand her own feelings about family. So often when she thought about her own childhood, she wondered whether she had a family or whether they were simply different constellations of people divided against each other one moment and regrouping to take care of each other the next. She and Daniel and Papa took care of Mama during her spells. She and Mama and Daniel buffeted Papa's dreams. She and Daniel schemed to take their parents back to Germany. What would she have done without Daniel? She picked up the stuffed animal, smoothing the fur over its face. She remembered the week on Long Island when she and Daniel played cowboys near the Joneses' store, just the two of them with the flies and mosquitoes, sloshing around in the ditch, lying on the side of the road, pointing their make-believe pistols at the passing cars. She recalled that Saturday in high school when they climbed to the top of Bernal Heights, she a length ahead of him and how, when they made the summit, they pointed to the land they would own one day. He had put his arm around her and said she wasn't bad for a girl.

Daniel had always tolerated her 'temperament' as the family called it. He was an easy-going kid who expected things to come his way, not obnoxiously, but confidently. He was sympathetic about her headaches, went with her to the first doctor about them. But she noticed he grew less solicitous as the headaches continued over the years. Stanford seemed like another world, one from which she was irrevocably excluded. And she felt as if she had gone through a divorce without the trial. There was so much now she longed to talk about with Daniel. So much she wanted to ask, to settle. A small cough distracted Ann.

The child was frowning, so deeply you would have thought someone had drawn a black crayon mark between her brows. The severe expression was incongruous with the soft tufts of blond hair. Was anything else this beautiful?

'Why so sad?' Ann reached for Leah's hand.

The child stood at the bottom of her cot and refused to move closer.

'Did something happen at play today?'

Leah stared, waiting for Ann to answer her own questions.

'You know we have something serious to talk about?'

'I don't want to,' Leah began, then stopped abruptly, as if suddenly recalling her resolution of silence.

'But we must talk.' Ann lowered her voice and moved toward the child. Leah's stubbornness reminded her of herself as a girl. 'There isn't much time to talk,' Ann told Leah.

Ann watched as the child's eyes filled with tears and then as the tears were swallowed back behind the pink rims. The girl had will.

'You remember Sarah?'

Leah was silent.

'And Mrs Goldman?'

Leah turned away.

'Listen, honey, they want to take you home with them. They want to give you a lovely room overlooking a garden. You'll have Sarah to play with. A big sister. You'll have a splendid time, just like I did with my brother Daniel. It will be ever so much more cosy than this dormitory.' Ann had no idea where these words were coming from.

'I want to be with you.' Leah was firmer than Ann could ever imagine herself being.

'That's just not possible. I have no home.' Ann knew her words were meager defiance to Leah's conviction. 'I live in a room by myself.'

'Then I'll stay here and see you every day. Like now.'

Where did this child get her calm?

'It's not good for you, love. You'll eat better there. You'll be more comfortable.'

'No, I won't.' Leah looked at her as if she were mad.

'Honey, we'll be able to see each other, to visit. I'll come down to Anerley Park and you can come here with Sarah and Mrs Goldman. We won't lose touch.'

'That's not the same.' Leah persisted quietly and backed away. 'I won't go.'

'Come give me a hug,' Ann said. 'This isn't getting us anywhere. Let's hold each other.'

The child stood rigid, shaking her head.

'I want to be your friend.' Ann smiled tentatively.

'I want you to be my mother,' Leah said quietly.

Ann began to cry.

'Don't do that,' Leah demanded. Her eyes were smaller now and tired.

'Give me a hug.' Ann beckoned.

Leah approached cautiously. She extended her hand and Ann pulled her close into her arms.

'It will be all right, you'll see.' Ann sniffed back her tears. 'You have your mother in Germany and Mrs Goldman and me. You have lots of people who love you.'

'No, Anna.' The child's voice was softer now, but just as tough. 'I won't go.'

Reuben came by at five o'clock, as he had promised. 'Hello,' he waved. Then, letting her get on with her work, he turned his large frame toward the bookcase in the corner. As he silently inspected the volumes, Ann considered his unobtrusive, yet distinctive presence. She lit another cigarette, upset to see that the Craven A box was empty. Wretched English fags; it took three of these to make one Camel. She shuffled the papers for a sense of movement, depressed that she hadn't accomplished anything substantial since the episode with Leah that morning. She ran a hand down her cheek, suddenly aware that she hadn't washed her face or combed her hair all day. What a sight she must be. But Reuben didn't seem to notice. He had regarded her as ever with that distant, somewhat quizzical affection. He was as guarded about himself as he was possessive of her. She didn't know whether to feel grateful or bemused. Sometimes she seemed unreachable. Tantalized and frightened, she often wondered why this man was drawn to her. After all, he had several university degrees. Before the war, he was on his way to being a prestigious professor of English. What did he see in a clerk-typist from America? Sure, they had had good talks; she was smart enough. But he would be better off with an educated woman like Marcia, who taught school, or his friend Myrna, the poet. Certainly he knew enough women. What did he see in her?

'I'm almost ready,' she said. He nodded. She needed to log the phone calls first, to give herself the impression of having done something real today.

Esther's head was bent over her report. Ann knew her friend would be here late and she felt guilty about leaving her. But Esther would get her reward tomorrow when they discussed this evening. She had been encouraging the romance – was it a romance? – since the beginning. Right now Ann was so exhausted at the idea of further emotional exchange that she would have been just as happy sending Esther off with Reuben.

Helping Ann on with her jacket, he noticed the hole in the lining and shook his head. He was a fastidious man, despite his parsimonious attitude toward himself. Ann wondered whether the concern was for her or for the coat. Did he find her sloppy?

'I thought we might take a long walk along the river,' he said, holding open the door for her. They both turned and waved to Esther. 'Maybe get a drink at the pub on the water?' He clicked the door shut.

'Yes.' She preceded him downstairs, thinking that she could do with a drink.

'So how did it go with Leah?'

'Oh, I need a beer in front of me before we launch into that.'

They walked silently, companionably, she noticed, recollecting that they had known each other for over a year now, and had been 'dating' for seven months. That was the term Esther used. They would have dinner once or twice a week. He never seemed to want more than talking. Of course, she kept telling herself, he would be reluctant to get too involved with his whole family left in Austria. To her relief, he hadn't ever elaborated on his offer to take care of herself and Leah. It was such a platonic friendship compared to the 'romances' at home. Or were they affairs? Could Reuben imagine that she had slept with two other men? Perhaps the first time with Stan had been more exploration than anything. But she had felt so passionate for Herb before he went to Europe. With Reuben, 'dating' was completely different, so much slower. Not that she hadn't fantasized having sex with him. But in real life, they only had kissed a couple of times. And even that seemed gesture rather than lust. She enjoyed his company, admired him and fancied an interlude. But she didn't want anything too complicated. After all they were both temporary refugees. And he was a difficult character.

They sat by the window and he went to the bar for drinks. She prepared the story. She knew he would be biased because he wanted her to take Leah. She would have to relate this carefully, to avoid his judgement without distorting the facts.

He walked gracefully for a big man, balancing her half pint and his pint. He always brought her a smaller drink even though he always wound up getting her a second half pint. Tonight this irritated her more than usual and she wanted to tell him. Then, most people followed this custom. How could she get so angry over a little thing? Reaching back to her neck, she was surprised there was nothing like the beginning of a headache there.

'She says she won't leave.' Ann tried to sound amused. 'A spunky little one.'

He sipped the foam and nodded.

'I think it will be fine once she gets down there and sees the pretty room Mrs Goldman has arranged. She'll be fine.'

'Yes?' He sounded genuinely curious.

'After a while.' She took a long drink.

'We'll see.'

She fell silent, angry again. She knew this was not the place to expect comfort or even advice. She had to persist with her own beliefs. And in a certain sense, she respected Reuben's intransigence. But that didn't quell her need for reassurance. She stared out at the Thames, so grey tonight. Dark and quiet and thick with the soot of centuries. It made her yearn for the Pacific. How she missed the sheer expanse. Would Reuben enjoy the roaring ocean? Would he be appalled? Maybe Europeans' personal expectations were smaller because their geographical inspirations were smaller. Were they more cynical than Americans because of the mean scale of their landscape? That and the fact that their continent had been ravaged by war for centuries. He was always calling her a hopeless idealist. Hope. That was the distinction between them. How could you expect to dredge up hope from the bottom of a river like the Thames? Now the Columbia River, that was another matter.

He brought her a second half pint and they discussed the new ideas being implemented by a woman at the Birmingham hostel. Then suddenly he offered, 'Would you like to have dinner at my place? I went shopping this afternoon and Manny gave me the two steaks he won in a lottery.'

She couldn't disguise her amazement.

'He owed me a favor.' Reuben spoke rapidly, as if she were waiting for an explanation.

This gave her time to say 'why not' to herself and 'yes' to him.

The walk to Henrietta Street was blurred by the beer. A pint on an empty stomach – suddenly she remembered that she had been unable to eat all day because of Leah – made the yellow street lamps shine like haloes over the pavement. Now that the blackout restrictions had been eased, you could travel short distances safely at night. She concentrated on the elegance of this city. London, despite all the destruction and deprivation, was still London. You could still see St Paul's in the distance, could still bicycle across bridges. A steak dinner, she repeated to herself. She hadn't had steak in six months, not since Esther's birthday when her parents had sent that generous check. Rare, she hoped, with mashed potatoes? This was almost enough to distract her from Reuben's intentions. It would be a lovely evening, she told herself. She was safe. She was a big girl. He was an honorable man. Did she want him to be an honorable man?

They climbed the stone steps to his flat, and she recalled the previous visit, one quick stop before they took the train to a meeting. So dark and spare. She remembered commenting on his asceticism and his consequent dismay. She loved these stone steps, worn in the middle from generations of tenants. She even liked the grimey stairwell. Sometimes wandering London at night, when the destruction wasn't so imposing, was like roaming through history.

He opened the door with a gallant flourish. She was startled by the brilliant ray of sunflowers on the wall opposite, a print of the Van Gogh painting they had admired at the National Gallery. Trying to conceal her surprise, she realized he had been studying her face the whole time. 'Beautiful,' she said, finally. 'It brightens the entire flat.'

He was a good cook, well-organized, proud of his menu, pleased to tend her. Taken aback that she also liked rare meat, he nodded with amused respect.

Ann enjoyed every morsel of the thick, juicy meat and the mashed potatoes. The Brussels sprouts left a little to be desired, but what could you do with these puny cabbages? The Cabernet was perfect and she tried to ignore how much the wine had cost him and where he'd found it.

'You're quite a chef.' She sat back from the table. 'Hidden talents.'

'There's a lot you don't see.'

'I've begun to understand that.' She laughed again. Why was she so happy? It had been a disastrous afternoon. In addition to Leah, Papa's horrible letter from yesterday continued to haunt her. And she had to get up early tomorrow to finish tons of paperwork. Maybe her mood came from the wine. Or maybe from the first good meal she'd had in a month. Maybe it was the strangely beguiling company of this taciturn man.

He pulled out a package of Old Golds and offered her a cigarette. She raised her eyebrow at the American label.

'My cousin George. He's stationed here with the American army. Aunt Rina's son.'

She nodded and wondered why she couldn't remember anything about Aunt Rina or cousin George. Was Reuben particularly loquacious tonight – yes, there was that – but in addition, had she been closed to his intimacies before this? How much had she shut out or forgotten? Her scrutiny was interrupted by his hand on her arm.

'Let's go smoke in the living room,' he said. 'It's more comfortable there.'

'The dishes.' She stood up, puffing furiously. 'Let me help you with the dishes.'

'Later.' He calmed her. 'There will be plenty of time for that.'

She followed dumbly, noting that she had always felt more sophisticated than Reuben. But he was in control tonight. She had been caught off guard. What guard did she need? Hadn't she been fantasizing about sleeping with him? But she had always imagined it taking place in her room. She had planned the lighting.

His own choices weren't bad. Candles on the table. The small reading lamp shining over orange Penguin novels and blue biographies. She sat on the couch opposite him and studied this room – the shelves of books in English, German and French; the neat bed with the brown cover; the two easy chairs that he had received from one of the foster parents last month: brown, beige, black. And the sunflowers. A blessing on this somber room, something like the light at the back of his eyes.

'I learned to cook from my father,' he said.

'Your father?' She was as much surprised by the way he was carrying the conversation as by the detail. Still, she never thought of old world men as cooks.

'Yes, Mama was busy at the store, from 5 a.m. to late at night. Papa was not much good at making money. He was something of a dandy. Grand clothes, grand manner, lots of friends, adored by all the ladies, but completely loyal to Mama. He went into the store for a few hours a day to preside over the purchase of new cloth. He loved textiles.'

Ann watched his intense face and listened to the casual urgency in his voice. It was more than the wine. He must have made a decision. Now that she was still for a moment, she realized he had made a resolution to open his life. She was very moved. Listening to his past tense, she thought about when her high school friend Carol died, how hard it was to refer to her as 'was'. Occasionally she thought about Mama as a 'was.'

'Then he would go out to lunch with the other merchants. He had friends from all quarters – Jews, Catholics, immigrants. He was invited to all the parties. Quite a catch to have Herr Litman at your celebration, so easy was he with the jokes, so chivalrous with the ladies. Mama never went along. She considered this socializing Papa's contribution to the trade. Anyway, when he wasn't at parties or dinners, he often would give our cook the night off and prepare family feasts. Mama would come in after we had finished eating and Papa would fix a special plate for her in the parlor, away from the noisy children.'

'There were six children?' She thought she remembered accurately. How horrible that he was the only one to make it out of Austria alive.

'Six.'

'So all the kids learned to cook?'

'I was most interested.' He smiled. 'The other boys thought it was sissy. And my sister Rebecca was too busy learning the violin. You should have heard her Chopin. It would make you cry.'

Ann nodded. 'Sounds like a remarkable, happy family.' She thought of Teddy and wondered what it would be like to have a large family. Could Mama have coped? Would it have taken her out of herself more?

'Happy, yes, well, in its own way,' he sighed. 'We didn't see much of Mama unless we went to the shop. Still, we were all encouraged to do what we wanted. There was no question about my going to university. If that's what I wanted, I would have it.'

'And Rebecca?' What did she look like, Ann wondered. Now that he had opened up, she didn't know how far to go. She imagined Rebecca tall and dark like Reuben, with a slight frailty around the mouth.

'She was auditioning professionally. They said she had a great career ahead of her.' He stopped abruptly and looked down.

Ann held her breath and cursed herself for pressing him.

'She was the pride of the family.' His voice grew stronger. 'Strange in a way for a girl. Still, we had the example of Mama. No one could stop Mama. That's why they didn't leave in time, you see. She wasn't going to let anything happen to her family. She would never have allowed me to take these courses in Britain if she thought the squeeze would come so soon. I mean if we were all there, holding up our home, it would be a fortress or something.' He stubbed out his cigarette and lit another. 'But here I have been chattering all evening. Tell me about your family, Anna. What were your parents like when you were little?'

'Anna.' She sighed, in spite of herself. 'Mama called me Anna sometimes.'

'Oh, I apologize. It just slips out. I always think of you as Anna. Do you mind?'

'No, I like "Anna". It's more lyrical. "Ann" sounds abrupt.'

'And your parents?'

She forced herself to talk. 'Quite a contrast with yours. I've already told you some things about them. Mama stayed home, almost hid at home, and Papa went out and engaged in the world. A real entrepreneur, my father. And a little successful. He came over – rather went over – to the States destitute and then worked his way to being a foreman at his factory. We had the latest conveniences.'

'But you got a strength from your mother, an integrity, didn't you?'

'I guess so.' She was touched again by his scrutiny. 'Part of Mama just refused to relinquish. Better to go crazy than to compromise.'

'I understand that. It's hard to surrender the identity from where you were born, where you grew up.'

'You've done that.'

'Yes.' He took a long drag on his cigarette and looked toward the window.

'You won't . . . go . . . back after the war?' She tried to control her fear.

He turned and rubbed her left shoulder. 'Never. That Vienna is dead. No, after the war, I will finish university here, if I can find the money.'

She shivered.

'You are still determined to return to America.' He considered her seriously.

'Yes,' she said, 'but that's different.'

Now he stared at the window. 'Not so different.'

This relationship was truly impossible, she realized. He was so foreign – from a completely different class, with different aspirations, different nationality, different language. The only things holding them together were being Jewish and their temporary refuge in London. Plus their loneliness. And perhaps a mutual affection and admiration and . . . she saw he was watching her as if she were a clock with a delicate balance wheel.

He finished the cigarette and stubbed it in the grey dish. She also killed her cigarette.

'More wine?' he inquired.

'No, thank you.' She looked down at her lap, aware of her torn cuticles. He had probably taken in her tattered hands as well as the rip in her coat. He was a careful observer. Why had she insisted on perceiving him as withdrawn and cool?

'Anna?' he asked. Of course he would ask. This was how she had imagined it.

'Yes,' she said, 'yes.' He knotted his arms around her. His face grew near and, as it did, he softened. His lips were gentler than she had remembered and more eager. She lay back on the couch and felt him lie on top of her, the whole length. 'Reuben, Reuben,' she heard herself call, although she wanted him to do the wanting. 'Reuben, tighter, Reuben.' Her body loosened and she allowed herself to feel the tears and the hunger beyond the tears and the hope beyond the hunger and finally the still satisfaction of being held.

She awoke at five the next morning, momentarily forgetting that they moved from the couch to the bed. She thought about last night's passion and turned to him, savoring the odor of their sheets. She felt glad he had moved his legs off her body for he would feel her wakefulness if they were touching now. They had been so attuned making love. The sex had been lined with an undercurrent of melancholy. Deferred passion? Hopeless future? Was she conjuring the melancholy to mask her happiness? Surely she had never felt so full as she had at moments last night. The questions left her tense and restless. Her neck began to ache and she knew that if she didn't get some tea and some exercise the headache would invade before she reached work.

Quietly, she slipped from the bed. Could he feel it? Was he pretending she wasn't leaving? No, he seemed genuinely asleep. This was one of the talents she admired, his ability to shut out the world. She had seen him do it during their walks and again last night. After he knew she was satisfied, he had fallen into an instant sleep. Gingerly, she made her way across the half-illumined room. It was sweet the way he had laid out her skirt and blouse so they wouldn't wrinkle. Still, here were her stockings, coiled over his socks. And his shorts peeking from under the couch. Carefully, she laid his underclothes on a chair and left a note: 'Dear Reuben. Must get to work. Thank you. Thank you. Your Anna.' Should she have signed it, 'love'? Should she have said thank you? There was no perfect note. She wished she had a dozen roses. She wished she could kiss him good-bye. Instead she stood at the door taking a quick, last look.

Covent Garden was just opening. She could hear the lorries as she walked down the street. And she approached the market even though it was in the opposite direction from work. Something about the purposeful chaos soothed her anxiety. She watched a woman unload fruit from the back of her husband's lorry. And over to the right, three men relayed large bouquets of flowers from a truck. Horns and screeching wheels and shouts back and forth across the stalls. One withered woman was laying out carrots and huge green cabbages and shiny apples. Ann watched two men gathering enough broccoli for a restaurant. 'Tuppence more for pinching.' The old woman winked. Ann moved closer, drawn to the bright red apples. 'One of those, please.'

'One?'

Ann remembered this was a wholesale market. They didn't do individual sales until the hospitals and hotels and restaurants were served.

Registering Ann's embarrassment, the woman softened. 'Of course, luv.' She reached down and considered several possibilities before picking one for Ann. 'The very best apple for a sweet girl who rises so early in the day.'

Ann smiled, paid the woman and walked toward the embankment, almost blanketing the street noise with the crunch of her red apple.

She loved the names of these roads: Long Acre, Floral Street, King Street, Maiden Lane. The Strand was beginning to draw traffic but it looked almost vacant compared to how it would be in an hour. Ann ran across the middle of the street, feeling a rare exhilaration about this city. Walking down Villiers Street, she contemplated the awkward elegance of Charing Cross Station. She followed the river toward Westminster Bridge. Then wandering past the Houses of Parliament, she was relieved to find the gate to the gardens open. She wished she had bought two apples.

Aside from several sleeping figures, she was the only visitor in the garden this morning. She felt pleased by the soft dawn light. The statue of Emmeline Pankhurst guarded the entrance like an avenging angel. Rodin's sculpture of the Burghers of Calais stood near the middle – simple and inspiring. Early sun struck a sharp sheen on the black bronze. She recalled the story of these men who, for the sake of their village, put themselves up for ransom. Reuben came to mind and she tried to suppress the image. He would do something like that. Just as suddenly his face disappeared replaced by Leah's.

Integrity, he had said. So what should she do? By all accounts, the child would be better off with the Goldmans. It made no sense to take her in, no sense at all. Was she mad enough to listen to a child? No.

A young couple strolled by. The man wore a US navy uniform. Ann held her breath for the girl, hoping she would be careful. There were going to be an awful lot of war brides. 'Would You Like To Swing On A Star?' And a lot of broken hearts. Why did she think she was any different from this English girl? Why did she assume she would be the one to leave Reuben? Ann stretched. She would have to get to work if she were going to finish the reports in time for Esther's meeting.

Still, she had so much to think out. Reuben was fascinating, brilliant, passionate. But he was also controlled. His story was parceled out in such precise segments. Would he always be regulating the doses of information and affection. He was, like Papa, a self-created man.

A wordly person like Reuben had made love before. And during the war things happened differently. People needed each other for solace and courage and distraction. Yet, even as she ran these notions through her mind, she rejected them.

Ann recalled Reuben's visit to her sick bed last winter and his strange encounter with Mark Speidel. Odd, how the two men had become friends, talking politics, attending football games. Also odd the affection she had developed for her fellow roomer. At first Mark seemed to have a crush on her. However his attentions flagged as soon as he recognized Reuben's place. Occasionally he still looked at her as if, well, as if he could be quite attracted. For her own part, she found Mark great fun and, if he had been Jewish and if Reuben hadn't been around, something might have developed. As it was, Mark played faithful friend to both of them, no doubt a tricky balance. He was one of the few people with whom she was able to discuss Reuben. Mark was much less sentimental than Esther. She recalled their last talk, as the two of them waited for Reuben outside a theater.

'He's got pluses and minuses,' Mark shrugged. 'He's a man of principles. But a moody man of principles.'

'He wants a family,' she said.

'Take it slowly. He'll wait. Your problem is that your confuse the two of them. You can adopt the girl without making Reuben any promises.'

'Sponsor. Not adopt. And even then, I'd have to get special permission.'

'If you made it over here, you can break through the red tape about Leah.'

'That's hardly the point.'

'What's the point?' he asked.

'The child's welfare,' Ann stammered, 'her. . . .' She was saved by Reuben's approach.

Now, Ann decided Mark was not the most responsible person with whom to discuss Leah. Besides she had made her decision.

She reached into her bag for Papa's letter.

Dear Ann.

Thank you for your last letter which arrived a couple of weeks ago. I think I mentioned this in my most recent letter, but perhaps one of yours got lost, so I thought I would repeat that I enjoyed your description of Southend. I remember Uncle Iz liked to go to the English resorts for holidays. I often think about Iz these days. I think he must have got out. But he was never much of a letter writer. He wouldn't think about his poor brother worrying about him, coddled in America.

Well, Mama is the same. Sometimes, it's a horrible thing, I think that she would at least show signs of life if she got worse for a day or two. I visit her faithfully and continue to read aloud the letters from you and Daniel.

I thank God Daniel is still fine unlike so many boys including tragic Howard Nakatani. I heard about that from Teddy and Moira, who came over last week. . . .

Your work there sounds very responsible. So, your agency has saved 10,000 children from Nazi persecution. Yes, that's worthwhile. But I wonder when you will return. There's work here too, Annie. Think about it. Think about the fact that Mama may not have much time left. . . .

Ann sniffed back the tears and cleared the anger from her throat, then the sadness and desperation. More couples strolled through the park now. She had better rush.

Chilled from the damp bench, she worried about catching another cold. Really, it was quite ludicrous to have sat there for an hour, mooning about her life. As she walked to Piccadilly Circus, she was disappointed to hear the lorries and buses out in full chorus. The city was rolling again, coughing, wheezing, roaring, functioning the way only London could function in this fog. She pulled her coat tighter and shivered again. Damn, she would be furious at herself if she got the flu.

Quickly, she bought a ticket and rushed to the northbound platform. Normally, she loved the long, curving escalators and carefully inspected the other passengers as they swooped deep into the safety of the Piccadilly Line. She often thought of what it was like when they camped out here during the heavy bombings. Despite its enormous size, there was something friendly about the station, even about the posters warning, 'Careless Talk Costs Lives'. Yes, she could imagine coming down here with her mattress every night. Not that she wanted to, not that she wasn't grateful she had missed most of the early danger and that Mrs MacDonald had quite an ample shelter. But there was something about the warmth of the station after the morning chill outside. Normally she would have stayed with these thoughts, marvelling that she was actually here in Britain. Ann Rose, American girl in London. But this morning she was irritated with herself for being late. She was in London all right and she was responsible to people and she had better remember that. The escalator let her off as the train was whooshing in.

The platform was crowded with weary people returning from their night jobs and with more alert folk on their way to work. She got a seat facing the direction in which the train was moving. Good. Ann rolled herself a cigarette and inhaled slowly. The smoke was harsher than last night. She did prefer Reuben's American brand. Peering out the window into the darkness, Ann watched the tunnel lights flash by, each one with a different face on it – Leah, Papa, Reuben, Esther, Mama, Mama, Mama.

Ann pulled out *The Horse's Mouth* and tried to read. But Reuben and Leah interrupted. The train pulled into a brightly lit station. She took another puff and stared down at the page summoning the sentences to distract her.

Chapter Twenty-Two

•

Late Fall 1944, San Francisco

ROOSEVELT PREPARES FOR FOURTH TERM

—————— • ——————

US COST OF LIVING RISES 30 PER CENT

•

STRASBOURG LIBERATED

'Concentrate,' Teddy told herself as she sat tall at her desk outside Mr Whitney's office. She inserted a familiar form into the typewriter, placed her fingers on the keys and was suddenly overwhelmed with a rush of Moira's soft pink skin. She closed her eyes and there was Moira lying next to her breathing evenly. She cleared her throat to conjure Miss Fargo. She tried to smell the teacher's carbolic soap and hear the tart instructions. 'Back straight; head to the side; fingers moving as lightly as if you were whipping a soufflé.' Nothing seemed to help. She was in a fog of happiness. Every time she thought of the new Moira in her life she had to stop herself from breaking into a grin.

'In the life,' was what Dawn called it. 'It ain't all roses,' Dawn had warned her yesterday. And for the first time in their friendship, Teddy was cross with Dawn, who wouldn't permit her to enjoy this love, who seemed to bear some kind of grudge against Moira, herself. 'Just watch out. You gotta be careful *inside* and *out* when you're in the life.' Teddy shook herself. Well, she did have to be careful, to pay more attention with the typing. Mr Whitney had brought back three forms this morning. That had never happened before. Never had Teddy received one complaint about her work at the Emporium. The strangest thing was she didn't know if she cared.

Moira was happier too, more relaxed, slower somehow. She had recovered quickly from the last phone conversation with Mrs Finlayson. Teddy had heard only half the exchange. But she could imagine Mrs Finlayson's sure, crisp voice when she insisted Moira surrender the baby for adoption.

'I will *not* sacrifice my child for your sense of propriety.' Moira had gripped the phone, staring at her tea.

'Selfish? How is it selfish to want to be a mother to your child?' Moira took a sip of tea and closed her eyes.

'Mother,' her voice grew higher, 'this is my life. And my baby's life.'

After a long silence, Moira said, 'Mother? Are you still there, Mother? Oh, damn.' She slammed down the phone. 'She hung up. That woman. Teddy, if she calls again, just tell her I'm not here.'

Teddy had thought Moira was kidding until several days later when Moira did, indeed, refuse to come to the phone. It had been weeks since mother and daughter talked. Teddy found this an unnatural state so close to the birth. Still, what could she do? And being so happy, she found it hard to worry, even about her father, who had been in the hospital again last week.

Startled by the sound of her buzzer, Teddy noticed her hand trembling as she pressed the button.

'Yes, Mr Whitney?'

'Time, Teddy. Have you noticed the time?'

Teddy checked the impassive moonface of the old wall clock. The black hands seemed like skis set at cross purposes over the lunar craters. '3.30,' she read with distraction. 'Oh, no, your tea. Sorry sir. I'll be right there.'

Concentrate, she told herself, concentrate. Yet even as she served Mr Whitney's tea, she was in a state of oblivion. She forced herself to check the number of sugars and to stir in just the right amount of milk. Grateful that her boss was too busy to talk, she returned to her desk and breathed deeply. The strange thing was that this happiness was much more distracting than trouble. She felt so excited all the time, as if she might spin off into the universe. As if she might throw up. She couldn't believe the fullness she felt with Moira, the joy and satisfaction of making love and the contentment of sleeping with her arms around the girl. She couldn't believe it. Yes, that was the problem. She couldn't believe she was so happy.

The phone startled her as if Teddy were in a deep sleep. She had to let it ring again while she caught her breath. Her stomach knotted suddenly. If she didn't get a hold on herself she would lose this job and a fine thing that would be now that Moira was on leave from the shipyard.

'Mr Whitney's office,' Teddy answered in her most polished secretary voice.

'Miss Fielding, please.'

Teddy couldn't quite place the woman's voice.

'This is Teddy Fielding.' What was it, bad news about Pop? Or Moira, had she already gone to the hospital?

'Teddy, this is Moira's mother.'

'Oh, Mrs Finlayson, how are you?' Teddy tried to restrain the panic in her voice. Instantly, she understood something about Moira. Just the sound of her mother's voice put you on alert.

'Fine, thank you. I am sorry to disturb you at work. I need to inquire about my daughter, about Moira. Is she all right? Has she, has she had the baby yet?'

'No, Mam. I mean she's fine and, no, the baby hasn't come yet.'

Mrs Finlayson sighed and spoke more slowly. 'Then I wonder if I might ask you a favor?'

'Yes, Mam?' Teddy said tentatively. She felt that familiar sensation of standing between Jolene and Pop.

'Please call me when Moira goes into hospital. I'd like to come up.'

'I, I don't know, Mrs Finlayson. That's something between you and Moira and I don't want to butt. . . .'

'Yes, dear, I understand. I wouldn't bring you into this if it weren't absolutely necessary. But you must know that my daughter refuses to speak to me at the moment. This is the only way. I do regret involving a stranger.'

Stung by the 'stranger', Teddy could only say, 'I don't know.'

'Of course, I appreciate your position.' Mrs Finlayson's voice was so tight Teddy thought it might snap. 'But please think about it. For Moira's sake.'

'Yes, Mam.' Teddy sometimes regretted her endless fund of

deference. The truth was Moira needed her mother at a time like this.

'Thank you, Teddy. I must let you get back to work now.'

Back to work. Teddy stared at the moon and watched the skis sliding past the minutes. Yet another thing to think about. Would she be betraying Moira if she called? Or would Moira be grateful to be saved from her own pride? No, it didn't seem right. But there were at least two weeks to worry about it. She stared at the form in her typewriter, drawing it into focus.

'Watch it. Be careful. Don't slip. Can't you see I just washed it?'

Teddy stared at the kitchen floor and then at Moira scrubbing her way out of the back door. A tilting, hennaed buddha banishing ancient stains.

'Yes,' Teddy said finally. 'I can see you. But I'm not sure I believe you. Didn't the doctor say that the point of leaving the shipyard was to rest, to avoid strain, to prepare. . . .'

'Oh, Teddy, I feel like a pressure cooker. If I don't do something I'm going to explode. Besides, I'm not due for two weeks.'

'But you push yourself too much and you might have the baby right here, while I'm at work.' Teddy leaned on the doorframe.

'Dear, that could happen anyway. The baby isn't punched into your timeclock, smart as any child of mine might be. Besides, Mrs Bertoli said she'd take me to the hospital any time. And Mr Minelli offered. He came around this afternoon with more eggs from his sister in Petaluma.'

'Well, a man with a heart condition isn't the best. . . .' Teddy stopped herself. Mrs Bertoli was reliable; she was always around the shop. Moira had it all under control. It was such a funny feeling – to see Moira cool at the helm.

'You're the one who needs to relax. Just go into the living room and read your mystery. Supper will be ready in half an hour. And,' she rubbed her back, 'so will I.'

After supper, they snuggled on the couch, listening to 'People Are Funny' on the radio. Teddy didn't follow the program at all, waking from her daze only when the audience laughed or when Moira shifted to a more comfortable position. 'Inside and outside,' Dawn's words kept coming back to her. She understood the outside problems – that this new life could cost the Emporium job and this house. Although Mr Minelli was remarkably tolerant of Moira's pregnancy, he would hardly accept homosexuality. But inside? No, Dawn just didn't like Moira, that was all there was to it. She – they – were perfectly safe here in each other's arms.

'Oh, oh, ohhhhh,' Moira gasped and sat forward.

'What is it?' Teddy demanded.

'You mean who is it?' Moira smiled, her upper lip beaded with sweat.

'Now? Already? Now?'

'Calm down,' Moira said, amazed at her own composure. 'Could be false labour pains, remember. We have to time them if they – oh, ohhh – yes, time this – ohhh – one, Teddy.'

Two hours later when the contractions were close enough, they borrowed Mr Minelli's car and drove to the hospital. Teddy had planned the trip a hundred times and proceeded automatically. She had planned where she would park, how long it would take to walk from the car to the hospital. Yes, she told herself, it was going to be fine. Moira was going to be fine. Concentrate, Teddy, concentrate.

Moira could not believe the pain. She had to control herself. She couldn't break down here in the car. Teddy would crash. She was an adult. Millions of women had done this. Her own mother at nineteen. Ohhhhhh, she couldn't believe the pain; she just couldn't. 'Teddy?' she heard herself ask.

'You all right?' Teddy maneuvered around a double parked car. 'Moira.' She turned quickly. 'You're not having it now. Not yet, not here, I mean if you have to. . . .'

'Teddy.' Moira's voice was steady now that the contraction had passed. 'I'm fine. But could you do me a favor? Would you call Mother for me? Tell her where I am and say if she wants to. . . .'

'Oh, that's a girl.' Teddy patted Moira's thigh. 'That's a good thing to do.'

Taken aback by Teddy's enthusiasm, Moira decided her friend was simply panicked. And this hysteria helped keep her on an even keel, herself. She twisted the plain ring Teddy had given her to wear for the occasion.

Teddy held Moira's hand as they checked into the hospital. She was distressed by the chaos: rolling stretchers, bustling nurses, ringing phones. Ten o'clock at night. Finally the nurse turned to Moira.

'Yes, your doctor called.'

'But where is he?' Teddy persisted. 'She needs the doctor to have the baby.'

The nurse studied Teddy and then turned to Moira. 'Your first, isn't it? Well, that'll take a while. Dr Emerson will be here. Hasn't missed a launch yet.'

Teddy carried the bag and followed Moira and the nurse down the hall.

Overcome with pain, Moira leaned against the wall. Teddy took her elbow, soothing her. Inside and outside, Teddy thought, holding on to Moira despite the nurse's stare. How much was she imagining?

The nurse cleared her throat. 'I think we should be moving on.' She took the satchel from Teddy and smiled kindly. 'The waiting room is over there. If that's what you want. It's likely to take quite some time.'

'Oh, yes, of course,' Teddy blushed. 'Yes, I will wait. Thank you.' Would Moira be all right? The girl was exhausted. If only she could stay and hold her hand.

Moira glanced back forlornly, her face suddenly overtaken by pain.

'I'll be right here,' Teddy called, using her will to restrain herself from hugging her friend good-bye. Oh, this was horrible. If only she could have the baby for Moira. She was so much better at handling pain. She stood in the hallway until Moira and the nurse had turned the corner, then rushed to the telephone.

Moira lay on the stiff bed feeling impossibly alone. Which was longer – the time between the contractions or the pain itself? Why had they left her here? What if the baby decided to come right now? No, she reminded herself, it took time. They had plenty of other people to care for. She tried not to hear the screams from the next room. Mother would be horrified if she behaved like that. Oh, why hadn't she broken down and asked for Mother? Still, they wouldn't let Mother in here. Yes, she would have to wait outside with . . . oh, dear, what had she done to poor Teddy . . . of course, it would take her hours to arrive. The baby would be born by then. The little girl or boy. . . . Oh, no, Moira tried to hold her breath against the pain, but still it came in waves of sharp determination. 'Owwwww,' she heard another scream from the other . . . no, not from the other room, but from this room, from her own mouth. Then she felt a

– 277 –

damp cloth on her forehead.

'Relax honey and breathe.' She looked up to the face of a new nurse and thought she heard a trace of South in her accent. Why had they given her another nurse? Had they discovered she wasn't married? Is that why she was in this room alone? Was this the unmarried nurse? The anxiety and pain disappeared as quickly as it had come. And so did the nurse.

This was so unfair; she hadn't asked for a baby. They had been careful. She was too young. She had been inducted involuntarily. Why did she think she was so special? Because Sister Lawrence had said so. A sin is a knowing offense against . . . she hadn't meant to get pregnant, so why was she having a baby? Sin, sin sin. Pregnancy was punishment for sex. No, that didn't make sense; it hadn't felt evil. It had felt right. She thought of Randy holding her tight, whispering – no, she mustn't think about him. Sex was a mortal sin, a very fleshy, very mortal sin. Oh, she would be punished doubly for this blasphemy. Her baby would be born deformed. Owww, the pain. Breathe, the disappearing nurse had said, breathe against the pain. Oh, the pain.

Anger coursed through her now. She did not deserve this. She had tried to do everything right, but there were no more reliable models like Susie Fitzpatrick and Cindy Patton. Whatever happened to them? Had they wound up here too? Were they, perhaps, the ones screaming in the next room? The married room, for no doubt they had done it right. You can't have models your whole life. At some point you just have to fly, to trust your instinct and your conscience. But every time she did that, she seemed to lose. She lost her acting chances when she went to the shipyard. She lost Randy after she gave him all she had. If you couldn't trust your judgment and there were no models, what did you have? A code of behavior, a sense of morality. She heard Mother's voice. Oh, the pain, the pains were getting closer.

Teddy leaned back and stretched her legs. On the couch opposite snored a young, expectant father. Teddy had learned he was waiting for twins. Might as well rest while he could.

Teddy picked up her cup of cold tea and set it down again. 4 a.m. She read her watch and shook her head. It was 5 a.m. in Arizona. Wanda would be asleep. Teddy felt overwhelmed with sadness, thinking about Wanda still stuck in that place. She was paralyzed with remorse that she had never made her visit. Of course Wanda wrote to say she understood that Teddy didn't want to leave Moira in her condition. Wanda understood. Wanda was called upon to understand a great deal these last few years.

Teddy stared down the empty hall. At midnight, the nurse had said it might be five hours yet, had told her to go home, but if Teddy knew anything about Moira it was that she was unpredictable. Well, maybe the child wanted to come at dawn. This was going to be some day. New baby. Reconciliation between Moira and her mother. Mrs Finlayson should be getting to town this evening. Good timing – allowing Moira to recover and freshen up and get to know her daughter. Why did she keep picturing a girl? She tried to think of a little boy. She had practiced saying Moira's favorite names: Tim, Bruce. This just didn't work. It would be a girl.

Teddy closed her eyes and imagined the three of them, Moira and the baby and herself, sitting out in the garden together. She loved children, hated to see her youngest brother and sister growing up. And now she was going to be a parent. Never had she featured herself as a parent. That was OK, wasn't it? True, she wasn't a mother, but maybe a kind of auxiliary mother or a step-mother. That's how Moira thought of it, wasn't it? After all, she talked about 'raising our baby'. Well, names weren't so important. It was the feeling they all had, the bond that counted.

Bonds. They had been through a lot together since July, she and Moira. First that horrible night with Moira lying at the top of the stairs. The frantic race to the hospital – this very hospital – and the agonizing wait while they ran tests. Then the coming-to-terms with her pregnancy. Then that wonderful night of Moira's birthday. The glorious days of loving since then. And now tonight, another birthday, any minute now.

Moira could not believe the wild, searing pain. The intensity. The endurance. How could it go on this long. There didn't seem to be any pauses between the contractions. But how could she survive if there wasn't some relief, some space for herself? She began to hate this thing inside her. Then she felt intense sympathy, because if this hurt her how did it feel to a tiny child? She knew she could not survive the pain much longer.

The nurse shook Teddy's shoulder. Startled, she almost knocked the woman getting to her feet. 'Is she born? Is Moira all right?'

The woman smiled and sighed. 'Progress, but no product. I'm going off shift now. And I've told Hazel,' she nodded toward the thin, young woman behind the counter, 'to keep tabs for you.'

Teddy blinked and yawned. 'Why thank you very much. Thank you for your help.'

Stretching, she noticed that the father of twins had gone, replaced by a younger man, smoking furiously. Teddy checked her watch and rushed to the phone to tell Mr Whitney that she was very sorry, but she had come down with a terrible case of stomach flu.

This is it, thought Moira, I'm going to die in childbirth. They had wheeled her into a different room. Dr Emerson had given her something for the pain, but she needed to remain awake to push. Push? She was already almost over the edge. Had they called a priest? She should have told Teddy to call a priest instead of Mother. Well, if anyone could get her into Heaven, it was Mother. Maybe they would say the rosary in the same church where they prayed for Uncle Willie. This time sweet, wee Jenny would hang on to competent Aunt Evie.

'Push.' The nurse was shouting in her ear. Poor woman didn't understand. Would the baby survive if she. . . .

'Push. Push. Puuuuush. Push. Pu. . . .'

Moira could hear the wails. High pitched and angry. So different from the deep howls of terror she, herself, had made a moment before. The child cried again. Her child. She raised her head and stared at the squalling, red baby. Girl. They told her it was a girl.

Teddy brought Mrs Finlayson a fresh cup of tea. 'It sure takes a long time.' She shook her head.

'Yes.' Moira's mother faltered. 'It's completely unpredictable. You must be exhausted, Teddy.'

'Yes, Mam. No more than you. Or Moira. Or. . . .' She saw the thin, young nurse approaching them. The man with the cigarette looked up nervously.

The nurse seemed to be trying to remember something.

'How is my daughter, Moira?' Mrs Finlayson stood tall.

'Well, Mam, it's a girl. The mother is fine.'

'Thank God.'

Teddy reached over and squeezed Mrs Finlayson's shoulder. She felt the older woman try to relax.

A girl, thought Teddy. And she was OK. Everybody was OK.

'When may I see my grandchild?'

Teddy looked on expectantly.

The nurse frowned as if she were still trying to remember something and said, 'Since you're the grandmother, I'm sure it will be all right. Just follow me.'

Teddy remained standing, confused and then disappointed. Well, she would get to see them soon enough. They were all right. Everything was going to be all right.

●

Chapter Twenty-Three

Early winter 1944–5, San Francisco

GERMANS RETREAT FROM ARDENNES

●

STRASBOURG THREATENED

●

HUNGARY AND USSR SIGN ARMISTICE

Streetlight filtered through the white shade as Moira tucked Tess into her crib. She stood in the darkened room, watching light play on her baby's face. Her baby. This sweet, small, chubby person. At once Moira felt wizened and weary and far too young to mother this child. Yet she knew Tess was hers by this love which was larger than anything she had ever experienced. Had Mother felt this way about her? The child turned with a low, gurgling sound. Moira held her breath because she didn't want Tess to waken. She had no energy to spare except for looking and loving. Is this why Mother never had a second child, because Moira had given her so much bother? She had often thought of Mother since Tess's birth – had found a new sympathy and forgiveness, at least the willingness to forgive.

A healthy wind blew outside, casting tree branches over the streetlamp and webbing shadows across the room. Moira watched anxiously for signs of movement in Tess, but all she detected was quiet breathing – in and out, slow and even. She studied the shimmering blond hair, the pink skin and the miraculous vitality that eased up and down beneath the knitted blanket.

When she noticed the baby's resemblance to Randy her heart

would catch. She stepped back and considered that she had stopped counting the months since she had heard from him. She had little sadness left, only a hard crust of anger. But it had all worked out for the best, hadn't it? Otherwise she couldn't have found this new love for Teddy.

Moira's eyes drew back to her own fingers, lightly gripping the edge of the crib. This skin was tougher since she had taken the shipyard job and her fingernails were ruined. What did Tess feel when she was washed? Did she feel Moira's rough, harsh skin? Did she sense security? Moira paused, remembering the antiseptic smell of Mother's hands after she purged their house with Clorox and the Bon Ami.

What would Tess's early memories be? Would she know anything of this war? Would she remember not having a father? Why was she thinking about Randy so much tonight? This wasn't a tragedy. Moira could not remember her own real father. And Tess wasn't an orphan. She had two parents. How much could the child feel? What could she taste? Did she perceive herself as separate from her mother? Surely when she was hungry, she squirmed and cried as if Moira belonged to her. So often Moira had the sensation that Tess was in charge. Her own arms were for holding; her shoulders for burping; her hip for carrying.

How long would their love be this strong? Moira had to restrain herself from tucking in her child again.

She worried about the desperate schism that tore her apart from Mother. Odd, how you could spend nine months surrounding a being, creating her, feeding her and then find out that you are completely helpless as to how that being develops, as to who she becomes. Would her hair remain blond and curly? Would those blue eyes turn dark? Would she be steamy or placid or dull or turbulent? Moira wondered if she were capable of being a mother since she had hardly learned the daughter role.

Tess continued to sleep peacefully, and Moira, concerned that her worries might disturb the child, blew a silent kiss good-night. Quietly, she secured the doorstop with her foot and proceeded across the hall to bed. Standing on her toes, she stretched the tension from her body. She had never imagined working this hard: tending a baby was tough enough; then the shipyard drained the rest of her spirit. They couldn't survive on Teddy's salary, generous as she was. The babysitter was reliable and she was blessed to have one.

Bending down to place her slippers under the bed, she felt a pain pulse along her waist. Must be the muscle she pulled at work yesterday. God damn, you think you've escaped these things and then they plague you. Still, she was luckier than some. She shuddered, thinking about Eleanor's eye and Nell's left foot. There wasn't enough attention to safety. Here they were building these ships tightly to protect the seamen so the seamen could bring supplies to the military who were protecting the civilians. But who was protecting the shipbuilders? This, if nothing else, had got her active in the union. She didn't care if people called her 'Red' with that silly double meaning in their voices, she knew she had a right to be paid fairly and treated carefully. After all, this wasn't Pan-O-Rama Studios; this was the American war effort.

She hurried into her flannel night gown, wistfully acknowledging that the warm spell was over. Opening the bed, she could smell the fresh sheets she had fitted this morning before going to work and the sweetness pleased her. The bed was cool, but it would soon warm up. Moira lay still, listening carefully for noises from the adjacent room. She decided to leave the light on.

Teddy tiptoed into the bedroom, worried about Moira, who had gone to bed early as she had every night this week. Well, tomorrow was Sunday and the kid could rest from at least one of her jobs. Undressing with dispatch, Teddy noticed Moira was wearing a flannel nightie. She reached into the bottom drawer and pulled out a long gown of her own. Then she stood beside the bed. Moira was as busy in her sleep as in every other moment of the day. Her round breasts rose and fell like ocean swells. Her curls tangled on the pillow like seaweed strung along the shore. For all her hard work, she looked well, more fit than in years. That nagging self-pity had disappeared. Maybe the problem had been she didn't have enough to do in that silly office job. Now she had responsibility upon responsibility and she was handling it beautifully. Ann should see Moira's self-sufficiency now. In many ways the girls were similar. She looked forward to Ann's return.

Teddy climbed into bed beside Moira, breathing in the scent of clean sheets mixed with Moira's lemon talc. She wasn't ready for sleep, so she picked up *The Glass Key* and turned to the chapter she had been reading last night. Moira's breathing remained deep and even. Teddy imagined it rising and falling in rhythm with Tess in the next room. She remembered nights when Moira still carried Tess inside her. The two of them would lie in bed timing Tess's heartbeat. Teddy leaned against the pillows and closed her eyes. How long had this been going on – how long had they shared the same bed, how long had they been 'lovers', as Dawn would say? How long? Of course she knew perfectly well because tomorrow would be their fourth month anniversary. Four months of holding Moira in her arms, of being able to look and smell and touch as closely as she wanted. Four months of skittish happiness. Teddy thought she could remember every detail of their first night. For one thing, Moira loved to relive that evening, talking about it moment by moment.

Teddy looked down at her friend and remembered her this afternoon, wearing the birthday dress, just to show that it finally did fit. Moira, yes, this was the same Moira who had waited for J.D. to give her a break in the movies. And she still fiddled with all that lipstick and nail polish. When Wanda and Ann returned, they would find the same person. They would recognize her. How long would it take for them to notice she had ripened? Of course they all had aged; they would expect changes. But Moira seemed so profoundly different to Teddy. She longed to share her happiness, but she knew, even as Moira warned her, that it wasn't the sort of thing you put in a letter. Wise as Moira was about the world, Teddy felt a little nervous in her general secretiveness.

Teddy couldn't keep her head in the book. She needed to remind herself that there were some friends she could talk to.

Dawn and Sandra were happy for her. Sandra more so. 'Welcome to the club.' Sandra had slapped Teddy on the back, as they sat in a corner of the Quiet Cat. 'You'll have to bring her along next weekend.'

'But you know, well, that she's different,' Teddy stumbled, unable to picture Moira in this place, reluctant to admit that Moira had already said she was too shy to come and that she herself was here only because Vivian and Moira had gone to the movies.

'Hell, that don't make no difference, some of those shy women are the most delicious and, if the dancing gets too rambunctious, we can all sit here at the table, the way we's doing now.'

Dawn held her peace, looking from Teddy to Sandra and rolling a cigarette.

'Well.' Teddy finally managed. 'It looks like you all will have to come visit us at the house. I reckon it'd be easier for everyone there.'

Dawn took a long drag. 'You be careful, honey.'

Sandra shot her a warning look, which made Dawn all the more determined to advise.

'Moira is a nice girl, we know that. But just take it easy.'

Teddy drew back, irritated by the smoke. Then, in spite of herself, she said, 'What do you mean?'

'I mean that straight ladies like to play games with us sometimes. They don't intend to hurt. But they can pull out anytime. And that leaves you holding a hole in your heart.'

'How do you know she's straight – or for that matter that I'm any more in the life than she is. This is the first woman I ever made love with . . .'

Sandra was shaking her head at Dawn. Dawn took another drag and interrupted Teddy. 'Honey, I know you. You're as queer as they come. I don't mean to sound superior, but I knew you liked women before you did. And that Moira girl, she does like men. Now would she be carrying around that bundle if she didn't like men?'

'It was an accident; she didn't mean it.' Teddy stopped, realizing how foolish she sounded, understanding that Dawn was voicing her own doubts. Still, Moira said that sex with her was gentler than with Randy. More fulfilling.

'Dawn McCormack,' Sandra whispered harshly. 'You don't know nothing about this affair. You don't know how people develop. Remember me five years back; I couldn't decide between you and Billy Walker. Besides, besides,' she turned to Teddy urgently, 'you deserve a little loving after what that Angela girl did to you. You take it while you can. These days you can't never count on tomorrow.'

Sandra hadn't made her feel better. That was the last advice from either of them. Sandra and Dawn wished her the best. She knew she could count on them for company if not for answers.

Teddy set her book on the bedside table next to Wanda's letter. She thought she had problems, well, what about Wanda? Her brother lost in combat; her boyfriend 6,000 miles away; herself completely responsible for Betty and their mother. Tomorrow Teddy would write to Wanda. Tomorrow as soon as she got home from work.

*

Vivian honked at exactly 5.45 the next morning. Moira was still feeding Tess her bottle. Someday she would get used to the fact that other people were punctual. She was supposed to be on time too, not eternally five minutes late. Teddy hurried into the kitchen, automatically lifting the baby from Moira. 'You go and get your coat and the basket; I'll finish feeding her.'

'Thanks, hon.' Moira kissed Teddy's cheek. As she raced into the living room, she had a queasy feeling that this was becoming like a marriage in the simple ways they relied on each other. Or had their relationship always been this way? Moira felt much more comfortable in a friendship than in a marriage. She smiled thinking about their traditional costumes – she in her heavy overalls and Teddy in her prim skirt and pumps. But she was really the mother of the baby. And Teddy was really the lesbian. Well, Moira guessed most people would call her a lesbian now. And she guessed that in loving Teddy that's what she was.

Honk. Honk. Vivian called from the car, 'Hey, Moi, get a move on.' Moira hustled across the room, taking Tess from Teddy's arms.

Moira settled into the front seat, quietened Tess with her bottle, then turned to Vivian. 'I'm sorry, I-I. . . .'

'So what else is new? Forget it. Just lucky we don't have to pick up anyone else today.'

'Right.' Moira caught her breath. 'I forgot Jay and Claire were taking a furlough. Good, we'll get to talk. It's been so crazy at work with the union stuff and the speed-up. Seems I only catch you coming and going.'

'Yeah.' Vivian tucked a stray hair beneath her neckerchief. 'You and Dot and I have to have dinner soon, that is if Teddy doesn't mind.'

'Why would she mind?' Moira asked, wondering if she were imagining the edge in Vivian's voice. 'We have separate friends.'

'Right.' Vivian's tone was more brusque.

'What's on your mind?' Moira checked on Tess as she often did when she, herself, was anxious. She wasn't clear whether her reflex was to protect her child or to find self-protection in motherhood.

Vivian stared at the traffic for forty seconds and began slowly. 'You heard from Randy at all?'

Moira blushed and resisted an urge to cover Tess's ears. Of course the child would learn about Randy some day. But while the war continued, Moira assumed a certain immunity. She was surprised at the intensity of her rage and underneath that – she was disappointed to find – of her sadness.

'No.' She shook her head at the universe. The anger was now tranferred to Vivian. 'How would I know if he's even alive?'

'Well, none of us have heard for months and months. Those things – those romances – blow over. You have to keep hope.'

'Of course I hope he's fine. But it's not like I'm planning any big homecoming for him. I've got a home. I'm settled, with Teddy. You know that. I'm surprised to be hearing this from *you* of all people. I mean, after you told me about your sister. I thought you said you were easy about lesbians.' Moira felt a twinge. Teddy would be pleased that she had used the word about herself. But how could she tell Teddy about this conversation without worrying her? Sometimes she felt so alone. When she was with Randy she could talk to all the girls about him. But Vivian and Dorothy were the only people she could talk to about Teddy and now Vivian was getting strange.

'Oh, I don't know, honey. I like Teddy. She's a real brick; everybody says so. Loyal, loving to you. God knows we all wish we had someone like that in our lives. Maybe I'm a little jealous. But I don't completely understand it. I mean my sister Abby has been that way all her life, a real tomboy, never dated. But you were the Belle of North Beach. You had men standing in line. And you loved every moment of it. Are you sure about Teddy? Does she "satisfy" you?'

Moira looked out at the street. The sun hit an old window of a semi-detached house, making rainbows in the watery panes. She thought of Mother's crystal pendant, lost for a minute in the colors. She sighed and turned to Vivian. 'You just finished listing her sterling qualities.'

'I'm not asking about character. I'm talking flesh and blood.' Vivian glanced sideways. 'Honey, you want this person for the rest of your days?'

'Why not?' Moira turned back. 'We love each other. We have fun together. I haven't been this happy in years, maybe not ever before.'

'Well, then, what about the kid?'

'What about her?' Moira held Tess closer. What had got into Vivian? Moira wanted to stop this conversation right here. It was as if Vivian were voicing all her fears about this new life and her courage to handle it. 'Tess will be a heck of a lot happier than I was as a child.'

'Don't you think she needs her father?'

'Her father?!' Moira's voice rang. 'And just how would you suggest I retrieve her father? Who knows where Randy is? When he returns, if he returns, who knows what he will think of Tess? And what other man would take us on? We're both very lucky to have Teddy. Besides I love her. We have a home.' Moira dug into her breast pocket for a handkerchief and blew her nose.

Vivian patted her leg. 'I don't know what's wrong with me. Maybe it's not hearing from Rick for so long. Somehow it's unnerving that you don't worry about Randy. Maybe that's it.'

'But you're married to Rick. And I-I-I have a home with Teddy now.'

'Maybe I just envy you your tranquility.'

Moira regarded Vivian through red, wet eyes. 'Me, tranquil?'

The two women laughed together. Vivian pulled over in front of a red brick house which functioned as a family home by night and a private nursery by day. It seemed ages until they boarded the ferry to Richmond and reached the yard.

Vivian managed to find a parking spot close to the fence. While they were collecting their gear, Moira tried to shake her anxiety about Tess.

'So are you still happy with the flanging? I mean you don't regret not going into chipping and burning?'

'You're kidding?' Vivian slung her purse over her shoulder and slammed the car door. 'You wouldn't catch me wearing all that gear. Safety boots and heavy gloves are enough for me. I feel like a snow woman as it is.'

Moira nodded, not really listening, eager to fill the time until the gate when she could part from Vivian. She regretted that they had already made a plan for lunch. It would be hard to forget the morning's conversation. Finally they got to the plate shop, a big building running the width of the shipyard. Moira raised her hand.

'See you at lunch.' Vivian smiled and walked on.

Moira nodded to Cliff and Samantha before going into the corner to pull on her heavy leathers and hood and thick gloves. Now, with the hot spell over, this gear was more bearable.

The shipyard folks were different from people at the office. Easier somehow. You didn't have to talk unless you wanted. Maybe that had to do with the concentration their work took. As a receptionist she was always on the alert to please, to say the right things. But here the job took you to another world, where words were not so important. Your focus had to be steady and clear. Moira had been extra careful with the torch since Tess was born. Today she would be working alone, although Cliff and Samantha remained in the same room. The morning passed quickly.

She almost missed the lunch whistle. She would have kept working if Cliff hadn't walked up and waved his hat in her face. Pulling out the earplugs, she looked up quizzically.

'I've heared of whistle-to-whistle workers, ladybug, but this is overdoing it.'

'Oh,' she smiled. 'It's the foam rubber. Much better than cotton. Can't hear a thing. Thanks, Cliff. Guess I *am* hungry.'

'Then get a move on, girl.' Vivian leaned against the doorframe. 'It's not as if we have a two martini lunch.'

As they walked out into the yard, Moira blinked at the intensity of the sun. Such a different light from her torch. When she was working, she enjoyed the flame's brilliance and her own controlled sense of power. Out here the sun illuminated everything equally, recklessly lending energy to ships and people and buildings. She wiped the sweat from her forehead and was conscious of weakness in her knees. 'Let's go over by the railing there, in the shade.'

Vivian nodded. So many people milling around. Such a difference from minutes before when everyone was disciplined to assignments from the inner bottom to the high steel rails. Moira felt dizzier than she had during pregnancy. Maybe her period was coming. She tried to concentrate on things outside herself as they walked and she considered how many more women worked in the yard now than when she first arrived. It was great to see hardhats with 'Barbie' and 'Gina' and 'Marie' and 'Maxine'. A lot more old people were also working, which allowed able-bodied men to join the service. As the sign on the latrine read, 'Be a worker. Free a worker.' She even saw one or two men who looked like they might have been wounded during the last war. Certainly there were a lot of Negroes. Dawn had told Teddy that thousands of colored women had left farms in the South to come to California for gold mine jobs. It helped Moira picture what home was like if they considered this a gold mine.

'You OK?' Vivian asked as they reached the fence. 'You're awful quiet.'

'A little tired,' Moira mumbled. 'And hungry.' She opened the baloney sandwich which Teddy had made this morning. What the hell did Vivian want after ripping apart her entire universe on the way to work?

Vivian bit into a carrot and shook her head. 'You know Cliff's family came to Richmond in the early 1900s and there were only a handful of houses. They say that at the beginning of the war there were 20,000 people here and now there are ten times that many.'

Moira nodded, conscious that Vivian was trying to be conciliatory. Ah, times were hard on everyone. Vivian was just taking out her worries on her. Moira had probably returned the favor a hundred times.

Vivian unlaced her boot. 'No, better not. I'll never get back into it.'

Moira bit her apple. 'How does the change from Liberties to transports seem to be affecting your crew?' She noticed the stiffness in her voice.

'Well, Miss Plushbottom, I haven't taken a comprehensive survey, but. . . .'

They both laughed.

'Truce?' asked Moira.

'Friend, I'm sorry. I didn't mean to butt in.'

'Truce,' Moira said more abruptly than she intended. 'And when are you coming over to the house for supper? You and Dorothy. Let's make it soon, OK?'

'Love it. You set the night.'

But Moira was distracted watching a crane swing a huge unit over by the plate shop. What were they doing with that thing, she wondered. The spectre of it swinging in mid-air, and the huge hole it would pound in the earth if the crane operator were an inch off, filled her with panic. Sometimes she felt as if she were living on the edge of the world.

Moira relaxed back on the elephant couch, feeding Tess her bottle and savoring the smell of Teddy's meatloaf. Would they eat as much meatloaf when Wanda and Ann came home? When Wanda and Ann came home – how much of that fantasy did she buy any more? Surely not as much as Teddy although they all wrote about the house 'returning to normal' after the war. Teddy's letters were full of plans about developing the garden and painting the house. Ann's letters seemed to nod in casual support. But Wanda hadn't shown much enthusiasm for anything since Howard died. Well, if they all did return, no doubt the menu would change. She tried to forget the conversation with Vivian and to concentrate on Tess.

The child seemed to feel completely secure in her arms. Did she think Moira had been a mother all her life? Would she ever see herself as a mother? Tess sucked greedily on the bottle. Moira wished she could breastfeed. But Mother warned that it created dependence. Besides, she had to keep up with the job. Mother always won the arguments, if indirectly.

Mother was less critical now that Moira had accomplished at least one expected task: she *had* produced a beautiful grandchild, if not at the proper time. Now the weekly phone calls were easier because they shared an interest. Moira learned to sort out Mother's helpful advice from her special obsessions. The sweetest moment of Mother's visit was when she declared that Moira looked just like this as a child, rosy and animated. Eventually the visit did become a strain. What would they have done without Teddy's peacemaking charm?

Moira rocked Tess and considered that it hadn't always been hard to be her mother's daughter. There had been wonderful weekends shopping and walking on the beach. Mother could never get her fill of those warm shores after the dour mists of Scotland. Moira remembered one long afternoon when the two of them walked miles in Long Beach. Daddy was fishing with his friends so she and Mother took the opportunity to hike along the shore as far as time would allow. Further. Almost lost in the dark, Moira felt more exhilaration than fear. She and Mother matched footprints in the mucky sand. At one point, they even held hands and skipped, Mother singing in her inimitably creaky voice, 'A Roamin' in the Gloamin''.

In fact, Moira reflected now, the two of them got along fairly well until Moira started high school. This was an important period, Mother reminded her, a time to study, to make the right friends. If only she, herself, hadn't quit school in grade six, she could have made something of her life. Home became more and more fraught. Sister Lawrence lectured about 'normal adolescence'. But Moira knew something else was happening, something to do with the whole family.

Early in the mornings when she was supposed to be sleeping, she could hear her parents arguing on the couch in the living room. Mother complained about Daddy's refusal to put himself forward at the factory. Daddy said he liked the men at work and he wasn't interested in becoming foreman. Gradually the fights cooled down. Her parents said little to each other for days at a time. Moira knew Mother's ambitions had shifted to her.

Tess stretched away from the bottle, whimpering. Moira flapped a diaper over her left shoulder and burped her baby. As she carried Tess upstairs she considered that she had no designs on Tess's life. Not yet. She didn't care what the girl did as long as she was happy. Was that any different from what Mother always wanted for her? Perhaps the difference was that Moira knew she had to maintain a future for herself.

'Urrrph'. Tess burped again and wiggled. Moira felt warm liquid filling the diaper and smiled to herself as she set Tess down on the changing table. How simple this part was. How easy to feed and burp and wash. She prayed she could keep up as the dance became more complex.

'Soup's on, Moi,' Teddy called from the foot of the stairs.

'I'll be right down,' Moira shouted over her shoulder as she placed Tess in the crib. She tucked in the pink and white blanket, which Teddy's Mom had knitted, and kissed Tess on the forehead. The child turned to the side and stared at the wall with a thin smile of satisfaction. Moira wondered how long Tess's sweet temperament would last. Everybody said two would be a terrible age. But then Tess might surprise her. Why was she always peering over the edge for pain? Why couldn't she simply accept the moment? Wasn't that what she was lecturing Vivian about this morning?

'Smells good.' Moira walked into the kitchen. 'And baked potato!'

Teddy kissed Moira on the cheek.

Moira collected her thoughts. 'Candles too. Must be a celebration.'

'Well.' Teddy spoke slowly, as she always did when she was trying to do one thing and talk about another. 'Hang on till I get this supper on the table and I'll tell you.'

Moira admired the steaming meatloaf, the salad, the potatoes oozing in oleomargarine and leaned back in her chair. It had been a tough day – that hard conversation with Vivian, the sweat of the plate shop, Tess's needs. Yes, she was going to enjoy this meal.

Teddy sat down with a plop. 'Ohhhh, long day, eh?'

Moira gave her a hand. Teddy kissed it and said, 'Well, the bond drive is a success. Mr Whitney called me in this afternoon and said we made 5,000 over the goal.'

'Terrific, honey.' Moira raised her water glass. 'A toast to the queen of the home front!'

Teddy clinked her glass and took a long gulp. Moira dug into the food, aware only after several moments that Teddy was neither eating nor drinking.

'Hey, pal, what's going on? Where are you? Supper's getting cold.'

'Yes.' Teddy smiled absently. 'You're right. It was just sort of a peculiar day at work.'

'What do you mean? Weren't you Miss Emporium?'

'That's sort of the problem.'

'What do you mean?' Moira set down her fork and observed her friend carefully.

'That wasn't all Mr Whitney said.'

Moira waited. Still, she wasn't used to Teddy's long silences. What to do while she waited to finish sentences? She had tried pointing out these lapses and this only flustered Teddy and made her speak more slowly. Sometimes Moira silently counted. Sometimes she recited poetry. Lately, she had avoided filling in the gaps because, when she did this, she was caught in her own thoughts by the time Teddy did get back to her sentence. Now she took a long drink of water.

'Well, he asked if I had a fellow.'

Moira choked.

Teddy stared, waiting for her friend to laugh.

Finally Moira did smile, 'Wha, what did you say?'

'I was too flabbergasted to be smart.' Teddy blushed. 'I just told him the truth. I said I didn't have a fellow.'

'Oh, no. Then what?'

'He invited me to the movies with him on Saturday.'

'Yes?'

'I told him the truth, that I had plans – remember Dawn and Sandra are coming to supper. And then my mind started to heat up, thinking of excuses to leave the office. But you know me, never fast enough. Mr Whitney comes over and puts his arm around my shoulder, real friendly like, and says, "Another time then?"'

'And?'

'Well, I decided to remain calm. I said, "Sure, I could bring along my friend Moira. We like going to the movies."'

'And he said?'

'You might have guessed. He said, "What does she look like? I

– 294 –

could find a date for her, too.'" Teddy grinned.

Moira giggled; then grew serious.

'Oh, Teddy, how can we laugh at this. It could mean trouble for you. You could even get fired. You might even wind up as Mrs Whitney.'

'Aw. Anyway, I thought up a good story for next time. I'll tell him I had a close friend who just died in the war. Now he's got to respect a girl's grief. I just wish I didn't have to lie. I just wish I could walk down Market Street with you hand in hand. All this deception – it's humiliating.'

'Yes,' Moira nodded. She stared at the back window, at the two spots of candle light shining against the blackness, like car head-lights funneling down a deserted road.

'But I do have some good news.' Teddy's eyes brightened as she pulled out an envelope. 'A thick letter from our friend in Arizona.'

She began to read.

> Dear Teddy and Moira,
>
> Thanks for the letters and packages. . . .
>
> The big story in camp is the government release, of course. It has only taken them three years to determine that we're not responsible for Pearl Harbor. Well, I shouldn't say too much in case I jinx it. We'll be on our way to California as soon as we settle things here.
>
> I got a letter from Roy last week which I'm still puzzling over. He says he's thinking about going to optometry school. Something about lenses of one sort being as good as lenses of another sort. Of course he thinks that there will be more financial security as an eye doctor than as a freelance photo-grapher. He feels loaded now with responsibilities to my family and to his own parents.
>
> Ann sounds like she's getting more serious about Reuben. What do you know about that? I wonder if she'll stay in London. . . .
>
> Thanks for the pictures of Tess. She's a doll. What I'd like now is some pictures of you two. God, I wonder how this war has transformed us all. . . .

Teddy finished reading the letter and closed her eyes. 'I can't believe she'll be coming home.'

'Now, don't get too excited.' Moira wanted to add that there was no telling what Wanda would consider home when she returned to San Francisco.

'Might as well hope,' sighed Teddy.

'So what's on for the rest of the evening?' asked Moira. 'Radio any good?'

Teddy moved her knee against Moira's. 'I was thinking we might retire. Might go to bed and see what we find there.'

'What a fine idea,' Moira smiled, taking her hand. 'We'll leave the dishes to the maid – or the morning – whichever comes first.'

After making love, Moira lay with her arms around Teddy's waist and her head on her shoulder. Funny, that they slept this way, Teddy often thought, since she was the bigger woman. But Moira rarely wanted to be held.

'You awake?' Teddy whispered.

'Yes.'

'I was thinking, but it wasn't important if you were falling asleep.'

'No, I'm awake, sweet, what's on your mind?'

'I was thinking about how I used to dream something like this. When I was little, I used to daydream about these two dolphins sleeping together in a cave under the Atlantic Ocean. And then when I was in high school and I had a crush on my math teacher, I used to imagine she would hold me, no falderal, only the holding.'

'Hmmm. Did you ever tell anyone?'

'Mom, once I told Mom.' Teddy's voice dropped.

'And what did your Mom say?' Moira felt a twinge of jealousy about Teddy's closeness to her mother.

'Not much,' Teddy said. 'I remember she was sewing at the time. She didn't look up from the mending, but her voice turned kind of funny. She said something like, "You'll probably grow outta that dear. But if I was you, in the meantime, I wouldn't go around telling folks."'

'What did you say?'

'Nothin. I stopped having those daydreams, although sometimes they stole into my mind at night. There was that warning in Mom's voice. I never did tell anyone either. Not until just now, not until you.'

Moira squeezed tighter. 'I love you, long one, you know that?'

'Yes.' Teddy sighed with a breath that moved through her whole body. 'I do know that.'

●

Chapter Twenty-Four

Winter 1944–5, Lion's Head

WARSAW LIBERATED

●

BURMA ROAD TO CHINA OPENED AGAIN

●

AUSCHWITZ LIBERATED

●

AMERICANS LAND ON IWO JIMA

It was too cold to sit outside, but Wanda leaned back on the bench and stared through the barbed wire to the mountains beyond. She had come here, as usual, for a good think and talk. Papa and Howard always provided good answers. If she needed a third opinion, she would consult Roy. Today she was filled with incredulity and exhaustion. The week before Christmas, three years after Pearl Harbor, and the Supreme Court decides in its infinite if tardy wisdom that it is a crime to detain loyal citizens against their wills. Who was going to pay for the crime? Who was going to resurrect Papa? Would they turn around and say that the war, itself, was a crime? Who would find Howard? Missing. Lost. Unaccounted for. Dead, she guessed he was dead. So did Mama, who now set flowers in front of his photograph too.

They could go any time. The United States was sorry to have detained them. They were free to go back. Back to what? Their farms and fishing boats had been sold from under them. Most people owned only what they could cram into their tiny cells here. They were free to return to California and start all over again as they had in 1910 or 1890 – three or four or five decades before. Not quite all over again.

What choices did she have? She could go now or later. Betty would hate leaving Mr Sasaki's lessons and her friends before the end of the school year. Mrs W. would be very disappointed to lose her. But Mama wanted to go as soon a possible. She ached to get to the coast, prepare for the journey to Japan and find the first ship leaving after the war. And Wanda? What did Wanda want?

Poking her stick in the cold ground, she thought about Ann's visit a year and a half ago. At that time, she might have known what she wanted. She would have been ready to leave this wilderness at the first opportunity. She thought about how she hungered after that college furlough Mrs Nakashima tried to arrange. How much she missed Stockton Street! How often she yearned to re-enter 'normal' life. But what was normal now? She couldn't live at Stockton Street because someone had to look after Mama and Betty. So returning to San Francisco without Papa and Howard, with Teddy and Moira and Ann, was like going to a strange land. Even living near Uncle Fumio's family would be strange, since they had been separated in different camps for three years. As mad as Mama's dreams of Japan were, Wanda understood her urge to control life. She understood the bitterness that made her want to leave this country for ever. But she doubted that she or Betty could ever become Japanese.

Her hands were red and chapped. She had become oblivious to the weather, finally withdrawing inside herself. The stifling heat of July and the frigidity of December were the same to her when she felt this numbness. After Papa's death, she had tried to stop feeling. She was surprised how much she felt for Roy, how much fear she experienced when he and Howard went away, how much anger she could muster against Mrs Wright, how much pain she felt about Howard's loss. Missing. Lacking. Absent. Astray. The day of that terrible telegram was the last occasion she had spent an hour feeling vulnerable. Since then, she squashed the slightest intimation of happiness or relief or sadness or regret. She had a hard time writing in her diary. What was the point? What was there to reflect upon? So the weather didn't faze her. She just made it through each day, teaching her class, tending to Mama, listening to Betty, waiting. Now that one of the things she had been waiting for was here, she was paralyzed. Maybe it would be better to finish the school year. Maybe it would be easier, then, for Betty, at least. Maybe Mama would change her mind about Japan once they were out. Wanda leaned forward on her stick and confronted the mountains, her eyes wide and her jaw set.

School was difficult to contain this afternoon. The kids were excited about the court decision. A quick civics lesson for reconstituted Americans. Mrs Wright had scheduled practice for the Christmas pageant and she could do nothing to cajole the students to concentrate on their lines. As Ricky and Bobby stumbled over the dialogue, two lost Wise Men, Mrs W. turned to Wanda.

'Wonderful news. You must be thrilled.'

Wanda nodded, somewhat surprised at Mrs W.'s enthusiasm and then abashed at her own surprise. Of course the woman wasn't evil, just a little dense at times.

'So many decisions for everyone,' Mrs Wright continued. 'I understand the children's excitement – about this. And then Christmas on top of it all. But the show must go on.'

Wanda nodded again. Theatres, she remembered, summoning the numbness.

'Ricky, Bobby.'

The boys recovered their lines from Betty, who worked behind the scenes on this production. She was saving her excitement for her own recital in February. Stanley, who Wanda thought looked more and more like his brother Roy since he got glasses, was practicing solemnity as St Joseph. Wanda ached to leave the classroom, to return to her spot by the fence, maybe to climb the fence, to lie down in the frozen desert. No, she pulled herself back.

Noticing Wanda's distraction, Mrs W. turned again, 'I hear that some families are leaving this week.'

'Yes.' Wanda wished she could fend off the next comment.

'I trust you will stay until the end of the school year – for Betty's sake, well, to be truthful, for all our sakes.'

'I don't know what will happen. It's been so long since we've had any choices.'

'I can appreciate your acrimony.' Mrs W. kept one eye on Ricky and Bobby.

Acrimony, Wanda pondered. If Mrs W. thought this was acrimony, she should know what Wanda had felt at other times.

Maybe the teacher could see it all. Maybe her numbness was so deep only she, herself, experienced it.

'The news is quite sudden. And the decision involves conflicts.'

'Ah, yes, does your mother still want to repatriate?'

'Possibly,' Wanda answered quietly. Had Mrs W. heard the plan from Betty?

'You told me some time ago,' Mrs Wright reminded her. 'The first day we met, I believe.'

Wanda turned her attention to a fracas in the corner. The children settled down.

'Wanda, I'd like to take you to lunch. I've always been reluctant to impose on your time, on your family obligations. Still, I would appreciate the opportunity to talk before you make a firm decision about leaving.'

'Of course,' said Wanda, conscious of the distance in her voice. 'How about after the holidays?'

'Good.' Mrs W. patted her hand.

Wanda compared the textures and colors of their skin. Mrs W.'s wrinkles and veins webbed together in a weathered pattern of experience. Her own hand was rough, but comparatively unlined. And the color was indistinguishable, both of them darkened by the desert to a light brown. Wanda thought of that man on the streetcar who scowled and moved away from herself and Roy on Pearl Harbor morning. Yellow peril. The desert had taken even her color.

Wanda sat a second longer, claiming her place, contemplating how alone she felt. Alone with Mama, with Betty, with Mrs W. She was a different person to each of them, responsible for important things. Who were her real friends? Carolyn, yes. But since the news about Howard, she was more a person to be taken care of. Two people to be taken care of now that she was pregnant. She longed to talk with Moira and Teddy. Now that the possibility was closer, that she might be in San Francisco within a few months, she didn't know if she could talk. She was out of practice. Correspondence was such a different form of communication. You orchestrated letters. No one looked back at you and said, 'Really?' or 'Tell me more'. It was just you and the letter.

February 1945

Wanda sat in the large, darkened room, holding Mama's hand. Together with everyone else in the audience, they waited for Betty to walk out on stage. Wanda could hardly believe this was the long-awaited February recital, so much had occurred in the past few months. Mama sat perfectly still, save for a slight fidgeting in her left hand, and her nervousness was unapparent to anyone except Wanda. This was the first time Mama had heard Betty play. She had refused all invitations to rehearsal, but Papa would have wanted her to attend the public performance. Wanda sat erect on the hard folding chair and tried to calm Mama with her own charade of serenity. Mama continued to fidget. She was eager to be free of this place, Wanda knew. Only three more weeks and they would be gone. This compromise had worked out best for all of them. Betty wanted to stay until the recital. Mrs W. had begged Wanda to wait until she could train another aide. Mama, herself, admitted that it would take time to arrange for a place in San Francisco and to pack.

A spotlight scanned the stage and, after a long pause, Betty walked toward the piano.

Wanda studied the pretty, poised girl and thought how much her sister had grown these last three years. She had come to camp as a shy, eight year old and now she was verging on an almost sophisticated adolescence. Bless Mr Sasaki. Betty would miss him. But Carolyn said she and her father would be coming West after the baby was born. It was just a matter of months. Oh, this moving was almost as painful as the evacuation from San Francisco. They had made close friends here. Wanda regarded her sister critically, as if she were a stranger. What a vibrant one, this Betty, who had taken to calling herself Lisa. She caught your heart with the joy of her movement. She was the kind of young woman who made you sit back in anticipation of gifts.

Wanda recalled a moment earlier this evening as they dressed together, the two of them standing before the mirror, giggling as they primped. Betty asked to borrow Wanda's rouge. Although the girl hardly needed it, Wanda handed her a small glass pot. As Betty applied red dabs to her cheekbones, Wanda thought about her own growing up. She remembered the thrill of being elected to Girls' League; her pride in the high school 'Nisei of Promise Award'; the fun of parties on Stockton Street. Betty was on the verge, full of potential energy. Wanda hoped that her sister could maintain this momentum.

Betty bowed gracefully before the crowd. Wanda turned to find Mama's eyes closed. Was she crying with sentimentality or was she still angry about her daughter playing *Hakujin* music? Was she thinking about Papa? Betty surveyed the crowd. Wanda's face grew more animated and she managed a discreet wink at her sister.

Chopin étude, Beethoven sonata, Liszt waltz: Wanda knew the program by heart. Betty had agonized over and over about which pieces to play in which order. At first Wanda couldn't concentrate because of the moving plans. Then she was distracted by everyone around her. The Watanabes off to the left. Mrs Nakashima sitting in the front row. Carolyn smiling brightly from the far edge of the room. Wanda took a deep breath and tried to enter the music. But she was fighting, resisting. It was beyond her. She didn't know how to appreciate it. Were you supposed to imagine a world painted by chords? Or did the notes fit together in a system you were meant to understand like mathematics? For several claustrophobic moments, Wanda imagined she would never fathom the music. When she had asked to learn the piano as a child, Mama had said it was too expensive. Of course Betty hadn't had to pay for lessons. And would she choose Betty's childhood here over her own youth?

The Beethoven was arresting and she felt Mama sit up. Wanda looked over and saw tears edging down her mother's cheeks. She took the old woman's hand in hers. Old, she was very old if you measured age by hardships. Wanda felt no response in Mama's hand, neither resistance nor acceptance. Since the telegram, only talk about Yokohama would revive her. Everyone tried to dissuade her now, saying the country would be ripped to shreds. Wanda also protested that there was no money for travel, that the conditions would be unbearable. She didn't want Mama to endure yet another defeat in Japan. She held on to the hand as if it were a rock that might come alive.

The stifled cough behind obviously came from Mrs Wright.

Wanda didn't need to – or want to – look around. It had been hard to think about Mrs Wright since their special lunch in January.

She had insisted on taking Wanda to town, to a small Italian restaurant where they ate too much minestrone and pasta. Finally, over tea, they got beyond the stiff exchanges about their favorite students.

'Have you decided about whether you can stay to the end of term?' Mrs W. bit her lip and stared over Wanda's shoulder.

Wanda shook her head. Actually, she and Mama and Betty had

decided the previous night that they would leave in February. But the war had taught them not to anticipate.

'Good.' The older woman's voice was softer now, and calmer. 'As you know I was hoping you would finish the term.'

Wanda nodded again. She observed this Japanese gesture – nodding gently with Caucasian people – and considered how she had acquired it at Lion's Head. Was she being obsequious or just maintaining her distance? Would she still do this on the outside? With Teddy, Moira and Ann?

'I have a proposal, well, nothing so grand, a suggestion, perhaps.'

'Yes?' Wanda listened politely. Why did she feel trapped? OK, so she was a chore to work for – fussy, erratic, old fashioned and formal – but these were not capital crimes. She was a kind, moral woman.

'I have taken the liberty of writing about you to my friend Robert Gorman, President of Salway College in Illinois.'

Wanda felt her insides clench.

'He has managed to arrange a full scholarship beginning next fall – that is. . . .'

Stunned, Wanda fixed her eyes on the checkered tablecloth. At first she felt flabbergasted at Mrs W.'s arrogance in organizing her life.

The teacher studied Wanda's tight jaw. 'That is, if you are still interested in college. It has quite a good journalism program.'

Wanda was touched by the generous concern.

Mrs Wright looked at the young woman carefully. 'That is if you are still thinking about writing as a career. Quite frankly, I think you'd make a grand teacher.'

Suddenly Wanda felt faint at the possibility of living near Mrs W. in Illinois.

'This is terribly kind of you.' Wanda cleared her throat. 'However I have responsibilities. Who would support my mother and Betty?'

'Surely, you weren't expecting to do that on your own?'

'No, my family, my uncles will contribute. And among all of us, we will manage.'

'But couldn't they do that without you? Don't you have a right to your own life?'

Wanda found herself growing furious as Mrs W. raised her own doubts and resentments. She traced the red squares on the tablecloth with her thumb.

'Well, could your mother come to Illinois? People there will be friendlier than in California. I'm sure we could find a grant for Betty at a good school. And the three of you would be welcome to live with me while you look for a place. There's plenty of room until Howard comes back, even after that.'

'Our home is in San Francisco.' Wanda held her voice calm.

'Yes, I understand you were raised in California. But there will be even more hostility to the Japanese there than in the past. Times have changed.'

'We hope to change the times.' Wanda was struck by her own forcefulness.

'Of course.' Mrs W. sighed. 'I thought you might respond like this. Well, if there's anything I can ever do to help. A letter of recommendation. A loan. Anything.' She coughed. 'Anything.'

Since the luncheon, it had been hard for Wanda to teach. The classroom lines had become unravelled. She would look up at the older woman and see through her discipline and control. Often Wanda thought she had liked the class better before.

Betty was embarking on the Liszt. Wanda relaxed. She would be fine now that she had made it through the hard pieces. Glancing at Mr Sasaki, she saw the old man smiling. Mama's hand had warmed up, or was she imagining it? Wanda shifted to find Mama's eyes were wide open, as if puzzling about the source of the music.

After Betty's performance, two more children played. Wanda tried not to be restless, but the chair was uncomfortable and she was desperate for some fresh air, even if it would freeze her lungs with the first catch. Soon enough it was over. She found herself standing beside her mother who was being congratulated by Mrs Nakashima and Mrs Watanabe.

Wanda searched the crowd for Betty and spotted her standing with a group of adults next to the stage – Mr Sasaki, Carolyn and a strange Caucasian man. As she turned to Mama, Wanda watched Mrs W. approach. Mrs Nakashima and Mrs Watanabe moved on.

'Mrs Nakatani?' The teacher spoke precisely since this was the first time she had ever talked directly with Mrs Nakatani.

'Yes.' Mama bowed, expressing the slimmest courtesy.

'I wanted to congratulate you on your two accomplished daughters. I have had the pleasure of teaching with Wanda as you know, and find her to be a highly intelligent, talented young woman. It's also been enjoyable to have young Betty in class. She's a bright, lively child, who obviously has a musical gift.'

Wanda clutched her hands behind her back, mortified for both women.

'Thank you for my daughters.' Mrs Nakatani barely spoke above a whisper.

Wanda regarded Mrs Wright with a mixture of sympathy and revenge. Finally someone who could make her mute. Leave it to Mama. The two older women watched each other closely. Wanda felt a surprising protectiveness for them both. Betty joined them, beaming, but she soon lost her radiance.

The Caucasian stranger joined their silent quartet. 'Hello again, young miss,' he nodded to Betty. 'I did admire your performance.'

'Thank you,' Betty grinned.

'And you must be the lucky mother.' He offered his hand.

Mrs Nakatani nodded.

Wanda smiled courteously and then wondered why she always felt she had to smooth things over.

Responding to the one cordial person, he said to Wanda, 'An older sister, perhaps?'

'You're talking to one of the best teachers in the country.' Mrs W. came to life. 'Wanda has worked with me all year and made a great contribution. By the way, my name is Adelaide Wright, and yours is?'

'Gardner, Hubert Gardner. Excuse me. I am a friend of Walter Knockman, the postmaster. Passing through on my way back from a concert in New York.'

Betty's face lit up.

'Walter told me you had a little virtuoso here. He was right. I presumed to intrude just now because I have a music school in San Francisco and I wanted to invite you, my dear,' he addressed Betty, 'to come and audition for me, if you wind up returning to the Bay Area.'

Betty beamed at Wanda.

Mrs Nakatani spoke first, surprising everyone. 'Thank you for our daughter. But we will not stay in San Francisco long.'

'I see.' He turned more sober.

Betty looked at Wanda beseechingly. Wanda was dumbfounded by Mama's outburst.

Again Mrs W. appropriated the silence. 'And where will you be going after San Francisco?' She inched closer to Mrs Nakatani as if to hear better, almost shutting Mr Gardner out of the circle.

Mrs Nakatani weighed the value of response. Finally, she looked past the teacher, across the room, and addressing the piano on the darkened stage, she said, 'My family returns to Yokohama soon.'

Mrs W. coughed. Mr Gardner smiled with nervous concern.

Betty began, 'Oh, Mother,' then looked at Wanda's shaking head and closed her mouth.

Mrs Nakatani, who had been virtually cloistered for three years, seemed to be enjoying her début. She looked around, taking in everyone's separate response. 'Thank you, Mr Gardner.'

Wanda stepped back, breathless from Mama's determination. She thought of times her parents would argue in Japanese in the kitchen. Mama might have gone through a long mourning, but she hadn't lost her voice. It was just a pity she had to make her appearance on the same night as Betty. Perhaps Mama was warning the child not to get carried away. Wanda would have a long talk with Betty tonight. Oh, she yearned for Papa and Howard. She considered Roy and shut her eyes. If he were still alive, that meant he could still die.

The next afternoon, Wanda found herself writing to Moira and Teddy,

Dear Friends,

We're coming back to San Francisco, for a time anyway. I still haven't been able to talk Mama out of Japan. But once she discovers the situation over there, once she realizes the hardship she'll have to change her mind. We haven't heard from Aunt Yuni for months. That may well turn fate. Oh, this is so hard. I feel responsible for Mama and Betty and they want/ need such different things. Will Mama survive if we don't go to Japan? Will Betty if we do? Before the war, I never appreciated how interconnected lives could be.

How is everything with Tess? I still can't believe you're a mother, Moi. (Carolyn is due in two months and then I'll be an aunt). When I think of mothers, I think of our mothers. And for my part, I don't feel ready yet. How on earth are you managing to work at the shipyard and take care of Tess at the same time?

And you, Teddy, as I said in the card, I was so very sorry to hear about your father's death. I know it was a terrible blow. In some senses he was a casualty of the war. Both our fathers died because of pressures, because there seemed no point in living through this madness. Both of them killed themselves in different ways. I hope you don't mind my going on like this, but I've been thinking about suicide a lot lately. It seems there are many ways of committing suicide. Fast like Papa, slow with alcohol like your Pop, and morally by giving up, by passing the days rather than living them, the way so many of us are tempted to go. Occasionally I do wish I were dead. It's so hard holding it all together. Now, don't get anxious that I'll do anything rash. But I sometimes live without any hope for days at a time. There are many decisions and all of them feel equally terrible. So I just accept despair. I know this isn't right. I look at Carolyn who keeps hoping about Howard. She's full of good projects.

And Ann – certainly she's faced impossibilities in London, yet she's plugging along. It was only three years ago that we were all dancing around the living room. And now look at us – so scattered. What will it be like when we meet again? Will we recognize each other? Teddy, I'm just kidding; don't panic. I'm sure we'll be friends for ever. But it will take time to see how the war has changed us.

Wanda set down her pen. No, this wasn't helping. It was making her more confused. She would simply have to find a peace in herself.

She watched Mama folding linen in the big trunk they had bought from Mr Omi. Mama enjoyed this packing ritual. Even though they weren't leaving for weeks, she sorted out some of her things each day. Betty sat in the corner reading or brooding; it was hard to tell. She had caught Mama's silence. The two of them had hardly spoken since the concert. Wanda had tried to mediate, but for the last couple of days she filled the silence with her own thoughts. Today, she felt stifled, unable to sit any longer under the wordless pressures in these rooms.

'I'm going for a walk,' she said to both of them. 'Anyone want to come?' They both shook their heads and she was relieved.

Strolling across camp, Wanda considered the changes that had occurred since the court decision. People knew they were going home – whatever that meant – and they no longer pretended about Lion's Head. For many this had always been an imaginary land which they fantasized into home with their small gardens and community activities. But now the gardens were wilting. Repairs were ignored. Furniture was being traded and sold. Lion's Head was assuming the air of a transient camp as the long hidden pain seeped out. Wanda found the dissolution depressing. The Hatas' porch was piled with suitcases and boxes. Wanda could feel tears welling inside her lids. She would miss the people here. She might never see them again. Funny, while she hadn't felt particularly Japanese before the camp, she now wondered how she would function in the white world. Well, she was dreaming if she thought she would go straight back to the middle of *Hakujin* territory. What with fires in the San Joaquin Valley and lynchings of those who went back to reclaim their land in Washington State, she knew she would live in a close Japanese neighborhood in San Francisco. Uncle Fumio had promised to find them a place. Then, of course, there were Mama's plans.

'Wanda, Wanda.' A voice trailed on the back of a strong wind. She turned to find Carolyn, hurrying after her with something in her hand.

'Hi, Carolyn, aren't you still at work?'

'Yes, I was just picking up in the lobby when I saw you.' She waved the envelope. 'But no one's been by to check your post today and I thought you'd want to know you got a letter from a certain party.'

Wanda inspected the envelope. It had been taken back to the States by Roy's friend Sam, if she were interpreting the return address correctly, and mailed in Arkansas.

Wanda stared at her. It had been ages. She had relegated the job of going to the post office to Betty.

'Well, girl, let's see how he is,' encouraged Carolyn.

Wanda looked at Carolyn, whose persistence was quite out of character. Carolyn must have sensed something. She was like Teddy in the way she perceived things before they happened. Wanda leaned against the wall of the mess hall and opened the letter. She didn't want to go home just now and she didn't want to be alone, in case, she didn't know, just in case. Her tears came with the first sentence. It was about Howard. Carolyn moved closer.

'Howard's death.' There it was in Roy's handwriting. Well, she had to find out sooner or later. Better this way than from the man in the Western Union truck. But why hadn't the government informed them? She turned to Carolyn.

'He's gone, Carolyn.'

'I know.' She stared at the letter as if it would keep her breathing. 'Does he say how?' she asked in a monotone.

Wanda looked up gratefully. 'Feel like a walk? Can you leave work now?'

'Yes, let me get my coat.'

Wanda watched Carolyn walk slowly back towards her, her coat barely buttoned across her huge belly.

They travelled to the far end of camp without talking. Since Roy and Howard left, Carolyn had often joined Wanda on the log. But she always waited to be invited.

'You want to read it?' Wanda offered.

'No, it's your letter.'

Wanda nodded, considering once again who was hurt more by Howard's death. You simply couldn't compare her history of growing up with Howard to Carolyn's future with him. Wanda wept and began.

Dear Wanda,

You will have heard about Howard's death by now. I wish I could be there to hold you and to comfort you and Carolyn and Betty and your mother. The next best thing, perhaps, is for me to tell you what I know and to promise that I'll be there soon to console you.

Howard was with a small platoon scouting the town before the rest of us moved in. We were told that the Jerries had left three days before by good local sources, who were grateful to have the Americans. Howard volunteered for duty because he had been down with fever several weeks before and felt he hadn't seen his share of action. Actually, during this period, part of the unit was lost for a while. And we heard some MIA telegrams were sent home. Typical army foul-up. Anyway, Howard went to town with several others. The story I got back was that he saw a Jerry pulling a gun from a window on one of our men and walked out from the wall to shoot. Then Howard was hit in the back from the west end of town. No one knows how the Germans still had men in the west end. As I said, they were supposed to be gone altogether days before. Well, our men got the German Howard was firing at and several others in the building. When they scoured the west end, they couldn't find anyone.

At first it looked like Howard might survive. He's a tough one. I still have a hard time using the past tense. Anyway, they brought him back to headquarters and operated. They got out one bullet and he was conscious for several hours. He talked about you a lot. 'Take care of Wanda,' he said. I told him I'd do that and he persisted. 'She needs you.' I kept telling him that he was going to be OK, but he knew he wasn't. He lost a lot of blood while they were bringing him back and then he lost more on the operating table. At one point he turned to me and said I should make sure you got to college. 'I'm sorry I took that away from her.' He was always talking about that part, Wan, about how you should have gone to college like Mrs Nakashima wanted.

Tell your mother and Betty he kept asking for them. I'll write to your Mama. He said he would think about all of you living back in San Francisco. He said to write to Carolyn, so I plan to send her a letter too. He loved her a lot as I'm sure you know.

Wanda put down the letter and wrapped her arms around Carolyn. The two women held on to each other, facing the cold mountains. Frozen earth stretched bare and grey to the base of the brutal peaks. Carolyn sniffed back her tears. Wanda stared, too tired and too empty to cry. She picked up the letter and continued reading aloud.

We had a ceremony on the hillside of this pretty town and sang some songs he liked. I guess they've notified you about all the official details. It was so terribly sad, Wan.

After that, we made our way up through Italy. I think this war will be over in the spring; the Nazis are falling apart. And believe me, I'm catching the first ship home. Well, there's a lot more I could say, but I think this is enough for one letter. We'll let this be Howard's good-bye. Remember I love you, Roy.

Carolyn took Wanda's hand. Their faces on the mountain, each woman wept.

'It's a good letter,' Carolyn said finally. 'So like Howard, right to the end.'

Wanda nodded, then buried her head in her friend's shoulder and sobbed.

The last morning was unbearably long. Mama had finished packing days before. Wanda had said good-bye to all the neighbors. But they had to wait for the Watanabes to return from town with some rope and one extra suitcase. It had taken some convincing to get Mama to drive with the Watanabes rather than to take the train. But it made more sense, since they had a station wagon and trailer and since the train was so expensive. At the back of Wanda's mind was that the Watanabes might talk Mama out of Japan. Maybe when she heard about their plans for settling in Napa, Mama would think about other possibilities. No one had been able to get through to her in camp because she walked away from conversations, but she would be stuck in the station wagon for four days.

Wanda couldn't stand their empty room, so she went for a walk to say farewell to the mountains. A surprise snow storm the previous week had left the peaks glazed in white. It was too cold to sit on the bench; she must be losing the numbness. She paced back and forth, in front of the fence, thinking about her visits here with Roy; the time Howard told her he was going to enlist; the visit from Ann; the talks with Carolyn. She knew she would remember this place more than anywhere in camp. She wished she had a photograph of herself here, but she would have had to have someone else take the picture and she wasn't willing to relinquish this solitude today even for that. So she took one last look and said aloud, 'Farewell mountains'.

When she returned to the barracks, Betty told her that the Watanabes would arrive in ten minutes and they should be set to go. Mama was counting the packages. Betty lugged them outside. Suddenly Wanda thought she might not be able to leave. She needed a cup of tea. Just one cup of tea. She needed to sit down and inhale the steam and ruminate for just 5 minutes. For the first time in weeks, she thought of her diary.

The horn was honking. Mr Watanabe was admonishing her to be happy. She kept thinking about how paralyzed she had felt the day they had moved in, just the four of them, carrying duffel bags, Papa dead in San Francisco. Who would have guessed that on leaving there would be only three remaining in the family? She reviewed the changes of the last three years – Howard's death, Roy's absence, Betty's blossoming, Mama's rage, her own callousness. How had she survived the loneliness, the responsibilities and the rattlesnakes? How much of her was left? Well, this was not the moment for personal reckoning. Betty called her. She carried a suitcase to the relay line – passing it to Betty, who passed it to Stanley, who passed it to Mr Watanabe, who placed it in the trailer behind the station wagon.

Once they were settled in the car, Mr and Mrs Watanabe and Mama in the front, herself and Betty and Stanley in the seat behind, Wanda peered out for her last glimpse of Lion's Head. Carolyn stood in front of the post office, waving. Then, as they headed down toward the gate, there was a line of people: Mrs Nakashima, Mr Hata, Mr Sasaki, Mr Omi and Mrs Wright – all waving.

Wanda recalled that damp spring morning in 1942 when Moira, Ann and Teddy came to the bus. She smiled at the image of Teddy lumbering down the aisle with gardenias. Dear Teddy. Teddy had travelled across the Southwest like this; she had gone much further in that truck packed with twelve people. Teddy. She would be seeing Teddy and Moira in less than a week. She was leaving Lion's Head and going home. Wanda reached for Betty's hand and kept her eyes wide as they passed out the gate.

•

Chapter Twenty-Five

Winter 1945, London

JAPANESE SURRENDER ON CORREGIDOR

•

FINLAND DECLARES WAR ON GERMANY

•

TITO BECOMES PRESIDENT OF YUGOSLAVIA

Ann walked meditatively through the park on her way to the tube. Most people stayed away from the park until the morning grey lifted, thus she could pretend this was her own estate. Of course, there were two men sitting on the far bench who still thought it was public territory. And there was that sad fellow lying near the entrance, bundled in his coat and hugging an empty green bottle. She was surprised when she saw people who looked more down and out than everyone else. This was one response to the turmoil, to let it pass you by.

Mrs Goldman said Leah had stayed in bed all week. There was no fever or vomiting. Nothing but a general listlessness. Ann wished now she hadn't promised to visit. Probably it would just make Leah worse. Why couldn't the child see that she was in the best place. Why did Leah keep insisting on being with her? Well, Ann had promised herself not to think about it until this evening.

She loved the hardiness of the park, despite the dreary weather, despite the endless war. This resilient green reminded her of the patched elbows on men's sweaters and the madeover dresses Esther and Sheila wore. On certain days, Ann felt as if she had no personal life; she simply lived for the news over the wireless about fighting on the Continent and the speeches in Parliament. And yet at other times she existed as if only the basics mattered – going to work, shopping for supper, drinking with friends.

Even on these mundane days she knew the war had burrowed deeply into British life. All women between eighteen and sixty were conscripted for the services, for nursing, factory work or other vital jobs. People donated their cooking pots for aeroplane aluminum. Signs in the butcher's shop read, 'Have You Registered For Meat?' It felt like an army of citizens, more dedicated than organized. Certainly there were rations and patriotic sacrifices in the States, but the war wore closer to the bone here. The bombings brought death, injury, damage. Churchill, himself, was much more of a warrior than Roosevelt. She often wondered how the man had suffered through Chamberlain's appeasement policy.

Ann breathed easier now. The further she moved into the park, away from the traffic exhaust, the more pensive she became. Perhaps it was because the oxygen was getting to her brain? While she felt involved in the war effort, she was continually reminded that she wasn't British. First, there was the language: lift, petrol, biscuit, barrister, wellingtons, spanners. Then her accent. Still, she was amazed when Londoners didn't understand her, for she spoke so clearly and slowly in comparison to them. Often she was grateful that she wasn't born here for she knew her class origins would exclude her from many circles. But as an American she was part of an international set which flowed in and out of various scenes. If she were to stay, would she lose that fluidity? Would she become British? She thought Reuben could make a more successful conversion than she.

Ann knew she could always count on the serenity of the pond, even this early in the morning. She thought about Wanda's letter reporting Howard's death. The Europeans who were so smug about Americans being unscathed by the war should meet Wanda and her family. God knew why it was Howard and not Daniel. They couldn't have been stationed that far apart. She had even written to Daniel suggesting the two boys try to meet. Why was it so important that all the pieces in her life fit together? Clearly she was losing rein on that. Everything was changing. Look at Moira, full of joy about baby Tess. Good for her. That kind of optimism counted for a lot when the world around you was falling apart.

There were four ducks today. Two stayed in the pond; two circled overhead and landed on the water. Where had the swans gone? Ann admired their alabaster certainty. She remembered how Moira used to tease her about being as aloof as a swan and now she had to wonder about her own arrogant presence around the house. So many questions crystalized now that she was leagues away from San Francisco. How much she wanted to return to Stockton Street, just for an evening.

She missed Moira's energy and Teddy's laconic good will and Wanda's political insights. She missed the fresh vegetables from their garden. She missed the sun. The stupid radio programs – even Jack Benny. The sense of possibility. Oh, the British were inspiring in their endurance. But they would call her American belief in progress quaint. Ann realized that this was more than another patch of homesickness. How could she convey the depth of this feeling to Reuben? If she were to stay in this country, she would always be alien. When she had first moved here she had revelled in the sophistication of the people, the historical buildings, the international references, the proximity of Culture. She thought she had grown up. Now she understood she had simply moved.

Ann pulled her hat over her ears and walked down the hill as fast as her straight, wool skirt would permit.

That evening, as she hurried to the train, Ann heard a distant air raid siren. She had got to the point that she knew where the bombs were falling, almost to the street. The sirens bothered her more than the explosions, with their eerie whining before and after attack. What was the sound? Melancholy, fear, resignation, resistance, outrage. Wolves howling in the bush. Women wailing in the kitchen.

Ann never worried about being hit. She knew people who had died. She had friends who had been badly hurt, who had lost their homes. But she felt immune. It wasn't rational, she understood this.

Once on the train, she prepared herself to be cool and professional with Leah. She would show her kindness through the book she brought and that was all. She would not fall for those big, brown eyes. She was going to reassure Mrs Goldman that the girl would be all right.

Mrs Goldman had prepared a generous meal. Sarah graciously helped her serve. Leah stayed in her room and Ann kept her resolve to attend to Mrs Goldman first. She would ignore the girl's sulking.

'Delicious,' Ann said. 'You're a splendid cook.'

'I worry about her appetite.' The plain, middle-aged woman spoke softly. 'She's a wee one.'

Ann looked at the fresh cake. 'She'll perk up. With such temptation, how can she do otherwise?'

'She does what she pleases,' said Sarah. 'Mum has tried everything. She doesn't care.'

'That's enough, Sarah, run along now dear.'

The girl walked out with dignity, turning at the door and casting a critical eye at Ann.

'She's very loyal to you.' Ann smiled.

'A lovely child,' Mrs Goldman nodded. 'Must have had – or have – a wonderful mother in Germany.'

Ann agreed, lost for a moment in the thought of Uncle Aaron's kids. She had never found out anything about her cousins. Could Sarah be her cousin? She was probably a little young.

'Leah is also a lovely child,' Mrs Goldman persisted. 'I'm just not sure this is the right home for her.'

'Are you asking us to take her back?'

'I cherish the girl. It's not me who's doing the asking.'

'We'll see.' Ann summoned Esther's confidence. 'She just needs time.' She changed the topic to practical matters of school and clothing rations and the two women managed to fill half an hour without mentioning Leah's 'condition' again.

'Perhaps I should say hello to Leah now,' Ann said, hoping she masked her anxiety.

'Right, this way.' Mrs Goldman led her to the back bedroom. Knocking on Leah's door, she called out, 'Visitor, luv, someone to see Leah.'

The door opened. Leah stood wrapped in a grey blanket. Ann looked at Mrs Goldman, who raised her eyebrows and ushered Ann into the room. Then she shut the door behind her.

It took all Ann's willpower not to open her arms to the child. She reached into her bag for the book she had brought. 'Hello, Leah. A present. From me . . . and Esther.'

Leah looked at Ann as though she were being presented with a dead mouse.

'How are you doing, Leah?'

Leah returned to the bed and pulled the covers around her. Ann noticed what a cheerful room it was, with a big window overlooking the garden, just as Mrs Goldman had promised. Ann waited several minutes for Leah's response.

Then she tried, 'It's a pretty room, dear.'

Leah stared at her in disbelief.

'Are you getting along with Sarah?'

Again Ann waited, leaning now against the bureau. Leah continued her silent reproach.

Ann was furious. Furious at the world forcing Leah to shuttle German and English and American mothers. Furious at herself for being so vulnerable. Furious at Leah for being so strong. She could think of nothing to say. So she turned and put the book on Leah's bureau. 'Good-bye then, Leah.'

She reached for the door and was split in two by the sound from behind her, a high-pitched wail.

Ann turned back toward Leah with a fearful admiration.

Ann sat in the chilly classroom, at the back near the door, because she didn't want to be conspicuous as she tried to catch up. She hadn't done this week's assignment because of the flu and the extra load at work. Were Virgil's *Eclogues* worth the effort? What was she doing studying Latin in the middle of a war? What good could this possibly do anyone? Ann stretched her neck, aware of an incipient migraine. Since she arrived in London, the headaches had diminished.

Professor Warwick was a small, white-haired man who looked as if he might have campaigned with Caesar himself. He had a fine Roman nose and aristocratic brows and, behind the stern veneer, a great store of kindness. It was kind of him to allow her to audit the course. Kind of him to see her before class because she couldn't come during the day. She felt remorseful tonight about being behind. Remorseful about school. Remorseful about work. She should be in the office now, finishing the new files. What use was it sitting in this cranky old room listening to Virgil's poetry?

Whose flock is that, Damoetas? Tell me, are these Meliboeus'
  sheep?
No, they are Aegon's. Aegon has just left me in charge of them.

Her last few days had been filled with questions about Leah and work and Papa and Reuben and now about this course. She hated the painful scrutiny.

Ann turned the page, consciously returning to the class. Yes, she followed these lines.

> Poor sheep, unlucky all the time! Aegon runs off to keep Neara warm, fearing she may prefer me to himself, while here a hireling shepherd milks his ewes every half hour, till the whole flock is dry and the lambs left without a drop.

She wasn't far behind. Ann looked around the room, appreciating the eclectic class: the young bank clerk in her starched white blouse; the middle-aged woman slumped behind her parcels; the thin, quiet, red-haired fellow who rarely spoke but who always seemed ahead of everyone. Yes, Latin appealed to a variety of people. Perhaps Professor Warwick was the attraction. Clearly he delighted in transporting his audiences through the centuries. She would like to do this one day. She imagined being in front of a younger group of students – exploring the psychological, spiritual and emotional textures of these poems. When she returned to San Francisco.

Ann felt a draught and pulled the coat around her. Teddy had been right about the value of a good wool coat. Only English rooms could be stuffy and chilly at once. Professor Warwick glanced in her direction. He seemed to be inquiring if she were taking care of herself, scolding her for sitting so near the door. That was a peculiar aspect of English personality – although they treated you formally at first, once they had got used to you they became overly solicitous. She smiled to reassure him, but by this time he had re-entered the *Eclogues*.

Teddy's letter was stuck in between the next two pages and as much as Ann tried to concentrate on Virgil, her mind wandered back to Stockton Street. Teddy sounded like she was running around with her head cut off, with her family and the Emporium. They were all overdoing it – Moira and Wanda too – but Teddy was stretched the thinnest. Nice to hear she had grown closer to Sandra and Dawn. Had she changed this year? Of course, they all had. They all changed in the sense of growing up: that didn't mean they were different people.

Oh, she would love to return to the slow Friday evenings and the lazy Saturday mornings, even to another dinner with the parents. Teddy always wrote encouraging her to come back, when she wanted. If they had another room-mate, they would tell the girl she could stay only until Ann's return. What would be waiting besides the room? Was Moira that much tougher from the shipyard? Would Leah and Tess get along? Leah, she had to stop thinking about her. Would Wanda be too bitter to return? How would they all feel about Reuben? No, she didn't want to think about him either. She wanted to. . . .

Chairs screeched across the wooden floor and Ann glanced up to find class over. She didn't dare look at Professor Warwick who knew, no doubt, that she had spent the evening far from Meliboeus' sheep. Carefully she collected her papers, as if they were her wits – slowly, neatly – and resolved to be better prepared the following week.

The next trip to Penge was less leisurely. Mrs Goldman had phoned, desperate about Leah not eating. On the train Ann's thoughts splintered into images of the Dachau victims and of Simone Weil starving herself in sympathy with the French people. Of course Leah was too young to understand any of that. Of course she was just being stubborn. Everything would be all right.

The train seemed impossibly slow. Ann tried to re-read a letter from Wanda. Then she started to write back. Then she put the pad in her bag and stared out the train window. How foolish to think she was immune.

Mrs Goldman let her into Leah's room and quietly exited.

Leah lay in the bed, her eyes closed, with none of the defiance of the previous month. Ann approached the bed cautiously, thinking she was crazy; she hardly knew this child, she had a life of her own. No, she reminded herself, this was not Mama; this was a stranger, a little girl who had a mother in Germany and another mother right here in England. Then Leah opened her eyes.

Ann expected anger, bitterness, demand.

Instead, the child smiled.

'All right,' Ann said. 'I'll ask if you can come home with me.'

●

Chapter Twenty-Six

Mid-winter 1945, San Francisco

AMERICANS TAKE MANILA

●

DRESDEN FIREBOMBED

●

SYRIA DECLARES WAR ON AXIS

Teddy stood on the front step, shaking out her black umbrella as Moira opened the door and bustled inside to claim Tess from the babysitter. Rainy Saturday, perfect time for a funeral. Teddy glanced at the Minellis' house. Hard to believe they were both gone now. She would miss seeing Mr Minelli thumping down the street with his cane. Of course she knew he wouldn't last long after Mrs Minelli went. What was it – ten months and he was gone. Mr Minelli had become a daily presence in their lives since his wife died. The Minellis had been good neighbors during the past six years. Lord, had it been six years since they had moved in? Teddy watched the water running in a small stream along the sidewalk. The street was slick and she could hear a screech of brakes from around the corner.

'Hey, Teddy, you gonna stand out there all day, heating up the sidewalk?' Moira called.

'Sorry.' Teddy hurried into the house, surprised by Moira's edge. She was probably just upset from the funeral. Teddy stood with one hand on the radio. The announcer was talking about the Marines on Iwo Jima. But Moira wasn't listening. She was paying the baby-sitter and twisting the lace collar off her black dress.

'How about some hot chocolate?' Teddy asked. 'Wouldn't that

warm you up?'

'No, there's too much work to do.' Moira was escorting the girl to the door, grateful for her report about Tess's good behavior.

Teddy started to turn off the radio, then followed Moira into the kitchen. 'What's so important? The breakfast dishes? I'll do those.'

'Why should you? You have your own life to lead.' Moira began running the water. Relieved to be back in the house with her daughter, she often worried someone would steal Tess while she was away.

'But you're part of my life. And those dishes are half mine.' Teddy draped her raincoat over a chair, listening to the radio with one ear. Iwo Jima, could that be where Virgil was?

'One-third yours. You did the vacuuming, the dusting and the cooking all week. It's my turn to do the damn dishes.'

'Moira, honey.' Teddy reached for her elbow, but Moira pulled away. 'You have enough to do with your job and Tess.'

'I'm sorry.' Moira nuzzled Teddy's shoulder. 'I know you're just trying to be kind, but I have to assume my own responsibilities.'

'Why can't you accept a little help? Listen, let's sit down and have a cup of something before falling straight back to work. It would be good to talk about Mr Minelli. We hardly got to talk last night with Tess's crying and such.'

'Babies cry, Teddy; it's part of the deal.'

Teddy didn't even attempt to answer.

'It's not my fault the child cries.' Moira could feel her spine tighten. 'If it bothers you, we can find another place.'

'Enough.' Teddy knew that when Moira got this upset she was hiding something. 'Just go into the living room and lie down on the couch while I make cocoa.'

Moira obeyed, shivering as she approached the old elephant. She had been upset all week, but it was getting impossible to contain. When she first saw the envelope from Randy, she felt relatively collected. Even after she opened it and read the neat block printing saying he would be home in a month, she thought she could handle it. Hadn't she practiced this scenario a hundred times? Of course Vivian and Dorothy always said he would throw over that girl in the end. But what did she care? She would see him once, explain that she was otherwise engaged, and be as low key about Tess as possible. He had no legal claims on either of them.

Moira half heard the gruesome details of the Dresden bombing.

Horrible, but necessary, everyone was saying. Necessary, did they have any idea what necessary meant when they entered this war? She tried to concentrate on a report about the Russians in Breslau. She had no strength to get up and turn off the wretched radio.

If he had been so anxious to see her, why hadn't he written for months and months? What was this about a minor wound, a medical discharge? Moira held her breath and told herself to forget it. Forget it. FORGET IT. What did she care? She was taken. Lesbian, he would hate that. She wanted to tell him as much as she knew she couldn't. She felt secure in Teddy's love but their very bond seemed like a terrifying dare to the rest of the world. Oh, hell, what did he matter?

She had managed to put the letter out of her mind all day Monday, but on Monday night she dreamt Randy was making love to her. She woke up, went downstairs for hot milk and later fell into another dream, like the ones that haunted her early in the war, about him bleeding on a deserted beach. She felt better on Tuesday after she saw old Vivian. Vivian said she had a right to be furious with the bastard. Then, as she was welding, Moira's mind wandered to the injury. What was it? Had it interfered with his writing? Maybe a blow to the head? His hands? The more Vivian defended her rights, the more guilty Moira felt. On Wednesday, she resolved to stop fretting about him and on Wednesday night she could not sleep for the dreams. Moira thought about telling Teddy, but she was so caught up with Mr Minelli's funeral and Mr Whitney's roving hands. However, the fact that she had a problem was becoming perfectly clear. Yes, she should tell Teddy. Tell her what? That she had heard from Randy? How important was that after all? There was no peace – in silence or in disclosure.

'It has been six days since Soviet forces took Budapest and a jubilant. . . .' the radio announcer insisted.

Teddy walked in with a tray and a tentative smile. 'We ran out of cocoa, so I made tea.'

'Fine.' Moira patted the seat next to her. 'Listen, I'm sorry, I-I-I. . . .'

'Don't worry. Are you feeling any better?'

'Yeah, some.'

'It's been a tough day.' Teddy sipped the tea and regarded Moira carefully. The poor kid had been strung out all week. She knew that the worst thing was to ask what was wrong. Moira would have to reveal that in her own time.

'Nice tea.' Moira smiled formally. Oh, God, this was ridiculous. She should just start talking. Probably all these nightmares came from holding back. Her silence was a lie, itself.

Teddy nodded, waiting for Moira to continue. From upstairs, they heard a low gurgling. They both listened carefully, but Tess did not cry. The gurgling stopped and the silence was more tangible between them.

Teddy didn't know why she felt frightened by the silence. She knew she should wait for Moira to say what was on her mind, but words spilled from her own mouth. 'I have some good news. I was going to wait for a respectable time after the funeral, still somehow it seems proper to mention it now.'

'Yes?' Moira watched Teddy's nervous hands, chopping the air to clear way for her words. These handsome hands always distracted her.

'Well.' Teddy pulled a manila envelope from her sweater pocket and slowly unfolded it. 'It seems Mr Minelli left us the house.'

'What?' Moira couldn't believe it. 'I knew he liked us, well, I'll be darned.'

Teddy grinned.

'Show me, will you.'

Proudly, Teddy handed her the envelope.

Moira skimmed the legal language and then stopped. 'He left it to *you*, Teddy. He left it to *you*. What do you mean, *us*? Of course he was always fond of you. And you deserve it. That's wonderful, wonderful.'

'Ah, the name is just a technicality.' Teddy shook her head. 'It's our house now. You can paint the outside that pale blue color you like.'

Moira shook her head and set down her cup. She didn't know whether to be amused or irritated. 'And I suppose you see it as Wanda's house and Ann's too?'

'Well, yes.' Teddy drew back. 'Don't you? Maybe you feel it'd be too small with Tess here. But I've been thinking of a little room next to ours on the top floor. When Hank and Arthur get back, they could build it in a flash. I'd like to try my hand at helping. I'm sure we'll all be fine again.'

'Teddy, you don't live in the real world. People's lives change. Wanda has family responsibilities. When she wrote she didn't say anything about coming back here after camp. And who knows what Ann's going to do about Reuben? What about Wanda and Roy? Most girls do get married, you know.'

'Most.' Teddy tried to raise a smile from Moira. 'But maybe our solution will be catching.'

'Catching,' coughed Moira. 'More likely they'll grow allergic and never talk to us again.' She was getting exasperated. How had she considered talking about Randy? This was not the time to talk about anything. She just wanted to do the dishes, maybe drop her head in the sink with them. 'Look, hon, it's terrific about the house. But it's important to remember that it says "Teresa Fielding" on that deed. To tell you the truth, I don't feel much like talking. This week – with the funeral and all – wore me out. Washing those dishes might just work away my jitters.'

Stretching out on the couch, Teddy closed her eyes. She felt paralyzed by conflicting feelings. Such sadness about Mr Minelli, but of course he was probably better off now than suffering through that dreadful loneliness. Teddy was very touched that he had left the house to her. Why couldn't Moira share the excitement just a little? Sometimes Moira was like that about financial details – so Scottish about who owned what, when it really didn't matter. She would be happy to add Moira's name to the title. Of course Teddy assumed Wanda would stay with her mother and Betty until the family got settled, but why wouldn't she return to the house eventually? It would take time for Roy to return, to make the wedding plans. Maybe Moira just didn't want to get her hopes up? Maybe Moira missed the old days so much that she couldn't face the loss again. She understood Moira better as she learned about that strained, solitary childhood. Moira never counted on a thing until three days after it happened.

Moira was right – people did change. Teddy could see Ann getting more and more sober in her letters. But there was a loosening too. She wasn't so fretful now that she thought she was doing important work. Maybe Ann wasn't meant to be a scholar after all. Maybe she was meant to help people this way. No reason she couldn't do that from Stockton Street. There were plenty of social causes in San Francisco, right in the neighborhood. Reuben, there was something in Ann's tone that implied she had only so much room in her life. That reminded Teddy, she should call Mr Rose. They had neglected him this last week.

Maybe Moira was right; maybe Wanda would be too angry to live with the *Hakujin* again. Teddy breathed deeply, thinking about the empty house next door. The Nakatanis couldn't return to their old place. But the Minellis' house was available. Well, she wouldn't suggest it to Moira just yet. Teddy listened to the water running like fury in the kitchen.

She picked up the deed and read, 'Teresa Fielding' with fresh pleasure. No one in the family had ever owned a house. Too bad Pop hadn't lived to see this. Teddy shook her head and touched a familiar place of remorse. He had failed at so many things – the farm, the move, the dock job. Drinking was the only world where he could let go of his responsibilities and preserve his hopes. Surely he knew toward the end he was killing himself. After that much liver trouble you don't keep up with the drink. Teddy sniffed, oh, they were all mixed up in her mind – Pop, Mr Nakatani, Howard – like Wanda wrote, they each died from the war in some way. She recalled that last conversation with Mr Minelli, the day before they took him to the hospital. 'Your father must have been proud of you,' he offered. 'In a way, yes,' Teddy answered to satisfy the old man. But she reckoned Pop was too busy being ashamed of himself to be proud of his children.

One good thing – the deed meant she could send her rent money to Mom. That would let Mom drop one of the jobs – she hated taking in laundry – and just keep on waitressing. She would call Mom tonight. No, she would go over there tomorrow. She wouldn't believe it unless she saw it with her own eyes. Teddy Fielding was twenty-eight years old and she owned a house.

She sipped the dregs of tea, playing with the bitter leaves on her tongue, and thought back to that last conversation with Mom. Just the two of them.

After dinner, they lazed around the kitchen, drinking the rich coffee Teddy had brought as a present. Mom looked tired, but satisfied as she described Jolene's new job at the shipyard, Jack's good grades in school, Susie's geography project and the letters from Virgil. Teddy noticed how her mother looked younger than she had since they left Oklahoma. Pop's dying had been terrible, but the death itself took a weight off his wife. There was a color to her cheeks and a lightness in her speech. Late in the evening, when they had run through everybody else's life, Mom asked quietly, 'So you happy alone in that big house with the other girl and her baby?'

'Yeah, Moira and I get along real well.'

She studied her daughter. 'You don't have no men friends? A girl your age'll be thinking about marrying.'

'Ah, Mom, I'm too busy. What with my job and the bond campaign and Tess, I don't think I could add a husband.' She concentrated an easiness into her voice, hoping Mom would drop the subject.

'I don't want to rush you honey, and God knows you didn't have the happiest example of man and wife here, but I want to make sure you're thinking of your future.'

'I'm fine, Mom, now when have you ever had to worry about me?'

'That's just it, Teddy, maybe I should have paid more attention. All these years you've been helping with the kids. And when did you ever get taken care of?'

'When I got the measles. When I had my tonsils out. When you told Pop I had a right to typing school.'

'All's I want is your happiness. Somehow I been worrying about you. You really like that other girl?'

Teddy smiled, looking for a deeper meaning in her mother's face. Since she got all her own powers from Mom, the woman must know what was going on. Teddy had told Moira that Mom said little things that indicated she knew they were lovers. Moira said Teddy was crazy, that Mrs Fielding was as conservative as her own mother. But Teddy knew Mom must remember that conversation about her math teacher.

'Yes, we really do care for each other.' Teddy paused, waiting for a nod or smile, but her mother just sat watching. 'We're happy.'

'That's what counts.'

Teddy slipped the deed back in the envelope and set it on the coffee table. She closed her eyes, listening to the clatter of dishes. Moira was slowing down; she could hear the radio again.

'. . . Forces, having crossed the Rhine. . . .'

She wanted to turn the damn thing off. She wanted to shut off the war – the shooting and burning and deaths and shortages and rations. Port Chicago and Normandy. She stared at the radio, willing it to say Virgil was on Iwo Jima and he was safe. Odd the way you listened to the news with two ears – one ear on the world events, one ear for relatives and friends. Like listening to a baseball game in which your family is playing, not caring about the score so much as about the individual players.

Two weeks later Moira was still fraught. She ran the vacuum in short, jerky movements, considering how every last thing was making her anxious. The union was driving her nuts; Tess was getting a cold; she, herself, was verging on the chronic bronchitis which always accosted her in the drear of winter. Despite all this, because of it, Teddy remained full of cheerful support. Ever since she had inherited the house, she acted as if there weren't an international problem she couldn't settle. She refused to accept rent payments for Tess and herself. Moira explained her fears of debt. Teddy kept insisting it was their house. Moira felt a funny claustrophobia about the idea of Teddy keeping them. She loved Teddy, yet didn't want to be beholden. She was so jittery that she even considered going to Los Angeles for a couple of weeks' holiday. LA? she asked herself again and again. Well, the sun would do her chest good. Daddy had never seen Tess. Still, Moira knew something was very wrong if she were considering Los Angeles.

At first she didn't hear the phone over the drone of the vacuum cleaner. Then, for a split second, she thought she heard Tess crying. She switched off the machine and registered the ring, ring, ring. Pausing to ensure everything was silent upstairs, she reached for the receiver.

'Hello.'

'Long time no hear.'

Moira was watching him dancing across the living room with Teddy . . . felt the warmth of his big hand on hers in the movie theatre . . . smelled the sweetness of his shaving cream.

'Randy.' He. voice was stronger by the second syllable. 'How are you?'

'Fine, just fine, and you, Moi?'

How could he do that, call her Moi as if there were no distance between them? She sat down in the armchair and stared blankly across the room. The low afternoon sun played angular shadows on the ceiling.

'Hey, Moi, you still there?'

'Yes, Randy.' Her voice was warmer than she intended. 'Yes, I'm fine.'

'Well, I was wondering why I didn't hear from you.' He paused. 'You got my letter?'

'I got one letter. Last month.'

'I'm no poet. But I did want you to know that you'd be seeing me home, almost all of me.'

'Thanks,' she said, using her entire willpower to keep from asking about the wound.

'Some greeting after those nights in the trenches I lay dreaming about you.'

The trenches, she recalled the trenches from when she was first pregnant with Tess, when she talked him to sleep. So he had heard her. No, no, she needed to get a grip on herself.

'Maybe you'll warm up a little when you see me. When can we get together, Moira? How about I come over this afternoon?'

'No, Randy, I don't think so.'

'Tomorrow, then?'

What was the hurry. After all this time, he had to pop over right away? She reached down and pulled up her socks which were creeping around her ankles. Teddy was right; she shouldn't wear these socks with loafers.

'I don't know, Randy.' She hated the warm feeling of his name. Her voice grew distant. 'I'm going down to Los Angeles to see my parents.'

'Wonders never cease.'

The bastard, playing on their old intimacy.

'Anyway, I'll be gone for a few weeks. Maybe when I get back. Will you still be in the area?'

'In the area! I live here. I didn't go to that Pacific swamp to set up a plantation or nothing. I was fighting a war. And now I'm back, grateful to be home, where I belong. With the people I care about.'

Her throat tightened. The baby began to cry upstairs. Or was this her imagination? She put her hand over the receiver, lest he hear Tess.

'Listen, Randy, I have to go. Maybe we can talk when I get back.'

'What the. . . .'

'No, please, I really must go.'

'There's some other guy, that's it.'

'No, Randy. I have to get off the phone. I'm glad that you're OK, that you're safe.'

'Gee thanks.'

'Good-bye, Randy.'

Tess was silent now. Moira sat with her head cocked, listening for her daughter. 'Almost all of me. . . .' She was angry at herself for caring. She listened for Tess again and, suddenly panic-stricken by Dorothy's story about crib death, she bounded upstairs.

From the doorway, she could hear Tess's quiet breathing. Moira tiptoed into the room. 'OK, hon, you're OK?' she whispered. Tess breathed in and out, in and out. Moira looked at the mobile Teddy had bought last week: the blue and green monkeys danced restlessly through yellow hoops. Moira noticed the window as open a crack. Should she close it? How much fresh air did a child need? Would she get the bronchial condition Moira inherited from her own mother? 'We're going to Los Angeles, Tess. How would you like that?' Moira watched her child, aware of a vague mutual protection. This baby was protecting her? Maybe Mother was right when she first heard about the pregnancy; maybe she was too immature to raise a child. 'We'll be fine, just the two of us.'

When Teddy came into the kitchen that evening, Moira recounted some of the day's events – that she had decided to go to LA – no sense upsetting Teddy about Randy, when she, herself, wasn't sure how she was going to get him out of her hair. She knew she was risking her job by taking another sick leave. She also knew she could not stay here. She poured Teddy tea and talked about the warm Southern California beaches. She told herself again that the two weeks would give her time to make plans and give him time to cool off. It would save Teddy a fortnight of worry.

'It's OK with you that I go, isn't it?'

'Sure, it's your health.' Teddy watched her closely.

'But more than that, I mean I have room to lead my own life?'

'Room? Yeah, why not? Say, Moi,' she reached over for Moira's hand, 'you OK?'

'Of course I'm OK, why are you always watching over me like a mother bird? I have a little congestion. The sun will do us good.'

'Us.' Teddy bit her lip knowing that she was not included in the 'us'.

'Sure,' Teddy said, 'I was only worried about you.'

'You're always only worried about me. Or about Tess. Why don't you worry about yourself for a change.'

'Is there something to worry about?'

'No. That's not what I mean. . . .'

'Worrying about you is worrying about myself.' Teddy paused. 'I mean you are in my life.'

'But we have separate lives too, don't we? I need to know I have a right to move, to breathe.'

'Sure.' Teddy was baffled; however it didn't seem safe to press Moira.

'It's just that we've been inseparable these last eight months. I need some time for myself.' No matter how hard she tried, Moira couldn't release the barrier. It would just get higher if she stayed in San Francisco.

Teddy sat erect, fear holding open her eyes. She gripped the edge of the kitchen table. Staring at her white knuckles, she spoke deliberately. 'Whatever is best for you, that's what I want.'

Moira cleared her throat. 'Do you think you could take us to the station tomorrow?'

Teddy returned from the station exhausted. She boiled some water, poured it into the tea pot to steep and set the kitchen timer. Then she stepped into the garden. Not bad for a winter crop: the cabbage and leeks and potatoes poked through the ground at different stages of green.

She missed working with Ann. Teddy could still picture them planting, Moira's radio blaring from the kitchen and Angela chatting over the back fence. She should stop by the store and check with Rosa for news of Angela. Maybe she would even send a card saying there were no hard feelings. She would love to tell Angela about Moira, but Moira insisted on close secrecy. Teddy didn't see any harm in telling a few people, but Moira said Dawn, Sandra, Vivian and Dorothy were the only ones who could know. If word got out, someone might try to take the baby away from her. Teddy hadn't considered that; Moira was often more savvy about worldly things. Their love was strong, but pressures from outside pushed them too tightly together. The timer clicked.

She poured milk into a cup and then filled it with rich, brown liquid, reassured by the strong color. She should eat something. Of course this was why she was tired; she hadn't eaten breakfast after insisting Moira have a big meal. Gingersnaps and cheese should do it. Sitting down by the window, she stared out at the garden again. Maybe Ann would revive her interest in it. Or maybe she could invite Dawn over this summer. Dawn loved to work in the earth and she had no chance in that tiny apartment. Sure, that was it, why was she always thinking of herself? She would have a lot to consider these next two weeks – trying to understand how she had driven Moira away – was it that or did she really just need a rest? – and how they might live together more happily.

Teddy was revived by the tea. Yes, this would be a good time for her, a chance to catch up on house chores, an opportunity to spend more time with Mr Rose and maybe visit Mrs Rose again. She might take off next weekend and go to Martinez to visit Sandra.

Teddy didn't hear the bell until it had rung two or three times. She rose slowly, reluctant to disturb her meditation. Here she was alone in the house for forty-five minutes and becoming a grumpy hermit already. Who could it be? Almost everybody they knew phoned first because of the baby. But Jolene did say she was going to be downtown shopping today.

Through the front window, Teddy could see a man's figure shuffling back and forth. She couldn't tell who he was, bundled up as he was in a heavy sweater, his face to the side of the house. Someone collecting for the Red Cross or one of those religious folks? Teddy felt a sudden panic, remembering Ann's story about a strange man barging into her room. You couldn't be too careful nowadays. Funny how Teddy never thought twice about danger when Moira was here – and it wasn't as if Moira were going to protect her – but now she was nervous about opening her own front door. Quietly she approached the window, trying to determine the man's identity. Then suddenly, he turned and stared her full in the face.

Randy Girard. Why, of course, why hadn't she thought about him. The hair was as yellow as ever and his cocky stance hadn't changed. Teddy stood still, staring, until Randy knocked on the window and waved.

She was glad Moira was away. It would be easier for her to hear about Randy's return from her. And by then, who knows, he might be gone again. He didn't look wounded or anything, so he was likely to leave on his ship in a short time. Please God, he would be gone by the time Moira returned. Now possessed by her reflexive hospitality, she moved directly to the door and welcomed her visitor.

'Hi, Teddy, how've you been?' He extended his hand.

'Fine, fine thank you, Randy, won't you come in?'

– 331 –

'Thanks.'

He wiped his shoes on the mat, a discipline he must have picked up in the service. She noticed his hair was trimmed more than usual. Usual? She hadn't seen him in ages.

Randy surveyed the living room with satisfaction and Teddy grew more defensive. She did not want this man in her house. As much as she reasoned that it didn't matter since Moira was on the train, as much as she lectured herself to be hospitable, she felt jumpy, as if the place had been invaded by ants.

'Well, aren't you going to ask me to sit down?'

Teddy noticed that he was much more nervous than she was. 'Yes, of course, how about some tea?'

'Is Moira home?'

'She's away a while. She left this morning.'

'Oh.' Randy looked down at his shoes. Teddy considered how odd he looked in these shiny regulation shoes and wondered whether he missed the fancy spats and bucks. 'Yes, I guess I wouldn't mind tea. With milk and two sugars.'

'I remember,' Teddy called over her shoulder, wondering at her sudden friendliness. In a perverse way, she thought, she had a special bond with Randy – she had always wanted to talk with someone who had experienced the full force of Moira's temper – and she was whistling as she served the tea.

Randy sat hunched on the elephant, his hands between his knees. She set his cup on the side table and he nodded thanks.

'When did you get back?' she asked, noticing for the first time how much older he looked, as if his face had been laid out to dry in the sun. It was as dark as a walnut and almost as shriveled in places, especially around the eyes. She had seen this happen to other men and she wondered how Virgil would survive the Pacific.

'Two days ago,' he said as if she had interrupted another conversation. Then, taking stock of his surroundings, he smiled ruefully, and picked up the tea. Teddy warned him it was hot, but he drank with the dispatch of someone used to consuming acid.

'You must be tired.'

'Worn out.' He shook his head. 'I guess she'll have a good rest in LA. So tell me, Teddy, how are you? Still at Woolworths?'

'The Emporium.' How did she know Moira was in Los Angeles? He probably just assumed she would be visiting her parents. Where else could she afford to go? 'I'm fine, Randy. Most, my family is OK.

But my Pop died.'

'Sorry to hear it.' He looked straight at her with those green eyes. 'I hear Howard Nakatani got it in Italy.'

'Yes,' Teddy nodded. 'That poor family. But Roy is all right.' They sat silently.

'And your brother?' she asked.

'Boyd was lucky like me, got out with a minor wound.'

'You were hurt?' Teddy listened to the worry and disappointment in her voice.

'You'd never guess. Knee injury. Hardly limp any more. That and the hearing in my right ear.'

'That's terrible, Randy. I'm so sorry.'

'Ah, I've seen worse. A lot worse, you can imagine. It's just good to be home now. So she did go to LA after all.' He shook his head. 'And she'll be back in a couple of weeks?'

'What, oh, yes, two weeks, that's right.' So much for her career with the OSS.

'She didn't sound exactly eager to talk with me.'

'What do you mean?' She flushed.

'I called yesterday. Didn't she tell you? Jees, this is worse than I thought. I suppose she also didn't bother to mention my letter last month?'

'No,' said Teddy, holding her back against the chair, 'but we're not exactly married.'

Randy regarded her carefully. 'Ha, not likely you and Moira,' he laughed shortly. 'How's what's-her-name, Antonia? Still in the WAFs?'

Teddy nodded stiffly. 'The name is Angela, but it is the WAFs.'

Noticing Teddy's change of mood, Randy smiled sheepishly. 'Hope I didn't hurt your feelings or nothing.' He leaned forward. 'Listen, Teddy, maybe you can get her to talk to me. I know it was crazy to have that fling. I know it was awful of me not to write. But I couldn't. I didn't know where I was. I didn't know whether I would come back. You lose perspective. The island is the only place that counts, the boundary of your life. I know it sounds nuts. But believe me, I wasn't the only one who couldn't write.'

'Life's like that,' Teddy said, or thought she said. She wished he would go. She needed time to think. Maybe Moira was hiding him to protect her. Surely she had no intention of seeing him again. Or maybe Moira was confused, torn between them. Teddy's heart

sank. This explained the weeks of hysterics. Vivian would understand. Did she know Vivian well enough to call her? Who cared?
The world was falling apart and this oaf was sitting in her living
room drinking tea.

'Well, I won't take any more of your time.' Randy's voice was
several degrees colder.

Teddy wondered how long she had been silent and then she lost
interest. She stood with him and walked to the door. He opened it
and she stuck out her hand. 'I'm glad you made it back safe.'

'Thanks. I think I'm glad, too.'

She clicked the lock, imagining him carrying Moira off in his
arms. Ann was right about not answering the door to strange men.

What was wrong with her? She stood in the middle of the living
room. She had been the one who lived with Moira all these months;
who had saved her after the botched abortion; who helped raise
Tess. She and Moira had built a life. At least once a day, Moira said
how much she loved her. Sure, they had been getting on each other's
nerves. That happened to any two people living together. She loved
Moira more than she could feature loving anyone. And Tess was her
god-daughter, almost her own child. This man with his flirty green
eyes couldn't swing in and whisk them away. She would have to
trust Moira. Walking into the kitchen for more tea, she tried to
concentrate on the week's plans, but she kept hearing the doorbell
ringing: she kept seeing that man dressed as a bear. Only one thing
would keep her sane and that was a talk with Dawn, who wouldn't
be back from Martinez for another hour. What could she do to hold
together for another hour?

The garden was cold but hospitable and she thought how she had
come to understand this subtle winter of California. She breathed
slowly, concentrating on the small plot of land, grateful for the
garden's distraction. When she first moved from Fortun, she
thought San Francisco had no seasons. Nothing like the Oklahoma
autumn which tugged on the branches and pulled off the leaves, one
by one. Nothing like the roaring snows and the bright white nights
when you could look for ever across the celestial surface of the farm.
Nothing like the luscious hot summer, sometimes so green you could
hardly breathe. But there were changes here. Indian summer led to
a rainy, cooler fall and then into a period when trees and grass
turned muddy grey. Everything looked asleep somehow, not dead
or disappeared as in Oklahoma, but in hibernation. So Teddy sat in

the garden considering the muted colors, thinking of the summer past and of the spring ahead. Maybe Moira was right; this garden would never return to normal.

The telephone roused her. Let it be good. Let it be Dawn. She ran into the house and the screen door smacked shut as she lifted the receiver.

'Hello.'

'Hello, Teddy?'

'Oh, my lord, Wanda, it's you. *Where* are you? Are you out?' Teddy bit her lip. Did Wanda use prison terms like that? She would have to learn a whole way of talking about that terrible experience with her. 'Are you in San Francisco?'

'Yes, yes, we're here.' Wanda's voice brightened, hearing Teddy. Some things stayed the same. 'We got here last night.'

'Yes.' Teddy tried to maintain her enthusiasm. 'Yes.' But she wondered why it had taken Wanda so long to call. Where was 'here'? Clearly she no longer considered Stockton Street as 'here' in the same way. Remembering her resolve from the garden – no regrets, just accept what comes – she thought how nice it was to hear Wanda's voice. Did she sound a little older? Or was she just tired? She wanted to see her so she would know she was really safe, really back.

'How are you?' Wanda asked. 'And Moira?'

'Fine, fine.' Teddy spoke rapidly, evading the bruise. 'Moira's down in Los Angeles visiting her parents.'

'Really?'

Teddy laughed. 'Really.' Eager to change the topic, to change the story, she asked, 'How are *you*? When are you coming back? I mean, when can I see you?'

'Soon, soon. We're not quite sure where we're going to settle.'

'Oh.' In spite of herself, Teddy plowed ahead with a subject she had resolved to approach slowly. 'I wrote you about Mr Minelli dying?'

'No, or maybe we didn't get the letter. Things got horribly confused at camp finally. How sad. I thought he wouldn't last long after she went.'

'But,' Teddy tried to keep her voice even, 'he left the house to us. And the one next door is empty.' It was coming out all wrong.

'That's wonderful for you, Teddy. He always liked you.'

Was Wanda missing the point intentionally or should she be more explicit? Teddy couldn't help herself. 'What I mean is that you and your family could think about renting the Minellis' old house from their niece.'

'Oh, Teddy.' Wanda knew it was going to be hard to settle back, hard to explain the changes she, herself, didn't fully comprehend. 'That's a lovely dream. Right now, it's more sensible to be with the family, to stay near Uncle Fumio.' She stumbled, stretching for the old intimacy. 'I want you to know how much I appreciated all those letters.'

'Appreciate. What kind of talk is that? I'm your friend. I needed to be in touch.'

'No, Teddy, you must let me finish. This is difficult to say.'

Teddy did not want her to finish. Her body ached enough from trying to hold on to Moira.

'I need some time to readjust before I come back to Stockton Street, before I see you all. I feel like I was wrenched away and that I need to decide when I return. Do you understand? I have to feel stable again, like I'm not walking in quicksand where I could lose my heart with a wrong step.'

'I understand. Sorry I was so pushy.'

'Teddy, you could never be pushy. It's just not time for us to see each other. I did want you to know that we were OK – Mama and Betty and me. Roy is, too; I just got a letter from him. So tell me how you are? The job? Your mother? The garden?'

Dawn was saving a place in the far corner of the cafeteria. What would Teddy have done without Dawn these last three weeks? Since returning from LA Moira had grown even more remote.

And it was impossible having Wanda so close and so far. Dawn didn't have any answers, but at least she was still here.

'Hiya, kid.' Dawn patted the metal chair next to her. 'Take a load off your legs on these commodious employee amenities.'

Teddy sat down, feeling like a stiff branch. The whole week had been a strain. Today she had a hard time breathing. She drank four cups of tea this morning, her mouth was so dry. Now she felt a dull ache at the base of her throat.

Dawn studied her drawn face. 'Nothing's better, I take it.'

Teddy nodded, looking helplessly at the egg salad sandwich which she could not possibly stuff down her throat.

'I see old Whitney hasn't given up.'

Teddy regarded Dawn curiously.

'I mean today in the hall he was saying how nice you looked in green and how you should wear it more often. Did he ask you out again?'

'To tell the truth, I don't know. I was too preoccupied to listen.'

'You can say that again. You looked like a tigerlily being buzzed by a giant bumblebee. Hopeless.'

Teddy shook her head. She would get into trouble if she didn't start paying attention. Before she knew it, she would have accepted a date with him.

'So let's get back to Stockton Street. What's going on? Has she seen him again?'

'Yes.' Teddy pushed away her sandwich and gulped down the tea. 'Third time this week. At first it was just to talk, you know to straighten out the past, to make a clean break. Then he wanted to see Tess. And tonight the three of them are going out to dinner like a, a. . . .'

'A family.' Dawn took Teddy's hand. 'Oh, child, I am so sorry.'

'You think this is the end? You think he's going to take her away? I keep hoping that she'll see through him. After all the things she said to me about him last year! I don't know what she wants.'

'Maybe she don't either, honey. Being in the life is hard. Not everybody is strong enough. You gotta see it that way. Maybe she's not making a choice between you and Randy but between safety and. . . .'

'But to have doubts after all the time we spent together, it just doesn't make sense.' Teddy ignored Dawn's point. 'I mean what can you count on in this world?'

'Yourself.'

Teddy looked at Dawn closely, wishing her to say anything other than that. Friends, principles, the truth. 'I know I know, you warned me to watch out. Maybe if I had listened, it would have been better for all of us.'

'For Moira?' Dawn pushed her glasses back on her nose.

'Yeah, for Moi, too, then she wouldn't have these pressures.'

'You get me; you really get me.'

Teddy began to cry. 'Oh I shouldn't; I'll embarrass you.'

'You go on, sugar. It's good for you. And there ain't nothin that could embarrass me in this place.' She held Teddy's hand tightly in her own. 'You gonna be OK. You got a lot of strength in that big self of yours.'

On Saturday afternoon, Moira set the table for tea. Four places – for them and Wanda and Roy's brother Stanley who had borrowed a truck to help move the Nakatanis' furniture from the house. What would it be like to have Wanda back here after all this time? For years, Moira felt that pieces of home were missing; but now she wondered whether it hadn't become a wholly different puzzle, whether Wanda and Ann wouldn't be the odd pieces out. Was this the same home it had been three years ago when Wanda left, eight months ago when she and Teddy got together, four months ago when Tess was born, four weeks ago when Randy got back to town? How would they all fit together again?

Moira wasn't sure Wanda would stay for tea. But she humored Teddy by setting the table. She was grateful for a dilemma unrelated to Randy. Could she concentrate on something beside her own problems for one afternoon? For the past month, she had been living two lives. When she was with Teddy, she felt loved and loving; it always seemed right for the moment. But in the long term, this life with its secrets and isolation seemed impossible. How could you raise a child like that? Was Tess just an excuse? Was she simply scared? Did it matter, if she loved Randy? When she was with him, the passion and affection and joy were tempered by doubt. How long would he stay this time? Did he really love her? He seemed to have grown up in the navy. He claimed he was completely devoted to her and to Tess. He wanted a family; he wanted to be a father. Did she love him or did she want a father for Tess? Horrible though it was, she sometimes wished the abortion had worked. Not that she would ever give up Tess. But if she hadn't been born there wouldn't be quite so many knots.

Moira swung back and forth. When she came home from an afternoon with Randy and sat down at supper with Teddy, she felt like a whore shifting camps. One of the most confusing parts was this man–woman business. When she was dating Randy the last thing she could have imagined was sex with a woman. And since she'd been with Teddy, she had stopped looking at men in a physical way. The urges seemed so opposite – the softness she felt with Teddy and the angular strength she enjoyed with Randy. But now, every day, she vacillated, unsure of whom she loved, unsure of who she was. Sometimes she could just forget one of them existed. Sometimes she pretended she was in a sane world and then one of them would break the rules and refer to the other. This usually happened with Teddy who needed reassurance. Randy was more confident because he didn't know the nature of her closeness with Teddy. Moira felt dizzy for although she was in control – both people wanted her – she felt completely unwound. Och if she could just put away all these feelings for one afternoon.

As she laid out the blue linen napkins Ann's mother had made, Moira was filled with nostalgia for the old times when they would sit around talking or listening to the radio. She felt nervous about seeing Wanda after three years. What would she be like? These grey and blue plates had been a gift from Mother. There. Moira stood back and considered the pretty table, suddenly distressed at having finished. She didn't want to talk with Teddy, yet she didn't want to leave her alone with the chores. As Moira turned into the kitchen, the sweetness of chocolate chip cookies wafted from the oven. Teddy was scrubbing the counters. Moira still marvelled at how Teddy could concentrate on other chores while cooking. If Moira were to cook and clean at the same time, surely the kitchen would incinerate.

The doorball rang and Teddy raced toward the living room, suddenly shy about her excitement in front of Moira. Terrible how guarded she felt lately.

'Oh, do you want to get it?' Teddy deferred.

'No.' Moira's voice was conciliatory, although she didn't know what she had done at this particular moment to upset Teddy. 'Let's answer it together. I'm sure that's what she expects.'

Wanda was not prepared for the changes in them or for the familiarity of the house. Teddy seemed smaller, broader, more settled into her body. Her smile was screened by a fine veil of tension. The shyness was at a further remove. Moira's face was fuller, her eyes alert rather than bright. She was wearing that green polka dot dress which was a little tight across the hips now. And she, too, seemed fraught. Well, there had been three years and a war between them. Wanda felt protected by this distance, but disappointed too. The house – with the elephant couch and the old radio and the rickety floor lamp – seemed the same, perhaps a little smaller.

Teddy moved forward first, her smile broadening as she hugged

Wanda. Moira put her arms around both of them. The three women started to rock and laugh. Their dance was disrupted by shuffling from behind. Stanley shifted as if trying to fade into the porch railing. Wanda turned. 'Oh, I'm sorry, Stanley. I want you to meet my old friends, Teddy and Moira.' She turned back to them. 'This is Stanley, Roy's brother.'

Moira shook his hand eagerly. 'You must be proud of your big brother. I understand he's won three or four medals?'

'Five,' Stanley grinned.

Leave it to Moi to say the right thing, thought Teddy, surveying the three of them. But she was distracted by Wanda's tone, by the phrase 'old friends'. It would have been easier if she had come home alone. Maybe not easier for Wanda.

Wanda couldn't believe how much older they each looked. Well, Moira was going on twenty-five and Teddy was twenty-eight. It made her feel the lost years all the more. Odd, how when she was a kid she always wanted to be older and since she was – well, since she finished Tracey Business School – she wanted time to stand still. Now she wanted to be younger, just a few years younger, three for instance. Age seemed to be a hedge that grew higher with responsibilities. Did Moira and Teddy feel this way? She wished she could collapse on the elephant and ask them scores of questions.

'Will you come into the dining room and have some tea?' invited Teddy.

Wanda looked at the table set with Ann's napkins and Moira's plates. She thought about their suppers and buffet parties. Light streamed in the side window, casting the shadows of live leaves on the faded, flowered wallpaper. No, she couldn't bear it yet. She needed to get the job done. What if she lost her nerve and claimed sanctuary here? 'Could we do the moving first?'

•

Chapter Twenty-Seven

Spring 1945, San Francisco

FINAL V ROCKETS HIT LONDON

•

ROOSEVELT DIES

•

MUSSOLINI IS EXECUTED

•

HITLER COMMITS SUICIDE

Wanda stared out the front bedroom window. The cold, drizzling day felt all the more miserable because this was supposed to be spring. She had forgotten the unpredictability of San Francisco weather and this forgetting unnerved her. Trucks droned monotonously down the street, occasionally switching gears and creating a screech that reminded her of Mrs Murakami's sick cat who screamed every time he had to urinate. Wanda could never understand why Mrs Murakami didn't put the poor thing to sleep. Although Wanda could barely acknowledge it to herself, she missed Lion's Head – the view of those mountains and the relative safety of camp. Often when she heard these gears screeching, she imagined something more ominous than the cat. She imagined firebombs through the windows and police arriving too late last month at the scene of Mr Hata's stabbing. At first, it was hard to believe the new violence against Japanese Americans. After all this. After three years. After loyalty oaths. After men fighting in Italy. After Howard's death. Still, no, it would never be still.

Maybe Mama was right about returning to Japan. It could be difficult there, but at least they would be free of this daily, hostile suspicion. On the other hand, Uncle Fumio was more determined than ever to recover his position at the cannery. Meanwhile, he was working with the rest of them at Hathaways Fish Company, cleaning and packing. Uncle Fumio's predicament made her understand Papa's decision. Below her a bus honked at two cars parked next to each other in the middle of the road. One motorist seemed to be giving directions to the other. The bus driver leaned on his horn again. Wanda felt at odds with the speed and impatience of the city. Where were they all going?

She missed Stockton Street all the more now that she was back in San Francisco. She belonged there. Moira and Teddy were continuing their lives as usual – well, not as usual, but at least with each other in that familiar house. And here she was, emancipated, now more imprisoned by this grim neighborhood and her dreadful job than she had ever felt in Lion's Head. At least in camp, she could imagine freedom. That was harder to do now. She reminded herself that the war had deprived everyone. Roy was still in Italy. Ann was in London.

Wanda pictured Roy sitting in the middle of a clearing – tall trees reaching up to the turquoise Italian sky. He would be exhausted, perhaps leaning against a log. She remembered him with Howard – for although she hadn't been there, she could remember it detail for detail – the two of them talking before Howard went off on patrol. Later, Roy bending over her brother.

Wanda picked up Ann's letter and shook her head. Would she formally adopt the child? She didn't get it. Of course Moira was a mother and if she could do it Ann could too. But where did her impulse come from? Perhaps she, herself, was unnatural. Perhaps she could change her mind in a few years. But she felt that she had taken care of quite enough people in her life, thank you very much. She watched Carolyn struggling with the baby and her new job.

Wanda wondered if Ann would feel like a failure to give up her classics study the way she, herself, would consider it a failure to abandon writing. Did Ann feel herself more Jewish in the way that she, herself, felt more Japanese? Wanda knew that so much of her acceptance in school had been a sham. The other kids probably thought of her as an imitation American girl. Had it been the same for Ann; had she suddenly understood her otherness? Had she been absorbed by Europe? Her thoughts about staying over there with Reuben and Leah were not so different from Mama's dreams of Japan. Maybe none of them belonged in America. What was this country, anyway, except the distorted fantasy of uptight Anglo-Saxons? She must not get carried away by comparison. She must remember that millions of Ann's people had been executed in those concentration camps. Their experience had been different. Yet alike.

Betty stood in the doorsill until Wanda noticed her. Wanda shook her head, distressed at how quiet Betty had become. Beautiful, vivacious Betty had grown shy and whiny recently in the new apartment and the new school. She had lost interest in the name of Lisa and resigned herself to Betty.

'Hi there, squirt.' Wanda waved her over to the window. 'What's going on?'

Betty looked down at the street. 'Noise.' She shook her head. 'I'll never get used to the noise.'

'I know what you mean. We'll save up for a long lost ocean villa, what do you think?'

'Which side of the ocean?' Betty studied the carpet. 'Mama has been going on and on about Yokohama this week. Wanda, what would we do there?'

'Live. Work. Eat.' She stopped herself and paid attention to Betty's long face. 'I don't know, honey, they're just people. We'd do pretty much what we do here. They're our people after all.'

'They're not!' Betty stalked back to the door. 'I'm an American. I am! I am!'

Wanda was struck by her sister's conviction. After all the kid had endured, Betty had no qualms about her identity or her loyalty.

'Say, sweet one, come over here and let me talk with you quietly,' Wanda beckoned.

'You're afraid she'll hear?'

'She is your mother.' Wanda heard Papa's voice. Someone had always defended Mama. How did she manage to be so vulnerable and commanding at once? 'Come here and tell me what's up.'

'Well, Mama may be Japanese, but I'm not. I mean, maybe I'm both. But I'm at least half American. Aren't you?'

Wanda held the child close. 'I don't know. I guess so. What brought on the big questions?'

– 343 –

Betty burrowed her head in Wanda's shoulder and said nothing. 'Something at school?'

'Well, sort of.' Betty held herself tight.

Wanda sat straighter. If anyone so much as grazed this kid with a pebble, she would personally apprehend the assailant. Damn. 'What? Tell me did someone hurt you?'

Betty shook her head in resignation. 'Nothing like that. The kids have been very helpful. Too helpful. Showing me the way to the playground, to the bathroom. It wasn't until yesterday, when I overheard two girls talking in the library, that I found out what they thought of me.'

Wanda held her arms across her chest. 'Yes?'

'One of them, a blond cheerleader, was saying to the other, who's on the student council, "That Betty Nakasoma" – they always get the name wrong, but I'm used to that – "she speaks English pretty good for a foreigner." A foreigner. I'm not a foreigner. I'm an American, right?'

'Oh, yes.' Wanda didn't know whether to laugh or to scream. 'Of course you are. That's why they released us from Lion's Head. The kids in your school – they're not much different from a lot of confused people. Things will change. You'll make friends. Wait till they hear you play the piano.'

'That's another thing.' Betty bit her lip. 'Mama doesn't want me playing any more.'

'I'll have a talk with her. She'll come around.' Wanda clenched her teeth.

'Oh, Wanda, I knew you'd make it all right.'

Wanda patted her sister's shoulder and coughed, to stem the tide of confidence.

'And do you think you could talk with her about the other part?'

'What's that?' Wanda was distracted.

'About the other side of the ocean?'

'That, oh yes. Let's tackle the piano first. The *world* may interfere with our trip to Japan. Shall we wait a while?'

'If you think so.' Betty smiled weakly. 'You know what's best.'

Wanda stared at the street as another bus rattled down the hill. 'Hmmm, we'll see.'

As Wanda waited for Moira in the café, she tried to stem her irritation. Moira had always been late. She would always *be* late.

Wanda looked at the small, sun-filled room. People sat in clusters, talking quietly. Were they discussing Roosevelt's death? She thought he would be president for ever. She could hardly believe that silly looking fellow, Truman, had taken his place. Not that FDR had been the great, competent father. He had been the one who sent them to camp, and she was annoyed at all the sentimental claptrap about his death.

Half the patrons here seemed to be sailors. San Francisco had grown a lot in three years. The war had put it on the map, had given it a big city feel. She didn't care for this new company. She tried to remember that Roy might be sitting in his uniform in an Italian café right now, but it didn't help. She was thoroughly cranky today.

Wanda checked her watch. Damn, she should have adjusted her schedule. She should have shopped first. Mama would be furious if she didn't get the best vegetables. No, that wasn't why she was upset. Wanda guessed that in some way she was angry at Moira because she had been in camp for three years. Although it was irrational, she resented the thought of those two safe and cosy on Stockton Street. She raised her hand to the waiter. To distract herself. Because she needed a cup of coffee. In these North Beach restaurants no one minded you sitting all day. No one noticed if you were drinking or not. Wanda didn't feel like taking any chances. She was going to rent her table, going to order a coffee before anyone came up and accused her of loitering. The waiter waved back and, a minute later, Moira rushed toward the table. Wanda imagined the table tipping over, the sugar and salt whirling across the floor, all eyes on them. But the world held still and Moira collapsed, breathless. Why was the girl always late if she were always rushing?

'Hi, hon, how are you?' Moira leaned over and kissed Wanda. 'Look, I know what you're thinking – that I'll never change. Yes, I'm very sorry to be late. But what with Tess and the errands, my resolutions get screwed up every day. Oh, you haven't ordered yet? Hey,' she called over to the waiter, 'André, two coffees and pastries.'

Wanda marvelled at Moira's ease and remembered that she, herself, had reassured Betty that she wasn't a foreigner.

'So,' Moira snapped her gum, 'how are you?'

Teaberry gum, Wanda smiled affectionately. 'OK, the job slitting fish throats is even farther from writing than my old position as bookkeeper. Still, it covers the rent. Mother and Betty are well. Tell me about you? And Tess? And Teddy?' Wanda noticed she always found it easier to open conversations concentrating on other people.

'Fine.' Moira sloughed off a fuzzy green sweater. 'Teddy misses you. Wishes you could come to the house. Doesn't understand why you'd want to meet me in a café, well, you know,' she shrugged shyly. 'Frankly, I think it's kind of nice to meet alone. Easier to talk in some ways. And I think I can understand your thing about the house.'

'Thanks.' Wanda was relieved that the waiter arrived with their order. She noticed how plain her beige dress was in comparison to Moira's green and blue outfit. Her taste had grown more subdued in the last few years. 'How are things at home?'

'Fine.' Moira spat her gum into a napkin and nursed the scalding coffee. 'Teddy's started the garden already. She's making salad for Ann's return. Tess is sleeping better these days. Everything is fine.' Moira stared into her cup.

'Doesn't look like it.' Wanda watched her closely. 'What's going on?'

'Well, it's confusing with Randy back.' Moira brought it up sooner than she had intended. Now she studied Wanda's face for traces of sadness about Howard or Roy.

'I can understand that.' Wanda broke off the end of a pastry. 'Does he want to get married?'

'How did you know?'

'It's the normal procedure.'

'Normal.' Moira shook her head and began tentatively. 'You know he and I haven't been talking this year. I had decided to raise Tess alone, even before she was born.'

'But times change, Moira. You can't be rigid.'

'To tell you the truth, over the last couple of months, I've come to love him again. I guess I do want to get married. It would be best for Tess. And, to be honest, best for me, too.'

'So?'

'So there's Teddy.'

'Surely she's happy for you. Oh, you mean she's upset that you'll be leaving the house. Of course.'

'More than that. She doesn't exactly know about Randy and me. I mean she knows what I feel for him. You don't get it, Wanda. Teddy and I became quite close, alone in the house, we. . . .'

'Yes.' Wanda frowned. 'You've been like family. And the war makes things tougher on everyone – separations, changes.'

'No, I don't think you understand.' Moira paused, wondering if she had given this enough thought. She had always supposed Wanda would accept better than Ann. She knew she shouldn't reveal anything without talking to Teddy first. Yet she was suffocated by these secrets. Did she and Teddy still have their bond if she were seeing Randy on the sly? Did one deception break the whole promise? Would Teddy care? After all, it had been Moira, herself, who had insisted on secrecy. Was it fair to implicate Wanda? Her stomach hurt. She needed to talk with someone. She had tried to sort it all out with Vivian, but Vivian didn't know Teddy the way Wanda did. Maybe she'd give it a try. 'Teddy and I have grown especially close this year.'

Wanda nodded, certain from the chaos in Moira's eyes that she didn't want to hear the rest of the story. Not yet. 'Well, whatever. You have a right to a father for your child, to a life of your own.'

'But, Wanda.' Moira reached for her arm. 'You don't get it. I'm trying to explain that . . . that. . . .'

'Waiter,' Wanda called, 'more water.'

Moira stopped at the expression on Wanda's face. She sipped the coffee. Well, she could talk about Randy and she would take any opportunity to settle some of her feelings. 'So you think Randy would make a good father?'

'Sure, why not? It sounds like he loves you.' Wandra drank the whole glass of water at once. 'He wants to take responsibility for Tess. Before the war, he was a little wild. But you say he's calmed down. What do you think, Moi?'

Moira shook her head, distracted by the 'Moi', for this was the first time Wanda had used her nickname since she had returned. 'I think you're right. At first I was suspicious – with his push me/pull you routine. Could I count on him this time? But he showed me the money he saved in the navy. He really scraped. And he's got that job at the garage. He's even been looking around at apartments for us.'

'Do you love him?' Wanda thought about a time when this seemed a simpler question. Did she herself love the person Roy had become? Did Mama always love Papa? Did Carolyn still love Howard?

Moira smiled at Wanda's perplexity. 'Yes, I guess that old feeling is there. I like his spunk. We laugh a lot. He's basically a kind man. And now there's the responsibility of Tess. I want her to have a family, a complete family, unlike mine, with brothers and sisters. And a father. I think Randy and I can make a home together.'

'Sounds good.' Wanda sipped her coffee.

'Well, we'll see,' Moira said. 'What about you? You'll get married as soon as Roy returns?'

'That's the way we write to each other. Now that the war in Europe is almost over. . . .' She paused, thinking how she believed that there were two separate wars. Sometimes she pretended the other one didn't exist. Although she had lost Howard in Italy; although she still risked losing Roy there, it was the Pacific war she wanted to be imaginary. 'Yes, I guess so. He's talking about moving to Berkeley for optometry school. And wants me to try to study writing.'

'Oh, Wanda.' Moira took her friend's hand.

Wanda pulled back. 'It would be better than slicing up fish all day. Often in the cannery, I feel like I'm on the battlefield, you know the way soldiers talk about depersonalizing the enemy.'

Moira grimaced. 'Yes, Randy said that about the Japanese.' She stopped abruptly. They had never really discussed about how to talk about the war. But what else could she say? They were the enemy. Besides, the Nakatanis weren't Japanese any more. She continued unsteadily. 'He said you had to get them before they got you.'

'Well, I don't feel endangered by those poor fish, but the job is my form of survival. And it's astonishing how used to the sight of blood and the smell of intestines one becomes.' She looked up at Moira, who had pushed her raspberry pastry to the side. 'Oh, Moi, I am sorry. Berkeley is a nice dream, isn't it?'

'Wonderful. But what happened to Roy's photography?'

'Not practical, he says. I tried to persuade him differently. But you know what it's like corresponding through the delay and the censor's scissors. I think he's lost heart. He insists that optometry will pay steadily and he can still play around with the cameras.'

'Still, you sound hesitant.'

'Mama is lost without Papa and Howard.'

'Won't she feel happy when she gets a grandchild?' Moira couldn't believe how evangelistic she had become about motherhood.

'She has one – Carolyn's baby, Winnie.'

'That's not what I mean.'

Wanda blushed. She could hardly discuss her confusion about children with Moira. 'Let's get back to you. When do you think you'll set the date?'

'July.' Moira startled them both with her alacrity. 'Rather, we'll have enough saved for an apartment by July.'

Wanda waved to Teddy across Union Square. Even from here she could tell the girl wasn't well. She sat slumped on the bench listlessly throwing crumbs to the pigeons. Last week, Wanda knew something terrible was wrong because Teddy cancelled their plans. She said she was under the weather, and, as Wanda approached, she saw Teddy's eyes were shadowed in dark circles and her hands twisted anxiously. Smiling faintly, she raised herself from the bench.

'Good to see you, old friend.' Teddy tried for her usual hardiness.

'And you.' Wanda impulsively put her arms around her. 'How are you?' Wanda could barely hear her own voice above the city noises.

'Still a touch of that cold, I reckon.' Teddy ducked Wanda's glance as if she were aware of the contrary evidence on her face. 'Shall we walk around this dinky old park. There seem to be some starving pigeons over there.'

'Sure,' said Wanda with concern. 'Let's walk.' At first, she thought that Teddy wanted to meet here to accommodate her. But now she knew Teddy needed to get out of the neighborhood as much as she, herself, needed to avoid it. Moira must have set a date.

'What's going on?' Wanda could not stand the suspense.

'They're getting married.' Teddy exhaled raggedly, as if she had ice in her lungs.

Wanda waited.

'Moira and Randy,' Teddy explained, for her friend seemed to have missed the significance. 'They're getting married in July.'

'I guessed that.' Wanda put her arms around Teddy who drew away automatically. 'How are you feeling about it?'

'It's the best thing for Tess. She needs a father. And I can always visit.'

Wanda shook her head in futility. Now that Teddy was letting Moira go, Wanda felt her own anger at Moira, who always landed on her feet.

'I feel so selfish.' Teddy surveyed the late afternoon shoppers and the sailors strolling through the park. 'I'm just thinking of me.'

'That's a beginning.'

'I don't get it.' Her voice grated. 'I did my best. I loved them both. Yet they're going. I have no say. It doesn't seem right. Doesn't seem fair.'

Wanda nodded.

'But it will be best for them, that's what I have to concentrate on. That's all there is to feel.'

'It's hard to be abandoned by your friends.' Wanda stared at the pigeons who were circling under the bag of bread dangling from Teddy's right hand.

Teddy looked at her, on the border of relief and panic. 'Oh, I don't know. I don't want to wallow in it.' Then, helplessly, she began to cry. 'I just don't understand it. First Angela leaves. Then you and Ann. Then Pop dies. Now Moira and Tess are going. Everybody seems to be disappearing. Oh, Wanda, I'm sorry, of course with your father and brother, you've suffered so much. I'm awful selfish, blubbering on this way.'

'No, perhaps not selfish enough. You're always talking about what's happened to other people. What's happened to you these last three years? You've run around taking care of your family and Mr Rose and Mr Minelli and Moira and Tess and the bond campaign and your job.' She sat down and tugged at Teddy's elbow. Her friend sat with a thud.

'Oh, but you don't know the half of Moira and Tess. Moira and I. . . .' Teddy stumbled because this would offend and frighten Wanda.

'I think I'm beginning to understand. Do you want to talk about it?' She was ready now, whereas she hadn't been prepared to hear about it from Moira. It wouldn't be easy, but they were her friends.

Teddy saw Wanda's lower lip trembling and knew she would just have to pull herself together.

'It's hard to be left alone.' Teddy opened the bag of crumbs, sprinkling them toward the parade of pigeons.

'We all left you,' said Wanda.

'That's not fair. It's not the same for you. You didn't have a choice.'

'In some ways Ann didn't either . . . or Moira.'

'In some ways.' She emptied the bag. 'Look, I'll get over it. People remain friends when they're living across town.'

Wanda nodded. When would they talk openly? She used to think intimacy became easier with age, but now she believed it was just the opposite. She was so much more aware of the vulnerabilities she wanted to hide. 'You will get over it,' she said finally, 'but give yourself time.'

Teddy crunched the empty bag into a ball. Then she turned to Wanda. 'You'll never guess who I heard from last week.'

'Miss Fargo.' Wanda peered at the leaves of a palm tree scratching the blue sky.

'How did you know?'

'No idea,' Wanda shrugged. 'Your tone of voice probably.'

'Well, a friend sent her that new article from the *Examiner* having to do with the bond campaign. Apparently when she received the letter, she was sick. Last week, she wrote to say that she knew I would go places. Not that I've gone very far. I think the Emporium is all of a mile from Tracey Business School.' She laughed self-consciously. 'Anyway, she asked after you, all of you.'

'Oh, yes?' Wanda's eyebrows rose.

'I think she's a little lonely, living in an old folks' home out in San Jose. I thought I might go down next week. You wouldn't be interested in joining me?'

Wanda looked back incredulously.

Teddy shrugged. 'Really, she did ask about you.'

'I got a letter like that last week.' Wanda changed the topic deliberately. 'From Mrs Wright, the teacher at Lion's Head.'

Teddy nodded.

'She's still urging me to enroll at her friend's school in Chicago. Wants to know how I am, how the family is. Funny when people keep in touch, people you'd prefer to forget.'

'Do you feel the same about me?' Teddy noticed all the pigeons had gone now.

Wanda frowned and shook her head. 'How can you even think something like that?'

'I don't know. I've just been questioning everything lately. The house, maybe it wasn't such a good idea.'

'What do you mean? We had a fine time.'

'But it didn't last.'

'That doesn't mean it wasn't good. We didn't end it because we failed.'

'No? Moira was just saying the other day that maybe it's not good for friends to live together, that they get on each other's nerves.'

'Everyone gets on everyone's nerves. That's crazy talk. Moira is upset. No, the house was wonderful. I often think that we were ahead of our time, or that it wasn't the right time.'

Teddy relaxed back against the bench. She knew Wanda was being honest and she wanted to agree with her.

Wanda wished she could explain to Teddy how much she respected her courage in living without a man, independent and unconventional. She even admired Moira for trying to live like that. But Moira obviously wasn't a lesbian. Now, what did that mean? And how could she admire Teddy for something that was simply her biological nature? Is that what it was? Just as well she didn't fumble through this out loud. Maybe one day they could talk about such things.

'You know that I admire you?' Teddy asked Wanda.

'Yes, ah, yes, enough of this. Let's talk about your family. How are your Mom . . . and Jolene?'

Wanda walked into the silent apartment, relieved to be alone. It was a tiny place in which it was easy to trip over each other. She looked around the living room, crowded with furniture from their house before the war. Before the war – would her life always be marked in two – before the war and after? It would have been easier in camp with spartan tables and chairs than to crowd with these old ghosts – reminders that the Nakatanis did not quite fit in San Francisco. The kitchen was the hardest room for Wanda because she had longed for a proper kitchen when they were in camp. She hated the mess lines and the cardboard dinners. But here she could never get used to the pink and lavender cabinets in this stuffy room several floors above the street. This wasn't a kitchen. Kitchens opened on to back yards with swings and gardens. But this was a boiler room hanging out over the loud, filthy traffic.

This morning she had opened a head of celery, horrified to find that the heart was brown and misshapen. Several stalks grew out of the twisted center and they, in turn, had been deformed, so that it only looked like a head of celery on the outside. It was ridiculous that this grotesque image haunted her all day.

Roy's letter lay in the middle of the dark table. At least she was alone with the letter now. Mama would be with Uncle Fumio for another two or three hours and Betty was rehearsing for the school assembly. She felt resentful that this letter was dropped in the open rather than placed on her bed or even left in the mail box. Out on the table like this, it could be everyone's property. She wasn't engaged to Roy. He was engaged to her family. He was the man of the family.

Mother and Betty already had expectations of him. Poor Roy. Dear Roy. Why couldn't they just have a romance, an engagement, a life that didn't hold so many people.

Two hours of precious solitude. Wanda stretched her hands above her head, then switched on the kettle. Sometimes what she missed most about Stockton Street was the feeling of being a self-sufficient working girl. But given all the catastrophes between Teddy and Moira lately, she knew that Stockton Street was part of the past for all of them.

Moira and Teddy. She had wondered about Teddy since the Angela days. But Moira? Was she using Teddy as a cushion against the loneliness? Had she really loved her like that? They had both been right in assuming she didn't want to hear much. She wished she had been able to reach out more, particularly to Teddy, who was so bruised. Perhaps she still could. Perhaps after Moira left and things were defused, they could talk more candidly. Certainly Teddy would need people then.

The kettle whistled and filled Wanda with a surprising pleasure. This was her favorite time of day, just as the sky was greying, while the air was still warm with the activity of afternoon. She filled her cup and walked back to the table with Roy's letter.

> Dear Wanda,
> I'm well. We've been in this village for. . . .

Wanda was always startled by the scissor marks stabbed into each censored line. Why didn't they trust their own servicemen? She understood that there were spies everywhere, but she hated the way the government stepped into the middle of personal lives. As was the way with the military, they didn't simply slice the offending word, but managed to cut into the other side of the letter, too, to excerpt the most innocent and sensitive correspondence. She sipped her tea and continued.

> It looks like things are going better and I may be home this summer. What do you think of that? I'm afraid to anticipate. What if I don't make it? Or what if we're delayed? Or what if you don't want me when we get there? Well this kind of rambling is silly. How is the family? I hear from Stanley that your mother is doing better, working at the cannery. And Betty's music? Tell her I expect a concert when I return. Tell

her sister I expect a lot of dances and quiet evenings strolling through the city and. . . .

Wanda stared down at the sidewalk which was littered with bottles and wrappers. She could almost smell the dog shit. When she lived on Stockton Street, she thought she lived in the city, but clearly there were city streets and city streets. What part of town did Roy want to stroll in?

She considered that long, dramatic hike they took through Golden Gate Park three-and-a-half-years before. Three-and-a-half years and still she had doubts about this marriage. Was he the right man? Would they have a good life together? These were the same doubts. However, marriage then was posed against an exciting career as a world roving reporter. Now it was posed against a past of commitment and a future of responsibility. They would get married as soon as he returned from Italy. Everyone expected it. At age twenty-seven, it was time for her to be married. Still, he was encouraging her journalism. After all, she had planned to write before she joined the reporter-photographer team. She did write. Why, during the camp years her diary grew as long as a book. Not that she would want to publish such private material, but it did show her what she could do. Earlier this week, she had five or six article ideas. But, it was impossible – how could she take care of Mama and Betty and go to school? Well, she had never known how they would make it through the last three years. Could the unpredictability of misfortune prepare you for the unpredictability of luck?

The phone rang.

'Hello Wanda, this is Carolyn.'

Chastened about her small worries, she forced herself to be bright. 'How are you, Carolyn? How's my beautiful niece? How's the job?'

'Oh, Winnie is fine. It's hard balancing work and home. I'm lucky to have Aunt Yoshiye to take care of her. I'm grateful for the job. And I keep my eyes open for you, Wanda. I've told my boss that you're a crack bookkeeper. When he starts to see our kind is trustworthy, I'm sure he'll interview. The man they have doing the books now is drunk half the time.'

'Thanks, Carolyn.' Wanda didn't want to raise her hopes. Besides, she wasn't sure Mama would wish her to leave the cannery. 'How's your father doing?' She stared at the front page of the

newspaper. 'Hitler Commits Suicide.' She had heard them screaming about it on the street. You couldn't get anything else on the
radio. She was only reading the newspaper now because Carolyn
made her nervous – one more person who thought Wanda had the
answers.

'Oh, fine, getting some of his former students back. But he's
particularly down today because he got a letter from Uncle Minoru
in Japan. My God, I had no idea of the extent of the destruction! And
the hunger. I should have known, but I've been concentrating on my
own woes. Anyway, hearing what happened to our family alone is
horrifying. Only one uncle left out of six.'

Wanda nodded silently. She wanted to go up to her room with the
tea and write in her diary until Betty and Mama returned. She had
so much to sort out today – about Teddy and Moira, about the war
closing, about Roy's return. But Carolyn was tense, going on
hectically, and she needed someone to listen.

'You know, as awful as that camp was, Wanda, I always feel kind
of grateful for it because it was there I met you. I know that's
cockeyed.'

'Not at all.'

'Well, it is a relief to be away from that place – to have a private
bathroom and kitchen and not to have to walk a mile to do the
laundry – but it's also hard sometimes. I don't know. I get lonely.
Lonely, after years of being in a prison camp, that's crazy, you
know?'

'I know.'

Chapter Twenty-Eight

Spring 1945, London

32,000 INMATES RELEASED FROM DACHAU

———————— • ————————

BRITISH OCCUPY LEBANON AND SYRIA

———————— • ————————

CHINESE MOVE INTO INDOCHINA

———————— • ————————

US TAKES OKINAWA

Anna Rosenzweig stood at the front door watching the parade on Chester Court. Everyone was outdoors tonight. Kids raced up and down the pavement. Neighbors who hadn't spoken for six years were chatting like old friends. Drivers weaved and honked, shaking flags from their car windows. It wasn't safe to be out tonight. Anna shook her head. If it was like this in Hackney, she could just imagine the West End. The radio announcer said Piccadilly Circus was exploding.

Victory in Europe. German Surrender. The end of war. Peace. Were they the same? What had been won – the remaining lives? Reports about the dead became more frightening every day. This was a war they would continue to suffer for years, as the details of the concentration camps were uncovered. For tonight, however, Anna forced herself to admit simple relief. The fighting was over. No matter how many Jews they had killed, this was the end. Reuben had rung and left a message for her to meet him at the Prince George.

She lit a cigarette and stared at her hysterical neighbors. She couldn't celebrate yet. She needed time to contemplate the conclusion and to absorb the idea of having a future. She also needed to watch over Leah tonight. For all his romance about family, Reuben didn't understand the responsibility of having a small child. He would be expecting her. And he would be angry.

Climbing the stairs now, she heard Leah moan from her dreams. The girl had been tired today – not sick, but slow – and she had always been able to sleep through anything. Peacefully curled on her cot in the corner of Anna's room, the child sighed as the door opened. Peacefully, this was such a relative term nowadays. Would a girl who had been ripped apart from her family at age two, only to find at age seven that they were all dead, ever sleep peacefully? Now that the war was really over, Anna would start formal adoption papers. Although this is what they both wanted, Anna worried that the official step would re-open the child's wounds. Yet she had to admit Leah seemed happier since she came here. She ate better and was even-tempered. Cheerful, the word for blessed Leah was cheerful. What would she think of the surrender? She could hardly remember anything besides war in her life. For Anna, peace raised a sheet of decisions about Reuben, about Mama and Papa, about where she and Leah belonged.

'Anna Rosenzweig,' she whispered. 'Anna Rosenzweig.' She was glad to have taken back the family name from the chopping block of Ellis Island. And although her given name was Ann – Papa would countenance no antedeluvian immigrant nomenclature in his American family – she knew she was Anna. Anna Rosenzweig looked out of the window this London evening and knew she would be leaving the city soon. Papa refused to notice and still addressed his letters to Ann Rose. Daniel was good about it, saying if that's the name she wanted it was OK with him, but he hoped he could still be her brother if he kept the Rose. The girls had tried. Teddy was the most consistent. Well, people would just have to get used to it. And she had a right to call herself whatever she wanted. Certainly these two years in Europe had been as much of a birth as the one she experienced twenty-seven years before. She had come to London and found her name.

'God save our gracious king. . . .' The voices would get louder and louder all evening. Eventually they would wake Leah. She turned to find the child still asleep. Of course she had had to sleep through much worse – the journey from Germany, the blitz, midnight screams from the other children in the dormitory.

They would all carry these last few years with them for the rest of their lives. Anna thought about her own despair and fear and exhilaration in London. She felt tougher and more compassionate. Somehow she was able to know the pain of other people in a way she had never been able to experience her family's pain. She wasn't afraid of catching it. This outside pain helped her to understand Mama's illness and Papa's intransigence. Anna looked out at the dancers and the cars. Yes, it was good that she had come here. She had contributed something and she had gained a lot – not the least of which was perspective on her family. But she couldn't assume that understanding better meant behaving differently.

Sometimes she daydreamed about introducing Leah to Mama, having Mama sit up in bed and hold the child. But most of the time she doubted that Mama would ever be able to respond again. If home were so horrible, she asked herself, why was she planning to return? She could stay here and marry Reuben. She could go to New York, visit Ilse Stein and start all over again. She could . . . maybe that's why this 'victory' was so ambiguous.

Now that the world had temporarily quietened, her choices echoed again.

'Telephone, hen.'

'Yes, Mrs MacDonald,' answered Anna. She knew Reuben would ring again, 'I'll be down in a second. Thanks.'

She took the stairs two at a time, thinking about that dreary day last year when she had the flu. She would like to see his sweet face tonight.

Reuben was more excited than irritated. 'Come on down, now, Anna. Lots of people. Esther is here. And Sheila. Everyone from the office. We miss you. I miss you.'

'I can't, Reuben, there's Leah. Someone should stay with her tonight. There's all this shouting and singing. It might frighten her.'

'Bring her along.'

'Children don't belong in pubs, friend.' She shook her head.

'Tonight she should be out. Several children are here already. The police are celebrating too. This is history, Anna, bring the girl along.'

'I'd rather be quiet tonight, myself,' she tried.

'Quiet, for quiet you'd have to travel to the North Pole. Pull yourself together. This is the end of the war, love, the end. We've won. You don't celebrate alone in your room.'

He was right. She would just get lost here in her morose family thoughts if she didn't go. And Leah would love the festivities. He was right. About this.

Leah held Anna's hand as they walked into the Prince George. 'So many people, Mummy.' Leah was amazed.

'Yes,' Anna stuttered, still unused to being called Mummy.

'Over here! Anna. Leah.' A familiar bass voice penetrated the din.

'There he is. Over by the wall.'

Reuben embraced the two of them and kissed Anna on the cheek.

She stared at this tall, handsome man all dressed up in his best black suit. He had shaved closer than she could ever remember and she was mesmerized by the tiny pits in his skin. Sometimes she was astonished by how strange men looked.

He didn't seem to notice her scrutiny. 'You two stay here and I'll bring drinks. Lemon squash?' He turned to Leah. 'And bitter?'

Anna nodded. An old man and woman squeezed together on the bench to make room for Leah.

'Thank you.' She smiled gracefully and accepted the seat.

Such a beautiful girl, thought Anna, bright and vital and so poised for a seven year old. She fairly glowed in that blue cotton dress, a much better choice than the drab brown one Anna had selected for herself.

'Where are you from?'

Anna turned to see Leah engaging her new friends in conversation. She smiled and leaned against the wall, following Reuben's bold movement through the crowd to the bar. As her eyes settled to the smoky atmosphere, she began to make out familiar faces. There was Esther sitting by the window. Yes, she was waving her to come over. Anna shook her head and pointed to Reuben. She had never known the pub this full and loud. She guessed it didn't matter if people couldn't understand each other because they were all saying the same thing.

Reuben returned with drinks. He handed her a whole pint of bitter. Had she made progress? No, he probably just didn't want to fight his way through the crowd for another half. She watched him chatting animatedly with Leah.

The warm beer was soothing on her throat. She looked around at the flushed British faces. They had endured a lot during six years of war. How could she have been so cranky about their songs on the street? She sensed Reuben standing beside her, his long body against her arm and thigh. He was always discreet in public. Not that anyone would mind tonight if they kissed passionately. Except Leah. She liked Reuben, but she was possessive of her mummy. Normal, Anna surmised, startled how normal they all were.

'I love you,' he whispered.

She smiled.

'We made it through together.' He smiled back.

'Yes,' she nodded and took another long drink.

'No reason not to settle down. Nothing to wait for now, except the rest of our lives.'

She stared across to the large, ornate mirror over the bar. She would have to make a decision sooner than she had imagined. Perhaps she had never imagined making a decision.

He moved closer. 'Tonight we live in tonight.' He clinked his glass with hers.

She reached up and kissed his lips softly.

Anna took another sip. Reuben was right. This was a night to forget the future and the past. Look at these people. They had all lost relatives and friends and limbs and homes and businesses and hopes to the war, but they were immersed in victory. She regarded Leah, sociably chatting with the old couple. She set her glass on the table and pulled out a cigarette. Reuben lit her tip with his.

He puffed studiously, blowing smoke rings into the hazy room.

'Balloons,' called Leah. 'Can you do a balloon, Mummy?'

Anna closed her eyes, concentrating on producing a smoke ring.

Reuben laughed as her balloons spiralled toward the intricately moulded ceiling.

The excitement continued at a fever pitch for days. Anna couldn't believe such giddy behavior from the British. They had even managed to drag her out of her own torpor. This week, she had gone dancing twice with Reuben. In fact, she got so far behind on work that she had to bring papers home on Sunday. What a blessing when Reuben and Mark invited Leah to the museum for the afternoon. The museum. Anna hadn't thought about museums for years. How many other usual activities had she ignored during the war?

She heard the doorbell ring and it took her a minute to realize she was alone in the house. Mrs MacDonald was at the Red Cross and the others were either working or enjoying their day off. She cleared her throat and reluctantly walked downstairs. As she opened the door, she saw the man walking back down the path. She stood frozen, but some innate sense of responsibility opened her mouth. 'Here we are. You have something for one of us?' As she spoke, she realized the telegram could be for someone else. The man swivelled and she noticed his shiny black shoes with the perforated toes.

'Glad you're here,' he called. The voice grew too loud as he approached. 'Didn't want to make another trip.' Too loud. 'Yes, this one's for Miss Ann Rose.'

She stared at his sandy hair and his flushed face. The man in the rooming house on Turk Street. He had found her again. No, he had been wearing a paper bag over his face. She remembered the wrinkled brown bag with a stain down the right side. But she had always imagined him to be fair like this.

'Miss Ann Rose,' he repeated.

'That's me,' she said, standing straighter for stability. Pathetic to quibble about names now.

'Sign here,' he said.

She returned his book. He waited. 'We're meant to see if there's a reply.' She heard his East End accent.

Anna read through the window of the envelope, 'San Francisco, California'. It would be about Mama. Or maybe about Daniel. Papa would hear first about Daniel. But the war was over; it was too late for casualties.

'No.' She turned to the man and found relief in his eyes. Horrible job. 'I don't think there'll be a reply right now. Thank you.' She dug into her pocket for a sixpenny bit.

'Ta, Miss,' he said hesitantly.

Anna crept up the stairs, holding the telegram in front of her. Collapsing into the armchair, she stared out blankly at the street. Mama or Daniel. Cruel roulette. What made her think she could get through the war unscathed? Sometimes she thought she had come to Europe to tempt fate, to put herself on the line, to assure everyone else's safety. She could hardly move her fingers. Slowly, she unfolded the telegram and read.

> Dear Ann,
> Mama passed away in her sleep yesterday. Funeral next week. I miss you. Love, Papa

No, it wasn't possible. Mama knew she was gone only for a short time. How could she leave like that? Anna read the telegram again. A mistake. How could she be dead? Her eyes filled with tears, held in by a skein of anger. Never again to see Mama. Never again to say, 'I'm sorry'. Never to say, 'I love you'; to say, 'I wish I could have made it better'. Never again to try for that bond that had been impossible while she was growing up.

Tears rolled down her cheeks; she wiped them away with her palms and then with the sleeve of her sweater. She thought of Teddy. Why did she have to be in London, for God's sake, so far from everyone? This failure she had been sorrowing about all her life was now irreconcilable. Mama was dead. Mama would never hear how she loved her. Mama could never tell her. Oh, Mama, Mama. Why hadn't she been in San Francisco? She might have been able to do something. Had Mama called her name? Did she feel Anna had abandoned her as everyone else had? 'Mama, Mama, I tried so hard to make it right for you. I wanted you to be happy. Mama, Mama. I love you. I'm sorry. I'm sorry.'

Anna staggered from the chair and found her handbag. They would return any minute and she couldn't bear anyone just now. She was tempted to leave the telegram on the table, to give them the shock she had received. Instead, she scrawled a note saying she would be home in a couple of hours. She tucked the telegram in her pocket where it felt warm. Lighting a cigarette, she scuttled down to the cool afternoon street.

She found herself walking toward the park where there would be fewer people. The swans, yes, she could go up to the pond. Still, she couldn't believe it. How could Mama be completely gone? How could she never introduce her to Leah, never tell her about the end of the war? Could it be a mistake? Doctors had been wrong before. Was Papa lying to lure her home? No, these were not rational thoughts.

Ahead of her, three children followed their parents across the grass. One of the little boys held on to his mother's skirt. She kept swatting him away until finally she turned and picked him up. Anna passed them.

The terrible sadness spilled over her face. She wiped her eyes and wished she had worn sunglasses. She remembered times as a teenager, feeling distraught that she lived in a different world from Mama. Sometimes she had wondered if her mother had died years before. Since the age of eight she had been Mama's mother – translating, running errands. Periodically Anna had cried herself to sleep, fretful about Mama dying. She had worried about and longed for Mama's death. These hot tears were so familiar.

The pond was deserted. It must have been months since she visited the park. Anna stood still, staring at the brown water and rolling another cigarette. The tobacco sliced into her lungs grounding her. She realized she hadn't eaten all day. She decided she preferred the sweet heat of the fag. She didn't know if she could hold in anything else. Daffodils bordered the path up the hill. Golden daffodils and narcissus. The scent was overwhelming. She followed the flowers to the crest and surveyed the remaining rooftops of North London.

Would Papa arrange a funeral at the synagogue? Or would he dispose of her body in a discreet Episcopalian ceremony? Her eyes filled again.

Anna thought about the day she and Mama had gone to Golden Gate Park, just the two of them. Such an expedition on the buses. Such an adventure to do something without Papa. The trip had lasted three or four hours, but it lingered in Anna's mind as a vacation might. The afternoon had been brilliant. She and Mama had walked along trails and sat on wooden benches, listening to an orchestra of men in red suits playing gleaming brass instruments. On the way home, she had held Mama's hand and listened to tales about bands in Frankfurt and about family trips to the countryside. That night she had felt a special bond with Mama. She knew how lucky she was. Anna took a drag on her cigarette. Now Mama was dead; Anna would never recover the bright brown eyes and the quick smiles of that once vital woman. Dead. Never again would Anna see her. The tobacco filled Anna with a vast ache. She crushed the cigarette out on the path.

The next week passed in a mist. Everyone was kind.

Reuben held her for three straight nights and let her cry and rant and collapse into muteness. Esther told her not to come to work. Mark said he would try to arrange an early passage home. She was numb to these attendants. She wished she were alone and then, when she was alone, she felt paralyzed. Of course she couldn't stay home from the office. She would go mad in complete isolation. Besides, every day they got more news from Germany about who had survived the camps. There was important work. No, she couldn't just leave, not yet. Papa would be able to deal with Mama's death alone. Her death was no harder to handle than her suffering in the hospital. She wanted to talk to Reuben about his parents, about how he had endured all the grief. She had never understood before. But Reuben's mourning was so caught up in his hatred of the Nazis. Strangely, Anna considered, she got the most solace from her daughter. At first Leah didn't seem to understand Anna had a mother. Then suddenly, three days after the telegram, the child crawled on her lap and simply cried. Anna rocked her, crying as well, and woke up, four hours later, to find Leah still on her lap.

Normally they both looked forward to commuting together to the hostel. It was a time to gossip and cuddle before the day ahead. But for the next few weeks, they moved silently through the tube corridors and on the long, rattling ride to the office. Anna emerged from her sadness in brief patches of clarity. She could think and behave sensibly for half an hour and then she would fall into a dullness in which life seemed to be going too fast or too slow.

One morning as they were seated next to each other on the tube, facing – as Leah preferred – the opposite direction from which the train was headed, Anna spotted a heavy-set woman with a child about Leah's age. Were they Jewish? Italian? Armenian? Dark and large and quiet – like Mama. Soon, Anna imagined, the girl would turn into her mother's caretaker. Already she seemed to be showing her mother a map and pointing to their stop.

Shame. Disappointment. Anger. Anna had started wishing for a regular mother when she was Leah's age – eight or nine. As a smaller child, she was always vaguely aware of Mama's weight. She thought Mrs Miller across the street was prettier and this disloyalty grated at her conscience for months. She admired the ease with which Mrs Miller walked down the street. She liked to go over to the Millers on Sunday nights for popcorn and soda. Mrs Miller cooked hamburgers and tuna casseroles. Mama didn't know anything except the heavy Yiddish dishes and Anna grew so ashamed of the *blintzes* and *latkes* that she didn't invite the Miller kids back. Funny, she couldn't remember their names or their faces and yet their mother, Marge Miller, was etched in her memory. And just as Marge Miller came into her prime as mother and citizen, Mama's shyness grew worse and worse. Her English deteriorated. Her weight increased. Her spells of anxiety and fatigue got longer. Mrs Miller had invited Mama to play bridge, had asked her to join the parents' group, had suggested that she come on girl scout expeditions. Mama shook her head and thanked their neighbor. Then she disappeared inside. Anna began to answer the telephone for her. She held her hand on the long nights Papa spent at the factory. Gradually Anna grew furious believing this was all his fault. They were trailing after his dream. There was no room for anger with Mama.

Anna felt a tug on her coat.

'It's our stop, Mummy.' Leah was looking at her with concern.

Anna searched for the heavy woman and her child, but they had gone. She turned to Leah and with all her strength responded, 'Yes, dear, let's get off the train.'

The weeks were formless. Gradually, she was able to immerse herself in work. Anna was usually aware of what she was doing, but never clear on *how* she was doing. Sometimes she could talk herself out of the grief. After all, the best memorial to Mama was a good life of her own. Besides, she was a woman in her twenties, not a child; God, she had a child. She had to remember her responsibilities.

The letters of condolence were the hardest part. Friends meant well, but they opened the wound again and again, '. . . your mother dead. . . .', '. . . our sadness at her death'. Just as she had climbed back to stability another letter would arrive – from people at work, from friends in the States. At least Wanda and Teddy and Moira included news in their aerogrammes; at least there was something to absorb the pain. Wanda seemed to be doing OK at the cannery although she had been worried about her mother. Separate letters came from Teddy and Moira. Moira was getting married, fancy that. What must Teddy feel; she didn't say much. Oh, poor Teddy, all alone now. Her father, gone, too. These past few years hadn't been kind to anyone.

Finally, a letter from Daniel. She hadn't heard from him since before VE Day. She raced upstairs to her room, grateful that Leah had made friends with the skipping-rope artists of Chester Court.

Dear Anna,

I feel sad about Mama. Where to begin? I wish we were closer, just so I could look at you. I never realized how important family was before the war. Poor Papa. I wish we could have been with him.

I've been dreaming about Mama every night since I heard. Dreaming about sitting in the kitchen each morning. One dream about *Chanukah*. But most of them are commonplace. I often think of her as a stranger, but she's deep in my blood. This isn't making much sense.

Let's try practical details. Tell me about your work. How much longer will you stay in London? Tell me about the girl, how old is she now? What does she look like? Kids change every day, I know. I've grown quite fond of several kids here in the village. Orphans everywhere. I can't imagine the devastation of Jewish families in the camps. I think you've done the bravest work, Anna, facing those stories straight on.

Don't know when I'll be released. There's a point system I'm sure you've heard about. Or maybe you haven't. American GIs think our news is the world's news. Well, you need eighty-five points for immediate release. You get one point for each month of service since September 1940; one for each month overseas; twelve points for each child under eighteen; five points for combat medals. See, this is the military – orderly disorder. I've got about thirty-five points, so it looks like I'll be in on the occupation for a while. I am tired.

Let's stay in closer touch. With the fighting over, mail will get easier. Maybe I'll get a leave to come to England. Remember I love you.
Your brother, Daniel

Anna put down the letter and sighed. Her brother a soldier who survived. Her brother loved her. She had always understood that, despite the way Papa's favoritism separated them. Daniel was right that the war made you weigh things differently. You saw past your own losses. Your blessings became visible. She was alive. Daniel was alive. Papa was alive. How could Mama have survived this war? Anna felt some kind of settling as she looked out into the cool afternoon at Leah who was turning the rope now and singing the song she learned in the hostel.

Jolly old sailor took a notion
For to sail across the sea. . . .

*

Reuben did his best. At first, he tried to listen, spending evenings inside her childhood. Then he tried to revive her, dragging her to the cinema. Then he tried leaving her alone as he went on several trips to other hostels. Then he encouraged her to take a trip with him. Never did he get exasperated. Never did he get tired. He had been through this before, she reminded herself – both parents, four brothers and a sister. He seemed to understand there was no solution. He would wait as long as necessary. And knowing he could outlast her grief helped.

Finally, she agreed to go to Cambridge with him. Mrs Mac-Donald was happy to take Leah for the weekend. Everyone thought a trip would be good for Anna. Had she turned into Mama, with all these people waiting for her to wake up?

The train was packed with families and soldiers. She felt self-indulgent, taking space for a country holiday when so many people had more pressing needs. Reuben got seats; she never understood his talent for such things. He set her down in a place facing toward Cambridge – for, if truth were told, she couldn't get used to Leah's preference for travelling backwards.

It was one of those clearly lit June evenings which wouldn't darken until 9.30 or 10.00 p.m. Secure in the long, late light, she considered the miles of lush green field and she imagined the war had never happened. She turned to Reuben who was deeply engrossed in a book, yes, *Der Zauberberg* by Thomas Mann. She felt illiterate. Reuben could read easily in French, English and German. Why had she given up her classics course? Would she ever catch up? Odd, how when she was with him she was stimulated to go back to school and study. And when she was away for a day or two, Latin and Greek felt like such luxuries. What was wrong with her? Didn't she have a mind of her own? She cleared her throat, this was going to be some holiday if she continued scolding. Look out at the farmland; she reminded herself that the earth was alive, that she was very much alive.

'You are all right?' He touched her knee.

'Sure,' she nodded. 'And you?'

'Fine,' he said, concern in his eyes. 'You seem a little nervous tonight.'

'Just the beginning of the trip. I need some time to unwind. You realize this is the first time I've taken more than a day's holiday since I landed here?'

'And think that we're doubling it now!' He shook his head. 'I hope you'll be able to bear all this leisure.'

She laughed and did feel more relaxed. He was a good man. He loved her. She loved him. She would remember that all weekend. She would enjoy herelf.

Saturday morning was spent in bed. It had been months since they had had such a luxurious time, since before Leah came to her. He was playful – tickling, touching slowly, teasing. As her laughter grew easier, she allowed herself to feel her extraordinary affection for him. They were both lusty this morning, as if the distance from London obligations granted permission to indulge. He came inside her once, twice, three times. And then sitting up, she moved closer to him, gently waking his penis again and drawing it into her vagina. They kissed and rocked and stroked and rocked and climbed together to a climax. Afterward, she held on to him like a buoy. Oh, she needed him. It was more than wanting. Petrified by this idea, her mind turned a joke, 'What if we're stuck?'

He frowned. 'Well, we'll just have to go to work like this. And that would end the whispering about whether we were "attached".'

'Yes.' She smiled and drew apart.

Reuben stretched back with satisfaction, lit a cigarette for her and then one for himself.

His smoke rings reminded her of Leah. 'Really, we shouldn't smoke so much,' she sighed and ran a finger down his temple.

'No "shouldn'ts" this weekend,' he said. 'This is R and R for you. For me too.'

'OK,' she said. 'Easily persuaded.' She held her mouth tight and blew circles to accompany his to the ceiling.

Late in the afternoon, they strolled across Midsummer Common to a pub that had been creaking since the sixteenth century. She thought how Mama used to talk about the ancient façades of Galicia and Germany.

She sat at a table by the window, overlooking the wide, green common. Reuben returned from the bar with his pint and her half pint. She sipped the beer, pretending to melt into the serene pasture before them.

'So I will meet your brother?' he asked.

'Maybe. He doesn't know about his discharge. I hope he comes in time.'

'In time?' His voice was thicker.

It had just slipped out and perhaps this was the best way to begin. 'There's Papa, Reuben. You know I have to go back at some point to visit Papa.'

'Visit?' He gripped his glass. 'Visit?'

She looked out at the grass again. How could she explain to him that she was indelibly American? After all, was he indelibly Austrian? What was a little homesickness in the face of history?

'I got a letter from the University last week,' he offered.

'The University?'

'Edinburgh,' he said impatiently. 'Where I was working. They asked if I could return in the autumn.'

'Oh.' She bit her lip.

'I haven't replied yet.'

She nodded.

'Well, perhaps we should try more immediate topics. Where would you like to have dinner? And shall we take that walk around the colleges?'

Had the weekend vanished already? She tried to stem the depressing thought. This was another late evening train, because they had made the most of Sunday – another turn in bed, a long walk in the country, a pub lunch, rowing down the Cam in the afternoon. Now it was 10 p.m. and they would be in London within an hour.

She was calmer on the way home. He was reading Thomas Mann again. Maybe she would take another class from Professor Warwick. That is, if he would admit her. That is, if he stayed in London.

'So, love, do we need to think about plans?'

She blinked, walking out of the bright classroom into a dark alley.

'Anna, darling, I'm trying to be patient. But I must know. I must tell the University.'

She bowed her head. 'Let's walk out in the corridor.' Silently, they moved the length of the carriage. They stopped by a half-open window, warm wind blowing across their faces.

'Come, Anna, we love each other. Come back to Edinburgh with me. We will make a family with Leah. Marry me, Anna, be my wife.'

'Reuben, I don't know. I just don't know. About Papa.'

'You must have a life of your own – it's not just Papa.'

'I shouldn't use him as an excuse. I don't know what I want. I don't know where I belong. I don't belong in London. But Edinburgh? And what would be best for Leah? I don't know. What about you? Did you ever seriously think of coming to San Francisco?'

'I have my studies.' His thick brows creased.

'Are my ties less important? What about my responsibilities?'

'You could bring Papa to Edinburgh.'

'You're mad. And it's more than that. It's a question of where I can work most effectively.'

'Are you saying you will marry me if we go to America?'

'I, I, I don't know. If only I could talk to Daniel about this.' She turned her back to the window, straining to look past their reflection into the night. 'If only I didn't feel so alone in this decision.'

'Alone?'

'Of course you're here.' She turned back to him. 'That's the point.' She stopped, afraid he would burst into tears.

'Darling,' he spoke more softly. 'I love you.'

Anna cried when she opened the package from Teddy. She was crying at everything lately – when a man held the door for her at Selfridges, when Leah presented her with a self-portrait, when Mark shared the rich chocolate his sister had sent from New Jersey. Teddy's packages were always so careful, containing food that was rationed, wrapped in neat, secure parcels. Today Anna cried at the dried apricots, at the sight and smell of California. She wanted to luxuriate in the memories and to banish them at the same time. Hot summer days driving through Merced to Yosemite. Miles and miles of fecund farmland. Dry, warm, pungent California. Could she afford such feelings? She told herself this was all sentimentality, that it didn't matter so much where a person lived as what she did with her life. What did it mean to be an expatriate? Did people belong to places or places to people? Papa, after all, considered nationality a question of choice and will. Anna pulled out an apricot and sucked in the tart sweetness. Slowly, she put away Teddy's flour and sugar and the precious gift of stockings. Setting aside the little package with Leah's name on it, she was curious about its contents, but conscious that it must be left for the girl, herself, to open. She noticed that she thought of Leah as a girl now, not so much as a child. Anna took another succulent apricot and resolved to share these with Mark, at least a dozen, in return for the chocolate.

'Mummy! Mummy!'

'In here, sweetheart, where did you think I'd be?'

'Oh, there you are. But you said in the garden. You said we would sit in the garden and read this afternoon.'

'So I did,' Anna stumbled, thinking how often Mama had forgotten plans and promises. 'Here – this is why I forgot. Aunt Teddy sent us a parcel. And she seems to have a special present for someone I know.' Leah seemed to like the idea of 'aunts' in the States. Anna did too.

Leah's eyes lit on her name written across green wrapping paper. 'For me. Just for me.' She pulled the package to her chest.

'Well, love, aren't you going to open it?'

'Did you get something special too?'

Anna regarded her closely. 'Yes, I got stockings. Aunt Teddy knows I wanted stockings.'

'OK. Yes, I'll open it.' Leah fastidiously untaped the parcel's seams, pulling out a white blouse with a lace collar. 'Ohhh, pretty.' She held the blouse to herself. 'What do you think, Mummy?'

'I think it's lovely. Really suits you. In fact,' Anna stood up and kissed Leah's hand, 'I think we should go shopping for a skirt to match.'

'Now?' The girl's eyes grew wider.

'What are Saturdays for? Not for moping around the house. Come on, it's a fine day. Let's find the ration book. And we'll go up the Holloway Road to see what we can see.'

A thin blue sky stretched over the spring afternoon. Anna could smell coal from the neighbors' houses as they walked to the corner. The pub was just opening its doors. Across the street walked a man with an umbrella and a bowler hat. She hadn't seen anything like that since the first weeks she lived there. Had they stopped wearing bowler hats during the war? What a peculiar form of rationing. Leah grabbed her hand as they walked along Seven Sisters Road. She chatted about her lessons and the end-of-term show. Anna half listened, her attention fixed to the exotic surroundings.

Holloway Road was chaotic with lorries and buses and cars and bicycles. She heard a horn behind her and another behind that. People shouted out of car windows. She imagined them in a

Gershwin symphony. Three women almost knocked into each other running for a bus. How precisely people avoided disaster, as if moving through a formal choreography. Such energy. Had she been immune to life these past weeks? She glanced at Leah, walking with perfect ease amidst the fray. Anna told herself she was emerging from the numbness.

Then she was enveloped in a memory of walking with Mama to Woolworths in New York twenty years before. A memory of Mama's determination to buy her daughter nice pencils and pads for school, despite Mama's own panic about the language. A memory of her own childish shame over this woman so unlike proper mothers like Mrs Miller. Woolworths had been relatively quiet that day, but still Mama did not stop sweating until they were safely back on the sidewalk.

Anna looked around now. Here she was in the middle of a big, foreign city, holding the hand of a child, her daughter. She felt strong, whole. She needed to let go of Mama.

'Mummy, do you like London?' Leah regarded her intently.

'Why, why do you ask that?'

'Mark was talking about going back to America. He said that it's hard to live here if you're not British. And you're American too. So I was wondering.'

She regarded Leah fully. 'What would you like?'

'I want to be with you.'

Anna nodded. 'Well, love, for the moment that means being here. And for the future, I don't know. Is that OK with you, to wait a little?'

●

Chapter Twenty-Nine

Summer 1945, San Francisco

UNITED NATIONS CHARTER IS SIGNED

● ————————

GENERAL MACARTHUR ANNOUNCES LIBERATION OF PHILIPPINES

———— ● ————

BRITISH LABOR PARTY WINS; CHURCHILL LEAVES OFFICE

———— ● ————

WHITE STUDENTS PROTEST SCHOOL INTEGRATION IN GARY, INDIANA

Teddy was startled by the cool blue of Moira's dress as her friend walked up the aisle past the stained glass windows and wooden confessionals. Suddenly the elegant Church of SS Peter and Paul seemed drafty and vacant. Why had Moira switched from her beautiful, soft yellow dress at the last minute? This tailored linen outfit was, of course, much more mature. Did she feel badly because Moira had changed or just because she had not consulted her? She was shaking as Moira reached the altar. Dawn reached over for Teddy's hand.

'It's OK,' she sniffed to Dawn.

Dawn held on a second longer. Teddy thought it was a good thing she had decided to sit by the far aisle like this. No point in making a spectacle. Moira did seem nervous, teetering on her heels. Teddy distracted herself by staring at the crucifix above the tabernacle above the white altar. She considered the image of Christ holding a book proclaiming *Ego Sum Via Veritas Et Vita* and thought about Moira and Ann swapping Latin over supper. She looked around the church at Mr Rose, Wanda and Mrs Nakatani, Mr and Mrs Finlayson, Randy's brother, Aunt Evie holding Tess, Vivian and Dot, the group of sailors. Some of the people Teddy didn't know. She turned to her own mother, seated stiffly on her left. What was going through Mom's mind? Did she wish her daughter were up there? Mom had been excited about Moira's wedding from the start. She said again this morning that she was surprised Teddy wasn't holding the reception at Stockton Street.

Teddy stared at her hands, at the long fingers Moira had so much enjoyed. No, she must erase those thoughts if she was to have any kind of relationship with Mrs Girard. Mrs Girard. Would she ever get used to it? Yes, she would have to. Maybe she had done the wrong thing in not offering the house. But she didn't think she could stand up all the way through the reception, knowing she was losing Tess as well as Moira. And after that, how would she get rid of the ghosts? As it turned out, the Finlaysons were happy to hire a hall. Moira explained her parents didn't like being indebted. But Teddy detected a touch of disappointment in her friend's voice. And she found a shard of revenge in her own subsequent silence. Maybe she should have swallowed her pride or resentment or terror. Dawn told her she was crazy even to consider offering the house. Dear, dear Dawn, what would she have done without her and Sandra these last three months?

Moira listened to the priest's words as if it were the first time she had heard them. This was it – she was getting married. It was suddenly completely clear. She hadn't reached the vows yet. She could still leave. Yes, she weighed her options. She could still leave this place a free woman. She thought of the nurse to whom she had lied and said her name was 'Girard'. In fifteen minutes, this wouldn't be a lie any more. She ached to be alone, not with Randy or Teddy or even Tess. She contemplated walking into the warm summer afternoon, all the way to the Bay. She didn't have the courage or imagination to escape, yet she would always remember this point in the wedding.

'We have gathered together. . . .'

Moira thought about her parents, together for almost twenty-five years. Would she and Randy stay together? She blushed, as if the others could hear her thoughts. She loved Randy. He loved her and their daughter. Concentrate. Concentrate Moira.

'Do you take this woman. . . .'

Why did they give the woman first? She was married and he wasn't. He could just walk out.

'Do you take this man. . . .'

He looked ten years younger and more afraid today. Moira's heart went out to him. Dear Randy was so determined to do the right thing – to have her parents like him, to bring her to a new apartment, to make enough money so she didn't have to work. She was very lucky. Some women had waited the whole war only to find their men dead or gone. He was growing more thoughtful each day. They would make a happy marriage. Yes, she must concentrate on their life ahead.

Wanda watched Teddy carefully. Her face was so tight it might crack. Poor Teddy, witnessing her love being given away. Giving herself away. It was the worst kind of torture. Almost like seeing someone die. Wanda examined her own neatly trimmed nails. This was her all over – composed, polished. She would never get herself in a position like Teddy. She wondered if Teddy were really braver than she. Why, she couldn't bring herself even to discuss the subject with Teddy. Moira didn't look so hot herself. She seemed to hold Randy's arm for support. Was the dress too tight or was that her imagination? Moira did want to marry Randy. It was all she could talk about for the last two months. Oh, she said she was nervous, worried about whether she could cook proper meals and so forth, but she never admitted the degree of sheer terror that Wanda saw on her face now. Wanda sensed Mama's stiff, small body beside her. Perhaps she was thinking about her own marriage in Yokohama thirty-five years before. Perhaps she was missing Papa. Wanda brushed a wrinkle from her pink flowered skirt. The suit was bolder than she was used to. She had worn the outfit for Moira – and the straw hat with the pink roses. What would Moira wear to her wedding? Years ago she had dreamt of bridesmaids – Anna, Moira, Teddy and Betty – carrying bouquets of daffodils, for it would be a spring wedding, early spring, outside with music and fancy food. Now she knew they could only afford something modest like this. OK. What mattered was that Roy return safely.

Moira stood in the reception line, praying that people would move faster. There would be plenty of time for chatting later. How could

Mrs Girard think of so much to say to each person? She felt silly shaking hands with Vivian and Dorothy. The bride role was easier to play with strangers, like Randy's sailor friends. As her brother-in-law, gawky Boyd, hugged her, Moira thought how she had always wanted siblings but now that she had inherited Randy's brother she wasn't so sure. She looked over Boyd's shoulder to check on the sandwiches, the cake, the champagne and the people clustering in predictable groups. Dot and Vivian were talking with the girls from the yard. Teddy and Wanda and Dawn were laughing in the corner. Aunt Evie and Uncle Benny and Aunt Flora were playing with Tess. They had all come to such different weddings. Dot and Vivian saw it as a farewell party. Her relatives regarded it as a passage. For Mr Rose and Mrs Nakatani and Mrs Fielding, it was another meeting of the extended clan. Mother looked softer than she had in years, luxuriating in public approbation of her daughter. Christ Almighty, this was her wedding, what did she feel? Maybe that would be easier to determine after some champagne.

Teddy left a circle of friends to check on her mother. Mrs Fielding was listening closely as Mr Rose told Mrs Nakatani and herself about Mrs Rose's death. When he saw Teddy, he drew her over.

'Such a fine daughter you have, Mrs Fielding. She visited me and my poor wife so very often during the past few years. We couldn't have asked more from our own Annie.'

Teddy smiled and stepped back slightly. 'Sir, have you heard anything from Anna?'

'Not in the last few weeks. Her letters, I don't know why, they've never been as regular as Daniel's. But the child is fine, so I understand.'

Mrs Nakatani looked puzzled.

'Her adopted daughter,' Mr Rose explained. 'One of the orphans from Hitler. Didn't you hear?'

'Oh, yes,' Mrs Nakatani recalled. 'She can bring the child here?'

'I think so.' Mr Rose tried to sound unconcerned. 'Her mother is an American citizen.'

Mrs Nakatani nodded.

'Ah, yes,' he caught on. 'Who knows, maybe we learned something from the injustices to the Japanese Americans. It never occurred to me that Ann couldn't come back with the child. Oh, dear.'

Teddy intervened. 'She said something about that in the last letter to us.' She paused, thinking that it would be the last letter to 'us' altogether. From here on, Anna would write to them all separately. 'She talked to somebody at the Embassy and it's OK.'

Mr Rose reached up and patted Teddy's shoulder. 'You are a helpful one to have around,' he smiled. 'Always with the useful answer. Always organizing things. Why, if it hadn't been for you, that house never would have got under way. I bet Moira won't know what to do without you.'

Teddy stared at her feet and shrugged, afraid that if she looked up she might cry.

Mrs Fielding spoke. 'Always that way at home, too.' Then, reaching for her daughter's arm, 'Did I tell you we got a letter from Virg yesterday?'

Teddy regarded her mother with gratitude, hugging her for the good news and for seeming to understand about Moira. No, she had never forgotten Teddy's crush on the math teacher. Maybe she could talk with Mom when this was all over. Why hadn't she thought about that?

'And our Daniel will be home soon,' said Mr Rose. 'We must have a party.'

Teddy watched Mrs Nakatani closely, but she seemed fine.

Observing Mr Rose's gregariousness Teddy considered how far he had come in liking the Stockton Street crew. She could hardly believe that he was suggesting to her mother that they hold a party together. But he had become much looser since Mrs Rose's death. Sad as it was, he was free to live his life – with the considerable energy he always had.

'Yes,' Mrs Fielding brightened, 'yes, that would be a nice idea.' Then, turning to include Mrs Nakatani, she said, 'Wanda tells me you're both working in the cannery. That sounds like rough work. I know how tired I get waiting on tables after eight hours. How can you stand in one place all day?'

Teddy watched Mrs Nakatani peering closely for the motive behind this question. Deciding it was safe, she answered. 'Yes, tiring. But like any job.'

'And it must be nice living near your brother again?'

Teddy thought how much easier Mom was in the world, now that she had an outside job. The shyness had almost disappeared. Clearly she wasn't needed here as much as she thought, so with a tap on her mother's elbow, Teddy withdrew from the conversation and walked back to Vivian, Dorothy, Dawn and Wanda.

'Teddy!' Vivian smiled broadly.

What was she thinking? wondered Teddy. Was she relieved to see Moira married? Teddy guessed that Vivian liked her alright, but that affection was mixed with a touch of sympathy.

'Hi,' she answered shyly, knowing all four women would be gauging her reactions.

Wanda thought Teddy looked fairly calm. Her hand was steady and the champagne glass was almost full. No, Teddy had never been one to drink too much, even in times of stress. Wanda's eyes went over to the circle with her mother, Mrs Fielding and Mr Rose. She was grateful to Teddy for checking on them. It was probably her own turn now. But she was enjoying these girls. She especially liked Dawn's sense of humor. How did she and Teddy become friends? Was Dawn a lesbian too? Maybe. She had a toughness and a self-containment and there was something in the way she stood.

'We were just talking about you,' Dorothy said to Teddy. 'Wondering whatever happened to that pariah you work for, what's his name?'

'Whitney,' said Dawn, patting Teddy on the shoulder. 'Is he still after you or what? You haven't mentioned it lately.'

'Oh,' Teddy laughed with relief. 'I think he's finally given up. I told him about "my boyfriend in the Air Force". That cooled him for a couple of weeks. Then when he started to pressure me, I mentioned that my aunt was sick and that I had to spend a lot of time with her and. . . .' She tried to sound lighthearted.

'Come on, now.' Dawn shook her head. 'Don't shrug it off. Tell them how he backed you into the filing cabinet.'

Wanda's expression turned grave.

'Or the time he said he'd fire you if you didn't "show a little company spirit".'

'Yes,' Teddy nodded, because Dawn was never one to let a trial pass unnoticed. 'It was hard there for a while. But he loosened up when another girl, Mary Anne, moved into the next office.'

The women shook their heads.

Teddy continued, 'I invited her to lunch next week.'

Moira listened to Mother's advice about when to cut the cake and when to throw the bouquet. At least she thought she had been listening, until Mother said, 'Moira, why do you keep staring at those friends of yours? Heaven knows you've been living with Teddy long enough and working with Vivian and Dorothy for years. You could spare a moment for your mother on your wedding day.'

Moira nodded sheepishly. How did she expect to be an adult, married woman when she couldn't get along with her own mother?

'And who is that other girl, the colored one?'

'Dawn; she's a friend of Teddy's.'

'I thought so.' Mrs Finlayson inhaled sharply.

'What do you mean?' Moira resolved to settle this peacefully.

'Well, I don't know where you would meet someone like that.'

'What do you mean, "someone like that"?' Moira lowered her voice. 'Lots of Negroes work in the shipyard. Besides, Teddy met Dawn at the Emporium. Negroes have been in America for a long time, Mother, longer than our family.'

'OK, I can see you want to visit with your friends. You don't have to keep your old mother company.'

Moira now noticed how tired Mother looked. The wedding is harder on her than on me, Moira reminded herself. Mother had worked for months organizing the buffet and the champagne and the flowers. She must be patient with her, and grateful. One did need a wedding to have a marriage.

'Mother, I've appreciated your help. Don't spoil. . . .'

'No, no, I didn't mean to sulk. And I apologize about Dawn. This is your day and you should enjoy it. Besides, I should say hello to Mrs Fielding, Mr Rose and Mrs. . . .'

'Nakatani, Mother.'

'Yes,' her voice was strained. 'I've been practicing the pronunciation.'

Moira tried to shake her irritation as she walked across to the girls. Vivian looked stunning in that white suit. Wanda's pink was marvellously daring. Dorothy's yellow shirtwaist was a little girlish, but perhaps, Moira thought, she was simply jealous that she couldn't fit into a size 6. Teddy looked trim in the dark blue. What would she think about her changing clothes at the last minute? Should she tell Teddy that Mother insisted on it? Should she bring it up in front of everyone? Dawn already thought she was enough of a jerk. But then Dawn seemed conscious of clothes today in that dandy red and grey suit. Dandy, could you use that word for a woman? Moira's eyes moved back to Teddy as she wondered how she was feeling. She looked calm, but you could never tell with Teddy unless you were close enough to be sure she was breathing.

'Here comes the bride,' announced Dawn.

Teddy checked Dawn for signs of hostility, but her face was impassive.

'Come to visit the old girls' corner?' laughed Dorothy, turning at the perfect angle for Moira to catch her slim figure.

'Come to see my friends,' Moira smiled, 'if I'm allowed to drop official duties for a minute.'

'Your outfit is super.' Vivian kissed her cheek.

'Congratulations, Moi,' Wanda winked. 'You did it, the first of us to get hooked. I always knew you would win first prize.' Suddenly she felt Teddy's presence, a heavy anchor beside her.

Teddy looked down at her hands.

Moira went on anxiously, 'I changed at the last minute. Mother thought this was more dignified. I'm sure either dress would have been fine. I was so nervous, I might have walked down the aisle naked if she hadn't been there.'

'That would have been a pretty sight,' Dawn smiled.

Dorothy put in quickly, 'Why should you be nervous? Do you feel different being Mrs Girard?'

'A little different. More's expected now. But I look the same as I did this morning, don't I, Teddy?' She bit her lip. It was unfair to force Teddy into the conversation.

Teddy raised her eyes and held Moira's glance, furious at her for playing on their intimacy and then furious at the others for not acknowledging it. Why didn't anyone ask if *she* felt differently – to be losing Moira, to be losing Tess? She cleared her throat, the force of propriety drawing her down. 'No, you look just as pretty, Moira.' Could they hear her anger? Were they waiting for her to say more? She thought she was getting along fine today, but her equilibrium depended on Moira's distance. In church, it had all seemed like a movie. Here, with Moira in the flesh, it was a nightmare.

Dawn intervened. 'So Vivian tells us you are all going to lose your jobs. Make way for the boys, huh?'

'Yeah, damned unfair if you ask me,' Vivian continued, somewhat high. 'How are we supposed to make a living?'

'But those men have been fighting for us,' Moira answered. 'They have families to support.' Her stomach constricted at the stupidity of her comment.

Vivian shook her head. 'That's all very well for you, honey. You have someone to take care of you. Now that Rick and I have split up, I'm on my own.'

Moira winced, feeling like a gate crasher at her own party. She had heard weddings brought out the worst in people.

'And some women have families to support,' Dorothy added. 'The war is leaving a lot of widows.'

Teddy glanced at Dawn's even expression as she followed the volley. Maybe she hadn't started this on purpose.

'But Teddy, you'll be OK.' Moira was desperate to detour the conversation. 'You and Dawn. No one is going to take your jobs.' She knew it was a stupid remark, but she didn't care. Why didn't they behave? Why didn't they act as if this were her wedding?

Dawn laughed. 'No man is gonna want to sell girdles at the Emporium. Women just got to get the right kind of job.'

Wanda nodded. 'And no one is standing in line to clean fish, yet. So I guess Mama and I are safe.' Did she sound too flip? Dawn was having an interesting effect on her.

'To tell the truth,' Moira leaned closer, 'I don't know how I feel about quitting. Staying home is a dream to some people. But I'll go stircrazy.'

'You can always have another kid,' Dorothy laughed.

Moira blushed. She glanced over to Tess who was sleeping in Aunt Evie's arms. Then she felt a tap on her elbow.

'Mrs Girard?' Randy said, 'Would you like to join me in cutting the cake?'

'Already? Yes, why not?' She turned to Dawn, in a last, strained attempt at friendship. 'It's such a great cake. Marble. Mother wanted white cake and Randy wanted Devil's food, so they compromised on marble, isn't that a kick?'

'Yes.' Dawn answered inscrutably.

Wanda closed her eyes, wishing the day were over.

Tess cried. Instantly Moira and Teddy turned.

Good old Aunt Evie, thought Moira, as the child was rocked back to sleep.

Teddy's eyes lingered on the baby. She had no words to express her sadness about losing Tess, losing her child. She had been there since the beginning, had sat up nights with her, had helped to support her. But how could a baby have two mothers? Her pain seemed illogical. She hadn't even been able to talk to Dawn about it.

Randy put his hand gently on Teddy's shoulder, 'So how are you doing?'

'Fine,' she said. 'Just fine.' She had to keep her anger – and her suspicion – in check. Moira had promised not to tell Randy about their relationship. Promised a little too readily. Did she consider it trivial? No, she was probably petrified he would desert her if he knew. This gesture of Randy's was just friendship and maybe a little recompense for her lost room-mate. No doubt they would be inviting her to supper soon, to make sure she wasn't lonely.

'The cake.' Moira looked from one to the other nervously. 'Let's go cut the cake.'

Teddy turned over in her bed which was cold and far too large. She knew it was early – six o'clock at most – from the light. Too early to get up. So what had wakened her? The silence. The emptiness. Of course – Moira was gone. Tess was gone. Teddy was alone.

She rolled over, digging one ear into the bed and putting her hand over the other. She couldn't close out the voices. Moira's. The priest's. Dorothy and Dawn and Vivian laughing over the champagne. Mr Rose congratulating the groom. Mrs Finlayson weeping as they cut the cake. Tess squealing in the late afternoon. Everyone clapping and cheering and giggling when the bride and groom descended the steps into the light summer rain. How did you silence echoes?

No sense lying here. She stuck one leg out of the bed, then another, feeling an odd memory of that morning Moira was sick in the bathroom. Would all the days be hemmed with memories? God, she felt wretched. Walking rapidly across the room, she threw on her robe and hurried downstairs. Surely her head would clear after breakfast. She had so much work today. She had promised to tidy up Wanda's room for Mom's cousin who was visiting from Fresno. Wanda's room. She supposed she shouldn't call it that any more.

Opening the back door, she stared at the garden. The beans and lettuce were flourishing. Also the zucchini. Anna would love the garden. Teddy had even put in some crookneck squash in case she made it back before September. If Mr Rose was right, she might just do that. Too cold for standing outside. Teddy shivered. She drew her robe closer and peered hopefully toward the melon vine.

Back at the table, she admitted to herself that Anna would

probably not return to Stockton Street. Reuben might be coming with her. Even if he didn't, Mr Rose had a big, empty flat. Now with Leah, Anna would turn toward family again. Teddy shook her head and then caught herself. At least she wasn't talking out loud. How ironic that it was she who was left alone. Anna and Moira had kids and Wanda, if everything went safely with Roy, would be married and having babies soon too. Of all of them, Teddy supposed, she herself was the most family-like and yet she was the one left alone. So, was it a tragedy? She did have her mother and brothers and sisters and friends. It wasn't as if she was in exile. She would have to calm down. Yes, she would tackle that room for Cousin Letty as soon as she finished breakfast. Come to think of it, she didn't feel much like eating this morning. Maybe she would go straight up there now and . . . and she broke down sobbing. The woman who was afraid of talking to herself was sobbing and beating the table and sobbing, at Moira's desertion, at her own loneliness, at the unfairness, at her confusion. Loud, ragged cries tore from her body. What had she done wrong? She had always tried to be good for Moira and for Tess. She had taken care of them, loved them. Moira had loved her, hadn't she? She hadn't pretended all that time, surely. She had changed her mind. Partly for Tess, she had explained. . . . Teddy ran through the story again. She had loved Moira with all her love and it wasn't enough. Did that mean she didn't know how to love? Sobs wrenched her body. She had tried. And she had done everything she could. It wasn't fair. No, damn it, first Angela. And now this. Her whole life had been taking care of people – brothers and sisters, Pop – and they all went off on their own. Leaving her, the capable one, alone. All alone in an empty house. She sighed and stood. This was getting nowhere. She didn't feel better. The tears brought more tears. The room, that was it, she would go up and check on the room for Cousin Letty.

As she climbed the stairs, she wondered why she had decided Letty should stay in Wanda's room, for surely it would be possible to put her in Tess's room, which had been Moira's room. Wanda, Tess, Moira, she felt like a madwoman in a house of memories. She paused at the top of the stairs, her eyes fixed on the spot she had found Moira that terrifying night. Teddy opened her mouth and a yell emerged, then a high-pitched scream, cauterizing her mind of pain. Yaaa. Yaaaaaaa. She needed to clear her memory and claim it back for herself. Yaaaa. Yaaaaa. Yaaaaaaaaaaaaaa. She leaned against the banister, waiting for a response.

Wanda's room looked out on a quiet street. The front room, that's what she would call it. And Tess-Moira's room was now the side room. And Anna's room? She would call it Anna's room until her friend reclaimed her belongings. The front room was empty except for an old double bed they had moved in after the Nakatanis took back their furniture. That and a small table with a lamp. Well, this would do. Letty wasn't expecting the Mark Hopkins Hotel. She would pull out the blue curtains from the linen closet and get the scatter rug from the basement and give the floorboards a good scrub. Yes, in a few hours, this would look like a real room. Teddy changed into work clothes and let herself feel briefly that it would be nice to have company again, especially the kind of company you didn't become attached to.

As she washed the back floorboard, depression descended again. Here she was at twenty-eight, a shrivelling spinster. Everybody else was going off and doing important things. What had she done during the war – nothing as useful as Moira or Anna. She stayed in her silly job and sold war bonds. She had stayed and taken care of the house. For what? She had helped Mom with the kids and then with Pop's death. She had visited Mr and Mrs Rose and the Minellis. Everyone's favorite daughter. How long did she think she could go on being the good girl? 'Grow up!' She heard herself shout. 'Grow up!! Instead of watching everybody else do it!' The yelling calmed her and she returned to the floorboards with renewed vigor. The scrubbing eased the tension, made her feel that she was accomplishing something. Maybe that was an illusion like the war bonds and the caretaking. What else was she going to do? Sit downstairs and cry all morning? No, she was going to finish this room, dammit, and maybe afterwards start on Tess's – on the side room.

It was hard to avoid the ghosts lounging invisibly about the house. What was she remembering, yes, those days in Oklahoma when she knew she was going to leave, when she knew she would lose the glorious sunsets and the acres of frozen flat fields and blue sky which kept her still and tranquil. She remembered Anita and their last visit together – at Anita's sickbed. She had promised to come on one last walk with Teddy and then had taken sick. Sick in the middle of the summer. They played dolls together. Anita's usually shiny brown skin had a dull, greyish cast. She looked at

Teddy with dark eyes and asked if she had to leave, asked why Teddy's family couldn't stick it out for just one more season. Teddy didn't want to go. These were the same questions she had badgered Mom with when Pop was out of hearing.

'Don't know, Nita. I don't want to go.'

'What's out there?'

'California.'

'Do you suppose there's oranges dripping off the trees like they say?'

'Maybe.' Teddy shrugged, not wanting to admit that she was looking forward to the trip. If only she could bring Nita with her. Surely Nita wouldn't be sick like this in California. People went there to get well. To get rich.

'And luscious ocean, I understand. Enough sun and ocean to keep you happy for a whole life.'

'Maybe,' Teddy shrugged. 'But what's that if you are away from home?'

'Home?' Anita sat forward from her pillow and examined Teddy's long face. 'You all are bringing your home with you – your parents, your sisters and brothers. You'll just have a new house out there, that's all.'

'Won't be home.'

'Sure will. What more could you want? Your folks, warm days and the sea.'

'You.' Teddy blushed but kept her eyes steady with Anita's. 'You and this land. I'll never forget.'

'You will too.' The ancient child leaned back on her pillow. 'Soon's you dive into that blue, blue water, you'll forget this parched place and everybody here.'

'Never,' vowed Teddy. 'We're blood sisters, don't you forget.'

'Me, I'm not likely to.'

Teddy leaned more heavily into the soapy scrub brush, swishing away the guilt. She had kept in touch with Anita, had written letter after letter – getting Christmas cards in between – promising some day to return to Oklahoma. Then one year there was no Christmas card. None the next year. Nor the next. When had they stopped? Teddy guessed it would have been when she was seventeen. Still, she herself sent cards until one was returned, stamped, 'Addressee Unknown'. What had she done about going to see Anita. She had never made it to Lion's Head to visit Wanda either. She was too busy holding down the fort at home until everybody deserted the fort.

Teddy stood and stretched, scrutinizing her work. The room smelled clean. And the floorboards fairly shone, making the blue wallpaper look even more faded. Yes, she should get around to re-papering this room and the hall. Must have been thirty years since the walls had seen any work. The tears welled again. Teddy imagined herself a seventy-year-old woman, alone in a beautifully renovated house. Year after year, Teddy thought, she could do a new, empty room. At this rate, each room would be redecorated four or five times. She stopped herself. Yes, she needed a cup of tea. That would shake her out of this, this . . . and she had a vacation coming. Mom could do without her. There wasn't any reason to stay here. God knows what the house would look like if she didn't get away. Yes, that's what she would do. She would take a train to Fortun. She would write, first, of course, to the Negro minister and to the school. But even if she didn't get a response, she would go back.

The tea canister was empty. One of Moira's chores. The girl had let so many things go at the last minute. Teddy pounded the counter. Her eyes filled again and her hands shook uncontrollably. She gripped the edge of the counter for steadiness. 'God damn her. God damn that selfish, lying bitch!!' She felt a little better. 'It will be all right. I'll get used to living alone.' She rummaged around the top shelf for cocoa mix. Ridiculous on a summer morning, but Teddy wanted something reassuring. Just as she stirred the powder into the hot milk, the doorbell rang.

Through the curtains she could see it was Mr Swerington, the mailman, with a package. He smiled broadly when she opened the door. 'Another present for Miss Finlayson, I suspect.'

Teddy stared at him. Didn't he understand Moira was gone? There was no more Miss Finlayson. Could she send back the package, 'Addressee unknown?' Miss Finlayson had turned into Mrs Girard. 'Addressee Deceased.'

Mr Swerington regarded her closely and repeated, 'Package. Can you sign for it, Miss Fielding?'

'Yes, sir,' she said reflexively in her Emporium voice. 'We'll' ('we' – me and the madwoman?) 'keep it for her until she returns.'

'That's right.' The mailman smiled again. 'She'd be on her

honeymoon now, wouldn't she? How was the wedding?' He waited, then noticing the strain on her face, filled in, 'Guess all weddings are about the same.'

She nodded coldly. She was truly sorry to be taking it out on Mr Swerington.

'Almost forgot,' he said with the cheer of conversations past. 'You also got a letter from England!'

'Oh.' Teddy let in a touch of lightness. 'Yes.' She reached for it, as if claiming the only good news that week. 'Thank you, thank you very much.' Still, she sounded out of control.

She brought the letter to the kitchen, retrieved her hot chocolate, opened the back door and sat on the top step overlooking the garden. Most of the morning fog had burnt off and she settled comfortably with Anna's letter.

> Dear Teddy and Moira,
> How are you? Still there, Moira? I hope this letter will arrive on time to wish you a happy wedding.

No, thought Teddy, this is not what she needed. Maybe she should read it another time. Might as well continue to the end of the page.

> And you, Teddy, how do you feel with everyone gone from the nest? I've thought about you often this week and hope you won't be too lonely. I know what lonely is. Even after all this time in London, I often feel abandoned by my family. Strange, isn't it, since I was the one who decided to come?

Teddy shook her head and sipped the chocolate which was now gooey and lukewarm. The letter would be good for her; how had she considered putting it aside? It was a fine, long letter. Anna was clever about getting so much on a page.

> It's been hard here since VE Day, in some ways harder than during the war. At least then, there was a sense of building to a climax, that we were suffering through something which would end one day. And here it is over, the war in Europe anyway, and we're still living in rubble and eating ersatz food. Of course people are grateful that their sons aren't dying and that we're not likely to be hit by another German missile, but the pain is more visible in many ways. I guess it's like how you feel after a long walk – while you're doing it you may be tired, you may even ache, but you keep moving because you know it will be

over. Although there were periods in the last few years when I feared the war might not end, I really knew down deep that it would. And now, after the race, you suffer all the painful bruises.

It's hard on us at work, now that we are getting reports about the children's parents. Almost all of them gone. After what these children have endured there will be no home! Will they stay here with the English families? The last word on one girl's relatives came yesterday. Not only were her parents gassed, but her three aunts and two uncles are gone too. How do the Red Cross people have the stomachs to gather these grisly statistics?

Reuben has lost everyone. He is sure now. And I feel so much responsibility to him. But now he refuses to come to America. What do I do? I love him, however the war has made me challenge so many of my old ideas about love. Feelings can pull you in different directions and the strongest ones at the moment are not always the most important. Do I sound too abstract? Yes, I suppose I am. But even this makes me question my bond to Reuben. Does that make any sense? Maybe I'll change my mind? Maybe he will change his mind?

One thing I have decided – but don't tell Papa yet because I haven't written to him; it seemed easier to tell you first – I have decided to return to California to live on Filbert Street. Teddy, I know this will disappoint you. And I know, I know, Papa drives me crazy. But this war has shown me so many Jewish families torn apart. I can't bear to perpetuate that. It will be good for Leah to have her grandfather and maybe I can persuade Daniel to move in with us. So this much is decided: Anna and Leah will return in November or December, as soon as we can get a ship.

Teddy stared across the yard to the fence. Anna had to do what was best for her. The neighborhood seemed uncommonly quiet today.

Now that the decision is firm, I have started to think about things I miss from the States. People come first, of course. You, Teddy, and you, Moira, and Wanda and Rachel and the family. And then the food! When I land I'm heading straight for the nearest hamburger and strawberry milkshake. But there are all sorts of ephemeral things – like the sense of humor. The

British laugh a lot, I guess, but there's always an edge to it, an irony, that I never knew in the States. Interesting, but not as silly as American jokes. Ours have more sense of possibility. British jokes are founded on despair disguised as indifference. Sometimes I spend an evening with Mark just laughing and laughing at the British self-importance, laughing at our child-hood riddles.

Lately I've become fascinated by the ways people behave. How did I think I could spend my whole life with Latin and Greek grammar? When Mama was going through her tor-ments, the academic world seemed safe. But I'm not as afraid as I used to be, to say, 'I don't know.' I'm not nearly so defensive, Moira, you wouldn't know me. But I do continue to smoke like a chimney.

Oh, what will happen to Reuben? I have made the right decision about Papa, yes, I think so. What will Reuben do by himself? Well, it's his decision, too. I hope you don't mind my nattering on like this – 'nattering', see I've picked up the language – I feel as if I haven't written a really good letter for ages. Just think of this, we'll all be able to talk in person soon. You'll meet my little Leah. And I'll meet Tess. I'm so excited. Great love to you both, Anna.

Teddy set the letter down on the stoop and glanced at the melon ropes. The garden would come and be gone by the time Anna returned in the fall. Anna was coming home. Home. To her own home. Teddy reached up to her eyes, surprised to find them dry. She didn't feel like arguing with Anna's decision. Had she become numb? She looked out at the garden and hoped she hadn't stopped caring.

Wanda sat in the living room with the newspaper on her lap, 'Bomb Destroys Nagasaki'. She stared down at the traffic noise. First Hiroshima and now Nagasaki. It was unimaginable, they said, the extent of destruction, the power of the flash, the number of people killed by one bomb. One bomb. Then why did they have to drop another? The surrender would have come. The Japanese were proud people; they just needed time. They would have signed the treaty in another few days. Unimaginable. But she had been dreaming about Hiroshima for nights. And now this. What went on in the minds of scientists divining these fires? Did they ever see children being ripped apart? Could they smell the flesh burning? Or did they stick to sterile calculation – so many ounces of bomb for so many lives? Wanda set down the newspaper and thought about Mama's silence this afternoon. What was she thinking? She used to talk so fondly of Grandpa's trips to Nagasaki and now the city did not exist. Not that there was much left of Tokyo or Yokohama. Gutted buildings and starving people. Wanda closed her eyes and imagined corpses littered on broken sidewalks. Japanese people dying in the fire of their own bones. What was going on with Mama? She must check, but not yet, she needed another moment to absorb the details. Officials had known about these bombs for months, withholding information to protect the national security. Here she was, safe and sound, Wanda Nakatani, secure American citizen.

When the phone rang, she grabbed it. 'Hello.'

'Hello.'

'Oh, hello, Moira.'

'Wanda, are you OK? I've just finished reading about that horrible bomb and I knew that you. . . .'

What did Moira think, that it affected you just because you had Japanese blood? Did she think there was something in the genes that could be touched across the ocean? No, of course not. This was a friendly call. This was Moira, her friend Moira.

'Would you like to switch plans for tonight? Would you like me to come over there?'

Plans for tonight. Wanda looked at her watch; of course, she was supposed to meet Moira half an hour ago. 'No,' she heard herself speaking. 'I don't think so. I need to stay here, with the family tonight. I don't think I can handle a dinner.'

'Sure, hon, sure. I'll call you tomorrow and check on how you're doing.'

Wanda tried to ignore the medical metaphors, tried to be polite to this person on the other end of the phone. 'Yes, do that. Thank you.'

Betty entered, admitting a breeze from the hallway. Wanda hated the door opened into the ugly, concrete stairwell, but she was revived by the air. How long had she been sitting here with the windows closed?

'Sorry I'm late, Wanda. I got held up at my lesson. Mr Sasaki was telling us the war is over. Isn't that wonderful? Isn't it? Now Roy can come home.'

Wanda hated her sister just now, hated her youth and her cheer and, most of all, her patriotism. 'Roy is in Italy, Betty, not Japan. You can count your stars he isn't in Japan because he would have been burned to a crisp with the rest of the Japs.'

'Don't hurt the child.' Mama stood at the kitchen door. 'Not her fault. Betty's right. War is over. Come, we will have tea.'

Wanda obeyed and followed Betty into the kitchen. Mama was serving special tea they had saved from before the war. She had set out five cups. 'First for Papa,' she said and then drank from his cup.

'Now for Howard.'

Wanda picked up her brother's cup and drank.

Mama raised her own cup. Wanda followed. Then Betty.

Mama pushed a letter forward. 'We're not going to Japan. The Red Cross could not find anyone in the family.'

Wanda tried to stifle the deep sigh travelling through her body. Was this definite? Would Mama change her mind?

Betty smiled thinly and took her mother's hand. 'We'll be all right here. You'll see.' She couldn't hide her relief, so she took another sip of tea.

'We will not be all right,' Mrs Nakatani spoke steadily. 'But we will live. And you will have children. Both of you. They will return to Yokohama.'

Wanda shivered at her mother's uncharacteristically prophetic tone. She looked at the old woman carefully and saw that she sat straighter, lighter than usual. Wanda hoped Mama did not plan to die soon. She closed her eyes, thinking about her diary and what she would write tonight. Details. She tried to steady herself on the details.

The blood covered Wanda's hands; she examined the thin, red line beneath her fingernails. Closing her eyes a moment, she saw queues of limbless people, some of them missing parts of their torsos – a hip, a breast. She opened her eyes again and smelled the ripe gore. She was not dreaming. All around her were pieces of skin, strips of spine, chips of bone. As much as she tried to convince herself to stay at the cannery – where else could she and Mama work side by side, where else could she even find a job? – she knew she would have to leave. After all that had happened during the last three-and-a-half years, she was not going to go crazy in a room of fish carcases.

Chapter Thirty

● ────────────────

Fall 1945, London

NUREMBERG TRIALS BEGIN

────────── ● ──────────

ARAB LEAGUE OPPOSES CREATION OF A JEWISH STATE

────────── ● ──────────

RATIONING OF SHOES, MEAT AND BUTTER ENDS IN US

────────── ● ──────────

DETROIT BEATS CHICAGO IN WORLD SERIES

Anna sat at Reuben's table and followed his swift movements toward the kitchen. She shook her head at his spirit – fixing an elaborate dinner after work and still unable to settle down. He had to make sure her wine glass was full. She reflected how comfortable she had come to feel in his flat this last year. She didn't notice the draft from the high Victorian windows or the clinking of the gas meter any more. How deeply was this atmosphere impressed on her memory? How much would she miss it after a month – or a year – in California? She took another bite of stew. Delicious, she couldn't believe she was eating so much; maybe it was to absorb the wine. She would regret the indulgences tomorrow but there would be so much pain then anyway. Tomorrow. No, concentrate on tonight. This was the last evening in London. Her last time with Reuben. She and Leah were boarding the ship tomorrow and sailing home. Home? Sailing to the United States. As her parents had done. She felt a trace of headache as she watched Reuben uncorking the new bottle. What was *he* thinking now? He seemed equanimous, even cheerful. Did he know a secret about the ship being drydocked or was he putting on a good show? She wished he would express his feelings; it would make it easier for her to let go. No, perhaps he was right to adopt this neutral tone. Where had he found this superb Cabernet?

'Sorry to take so long.' He smiled shyly. 'The corkscrew. Some of these bottles barely survived the hostilities. Perhaps that's why the cork didn't want to come out.'

She listened to his elegant Viennese accent, wondering if it had always been this strong. Often during the war she felt numb to certain sensations. It took an effort to hear and to see clearly.

'Thanks.' She held up her glass greedily. Yes, she did know him well enough to be greedy. He looked so dark tonight – that had come with a summer in which he had finally allowed himself sun.

'You are all right?' He examined her closely and held the back of his hand against her forehead.

'Yes,' she laughed. 'I was just thinking about Leah. I'm sure she'll be OK with Mrs MacDonald tonight.' She should tell him she was just pretending to be a cordial stranger to stem the grief. She was afraid to look at him and took another long gulp of wine.

'Yes, she will be fine,' he said. 'More stew?'

'It's delicious, but no thanks, love. Really, this was beyond the call of duty.'

'Duty?' He shrugged and opened his mouth as if about to continue. Then distracted by the flapping window shade, he stood to adjust it. 'Your father has all the details of your arrival.'

'Yes,' she nodded. 'Yes, he knows. Do you want to talk more about this, Reuben? Is there something you're trying to say?'

'I've said it all.' He smiled ruefully. 'I won't stand in the way of your decision. And I'll come visit you in America as soon as I have saved money and things are sorted out at University. I will bring you back here. That's why I can be festive tonight. I cannot love you by holding you here. But I know you love me and you shall return.'

She tried to hear devotion in his voice. Instead, she was unnerved by his certainty, by his silence about tomorrow. Oh, for God's sake, what did she want from the poor man? Here he was trying to let go generously. He had cooked a sumptuous meal. He would escort her to the ship.

'To love.' She lifted her glass as a toast and drove confidence into her voice: 'To us.'

It felt like years before she was allowed to go to bed. They talked and talked about friends and music and seasickness. They consumed chocolate cake and coffee and brandy. The evening inched by with excruciating anticipation. Anna was at once sad and exhilarated, wishing to stay in London forever and desperate to leave. First, what time was it, oh, better not look at his wristwatch, no, too late, 2 a.m., they went to bed.

She crawled between the sheets, exhausted, and waited impatiently, listening to the rush of water in the bathroom. Why did he insist on brushing his teeth tonight of all nights? But that was the point. The last night. He was feeling everything while she had grown numb.

He stood at the door, bathroom light shining on to the bed. 'You are beautiful, my Anna.'

'Come to bed, love.' She patted the sheet beside her, suddenly alert and aroused. 'No, don't,' she said as he reached for the light. 'Tonight, let's just leave it on, OK? Let's remember each other clearly.'

'For that, I don't need an electric light, but as you like.'

When he opened the sheets, she smelled the heavy sweetness of his armpits. She could almost feel his bear arms around her. He moved closer, but she held him off gently, relishing the image of this big man in the soft light. He lay next to her, stroking her arm and leg. Her insides swelled and melted.

He shifted on top of her. She accepted the silent weight, protecting her, holding her, engulfing her. She imagined flowers opening each other in spring. She could feel his penis grow stronger and harder against the inside of her thigh. Just once, she would like to experience that kind of expansion in herself, know something grow so rapidly and perceptibly. What did he think when this happened? How much control did he have over it? Did he ever resent her for 'doing this to' him? She could feel her own liquid web weaving wildly. She grew wider inside and then spread her legs. He moaned, stroked her hair and reached down to her breasts with his mouth. Dizzy, she grew hungry for him. But he continued licking back and forth, back and forth. She bit his ear and he breathed with satisfaction, rocking his lower body against her moans. 'Yes,' she whispered, cutting the silence. 'Yes.' He raised his face over hers and watched carefully, smiling, seeming to take in a dozen aspects of her face before he kissed her lips and moved his penis closer. Just the touch caught her breath. 'Yes, yes,' she heard herself saying. He moved inside her slowly, as if tasting the temperature. He pulled out carefully and then returned. Deeper, he entered and deeper and she raised her buttocks off the bed so he could enter her deeper still. Where was he, how far from her heart, from his peak? At moments like this, she wished she could unzip herself and draw him into her skin. So close, almost merging, almost merging and then – the distraction of his rhythms, of his consuming lust. 'Yes, yes.' His voice. 'Anna, oh, Anna.' The hot, tense excitement suspended her above the bed until she felt circles within her, reaching from the lips of her vagina to the base of her belly. He climaxed right after her, magnificently loud and sweaty and completely spent. He remained on top of her and they lay together like sun bathers lapped by a salty ocean. His breathing was so even that Anna wondered if he were asleep and, as the thought crossed her mind, he shifted slightly.

'Are you OK?' he asked.

'Mmmmm,' she said, unsure about whether she wanted to sleep like this or whether she wanted him to move immediately so she could bathe and go home. Crazy she was tonight.

He drew apart slowly and she became more aware of the moisture between them. Chilly now, she snuggled into his arms.

Stroking her hair, he softly issued her name, 'Anna.' His breathing grew steady and she knew he was asleep. Why did she feel deserted? They had talked until 2 a.m. They would talk more tomorrow. She was leaving him. She backed closer against his body; his arms tightened around her.

She could not sleep. Sometime later – half an hour – an hour – she moved toward the edge of the bed and placed the pillow over her head. She still liked to sleep under the pillow like this although the night sirens had ceased months ago. Tonight the pillow seemed filled with memories of London. Her first morning in the office when she wondered how she would survive in such a dreary, cramped, freezing room surrounded by those immense files of irresolvable troubles. The day she met Leah's enormous brown eyes. The time Mark apologetically returned her letter and commenced their friendship. Reuben's precipitate visit to the house. The hours spent on tubes, crushed between people figuring out crosswords or reading about the royal family. The phone calls, articulating her words scrupulously until they could be comprehended by London ears. Did she have a British inflection now, or was Mark just teasing her? The walks through Finsbury Park.

Now she was scuffling around the pond. It was a cold, spring afternoon. Spring? They said it was spring in London, but it could be Greenland, with this Arctic wind. Alone. Not alone in the park, surely. But alone by the swans. 'Love.' The voice came from behind her and when she turned there was no one there. 'Love.' The voice came from the side and again, when she turned, she was completely alone. 'Love.'
'What?' Anna asked.
'Love?'
'Who?'
'Owl?'
'Is this some kind of game?' She whirled around. A fierce wind blew across the daffodils, knocking several to the grass. Stopping to collect the flowers, for surely they would die here with their stems broken, she felt another wind from behind. And she was lifted into the air, surrounded by white and a great flapping sound. She was flying above the pond thinking, oh, good, I always wanted to see the house from here and suddenly. . . .

She was beneath the pillow again, tossing, amidst the rich fragrance of sex. She listened to Reuben's breathing, hoping that it would make her sleepy, but it only made her more anxious. How could he sleep like that, so peacefully, without moving? Well, he wasn't journeying 6,000 miles. Already, she could feel the hangover – that thick, stuffy feeling behind the eyes. Her mouth tasted of wine-turned-to-piss and her teeth were scummy. Would she wake him if she went to the bathroom? No, this was ridiculous, she would just wake herself more. She needed sleep. Ann reached for pleasant thoughts: the geraniums in her windowbox; the sun on Parliament Hill yesterday; the aroma of Reuben's splendid dinner, but every piece of gratitude was stalked by mourning. Tomorrow. Panic coursed through her stomach, dissolving the sexual satisfaction. She had packed a week ago and in the ways she was not ready she would never be ready. Closing her eyes again, she tried Esther's meditative breathing, one-two-three-four-three-two-one. This only bored her.

The fur on her teeth was driving her nuts. She would slip out of bed quietly and he wouldn't notice.

'Anna, are you all right?'

'Yes, Reuben,' she called from the bathroom, opening the door. 'I'm fine. Now go back to sleep.'

'Back?' He sat up, watching her watching herself in the mirror. 'I've been awake for the last hour. How can I sleep with you so worried?'

Surprised at her tears, she told herself he wasn't scolding. He was concerned. She finished brushing her teeth and switched off the light. He clicked on the bedside lamp.

Climbing back to bed, she tried to pull him beneath the covers. 'Come on down, bear, you'll catch your death up there.'

'What's the use pretending?' he asked. 'Let's talk a while.'

She sat up, pulling the sheets over her breasts, and reached for a cigarette. She offered it to him and he sucked hungrily. 'There are more.'

'No.' He shook his head. 'I'd rather share yours.'

'They go faster this way.'

'But it's more fun.'

She carefully observed him – quiet, sober Reuben. Very few people knew what a boy he was, how charming, how spontaneous and silly.

'So what's on your mind?' He rubbed his chin with his thumb.

'Guess.'

'The trip will be fine. Those ships have made it through rougher seas these last six years. . . .'

'I'm talking about. . . .'

'And we've made it through a lot,' he laughed. 'We'll be fine. Just wait until I bring you and Leah home.'

'Reuben, don't convince yourself of anything. None of us knows what's going to happen.' But she didn't want to be the voice of doom. Just because she was leaving, she wasn't responsible for everything. 'Who knows, when you make that famous trip to the States, you might decide to stay. You know, California wine is superior to your French juices.'

'Hang about now.' He looked at his watch. 'Hmmm, 3.30. No, even the hour can't explain such delusion. California wine couldn't begin to compare. I'm sorry.'

'You're not sorry at all,' she grinned.

'Not about that, no.' His voice cracked and he turned aside.

'Oh, Reuben.' She reached for him, but he moved away.

'Love, don't.' She took his arm and felt his whole body shake. 'Sweetheart, I'm sorry. I'm really sorry.'

He turned and settled his head on her breasts. His tears ran through the sticky sweat that enclosed her body and she imagined herself turning to salt.

'It's no one's fault.' He had stopped crying, but his breathing was weighted. 'Not your fault, not my fault. . . .' His lips trembled again.

They both broke into sobs now, rocking back and forth in the old bed.

She squinted at him through the tears. Wiping off her cheeks, she sat straighter and sniffed. 'The two of us!' she tried to laugh.

He tried to laugh.

'Sleep?' she suggested.

He checked his watch. '4.15. That leaves us a little time. Why not?'

As they slid beneath the covers, she tried to feel safe by picturing the light rising outside.

Anna opened her eyes that morning, glad of the cold she felt on the tip of her nose. She would hate to leave London on a perfect day. Not that she believed in omens, yet she noticed that, since Mama died, she was sounding more and more like her. Reuben was still sleeping beside her. She didn't want to waken him, but there was so much work to do before they got to the ship. Tentatively, she moved her hands from the warm vapors of the bed. Cold, yes, it was going to be one of those dank London mornings. She could see fog shrouding the steeple down the street.

'You awake?' He opened one eye.

'Yes, it's seven o'clock already,' she said absentmindedly, realizing she would have to get her own watch repaired now that she was leaving Reuben. She had wanted him to bear the temporal responsibility in their relationship. Temporal. Spatial. This would be so different tomorrow. Could space invade time? The past? Which was worse, being far apart or being long apart?

'Then you must be ready for breakfast.'

'Breakfast?' She felt the full impact of her hangover. Who was he, the mad chef?

'Yes, I made pastries yesterday afternoon. And I managed to get some of your favorite coffee from Emilio's.'

'Coffee would be terrific,' she said, noticing how American she sounded already. 'I just don't know if I could do justice to your baking right now.'

'I suspected that would be the case, so I wrapped some for the sailing.'

Where did all the good will come from, she wondered. Had he always carried the cheer for them as well as the watch?

By the time he had prepared coffee, she was ready to leave. She forced herself to sit down and drink the cup of coffee with milk and cinnamon. It did revive her. She knew she should linger, and she should at least give him the chance to eat his own pastry, but she had no room for consideration. She was worried about Leah and felt an irrational need to get going.

'You don't have to drive me, you know. The tube will get me home in half an hour and what will you do waiting around for me all morning while I pack?'

'Watch.' He smiled.

'Hmmmm.' Watch her sorting through the final threads of her London life? Watch her cry as she said good-bye to Mrs MacDonald and Mark? She knew he was being romantic; she knew he was being kind. Surely this must be more terrible for him. Why was she so angry? Was it that she couldn't admit it to herself that she wanted to be alone this morning, that she would actually prefer to ride the tube in solitude and have one last walk in Finsbury Park? He wanted to spend the morning with her for the same reasons she wanted to spend it alone. He wanted to catch last glimpses, to preserve last moments of their time together.

'OK.' She shrugged her shoulders, for there was no satisfactory solution. 'You win. Come along for the picture show.'

The street was alive with horns and screeches. Anna kept staring out of the car window, startled by the clog of automobiles and lorries and taxis. She had never been driven through rush hour before. She had always taken the underground. How different the city was up here. She didn't like the sensation of everyone segregated by automotive steel. At least on the tube, you could look around and see the colors of people's shoes and the weave of their coats. Here, she felt like part of a carnival ride, closed off with Reuben in their little seats, imminently risking collision. Still, it was fascinating to see the journey directly: Covent Garden to Holborn to Euston to Camden

Town to Hackney. Elegant buildings next to blackened holes.

Ahead of them a crowd of people walked into the street because the pavement was cordoned off. Anna watched one woman trying to pick her way through the broken concrete and twisting her foot. She stood against a building, holding her ankle. Anna could feel the sharp pain and turned to Reuben to ask if they might stop and offer the woman a lift. He was completely absorbed in the obstacle course ahead. Behind, a bus driver leaned on his horn. Anna decided to leave the woman to other good neighbors. She knew she would remember this incident for years even though it was neither tragic nor dramatic. Here was London crystalized: the arduousness of daily movement; the resourcefulness of the people; the ways strangers helped and confounded each other; the individual picking her personal direction through confusion. Anna recalled newsreels she had seen of London before her arrival – pictures of the Blitz and of the crowded hospital corridors. This had led her to expect a grand and bloody theatre. Instead she found the challenge more prosaic: navigating the way to work; juggling rations of clothing and food; negotiating the electricity shortages; worrying about the children; communicating with people back home; living on the edge; trying not to look over the edge.

'How are you?' Reuben was more relaxed now that he had escaped the bus and was driving twenty miles an hour up the Holloway Road.

'Just lost in thought,' she smiled.

'That sort of day.'

Why was he so damned understanding? Where was the old, feisty Reuben? This cool was his way of coping with the departure. And he was no fool; he knew he was making her feel guilty.

'How are *you*?' She played with the handle of her handbag.

'Sad. But fine,' he said and then concentrated on the traffic ahead. Seven Sisters Road was congested with shoppers and people rushing to work. 'Almost home.'

Home. She realized how much she would miss this respite. How much she had looked forward to returning to this creaky Victorian house. As a child, home was alternately a nest and a prison. Stockton Street was fun and fulfilling and a place for coming into her own. This house had been her refuge, the only place in London she felt safe. How she would miss the long walk from the tube, the lilac that bloomed in the Irish woman's yard each spring and the kids who skipped rope beneath her own window.

Reuben pulled up to the house. Before Anna could open the car door, Leah came dashing into the street. 'Mummy! Mummy! We're taking a ship today.'

Behind her, Mark followed, a frown on his tired face, his hair touseled and his bathrobe hanging loosely over his pajamas. He had lost a lot of weight these last two months from overwork. Anna knew she should have badgered him more. What would happen when she was gone? More to the point, what had happened to him this morning?

Reuben raised his hand in greeting. Anna was pleased, as ever, by the friendliness between the two men who were quite alike in their bluff sensitivity.

'Has she been keeping you up dancing all night?' Anna inquired.

'Oh, no,' Mark said sleepily. 'Mrs MacDonald got an emergency call from the Red Cross yesterday, so she asked if I could keep an eye on her until you returned.'

'We've been playing ship!' Leah was delighted in the spotlight. 'We've been playing shuffleboard and watching for albatrosses.'

'Albatrosses?!' exclaimed Anna.

'Well, it was early and I'm not much of a sailor,' squinted Mark. 'Albatrosses were all I could think of.'

They walked into the house. Anna shook her head at Leah's exuberance and patted the girl's jittery shoulders. Did the ocean seem vaster to a child? Certainly the journey would be longer since she didn't know what was on the other side.

'Tea?' Mark asked Reuben. 'Why don't you come into the kitchen for tea while the ladies pack.'

'Ladies!' squealed Leah.

'You've won her heart,' Anna laughed. 'She won't want to leave you next thing we know.'

'You mean you don't want me coming along?'

'Say,' Reuben coughed, 'I believe I should have first shot at that.'

'You can both come,' Leah laughed. 'I'd like two daddies.'

Surprised by the blush crossing her own forehead, Anna said, 'Enough! You're all trying to confuse me because I'm tired. Speaking of which, Miss Muffet, when did you go to bed?'

Leah's eyes rolled toward Mark.

He answered. 'Well, I figured it would be her last chance to hear the BBC. Then we got to talking. I'm afraid it was rather late; one might even say early.'

Anna shook her head. 'Men! Come on, Queen Leah, let's leave them to their teapot.'

Anna followed Leah. Where did the girl find such energy? How had Mama kept up? A heaviness gathered in Anna's chest; she had been moving with Mama all day.

Leah waited at the top of the stairs, her hands on her hips, exasperation lightly tracing her lips, as if the day – and certainly her mother – were moving too slowly.

'I'm right here, honey,' she called. 'Now did you pack your toys in that box?' Anna caught up with Leah. She opened the door and wanted to shut it immediately because the room was so spare. It hadn't looked like this since the spring day when Mrs MacDonald asked, 'Will this do?'

'Yes,' Leah said, almost inaudibly, speaking lines from another stage. 'I did it all before we told ghost stories. Mark said I had to follow your orders.'

'Then maybe you could help me by, uh, by sweeping. Go get a broom from the kitchen, sweetheart.'

She could hear Leah bounding down the stairs. Then the men's voices greeted her. And the laughter. Such a charmer. Anna looked around the room again, at the stacks of boxes piled in the corner – the open suitcases; the cleared closet. All that was left, really, was moving their clothes from the drawers. How would that fill four hours? She'd been crazy to start so early. She hadn't been this manic when she moved from Stockton Street because, of course, she had much less to bring. Little could she have imagined returning with a daughter. And these first editions of novels and strips of lace and fragments of jewelry from the street markets. Why had she collected so much?

'Mummy.' Leah stood with one hand on her hip and the other holding the broom like a lance. 'I'm back.'

'So you are, my inspiration. Why don't you start over there, in that corner, and then work your way across the room?'

The broom was really too large. Anna pictured the girl dancing with Ichabod Crane. Still, it was good for her to have a sense of purpose, good for the men to have some time alone downstairs, good for her to have company here. Now where to begin – the underwear or the sweaters? She stood, staring at the bureau. What was wrong with her, did she expect them to get up and move of their own accord? She opened a drawer, lifted a pile of – yes, nightgowns – and laid them in the suitcase. Then the slips and. . . .

'Doorbell, Mummy, may I answer it?'

'Yes, love, but don't race down those stairs. You'll break your. . . .' Mama again, well, it was fitting.

'Anna, Anna.' The breathless voice was Esther's. 'I'm so glad.' She entered the room, holding a box tied with a red ribbon. 'I was so afraid I had the time wrong, that you'd be gone. I still don't want to believe you're leaving.'

Anna watched Esther's nervous eyes. This was so unlike the collected Esther who supervised her trials with Reuben and her anxieties about Leah.

'Perhaps we're not. I seem to be paralyzed between the sweaters and the socks. We could miss the ship at this rate.'

'Oh, Mummy, no, let me help, we can't miss the ship.'

'All right, sweetheart. Enough from you for the moment, why don't you run down to the shop and buy yourself a drink? Wouldn't you like that?'

'Yes, I, I, I guess so. But promise me we'll make it to the ship. Promise me you'll finish packing.' She looked at Esther accusingly. 'You'll let her pack, won't you?'

Anna didn't know whether to be amused or annoyed. 'Off now. I guarantee we'll make the ship. Let Esther and me say good-bye.'

As the girl bounced down to the front door, Anna turned to her friend and surprised them both by weeping. 'Esther, I'll miss you. What will I do without you?'

'Eat sweets for a while,' she grinned, extending the box.

'Thank you, Esther, it's lovely.'

The two women embraced and then, embarrassed, they moved apart and regarded each other in silence.

Finally Esther said, 'Here, we've always worked well together. You do the socks. I'll take care of the sweaters.'

Esther and Mark helped load the car. Reuben invited them to come: people could squeeze; laps could be sat upon. No, they both declined, insisting it was better for Reuben to see them off alone. Esther sniffed into a pink handkerchief. Mark bent down and made

– 403 –

funny faces at Leah. Finally Reuben started the car. And so they left Chester Court, Anna sitting in the front seat holding a box of books and Leah in the back with her ragged bear. Anna checked her turquoise hat in the rearview mirror. This would have been the perfect outfit for Moira's wedding. Leah turned and waved to Esther and Mark, long after they were out of sight.

They were silent until the bridge. Reuben cleared his throat. Leah tried singing. Finally, Anna spoke. 'It was kind of them.'

'Yes.' Reuben nodded.

'What?' demanded Leah, 'What was kind of who?'

'Oh, everything,' said Anna, 'Esther and Mark helping us pack, saying good-bye. . . .' she trailed off. 'Leah, honey, will you sing that song again?' Time seemed to dissolve.

When they reached the dock, Reuben couldn't figure out where to park. Anna was overwhelmed by the crowds, by the colors and racket. She hadn't considered how packed the ship would be even though she knew that thousands of people were leaving for the States these days. Leah fretted, 'We're not going to miss the ship; we're not going to miss the ship, are we?'

'No.' Reuben's temper broke. 'Be quiet, Leah, we've got an hour before sailing.' He recovered a softer voice. 'Now help me by keeping your eyes open.'

We've got an hour before sailing, thought Anna.

A uniformed man led them down the grey metal stairs toward their cabin, then down more stairs, and more. Anna grew more claustrophobic with each step. She felt the fringe of a headache on the right side and cracked her neck to loosen the tension. Well, Mama and Papa had travelled in steerage, so this would be OK; they would be OK. Mama, are you still with me?

'Mummy?'

Anna blinked and looked around. Where was Leah? Her heart pounded. Where was the child? 'Reuben,' her voice was alarmed, 'Where, where. . . .'

'Don't panic,' he said, nodding at the stairwell below. 'There's Captain Hook.'

'Mummy, I've found it, 20B. Our number. Our cabin.' She dashed ahead.

When Anna and Reuben arrived, the cabin door was wide open and Leah was sitting on the bunk talking to an older woman.

'Mrs Birnbaum,' explained Leah.

Anna regarded the elegant woman. Mrs Birnbaum held herself like a figurine, poised and delicate, handsomely turned out in a black hat and a blue tweed suit. The material was of fine quality, but a little threadbare. The woman kept her finger in her book, as if the interruption would be temporary.

Mrs Birnbaum smiled. Anna smiled back, noticing the book was *Yankee From Olympus* by Catherine Dinker Bowen. Perhaps they could swap books during the journey.

Mrs Birnbaum slowly examined the strangers. 'No one told me there would be a child.' She had a light German accent.

Anna wanted to cry. No, not at the beginning, please not trouble now. She noticed that the woman had taken the best bed in the cabin, the bottom bunk on the right. Fair enough, but let her be tolerant of children.

'This is no ordinary child.' Reuben moved forward. 'Permit me to introduce myself, Reuben Litman, a friend of . . . of the family. This is Anna Rosenzweig. And I see you've already met her daughter, Leah.'

Mrs Birnbaum unclenched her hands and sat back against a pillow. 'Mr Litman, you will be travelling too?'

'Not on this trip, I regret.' He offered his most winning smile, reminding Anna of his shy cordiality two years ago. 'But in Leah, you will have the most amiable of companions. A good conversationalist who knows how to be quiet when appropriate.'

Mrs Birnbaum laughed. 'Excuse me, one does get tense at times like this. I'm afraid I've been horribly inhospitable. Welcome, both of you. I'm sure we'll all become friends.'

Leah offered Mrs Birnbaum a sweet. Meanwhile, Reuben dispatched the boxes and suitcases from the corridor. They sat and chatted for a few minutes. Then, suddenly, too soon, the whistle blew and a man's voice announced over the loudspeaker, 'Twenty minute warning. Will all visitors please leave the ship.'

Anna stared, petrified at the white loudspeaker, noticing that paint had stuck in some of the tiny holes. Reuben moved closer on the bench and put his arm around her.

Mrs Birnbaum looked at Leah. 'Why don't the two of us take a stroll? You can show me the ship. Do you know where the lounge is?'

'Yes.' Leah jumped up. 'We passed it on the way down, didn't you see it? Let me show you. Is that OK, Mummy, is that OK?'

Anna nodded and smiled gratefully at Mrs Birnbaum. 'We may just take a stroll ourselves.' Turning back to Leah again, she whispered, 'Do you want to say good-bye to Reuben now, love.'

'Yes, yes, yes. Oh, Reuben, what will we do without you?'

Anna wondered which movies Mark had been taking her to. But the girl was crying, her face caved in with grief, as if this were the first time she had realized the adventure involved sacrifice.

Reuben picked her up. 'We'll meet again, beauty, you'll see. I'll come for you in America.'

Leah regarded him questioningly and then threw her arms around his hair. Reluctantly, she climbed down and escorted Mrs Birnbaum to the deck.

Anna couldn't speak. She took his hand and stared at his large brown eyes.

He drew her close and they held tightly, rocking, sighing, rocking, sighing. Pulling slightly apart, she studied his face and trembling lips. Her hat fell on the floor and he retrieved it with a gallant flourish.

'Ten minute warning, ladies and gentleman. All visitors must leave the ship at this time. Ten minute warning.' A second whistle sliced across the cabin.

Wordlessly, they walked toward the stairs. Anna stopped abruptly and returned to lock the room, castigating herself for being so irresponsible. Here she was, not yet even embarked, letting another woman care for her child and leaving their cabin open to intruders. He took her hand; quickly they climbed the stairs.

She had counted on a long line at the gangplank, but most of the visitors had already departed. The whistle shrieked again.

She gave him another deep, rocking hug and whispered into his chest, 'I love you, Reuben. I will miss you, bear. Thank you, oh, thank you.'

'I love you.' He struggled to keep his voice steady. 'I'm coming for you, I promise. What's an ocean?'

'Yes, yes.' She nodded and kissed him passionately. They held each other until the next whistle. Then slowly they let go. He walked down the gangplank, turning every third step to wave and smile.

She squeezed into a place by the rail, keeping an eye on him. At first he didn't see her. She waved frantically, knocking her hand into her hat. Impulsively, she took it off, let it go and watched the hat float down to him. He managed to catch it. Laughing, he put it on his head and waved broadly. She waved back, recalling Wanda on that awful bus trip to camp. The tears streamed down her face as she thought of all the subsequent departures of these last few years. She missed Mama so badly. They seemed to be moving, no, that was just the rocking of the ship, which, she realized, had been going on since they boarded.

'I love you,' he called. 'I love you,' she shouted back. She kept her eyes on him – silly, dear man in the veiled, felt hat. The turquoise bow looked ridiculous.

'Drive safely,' he called.

'Yes.' She waved. Oh, how could she be leaving him like this? He was right, there was so much work to do here. So much unsettled about the children. Her chest ached. Well, she could still stay. She could run down the gangplank. Yes, she thought, that would be the braver choice, to stay in London. She started to turn from the rail.

Then she remembered Leah. She had made her decision. No matter where she lived, she would be leaving someone. The next whistle was almost drowned out by the wrenching screech of engines as the ship inched away from the dock.

— • —

Chapter Thirty-One

Christmas 1945, San Francisco

CHINESE AGREE TO AXIS TREATIES PROPOSED IN MOSCOW

— • —

TWENTY-EIGHT NATIONS ESTABLISH BRETTON WOODS BANK

— • —

GENERAL GEORGE S. PATTON JR BURIED IN LUXEMBOURG

— • —

US NATIONAL CHRISTMAS TREE LIGHTED AT WHITE HOUSE FOR FIRST TIME SINCE 1941

Teddy stood before the tree which was a truly grande dame in skirts of tinsel and popcorn, sparkling with red, green and blue balls. Elegant. Spirited. It reminded her of the trees they used to cut in Oklahoma. Pop lost interest in big trees once they reached California; he claimed trees didn't know how to grow out West. But Pop, Jolene would argue every Christmas, they had got the biggest trees in the world out here. And, every Christmas he told her not to sass him as they put up a scrawny four-foot bush in the corner of their living room.

One thing Teddy had always loved about Stockton Street was the big trees, why you couldn't fit anything else in these high-ceilinged rooms. The other girls didn't really care. Anna and Wanda had never celebrated Christmas and Moira laughed, trying to explain

Southern California Yule on the beach. So each year Teddy would drag in a big tree like this – 7 or 8 feet – and they would have a party decorating it on Christmas Eve. At first, she knew, they indulged her. But it had become one of the Stockton Street rituals. She shook her head, maybe she should have waited and let them decorate the tree, but she had wanted it to be perfect when they arrived. It was a spur-of-the-moment decision to invite them, for she hadn't known until the last minute that Moira would be in town. Everybody said it was a great idea and that they would try to make it. Perfect. She checked her watch. 8.00. She told them to drop by any time after eight. She hurried back to the kitchen for the cookies and eggnog.

She wasn't sure about the eggnog. It seemed the sophisticated thing to serve. Had she used enough rum? Or maybe too much? Wanda wasn't keen on alcohol. Should she be serving it in this old punchbowl set, with two chipped glasses, or should she have settled for paper cups? Somehow the paper ones didn't seem right.

Teddy closed her eyes, wondering who would arrive first. Probably Anna or Moira, because the kids would have to go to bed early. But then Mrs Nakatani didn't like late hours either. Teddy was worried about the presents. Had she found the right doll for Leah? She was such a little mother, so unlike Anna in some ways. Teddy had opted for the doll that drank water and then released it through both ends. Tess seemed too young for a doll, so Teddy had chosen a furry brown monkey. It was even harder to select presents for their mothers. The blouse for Moira – she did still like green, didn't she? What a ridiculous question; it had only been a few months since she left the house. Would Anna wear the earrings and would Wanda use the fancy pen? She had been careful – personal and generous – but not extravagant in case they would be embarrassed. Well, if anyone complained, she would say she got a good discount at the Emporium and she had a little extra money to fiddle with since she didn't have a kid and her rent was free. Worry. Worry. You could try enjoying Christmas, Teresa Fielding. 8.30.

The doorbell rang twice, quickly. Must be Moira, she sighed; only Moira was that impatient. Teddy noticed that she was both relieved and nervous because she doubted that Moira would actually show up. Smoothing out the front of her dress, she hurried to the door. Teddy wished she hadn't invited Randy, but what else could you do on Christmas Eve? She would be polite and ask him about the garage.

Four young carollers stood in the cold, singing 'Away in a manger'. Sweet, thought Teddy, concealing her disappointment. She leaned against the doorframe, shivering, not wanting to get a sweater, not wanting to encourage them to prolong the singing.

'Thanks,' she waved and dug 50 cents from her pocket. 'Merry Christmas.'

She sat back on the couch and poured herself an eggnog. Really, she should wait. But this would help her relax. She hoped the girls didn't mind that she had asked Dawn and Sandra. Of course, they would all bring other people too. And even though Dawn and Sandra weren't part of the family, they had been a big part of this house during the last few years. It was nice of them to change their plans tonight, she should think about it that way. Oh, what was she going to do when they moved away? Sometimes it seemed as if everybody moved except her. Everybody had gone through enormous changes and here she was in the same house, with the same job. No, no, this was exaggerating. She had shared a lot with Moira and she had grown up since then. She was more sure about being a . . . lesbian. Yes, there were some times with Dawn and Sandra when she felt quite special being a lesbian. So what if she still lived in the same house. Progress didn't require geographical movement.

8.35. When *were* they going to arrive? It wasn't the wrong night or anything? No, the carollers had come; this was obviously Christmas Eve. Should she have held an open house all day tomorrow? Would that have been easier on people? But they might have missed each other that way – some coming at noon; some coming at 5.00. Tonight would be the first time they had all been together since Wanda left.

This had seemed like a good idea – people dropping by for a drink. A few toasts, a couple of photos, maybe a song and then people could drift back to their own lives. 8.37. She couldn't wait any longer, so she walked over to plug in the lights. Standing back, admiring how the white bulbs winked like candles in the colored glass balls, Teddy was filled with nostalgia for her family Christmases.

The doorbell rang again.

Wanda sat in the living room waiting for Mama to make up her mind about Teddy's party. Should she remind her that they were supposed to decide by 8.00? Would that set her off again? Bad enough that Betty should go carolling with her high school friends, leaving Wanda to umpire as usual: Mama wanting to protect her younger daughter from the vulgarity of Western culture and Betty demanding 'a normal American life'. Sometimes Wanda let the two of them argue. She had thought about going alone to Teddy's house. Tonight it didn't seem right to leave Mama solitary in her principles. Not that Christmas was an important observance in their house, but this afternoon Mama had put fresh flowers in front of Papa's and Howard's photographs.

Wanda turned to the Christmas cards on the living room table. The blue and white Madonna was from Mrs Wright, who was so happy to have her husband back in Chicago. This was, what, the third or fourth time the woman had written and Wanda needed to respond. Mrs. W was always gently urging her to accept the scholarship at her friend's college. She wasn't such a bad old bird, Wanda knew, and she felt touched by her persistence. Still, the woman did not understand her family responsibilities.

The red Santa was from Carolyn. Wanda had read this card over and over; at first her delight was edged with jealousy, but now she felt mostly pleasure.

> Really enjoying the term here. The baby has only been sick once and the Andersons take her while I'm in class. You'd love Portland, Wanda, right on the water, with beautiful bridges and parks. I miss the San Francisco weather, but most of all I miss friends. Any chance you could come up during Christmas break? How is your mother? And Betty? Is she still practicing? . . .

It was good for Carolyn to get away. She had to start a new life. Carolyn needed school in a way that she, herself, didn't. She had Roy. He would be coming home soon.

At least that's what his card said.

> Spring, that's the latest word. And I've never considered what a long season spring could be. Will they send us back in March or June? Well, either way, dear one, I'll be spending the summer with you. That will give enough time to prepare for optometry school in the fall. The government money should cover us, in case you wanted to quit work and start a family or something. I can't believe I'm writing this boldly. One thing the war has done – it's taken away a lot of my silly shyness. I mean

we do have to talk about things like this, don't we. We're not getting any younger. Oh, Wanda, I can't believe we'll see each other in – at most – six months. Can you believe it?

No, she couldn't believe it. She wanted to see him now. Then again, she didn't want to see him for another year or maybe two. This was the man she had been longing for. They had waited for the war to end. And now it had. They could get on with life. But that meant a lot of decisions.

It was difficult to move from a period when time seemed to control you into a freedom where you owned time, where you made decisions with it. For four years now, she had concentrated on getting through the day, through Papa's death, through the camp drudgery, through Howard's death, through the relocation to San Francisco. And now everything was supposed to return to normal, where she made normal choices about what to do with her normal life – when to get married, when to have babies. Why was it happening so quickly? Teddy would be a good person to talk to about this. Nothing ever went too quickly for her. Teddy, yes, she really had to phone.

Mama carried a tray of cookies. Oh, dear, she has forgotten the party, thought Wanda. Lately it felt as if Mama had given up. Papa and Howard gone. Dreams of Japan gone. She carried isolation low on her shoulders and moved like a faint shadow.

'Thank you, Mama. I would have got this for us.'

'You rush around all day. Time to take care of Wanda.'

Wanda watched her mother carefully.

'Reading cards again?' She handed Wanda a cup of tea.

She nodded. 'I wonder if cards don't make the season harder. People mean well, but. . . .'

'It's more than lonely you feel, isn't it, daughter?'

'What do you mean?' Wanda thought about the conversations they used to have when she was a teenager – her mother encouraging her to strike out on her own, not to be traditional like the other Japanese girls. Here was that familiar tone of voice – ironic and challenging.

'Do you miss friends so much – or your old self?'

'Sorry?' Mama was metamorphosing too fast.

'Do you miss your choices?'

'I still have choices, Mama.' She tried to steady her voice. 'The

– 412 –

problem is that there are too many choices.'

'Which are?'

'When Roy and I get married. When we start raising a family.'

'What about Wanda's choices?'

'Those are *my* choices.'

'Married choices. What about your own choices?'

'Mama, could you be more direct?'

'Writing.'

'Those old dreams. The war changed the old dreams.'

'Changed? Ruined?'

Wanda stared at her mother.

'I have been thinking a long time. You should go to college now.' She held up her hand. 'Don't interrupt. You have your own life, even if you are going to marry.'

'But, Mama.' Wanda tried to breathe normally, wondering if Mrs Wright had suddenly possessed her mother's body. 'How will we support the family?'

'You're smart enough for scholarships.'

Wanda shook her head. 'But how will you. . . .'

'I earn enough for Betty and me. And if you get a scholarship and a part-time job, well, we can make it.'

'Mama.' Wanda tried again to contact the familiar spirit. 'Really?'

'Don't be surprised. Anger gives strength. After time. When I gave up Japan, I put my mind on living here. No sense otherwise. Papa would say there is no sense living, unless living well.'

'Oh, Mama, I love you. I, I. . . .'

'Yes. You have waited a long time for Mama to return to the family.'

Wanda shook her head, wishing all the more that they were going to Teddy's tonight, so she could discuss school with her friends. But Mama looked settled and she didn't want to spoil the mood by nagging about a visit to the *Hakujin no* girlfriends. Teddy would be OK. Anna would show up, probably with her father. She would call Teddy and explain later, after she and Mama had a chance to talk.

Anna sat back in the chair, exhausted, growing more tired by the minute as she watched Papa and Leah play. For a child with a bad cold, Leah had a lot of energy. For an old man, Papa could keep up the pace. Why was *she* exhausted? She didn't know, but she felt one of the headaches coming and, if she pushed it, they would be in

– 413 –

trouble, so she just sat back and watched.

She was lucky they had taken to each other so well. Not that she was surprised that Papa would love Leah. Oh, at first, she imagined he might worry that she wasn't his flesh and blood, might feel squeamish about her calling him Grandpa, but he had adored Leah from the minute he saw her at the train station. 'She's so like your Mama,' he had said cryptically; Anna still had not asked him to explain. Leah liked him hugely, and knew how to draw him out. It hadn't been unqualified peace since they returned home. At first Papa had had a hard time with the child's noisy exuberance. But after years of Mama's muteness in the house and more years of her absence in the hospital, he had been relieved to relinquish the quiet.

'Papa, will you have more tea?' asked Anna.

'Yes, Mummy. I'd like some tea, with milk and sugar, please,' said Leah.

'Not you, Miss, you should be in bed.' Anna shook her head.

'Give her half a cup, Ann dear, it will help her sleep. Besides, we haven't finished here. Mr Fox must escort Miss Rabbit back to her hutch.'

Anna shrugged and checked her watch. 8.45. She really should call Teddy and tell her they wouldn't be coming. She would be terribly disappointed. Maybe they would be able to stop by tomorrow – or did Teddy say she was spending Christmas with her mother? These tangling personal ties were the most difficult aspect of being back in California. In London, life had seemed simpler – because the demands were clearer. Work came first. After she adopted Leah, Leah was first, then work, then Reuben. Reuben – she had managed to avoid thinking of him for an entire hour. Perhaps he would just slip away if she went for the tea. Of course Moira would be at Teddy's with Tess and Randy.

Anna put on the kettle, thinking about Teddy's criticism of Randy. Neither Teddy nor Moira had ever explained, but she was sure the women had been lovers. There was an urgency in the way they talked about each other. She hadn't seen them together since she had been back. She could imagine their attraction and the intensity of such a relationship. She could also imagine its crash. Not that she knew much about that sort of thing, but she thought Moira was indelibly heterosexual. The door banged. Daniel back from his friends. She supposed she could go to Teddy and leave Leah with the men. No, she was too tired; she would call as soon as she brought in the tea. She fished around in the cabinet for an extra cup and walked into the living room.

'Anna, just what I need.' Daniel smiled and took the tray from her.

Her brother was a handsome man, with his dark brown hair, thick brows, pensive eyes and wide, brilliant smile. Yes, he would probably be married and out of the house too soon. She should enjoy all of them together while she could. She watched him fondly as he collapsed on the couch.

Daniel swallowed the tea in one gulp. 'Really, Anna.' He spoke loud enough for Papa to hear, 'You must enroll in one of those courses.'

'You're a broken record.' She tried to shush him. 'Picking up where you left off.'

'It's easy,' he continued, 'everyone is going to school.'

'I told you Daniel, I'm not so keen on classics any more.' She sat down with a thump and reached for the tea. 'I like my job.'

'Jewish social work!' he exclaimed. 'You don't want to stay in a ghetto for the rest of your life.'

'It's not a ghetto if you choose it. I like working with my people.'

'Your people, your people? Why are they your people any more than other Americans?'

'Now you sound like Papa!' She lowered her voice, grateful Leah and her rabbit hutch were in the dining room, so Papa was out of earshot.

'No, it's completely different.' Daniel poured himself another cup. 'I'm not transforming you into Loretta Young. I'm just saying you have lots of opportunities. Why are you sticking to such a, a, I don't know, such a womanly occupation? Taking care of people. Your whole life this is just what you said you weren't going to do. You were in love with Latin and Greek. Professor Rothman said you were a star. And here you are, stuck in a little agency, helping people set up house.'

'"Setting up house" is a big task for someone who has travelled 6,000 miles, doesn't speak English and doesn't know North Beach from Portrero Hill. We're not talking about dolls here, Daniel; we're talking about people's lives.'

'OK, OK, so it's useful work. But you've been doing that kind of thing for the last two years. You risked your life in London. Aren't you at peace yet?'

'Listen, Daniel, I'm not sure where you're going with this, but I don't like your tone. I'm working because it's necessary and because I like it.'

'Bull.' He lowered his voice too. 'What do you like about the late nights and the constant worry?'

'I like stories of people's lives. I like to see them pulling through. I feel satisfied being of use. Really, Daniel, I know you mean well, but I'm happy with my job.'

'You'll not go and run off and leave us for that young man in Edinburgh, after all?'

She looked at her watch. 9.15. Another half-hour without thinking of Reuben. 9.15. She had better call Teddy. She would be so disappointed. 'I don't know, Daniel. I can't see going back to Europe. I do miss him. I try not to think about it. When we left he promised to come to get us. One part of me didn't believe it and another part counted on that happening, sooner than he said. In a certain way, I've begun to appreciate Papa's ideas about this country. Yes, he's a little wild-eyed, but he may be right about the chance to start over again here. I dream of Reuben getting a job in an American university. That's the only way I can picture us together. Does that sound selfish?'

'Selfish isn't a word I'd associate with you, Anna. Idealistic, perhaps, but not selfish.'

She sipped her tea and felt even more tired.

Teddy walked from the dining room carrying fruitcake for her friends. 'That was Wanda on the phone. They can't make it tonight. Her mother isn't up to it.'

'Oh, too bad,' said Sandra, playing with the red lace on her collar. 'I wanted to meet her. I had a friend in one of those camps and I think she might have known her. Lion's Head, right, in Arizona?'

'Yeah,' Teddy said blankly, trying to shake off the disappointment. It was after 9.00 and no one but Sandra and Dawn had arrived. Well, it was a last minute invitation and they had all been iffy about coming. She should have listened more closely to their voices. Anna had sounded worried about Leah when she called.

'Still some chance Moira will show up,' she said cheerfully. The idea of Randy trying to socialize with Dawn and Sandra gave her a perverse pleasure.

'Don't worry, honey.' Dawn looked at her steadily. 'You don't got to provide us with no entertainment. We came here to celebrate with you.'

Teddy blushed. 'Speaking of which, have some of Mom's fruit-cake. She put lots of brandy in it. An old family recipe from the days when we made our own "brandy".'

'Your family too?' laughed Dawn.

'Well, I know you're all trying to be polite,' said Sandra, 'but I think it's a shame they left you stranded. I'd like to know why they didn't come. Are they afraid to be back together?'

'Afraid?' repeated Teddy.

'Afraid that they'll see how much they've changed or something.'

'But they haven't.' Teddy shifted in her seat. 'I've seen all of them. They're all still. . . .'

'No, maybe Sandra has a point,' said Dawn, pulling a green thread from her jacket. 'Maybe they don't want to face all they've lost.'

'It's just circumstances – people being busy during the holidays,' Teddy sighed. She poured more eggnog. The silence became uncomfortable. Finally, she said, 'Tell me you've changed your minds. I can't accept the two of you leaving town. What will the Quiet Cat do without you?'

'Not much choice,' Sandra shrugged. 'You know I can't find a new job. Hard enough to get work if you're a white woman, but for a colored woman with my kinda skills. . . .'

'I still think you should let us try to find you something at the Emporium.'

'You're crazy,' laughed Dawn. 'We'd be arrested for cuddling in the corridor the first morning. Besides I'm tired of this place and its fuzzy liberals. No, we're moving on. To Seattle.'

'Seattle?' asked Teddy.

'I've got an aunt,' Sandra explained, 'runs a little café near the bus station. She's getting on in years and could use help. I figure Dawn would be great at the books and I could handle some of the practical things. It'll be fun, having a small place like that to run, you know what I mean.'

'Sure, sure,' said Teddy, on the verge of tears.

'And of course if you're ever in the neighborhood,' said Dawn, 'I'm sure we could find a position for you.'

'As typist!' Teddy tried to laugh away the heaviness in her chest. 'When do you go?'

'Oh, we've a lot of partying to do before then, honey,' grinned Sandra. 'Not until spring, not until the rains stop.'

'Enough mournful talk.' Dawn raised her cup. 'How about a little dancing? As the owner of this establishment, Miss Fielding, you don't have to worry about being evicted for lascivious behavior. May I have the first dance?'

'To "Jingle Bells"?' Teddy winced.

'A good dancer can rescue any music.' She pulled Teddy to her feet.

What would Moira think if she walked up the front step with her baby in one arm and her husband on the other? Teddy smiled.

Moira cleared the table, distressed by the sight of the half-eaten meatloaf on Randy's plate. He said he liked it, but she could tell he was just being polite. Last night it was the same with the baked spaghetti. Too much salt then. Not enough tomato sauce tonight. She had never been a great cook, but lately she had been horrible, forgetful and clumsy. Earlier she had dropped a whole bottle of pickles and now she cringed thinking about those delicious dills floundering around the shattered glass on the kitchen floor. Randy had been terribly understanding, said it must be hard to set up house on your own and take care of a couple of people suddenly, but to tell the truth she wasn't bothered so much by the extra responsibility as by the boredom. What does a person do inside an apartment eight hours a day? Tess was getting on her nerves in ways she never did before. Moira knew she should be grateful, as Mother pointed out, that she had a man who loved her and was eager to support her. Yes, she would just have to get used to the luxury. This was the easiest part she would ever play, wasn't it?

She watched Randy in the living room finishing the log cabin for Tess's Christmas present. Do girls like log cabins? she had asked. Of course, he said, it would make a perfect dolls' house. Right, well, she was lucky he was such a devoted father. Tess loved roughhousing with him. Moira reminded herself that Christmas Eve was a night to count your blessings.

She glanced at the clock. 9.30. Christ, she should call Teddy and explain they weren't coming. She had known this all afternoon, since she counted up the number of presents to be wrapped and the cookies to be made for Randy's family party after midnight mass. She was also behind on preparations for tomorrow's supper with

Aunt Evie and her parents. She plopped down in a chair and scraped the dishes. Tess's plate was a mash of potatoes and carrots and tiny pieces of meatloaf. Had she eaten any of it or just cleverly redistributed it? Oh, she leaned back and stared at the ceiling, imagining Anna blowing one of her marvellous smoke rings.

Anna, it was good to have her back in town. What a comfort to have someone besides Mother to discuss Tess with. Moira didn't feel like a failure around Anna. They had lots of good laughs – more than she could ever remember from Stockton Street. Anna had softened some; maybe part of that was having a kid, but Moira suspected it also had to do with her mother dying and her experiences in London. How could she have left Reuben in Europe? At first Moira imagined Anna didn't love him enough, that theirs had been one of those passing war romances, but now she thought Anna was quite in love. She had been drawn back here by her principles, by responsibility and a sense of identity. It was so unfair. If anyone deserved to be happy, it was Anna, after all the pain. Boy, that was a Catholic judgment, thought Moira. Of course we all deserve to be happy.

She walked to the sink and turned on the water. Well, Wanda looked like she was on the road to being happy. Everyone's life had turned out differently than expected. Things were settled with Roy, although she seemed disappointed he had switched from photography. Actually, Moira reminded her, it would be easier to raise a family on an optometrist's salary. Wanda remained uneasy. 'Don't be in such a rush to have kids,' she had told Wanda. 'You can still do it after four years in school.' Moira worried that she had said the wrong thing. Often she felt like a dope around Wanda, who was by far the most sensitive of the four women. It had taken her longer to revive the friendship with Wanda than with Anna. But things were improving. They had had a good visit on Wanda's last day off.

So strange to wait to see someone on her day off. Moira felt as if she had no day off – although most people wouldn't see what she was doing as working. She saw more friends when she had a regular job. Certainly she saw more of Vivian then. Lord, with Vivian's new job out in Castro Valley, they were lucky to get together once a month. The poor kid was barely making it on her typing salary. Moira finished washing the plates and stepped back slowly. She had been very tired lately.

She shuffled to the phone, worrying how to explain her absence to Teddy. For so many years she and Teddy had been family to each other. Her stomach fluttered as she raised the receiver. No, she put it down again. She should think this out carefully. She had got in big trouble these last five months calling Teddy on impulse. She always thought she knew what she was going to say, but it would come out wrong. Crazy the way they had expected to carry on seeing each other as friends. After she returned from the honeymoon, they would meet for coffee every couple of days and dissolve in tears. Moira was sure she had made the right decision. Absolutely sure, but when she saw Teddy old feelings bubbled up. Teddy never accused, never complained; that was the tough part. Moira would fight back, but she couldn't cope with the regret and the remorse. Was it her fault that she loved two people? That she had chosen one of them? That her child needed a father? Did that mean she had to lose Teddy? Plenty of people saw their old flames. OK, it was different because Teddy was a woman. Moira knew she had left her in the lurch, moving to a more acceptable life. But she had a duty to Tess. She tried to tell Teddy how she still loved her. Teddy would sit there listening, never saying a word. Then they would both break down weeping. Crying seemed the only way to communicate. Yes, it had been wise to take a rest from each other. And tonight would have been their first time together in two months. Moira closed her eyes, how could she explain to Teddy? She stared down at her belly, wondering what her friend would say about this new baby.

Teddy walked stiffly back from the telephone. 'Moira can't come either.' She looked at Dawn and Sandra quizzically. 'Too many plans for the family dinner. She might drop by tomorrow after her folks go back to Aunt Evie's.' Teddy realized she was going on a bit, but she felt safer talking. 'They all said that – maybe tomorrow. I guess this party wasn't a bright idea. People are busy during the holidays. I was stupid to suggest it.'

'Now sit yourself down and have some of this delicious food,' Dawn said, patting the couch next to her. 'This is a party, not a wake. You're right, it's a crazy night to get people together. Unpredictable. But you're not stupid, just good hearted.'

'Yeah,' said Sandra, filling a cup for Teddy. 'They're all probably sad, too, but people have responsibilities.'

'Responsibilities. Do you think it was juvenile of me to try to get my friends together? They seem to forget this part of their lives. Why do I care so much about the time we lived together? Is something wrong with me?'

'No honey,' said Dawn. 'It's only a different way of living. Maybe braver in some ways, setting your own turf.'

'Like I said earlier,' Sandra shook her head, 'they're probably all a little shy with each other. It's hard to have a party like this – who knows how disappointed they might be if it wasn't the same as before? It's more to do with them, honey, than anything to do with you.'

Teddy nibbled the sugar beads off a snowman cookie she had made for Leah. Maybe they were right, maybe they were just being kind. Who knew? The cookie was too dry.

Moira had sounded tense. Was that because they hadn't talked for two months, or was something wrong? Was Randy treating her right? She hoped nothing was wrong with Tess, but surely Moira would have said. Maybe it was just the Christmas pressures. Glancing at the tree, she couldn't help seeing the decorations – angels and soldiers – she and Moira had collected over the years. She should have returned Moira's share of the decorations. She just wanted one last Christmas with them all together. Maybe she had wanted too much. She saw Dawn and Sandra consulting their watches. Teddy realized they would be late for the Quiet Cat. 'Listen, you two go on. I've got plenty to do here. And I'll be with my family tomorrow afternoon. I'll be fine, you don't have to babysit me.'

'Babysitting isn't the question,' Dawn said. 'We've been enjoying your company. That's what friends do with each other – enjoy company.'

'We were wondering, do you want to join us?' asked Sandra. 'Come on down to the Quiet Cat. It's not gonna be as crowded as usual. A private party – with a dozen girls – you know, Hannah, Mary Ellen, Lucille, some others. In fact Gretta has been dying to see you.'

Teddy shook her head, to hide the sadness, to give herself a moment to consider. Maybe it was crazy to sit alone like this. And they didn't look like they were going to budge until she agreed. 'I wasn't directly invited.'

Dawn laughed. 'Just like Teddy, to accept an invitation whole-hearted. Look, if it makes you feel better, I'll call.' She walked to the phone before Teddy could protest.

Sandra turned to Teddy. 'So things worked out OK with your brothers, I mean they'll be coming back soon?'

'Oh, yeah, you know Virgil's back already. Got himself a job on the docks. And a girlfriend; they're getting married in the spring.

Just leaves me and Jack unattached.'

'I wouldn't count on it,' smiled Sandra. 'Pretty lady like you ain't gonna be unattached for long.'

'You are good for my spirit, both you and Dawn. Don't know what I would have done without you these last few months since Moira left. You've saved my life.'

'Doubt that.' Sandra stared at her lap. 'You're a strong one, you know that, a tough woman.'

'The one I worry about most,' Teddy was distracted again, 'is Anna. I mean, you talk about me taking care of folks, but there she is looking after Papa and Leah and cooking for Daniel. Leaving her man Reuben behind. I just worry she's wandered too far from her heart.'

Sandra turned to the doorbell. Startled, Teddy checked her watch. 10.15. Who could that be? Had Moira changed her mind? Or had Wanda's mother gone to bed? Her heart beat fast as she walked to the door.

She didn't look much different really, maybe a little broader in the shoulders and her dark curls were cut into a neat pageboy. But her eyes were the same deep brown color and her smile was radiant.

'Merry Christmas.' Angela offered her gloved hand.

Teddy stared, smiled and returned the strong grip. 'Merry Christmas.'

'Mind if I come in? To share a little cheer with you?'

'No, why, of course not. Welcome home, I don't know what's the matter with me. Come on in. We have,' she paused – 'we', always the 'we' – 'eggnog and cookies and some of my friends have dropped over. Sandra,' she nodded and shut the door, 'this is my friend Angela.' Was this really happening?

'Who else could it be?' said Dawn, walking in from the phone. 'Why Angela, old girl, nice to meet you after all this time.'

Angela regarded Dawn carefully.

Dawn took Sandra's arm. 'This is Teddy's old friend who's been in the WAFs.'

'Didn't think it was Santa Claus.' Sandra shook her head.

Teddy watched them figuring each other out. She wanted to laugh, to stop the scene and explain everyone's position, but she simply stood back, grinning.

'New room-mates?' Angela helped herself to eggnog, a little

studied in her casualness. 'Mama told me there've been big changes with Wanda, Moira and Ann.'

'Doesn't sound like you two have been in touch.' Sandra laughed.

'No.' Teddy waved Angela to the couch. 'I always meant to write, after you told me about Mabel, but things got hectic and, well, a lot has happened.'

'Mabel, that was a long time ago.' Angela sighed. 'Yeah, I suppose I should have written more too. I don't know, well, here we are.'

Teddy didn't know where to begin, with Moira's baby or with Wanda's family or with Anna in Europe. Had she ever written Angela about Dawn? Yes, of course she had.

'Your family pull through OK?' Angela asked Teddy.

The next hour was a rapid exchange of sad news and memories and mild surprises. Angela described Texas in detail. Dawn had some friends in the WAFs and Angela knew two of them. Everybody seemed to be getting along fine. Teddy rested her head back on the chair, looking from the tree to Sandra, playing with the folds of her brilliant red dress, to Dawn clapping her hands on her knee in exclamation to Angela's widening grin. She closed her eyes and listened to Bing Crosby singing carols on the radio. She didn't care if this weren't really happening; she would simply enjoy the fantasy.

Dawn listened to Sandra and turned to Teddy. 'Looks like we should be getting down to the Quiet Cat. You and Angela are welcome too. When I phoned Gretta, she was ecstatic, and she can handle the newest development. Will you come?'

'The Quiet Cat? That place still going? And is Tommy still standing in a parking lot dishing out gossip?' Angela stretched out on the couch. 'I don't want to interrupt your evening plans.'

'No.' Teddy couldn't help smiling. 'This evening has no plan.'

She stood and hugged Dawn and Sandra. 'Thanks, but I think I'll – we'll – just stay home after all.'

Teddy got her friends' coats, walked them to the door and stood waving as they drove off.

She paused on the stoop, staring out at Stockton Street and reminded herself to take it easy. She could hear Angela nervously swishing the radio dial. Teddy look a long breath of cold night air and savored the warmth of the living room at her back.

Chapter Thirty-Two

———————————— • ————————————

Spring 1946, San Francisco

400,000 AMERICAN MINERS GO ON STRIKE

———————————— • ————————————

WAR CRIMES TRIAL OPENS IN TOKYO

———————————— • ————————————

SIAM APPLIES FOR UN MEMBERSHIP

As Wanda walked up Stockton Street, she thought how much the neighborhood and the city had changed. Now it was crowded and noisy. A lot of servicemen and their families had decided to stay in San Francisco. More and more, she toyed with Roy's idea of moving across the Bay to Berkeley. But that was predicated on so many ifs. If she got a scholarship. If Mama would live with Uncle Fumio. If Betty wouldn't feel deserted. Moira said that she took too many people into consideration, but Moira had a different sense of family.

Wanda had almost reached the front door before she saw Teddy waving from the front window. She was in an abstract mood today and her mind turned to the metaphor of the window – despite the illusion of intimacy, both people were separated by the pane. Despite the semblance of reality, glass could distort the image. And if you pressed too hard, the window would shatter, cancelling the picture.

Teddy was running down the steps to welcome her.

'Thought we might have lunch inside and then maybe it'll be warm enough to sit in the garden with a cup of coffee?' Teddy tried to restrain her enthusiasm. After all, it was just lunch. But this *was* the first time Wanda had been back to the house since she and

Stanley moved out the family furniture last year.

Wanda shook her head fondly. 'Sounds good to me.' Sometimes she felt pressured by Moira and Anna to restore their old familiarity, but Teddy had always been so tentative about intruding that she felt safe here.

Teddy observed her friend carefully, noting that she seemed more rested. Well, having Roy home must make a big difference.

'Oh, Teddy, these salads look delicious.'

'Mrs Bertoli. She's opened a deli counter at the store. The potato salad is my favorite. That and the coleslaw.' She wanted to tell Wanda about Angela moving into the house, but she didn't know how her friend would take it.

They caught up on news about Anna and Leah and Moira and Tess and the new baby, Clara. They each grew more comfortable as they finished lunch.

Wanda said something that had been on her mind. 'I hope you understand about the wedding, Teddy, about why we kept it small, kept it to family.'

'Oh, sure,' Teddy shrugged. 'Made sense to me. Besides those weddings are expensive. Mom just about went under catering for Jolene's. She over-calculated on the soda pop and she still has a case of Coke in the pantry.'

Wanda laughed.

Uncomfortable with the silence that followed, Teddy blurted, 'I'm gonna have a new room-mate next month.'

'Angela?'

'How did you guess?'

'Well, I knew space was tight at the Bertolis' now that the youngest girl has brought her husband home. Besides, Angela has been itching to work in this back yard since your Victory Garden days.'

'Speaking of gardens,' Teddy said, 'it's warmer now. Let's go out back.'

Discreetly, Wanda checked her watch. She knew Teddy would be disappointed yet she had so little time, lately – being married, working at the cannery, helping Mama and Betty, taking night classes. She felt she had stolen this couple of hours for lunch. She knew it was important to Teddy that she see the garden.

'Now, you can't go yet,' Teddy smiled. 'Come have some coffee.'

'Yes, of course,' said Wanda, hoping that she could finish her shopping and make it home by five to fix dinner.

Teddy had built two wooden chairs and a small table and placed them next to the rose bush. Was this the same city where her family lived cramped in a two-bedroom apartment splintered by traffic noise? Stockton Street. She looked around at the weathered wooden fence and the neat rows of recently planted vegetables and wished that she had never lived here, had never felt such possibility.

When Teddy returned with the coffee, she could tell Wanda she didn't feel like talking. She relaxed, glancing out across the fence. She could hardly believe that *this* house would be Angela's home in just twenty-five days.

'So tell me about the night classes.' Teddy put down her empty cup.

'Nothing much to say.' Wanda frowned, unsure about whether she wanted to get into this subject. 'Both my English professors say I can write. They're flattering.'

'And Roy got accepted at optometry school, so what's the problem about moving to Berkeley?'

'Mama, of course, and Betty. Mama wouldn't want to leave the family. And Betty shouldn't be torn away from yet another school.'

'So that's a problem? Sounds like everyone is getting along just fine. Your Mama and Betty can stay in the City.'

'But it's selfish. I mean Roy and I would barely be making it with his GI bill and my uncertain scholarship. We couldn't contribute much to Mama and. . . .'

'Wanda! You've been living your life for other people for years now. If you don't do this, if you don't find a way to express your talent, it will be, I don't know, a waste.'

'Just what I needed, another moral mandate.'

'Wanda, I didn't mean it that way.'

She reached for Teddy's hand. 'No, I understand. And I think you're probably right about school. It's what everyone says – Roy, Mama, Carolyn in her letters. Yet, here I am – twenty-seven already – and I should be getting on with a family. I have a husband, other people who love me. Who do I need to change, to get a degree? Look at you, you've been in the same house for seven years and the same job for six years. You're not champing at the bit?'

'But I'm happy with my life,' Teddy said softly. 'And,' she poured Wanda more coffee, 'I chose this life. I wasn't locked up for three years.'

Wanda was surprised by the shame welling up inside her. She hated it when any of the girls mentioned Lion's Head.

'Something I need to say,' Teddy pressed on awkwardly.

Wanda glared back, silently warning her to be quiet.

Teddy persisted. 'I am sorry, real sorry that I never made it out to visit you in Arizona. I was tied up with Moira and then the baby, but still, I could have arranged something. And I'm sorry.'

Wanda's stomach was tighter now, embarrassment wound into rage. But she knew that when she got home she would be glad Teddy had spoken. She had been waiting almost two years to hear Teddy say this.

Wanda sat on the streetcar, balancing two bags of groceries and calculating the amount of time it would take to prepare dinner. Of course it wouldn't matter that she were fifteen minutes late. It wasn't just tonight's meal that bothered her. It was all the juggling and accommodating and shifting of schedules and priorities and . . . she felt she were living two lives, maybe three and none of them for herself. Teddy was right. She should go to Berkeley. She could always have children later. And well, the writing wasn't simply for herself. She could do a lot with her articles. Help people communicate with each other. Interview men of influence and print both sides of the story so readers could think clearly and decide for themselves. The streetcar was inching along. She was going to be terribly late.

Wanda considered that Teddy could never understand why it was important for her to contribute to progress, maybe because Teddy didn't see the need for social change. Maybe because she approached it on a more personal level, for everyone knew Teddy was a generous woman. But why was she going back and forth, back and forth? She had everyone's permission to return to school. Perhaps she was afraid of having this freedom and losing it again. The streetcar windows rattled. She held the grocery bags tighter.

In comparison to herself, Wanda reflected, Roy seemed directed. He would become an optometrist in two years. He would set up a practice, save money for a house, help support their parents, raise beautiful children. He was terrifyingly organized as he compensated for the lost time. He refused to look back – refused to talk about the war. Everything was possible – if you concentrated on the future.

Wanda stared out at Market Street now, bustling with Saturday shoppers and traffic. She could hardly believe the increase in automobiles. She thought about that ride to Golden Gate Park on 7 December, 1941. 7 December. Their immunity to history that morning seemed incredible to her now. She remembered the man who squinted at them and moved his seat. She spent months hating that man until he melted into a hundred other scowling Caucasian faces. Both she and Roy had been so nervous that day – and so innocent.

Wanda worried that Roy never talked about the war. After he described Howard's death to Mama, Betty and herself, that was it; he shut the door on those years. He refused to go to reunions with his army buddies. Refused to read about the war. Even refused to talk to Betty and Stanley for their class assignments on the war. Wanda understood his need to forget. However she didn't think forgetting was possible while the wounds still suppurated.

Roy had amputated his memory of the war and his interest in photography. He gave Stanley the camera. And when he moved from the Watanabes' house, he left all his photography books behind. 'Too busy' he had explained to her. Too desperate, she thought to herself. No shutter speed would be fast enough to protect him against an aperture opened on imagination. Optometry made perfect sense for he was passionate about vision. He would concentrate on clarity, on technical precision, and leave the imaginative business to her.

Wanda shifted the grocery bags to a more manageable position as she climbed up the hill. Turning the corner toward their apartment house, she saw Betty sweeping the sidewalk. Wanda had told Mama a hundred times that this was the superintendent's job, but Mama was never satisfied with his once-a-month sweep. Upstairs she could see Roy standing on a ladder – please make him be careful – tacking in the wall molding. And there was Mama in the kitchen, washing the windows. She thought of her family like a school of fish, swimming together for safety, yet endangered by their visibility. She wondered how the years of hardship would finally affect them. Would Roy grow cold and distant from his feelings? Would Mama despair again? Would Betty become a gung-ho American to prove her acceptability? Mama was scraping away at a particularly tough spot on the window and Wanda was afraid she might break the glass.

But she never had. In decades of scouring windows, Mama had never broken the glass. Wanda snapped out of it. So why did she have to worry; why did she insist on watching through her past uncertainties? Why couldn't she concentrate on how they had survived? On Mama's endurance; Betty's resilience; Roy's optimism. Wanda leaned against a telephone pole, readjusting the grocery bags. She was filled with a great admiration for these people who were her family and with a new determination.

•

Chapter Thirty-Three

Spring 1947, San Francisco

GREEK RESISTANCE FORCES FIGHT RIGHT-WING DICTATORSHIP

•

JACKIE ROBINSON SIGNS CONTRACT WITH BROOKLYN DODGERS

•

GENERAL ANASTASIO SOMOZA TAKES OVER NICARAGUA

•

NEW JAPANESE CONSTITUTION IN EFFECT

Moira sat back in the overstuffed chair and watched her two daughters playing together. Her daughters. Still, sometimes, she found it hard to believe that she was a mother. She was the mother of these two beautiful – sometimes exasperating – but mostly exquisite children. Tess was more gentle with Clara these days: the two-and-a-half-year-old girl taking care of her one-year-old baby sister, carrying toys to the blanket, clapping and laughing. No doubt this idyll would last only two or three minutes, but Moira was determined to enjoy it. She listened to the sound of Randy's shower, beating steadily against the bathroom wall. This strengthened her calm, more than it might have last month when the pipes were leaking into the apartment below. But leaks could be fixed. Emergencies could be met. Lost safety pins were found – far from delicate gullets. Fights could be patched and marriages continued.

Moira felt she lived in a steadier place now. While she hadn't exactly planned this family, she had always wanted more than one child. After her own experience, she would never condemn anyone to only childhood. Sometimes now, she wondered if the reason she loved Stockton Street was that it provided her with sisters. Occasionally she daydreamed about them all living together in interconnected units. At night after they tucked in their husbands and children, they could sit around the old elephant couch and talk.

Clara screamed. Moira looked up to see Tess pulling away the doll from her sister.

'Share, Tess; remember what I told you about sharing?'

'Baby bite doll!' Tess was outraged.

'It's OK, honey, we'll wash the doll's face before we put her to bed. Be kind to your sister.'

Miraculously Tess obeyed and sat down on the blanket with Clara.

Moira closed her eyes and smiled, pleased with her maternal wisdom, which seemed to evolve from one second to the next. Her own mother, the supreme sage, must have improvised just like this. That knowledge added a certain proportion to life. Having these children brought Moira enormous pleasure – in the love they expressed, in the competence she felt. Of course life wasn't all satisfaction. And she did wonder what she would do when the children were in school. She wondered this, especially, after a visit with Wanda, who seemed to be sailing through her classes at Berkeley. In a couple of years Wanda would be out in the world writing articles and Moira, Moira would be hanging up clothes on the back line. They'd have to move first. The only place to hang clothes in this apartment house was the basement.

Not that Moira regretted her choice. Being a good mother was important. And when the girls were in school, why there was no reason she couldn't do part-time work, maybe even return to school herself. Moira turned the shadow of an idea – which she didn't yet dare share with Randy – that she might become a teacher. She never imagined that she would like children so much. Everyone said she had a flair in groups. Maybe she would mention it to Anna when she came to supper tonight. Anna never laughed at her ideas.

Randy stood over the children, his hair still wet, reaching out to Tess. 'You going to be good while Daddy is bowling?'

'Yes, Daddy.' The child allowed herself to be picked up and

swung around.

Now Clara was crying. He stopped to lift her and danced them across the room to Moira. 'When's Anna coming? You want me to help you tuck them in?'

Moira looked at her watch. 'No, you'd better leave or you'll be late for the team.' She kissed him on the cheek. 'Say 'night to your Daddy.'

''night Daddy.' Tess kissed him.

Clara laughed and clapped her hand over his face. She watched him take the girls back to their blanket and then pick up his bowling ball. He was still handsome although his hair was receding and he was adding a little paunch. Bowling probably wasn't the best exercise, but he liked going out with the boys once a week. She closed her eyes. She never imagined that Randy Girard would grow tame. No, that wasn't the right word. He hadn't become dull, just lost a little of his spark. Wanda said Roy was like this and, in funny ways, the men were similar. Neither one would talk about the war. At least Randy didn't talk to her about it; maybe that was what they discussed at the bowling alley. Both Randy and Roy seemed to have more of a sense of their limits and their purposes than they had a few years ago. Well, that was all to the good if you had other people to support, supposed Moira. Randy picked up his jacket and waved good-bye.

'Perfect timing,' Moira said as she answered the door. 'I've just got the second one down.'

'Good.' Anna was out of breath. 'Actually, I'm a little late. I had to drop Leah and Papa at the movies.'

'Now just sit and relax,' Moira said. 'Drink before supper?'

'Just ginger ale, if you've got it.'

Moira frowned, fixed herself a gin and tonic and brought Anna her soda.

'Thanks, Moi. Actually, I'm sorry I missed the kids. I haven't seen the girls in months. Do you have pictures?'

Moira took a long sip of her drink, considering that Wanda had not asked for pictures, had not seemed interested even in seeing the real thing. She hoped that her motherhood wasn't going to separate her from Wanda. 'Since you ask.' Moira smiled and pulled out an album.

Anna sipped her ginger ale and she paged through the album.

'Oh, here's your mother. She is looking good. In love with her grandchildren!'

'You think so?' Moira was taken aback by her own pleasure. 'Yeah, she does enjoy visiting. The miracle is that I almost enjoy having her.'

'Yes, Papa is in love with Leah. And Daniel is good for her too. Speaking of which, I have news – about a forthcoming member of the family. . . .'

Moira finished her drink. 'Reuben? He's coming?'

'No,' Anna sighed. 'That conference fell through. But,' she brightened. 'Daniel. Daniel and Rachel are getting married.'

'Rachel? You mean the one who used to come to the house? And she was in that group with you? I thought you lost touch.'

'Right. She moved out of town while I was in London and then . . . well, anyway, she saw Daniel's new law shingle several months ago. She works in the same building. So she knocked on his office door in search of his sister. And fell in love.'

'Isn't that something. Hey, come tell me more over supper.'

Moira nervously brought out the baked potatoes and chicken. Everything was intact. She pulled the salad from the ice box and poured them each a glass of water.

'But before we get to Daniel, let's go back to Reuben for a minute. Are things all right?'

All right. How could she answer that question? Reuben was well. He wrote every two weeks as did she. He had phoned on her birthday. He was still planning to come over and rescue them, but the realities of distance and time were more imposing now. She found it was harder to conjure his face at night, so she had taken to looking at his photo before she fell asleep. How much could she tell Moira?

'It's hard being apart.' She cursed her own restraint. 'But he promised that he would come over in late summer or early fall. He suggested we meet in the Grand Canyon.'

'The Grand Canyon!' Moira gulped.

'Yeah, that's sort of what our relationship is like, with the canyon growing grander by the moment.'

'Oh, Anna, don't be sarcastic. You love each other. You'll find a way to be together. Just wait.'

'That's what I've been doing.'

'But, but. . . .'

'Listen, Moira, what choice do I have? I have other responsibilities. If Reuben and I can find a way to bridge the ocean, that will be wonderful. If we can't, we'll survive.'

'That sounds so detached and objective. But I guess you think I'm a hopeless romantic.'

'Yes,' Anna smiled. 'I guess I do.'

Moira looked down at her meal, consoled that at least the dinner had been edible.

'It's one of your charms, Moi.'

Moira pulled a face. 'People don't take me seriously. They don't think I'm serious.'

'Oh, quite the contrary.' Anna's eyes filled with affection. 'If anything, you're more serious about more things than anyone I know. You're passionate and you throw yourself into life. I respect that. Although sometimes I worry about you.'

'About me? I always land on my feet,' Moira winked. 'Don't worry about me.'

———————— • ————————

Chapter Thirty-Four

Spring 1948, San Francisco

USSR AND WEST BATTLE OVER BERLIN TRANSPORTATION

———————— • ————————

RACIAL DISCRIMINATION IN HOUSING DECLARED UNCONSTITUTIONAL BY US SUPREME COURT

———————— • ————————

ISRAELI INDEPENDENCE WAR BEGINS

———————— • ————————

200,000 JAPANESE WORKERS WIN STRIKE FOR HIGHER WAGES

Teddy knelt in the garden, lifting the fledgling lettuce head from the planter where she had grown it from seed. Wanda's suggestion, she remembered. Last year all but one of the lettuce heads survived. Anna kept calling her a 'brilliant gardener', but she knew as well as Teddy that all it took was a little patience and common sense. Teddy inhaled the scent of rich, black dirt and felt the relief of spring. Teddy never counted on a new year until the heavy rains ceased and the ground warmed.

She shifted a few feet and dusted the roots of the next tiny lettuce plant. It was so peaceful here today; she just wished she were sharing it with someone. Perhaps she was destined to garden alone. She knew Anna would enjoy getting her hands dirty, if only she didn't have so many obligations. Leah was growing into a fine companion for Anna. Where the child found her light after such loss, Teddy still wondered. Anna did seem relaxed, despite the huge work load. Moira said she had noticed this, too, when Anna and Leah came over for Clara's second birthday party.

Two years old. Well, Teddy reflected as she sprinkled water on the new plant, it had been ten years since they had all met at Tracey Business School. Ten years, she closed her eyes. Why did time accelerate as you got older? People said it was because you saw time more in proportion to the rest of your life. The longer the past was, the shorter the present seemed to be. But Teddy suspected that it was also because she wasn't paying as much attention as she used to. She didn't anticipate events in the same way; she didn't savor them; she didn't recall them in the same loving detail. She took too much for granted, that was it. Of course this meant that she didn't worry as often, which was an improvement.

One thing she didn't worry about was her tie to Moira. That seemed to be strengthening steadily. She loved Tess and Clara enormously and prided herself on being their favorite aunt, although this was probably just because she had more time for them than Wanda and Anna. It helped, of course, that both the girls looked like Moira rather than Randy. She should get used to Randy. She should practice.

Hummph. She stood to shake the frustration and decided to dig the bed for squash. She enjoyed such physical labor after a week of typing and filing. The soil was loose and moist today, perfect for planting. Of course it wasn't as lush as Wanda's garden, but Wanda got more sun in Berkeley. How proud Wanda had been to show her their garden and the house last week. Teddy would have stayed longer if Angela hadn't been waiting in the city. People never thought to invite Angela with her although she invited their husbands with them. Roy had already been asked to join an optometry practice when he graduated in June. And Wanda was almost finished with classes herself. Teddy wished she could explain to her friend how much she admired her. Wanda still seemed to be questioning her decision to go back to school!

'Teddy. Soup's on.' Teddy straightened and pulled the shovel from the ground, lost in memories of Moira calling from the kitchen and Angela hanging over the back fence.

Now it was Angela calling from the kitchen and lest there be any mistake about it, the fog horn sounded again. 'Last call, Teddy. It's getting cold.'

Teddy waved and smiled, picking up the trowel and carrying it with the shovel to the back porch. It would be nice if Angela joined her in the gardening, but when you gardened all week for a living, fixing ravioli was more relaxing. And how could Teddy complain? No one could complain about Angela's cooking.

'Nothing is worse than cold ravioli.' Angela stood with her hands on her hips which had grown considerably broader over the last two years of domestic bliss. Teddy considered Angela affectionately, deciding that the girl could use even more exercise than she got working for her brother Mario's gardening company. It was a healthy, steady occupation. But Angela was still stinging from the months of rejection after returning from the WAFs. All the airline jobs, all the mechanics jobs, went to ex-servicemen. Angela said most of her WAF friends had wound up getting married or doing office work. Teddy wondered what was happening with Vivian.

'Except perhaps your cold fury,' teased Teddy. She marvelled at how comfortable she was with Angela, despite the woman's unnerving tendency to take care of her.

'Jolene called while you was in the garden. The baby cut a tooth today.'

Teddy shook her head. 'I can't believe Jolene has three kids already. I thought that like Moira she was destined for stage and screen and. . . .'

'Maybe she saw a little too much drama when you was all little.' Angela dug into her ravioli.

'Too bad Hank didn't learn the same lesson.'

'Drinking again?'

'Yeah, Mom called last night when you were out. Arthur had to go over there 'cause Hank was threatening to clobber Beverly. I guess I was kind of silly to think that the drinking died out with Pop.'

Angela regarded her with concern. 'But Hank's the only one, right? The rest of the Fieldings are doing great. Look at your Mom. She seemed ten years younger than when I first met her. She's loving that little apartment.'

'Yes, you were right about not pressing her to live here.' Teddy shrugged. 'Still, it seems a waste to have this place all to ourselves. Just two people.'

Angela raised an eyebrow, wary of the routine conversation. 'I guess you don't like the food, eh? Not up to par?'

'No, Angela, it's delicious. I'm sorry. But what's going on with you. You're hiding something. I can tell by your expression.'

'Where did you learn to read minds?' Angela was annoyed, then amused. 'All right, I was going to keep it for tonight. But I got you a surprise. For our anniversary.'

Blushing, Teddy accepted the envelope. She opened it slowly. 'Tickets. Train tickets.' She was bewildered.

'To. . . .' Angela prompted.

'Seattle!' Teddy exclaimed. 'To see Dawn and Sandra. Oh, Angela, this is too expensive. We can't afford . . . I don't know if I can get off work . . . I. . . .'

'Non-refundable.' Angela sat back, with her arms across her chest. 'You'll just have to ask old Whitney to let you off. Listen,' she leaned forward, 'you've been promising to visit them for years. And we've never gone on a trip together. Why I don't think you've left this house for more than a weekend since you moved in.'

'Not for more than a night.'

The phone rang. Teddy jumped to escape the explosion of feelings. It was a wonderful surprise, she insisted to herself as she hurried to the phone. It would be terrific to see Dawn and Sandra.

'Hello,' she said absently.

'Teddy, you OK?' asked Moira.

'Yes, and you, Moi?' She wondered how Moira always managed to call when she was in the middle of a serious discussion with Angela.

'Fine, only wanted to say hello. Is this a good time? I waited until Saturday because gruesome Mr Whitney shriveled me through the phone the last time I called you at work. I'm sorry if this is the wrong moment.'

'Moira, you're never going to stop apologizing, are you?' How could she excuse herself when Moira was so nervous about phoning at the wrong time. Now, as so often, she felt she had to choose between annoying Angela and hurting Moira. 'I'm fine, just fine. Angela just bought two tickets for us to visit Dawn and Sandra in Seattle.'

'That means you'll leave the house?' Moira's voice was cool.

'Just for ten days or so. Don't you think it's safe?' Teddy felt the anxiety rising again.

'Safe, yes, of course, I'm just being silly. I've never known you to leave the place and I guess, I don't know, I guess that I like to think of you there. . . .' Covered with embarrassment, Moira abruptly shifted gears. 'The girls are fine. Tess seems more of a lady every day now.'

'Yeah, sorry I couldn't make Clara's birthday party. Did she like the doll?'

'Oh, Teddy, I'm sorry, of course that was one of the reasons for calling you. Yes! She loved it. She's playing with it right now. God, you know I can't believe sometimes that I have responsibility for these two human beings and that I *like* it. I bet you never would have thought.'

'I always knew you were loving,' Teddy said. 'You just needed to get used to people needing you.'

'And you needed to get used to people not needing you, to living your own life after taking care of your family and the Stockton Street girls.'

'Hmmm,' mused Teddy.

'So I think the trip is a great idea.' Moira's voice grew stronger. 'Anyway, tell me, how is Angela?'

•

Chapter Thirty-Five

Spring 1949, San Francisco

ALGER HISS ON TRIAL IN NEW YORK

•

SOVIETS END BLOCKADE OF BERLIN

•

UNIVERSITY OF CALIFORNIA, BERKELEY FACULTY TOLD TO SIGN LOYALTY OATHS

•

US POST-WAR OCCUPATION TROOPS LEAVING KOREA

Anna was reading by the window, enjoying the warmth of the sun on her neck. Closing her eyes, she listened to the light strokes of Leah's pencil across the sketch book. Saturdays. She must be getting old because she ached for the weekends now. She still loved her job, she reminded herself. Refugee work was important; there was so much to do. But she did get tired by Friday night. And why not, Dr Trubo had said; she worked a full week and took care of a lively child and an irrepressible father. Papa would die if he knew she was seeing a psychiatrist, so she went during her lunch hour. In fact he wouldn't be too pleased to see her leafing through Karen Horney's *Our Inner Conflict*. But she wasn't going to censor her reading for his peace-of-mind. Conflict. Dr Trubo said Anna was always creating conflict before it happened. She glanced out the window at the fog and clouds moving in from the Bay.

Leah looked so comfortable there on the rug drawing, what was it, oh, a coastal scene from last month's trip to Marin. They should take more outings like that. Leah was growing by yards, but then she was almost eleven. Anna was astonished last month when the child, the girl, her daughter, came to tell her about her first bleeding. It was all happening too quickly. She, herself, was thirty-one. Thirty-one. No, she wouldn't think about that, either. She was relieved to see that the clouds had passed and the sun was streaming down again.

'All right daughter, I'm off.' Papa bustled into the living room with his coat and a paper lunch sack.

'Not on Saturday, Papa, you promised. You'll wear yourself out.'

'Enough. I'm lucky I can work. Besides, we're still trying to recover from that shutdown last month. I'll be back by six. And your friends are coming to dinner at seven?'

'Yes, Papa.' Anna sighed in resignation.

Leah stood and kissed her grandfather's cheek. 'Bye, Grandpa.'

The door shut and Anna was overcome with suffocation. Of course this was what it had always been like in her childhood: Mama saying, 'Don't go, David.' And Papa saying, not to worry, he would be fine. Obviously Papa would be fine. He was born to explore the Northwest Passage or the South Pole. But Mama would not be fine. Anna realized that it had been this time in her own life – when she was about Leah's age – that the family moved West, that Mama closed the doors permanently. She walked to the front window. No, she was not her mother. They had got to the crucial time of Leah's womanhood, and she was not going to turn into Mama. Leah didn't even call her Mama. At first it had been Mummy and now it was Mom. Such an American, her daughter.

Leah had returned to the pad, shading the trees with green pencil. Anna was struck with nostalgia about the drawing Leah had given her in London when she had come back after the flu – the portrait of the two of them together. She thought, quickly, of that other artist in her life. But Carol's pictures were so much more dramatic and disturbed than this. No, she reassured herself, she wasn't Mama and Leah wasn't Carol.

The phone broke Anna's reverie. Leah raced for it and then ran back. 'It's for you, Mom. Aunt Wanda.'

Anna shook herself and walked into the hall. 'Wanda, hello, how are you?'

'I'm fine, Anna, thanks. But Mama has come down with something. So, I'm sorry, but we can't make it to dinner tonight. I think Roy and I should drive in and spend the evening with her.'

'Oh, I'm sorry to hear that, Wanda. Do you think it's serious?'

'Hard to say. She's been slowing down lately, but we all thought it was age.' Wanda hoped Anna would accept this. She didn't want to think any more until she saw Mama for herself.

'Give her my good wishes. How are you and Roy?'

'Roy's fine.' Wanda's voice eased. 'The practice is going well. He's working too hard, but we expected that the first few years.'

'And Wanda?'

'Fine.' She held back. 'Just fine.'

'And why *so* fine, Mrs Watanabe? You're hiding something.'

'You know that article Professor Washington sent off to his friend at the *Saturday Evening Post*?'

'You're getting it published!'

'Looks that way.' Wanda was grateful, after all, to tell Anna, so she might experience the excitement her own modesty inhibited.

'Congratulations. You know I really admire your determination. You're something – pushing ahead despite everything – getting your degree early because of those night classes. I look up to you, you know.'

'Thank you.' Wanda had had enough. If she could only switch off Anna's enthusiasm when it became unbearable. She knew if she didn't change the topic, she would start tripping over her own embarrassment. 'How are Daniel and Rachel?'

'Fine, fine. In fact, I was going to tell you tonight, but I'll tell you now. I'm going to be an aunt!'

'That's wonderful.'

There was a listlessness in Wanda's voice that Anna couldn't place. Perhaps because she hadn't been concentrating. 'You must be worried about your mother. May I call tomorrow and find out how she's doing?'

'That's kind of you, Anna, but you don't have to. . . .'

'I know I don't have to.'

'Yes, well, thanks, and maybe we can have a real talk then. I'll be more in the mood.'

Moods were curious, Anna thought, returning to the living room, which was once again drenched in shadow. Moods could transport you to a completely different world. Most of the week she had spent recalling London, perhaps because it was this month, six years ago when she arrived in that sooty, cramped office, lit up with Esther's ebullience and Reuben's implacable curiosity.

Sometimes she remembered London so strongly that she could taste the beer and smell the coal fires. She could touch the gleaming fruit in Covent Garden. One memory would trip another and she couldn't remember why she left London. Oh, how she missed the sophistication of the place – the slightly seedy atmosphere of experience that permeated the numerous cracks of a difficult but fascinating daily life. She missed Esther and Mark and Mrs Mac. And Reuben. She was almost able to place his name with the others now. Almost able to relegate him to memory. Oh, he was still promising to meet her in some National Park or other – so European to perceive the United States as a vast wilderness adventure – but she knew he could never permanently settle here. And how could she leave San Francisco again? In London she learned she was immutably American. No matter where she lived there would be loss. She felt more wistfulness than pain over this now.

Anna sat down, but could not concentrate on reading.

Sometimes she imagined a reunion of all the Annas. The Anna who stayed in New York with her parents and grew up to room with Ilse Stein at Barnard; the Anna who went back to New York and lived with Carol Sommers; the Anna who lived on Stockton Street and attended San Francisco State; the Anna who remained in London and married Reuben; the Anna who adopted Leah and returned to the States. Would they all get along with each other? Would they respect each other? Sometimes Anna felt that she was the composite of all those experiences and possibilities, more mature and complex for the variables faced and chosen. Sometimes she felt that there had been no choice, only chance, and that she would be better off as one of the other Annas.

But if she had stayed in London she probably would have lost touch with Wanda and Moira and Teddy. And she valued this remarkable friendship. She occasionally wondered why they had stayed so close despite their different directions. But the answer to that question was why they had become friends in the first place: something in each of them transcended parents and religion and ethnicity and marriage and children – a common independence and a shared sense of potential. Perhaps she would have to settle for a reunion of the Stockton Street women instead of a reunion of the

Annas. The friends would meet as a group in good time. They would meet together when they were comfortable enough in their own lives to talk about their differences and similarities.

Leah entered with a pot of fresh tea. 'What did Aunt Wanda say, Mom?'

The room was small and dark, remarkably dark for noon in the Golden State. A lamp shone on the red curtains which, Anna noticed, were never dusty. Dr Trubo was usually listening to classical music when Anna arrived. Once she had left it on during the session, but they both found it distracting. The darkness comforted Anna and disturbed her. She understood that Dr Trubo couldn't really open the curtains because her basement office was on a busy street and the patient would be watching feet clomping down the sidewalk outside instead of concentrating on her own inside. Inside: the warm room glowing red from the curtains seemed a blatant metaphor. Yet Dr Trubo had seemed more pleased than annoyed when Anna mentioned this.

Today Anna stared at the fragile, dark psychiatrist, considering how she liked her seriousness, her precise attention, her crisp responses. They had been talking about Anna feeling guilty spending therapy money on herself. And now Anna considered how much she enjoyed it, how she had no intention of giving up therapy so she would just have to give up the guilt.

Abruptly, Dr Trubo cleared her throat and this alarmed Anna for the woman never spoke except in response.

Panicked, Anna decided that she should speak. And she could not help what came out next. 'I've been wondering if it wouldn't be such a terrible thing if I didn't get married.'

'Yes?' Dr Trubo sat, her head almost touching the bottom of the frame of a playful Miro print.

Anna lit a cigarette. 'I don't mean I'd never marry. But we keep talking about marriage and perhaps there are other decisions to make first.'

From outside the window, Anna could hear the slow, heavy gait of someone she imagined to be an old woman.

'I mean I feel fulfilled with Leah. I've also got Papa and the job. Well, the job has been wearing lately. Perhaps I need to get away from people. Perhaps I have been too involved in their lives. Perhaps I delve too deeply.' She took a long draw on the cigarette.

'Too deeply?'

'Or not deeply enough.'

Dr Trubo waited.

'I've been thinking about going back to school.'

Anna thought she could see a flicker of approval, but she was quite unsure of her next remark.

Anna exhaled the smoke. 'To study psychology,' she said bravely to the red curtains.

Chapter Thirty-Six

●

Spring 1950, San Francisco

HYDROGEN BOMB REPORTED 1,000 TIMES MORE POWERFUL THAN A BOMB

●

CHEROKEES LOSE $6.5 MILLION SUIT AGAINST US GOVERNMENT

●

MOSCOW CRITICIZES US ATTEMPT TO REMILITARIZE JAPAN

●

US SIGNS MILITARY AID AGREEMENT WITH FRANCE, VIETNAM, CAMBODIA AND LAOS

Teddy slowly set the table. She was savoring the afternoon and fearing it. Although she had lived eleven years in this house, it felt like alien territory. Stepping back, she considered the four adult places at the big table and the three places for the girls at the adjacent card table. Children preferred to be on their own, didn't they? Carefully, she smoothed each of the burgundy napkins. Would Moira be disappointed that she wasn't using her mother's Belgian lace, even though there weren't enough to go around? After all, she was using Ann's butter dish and Wanda's silver serving spoons. But the vase – the milkglass vase – that was Moira's. She would notice that.

Turning to the sideboard for knives and forks, Teddy caught her reflection in the mirror. A thin, middle-aged woman with wrinkles around the eyes and streaks of grey in the hair, well, maybe she was exaggerating – she was only thirty-three – a few silver strands here and there. She pulled down her purple sweater, noticing how bony her shoulders seemed. Perhaps she should change into that new paisley blouse. All in all, not a bad sight, Teddy smiled to herself. An almost wise smile. She enjoyed getting older because she felt she had always been in her mid-thirties. This body suited her better now than in her youth when it seemed a lanky Abe Lincoln model. Lanky was all right for men, but she had looked downright undignified until the last couple of years. Dignified! She smiled again. Her attention was caught by the color on the wall opposite, a soft, apricot shade. Angela's choice. She wasn't sure she cared for it, but as Angela said, this was her house too and she had a right. What would the girls say? Some day they would talk about all of it. One thing at a time. Lunch first. Please God they would make it through one lunch. It would be good to talk to Wanda and Anna about Angela with the ease with which they discussed Roy and Reuben. She missed Dawn and Sandra so much. She was happier with Angela than she had been in her whole life. The house was cozy, full of laughs. Just occasionally, she wanted someone to protest to, someone to ask advice from. Just occasionally. Teddy looked through the mirror at the living room, pretty much the same room for eleven years, except for Angela's brown rug and her framed prints. It was a homey place, Jolene said.

'Admiring yourself, Cleopatra?' Angela entered from the kitchen.

Teddy turned, flushing.

'Listen, I'm not complaining. I admire you all the time, myself. I know that you want to make sure you're in top shape today.'

'Still sulking?' Teddy kept her voice light.

'Na, who cares about being excluded from your old girls' club, your sorority? I'd never worry about Wanda and Anna and Moira, well, Moira is three months pregnant.' Angela laughed and then caught herself. 'But I guess she was knocked up when you fell in love with her.'

Teddy shook her head. 'Would you please watch your language. And get out of here before I throw something.' They were laughing now. Angela turned and bumped into Wanda who was walking through the dining room.

'Oh, I'm sorry,' Wanda blushed. 'I found the door open. I figured you wanted us to. . . .'

'Fine, Wanda, fine.' Angela took her tray. 'Mmmmm *sushi*, I'm sorry to miss this, but I have a vital engagement.'

Teddy rushed forward and hugged her old friend. She couldn't get over how much more like her mother Wanda was looking every day. Even her movements and her voice seemed to have become, well, more Japanese. Did Wanda notice it, too? Teddy took the tray from Angela and said good-bye. 'Come into the kitchen, Wanda, and help me finish up.'

Wanda followed through the swinging door, reflecting on the distinctive smell of this house – a combination of the bay leaves that Teddy hung in the kitchen and a general Northern California dampness. Really, she had been silly refusing to visit Stockton Street more often.

Teddy set the *sushi* tray on the shiny linoleum counter. She had cleaned the kitchen for days and still all she could see were spots and stains. Wanda's plate was exquisite: the tuna, salmon, squid and crab arranged delicately on beds of rice and seaweed, so much more attractive than her own lump of meatloaf that was simmering in the oven. Would the menu fit together? She had wanted to organize things more tightly, but Moira said it would be fun if everyone brought her favorite dish even if they wound up with four jello molds.

'Oh, Teddy.' Wanda looked out at the garden. 'You've already planted. You'll have the first lettuce in the city. I feel so sentimental.'

'Really? I never knew how much you liked the garden when you lived here.'

'I loved watching you and Anna plant it. But I never felt as competent.'

'You incompetent?' Teddy's eyes widened. 'Our star? Wanda Watanabe, famous journalist!'

Wanda shrugged.

'Wanda, whenever I see your name in a magazine, I'm thrilled. The other day on the streetcar, I bent over a man who was reading *Colliers* and said, "I know the author of that article".'

'You didn't.' Wanda gripped the edge of the counter, taken aback by her own discomfort.

'I did, and he told me it was a very fine story. When I got home, I read it and he was right. You know, it was the one about deaf people. You must be so pleased, Wanda, after all your effort.

Everything is going great in your life – the articles, Roy, the new house.'

'Yes.' Wanda stared at the garden as Teddy continued her praise. She knew they would all say something like this. Yes, she was happy, at least happier than she used to be. She loved her work. Roy was a good husband. He had stopped pressuring her about children, although it was clear he would be ready any minute. After all, family was important to a *Nisei* couple. She knew no other Japanese woman her age who was childless. It would work out; it would all work out.

'I've been lucky in a lot of ways.' Wanda studied Teddy's comfortable face. 'Not the least of which is the loyalty of my friends.' She walked over and hugged Teddy, embarrassing them both.

They were relieved to hear the doorbell.

'Guess. Guess who will be next.'

'No contest.' Teddy laughed over her shoulder. 'The day Moira shows up on time is the day I turn into Imogen Coca.'

Leah was at the door with a bowl of salad. 'I made it myself,' she announced and stood on her toes to kiss Teddy. 'Mom went back to the car. She forgot the bread. She's always forgetting things.'

Teddy returned the kiss. 'Why child, you're almost a lady. I wouldn't have recognized you. How old are you now?'

'Twelve.' Leah smiled triumphantly. 'Hello, Aunt Wanda.'

Wanda bent down to receive a kiss.

Anna panted up the walk, her arms filled with bread and a hot dish Teddy knew would be *kugel*. Teddy was overcome with nostalgia, so happy she wanted the day to stop here. She hadn't eaten *kugel* since their dance party centuries ago.

Teddy called out, 'Anna, can I help you?'

'Don't think so.' Anna smiled anxiously. 'It's a delicate balance. Just clear me a way to the kitchen.' She hurried in the door, thinking how good it was to see everyone, almost everyone. No doubt Moira would be as late as ever. 'Leah,' she called ahead, 'please make a space on the counter.'

Wanda and Teddy followed.

'Mom is always trying to do too much.' Leah shook her head. 'Grandpa keeps telling her, but she won't listen.'

'She's right.' Anna was chastened. 'Sorry I'm late but I had a case this morning and then Papa's lunch had to be fixed and then, well, if it hadn't been for Leah, we wouldn't be out of the house yet.' She

leaned on a yellow chair, lit a cigarette and took a long, slow drag.
'That's better. Oh, sorry.' She moved the cigarette down at her side.
How good they both looked: Teddy relaxed and strong; Wanda so
stylish and purposeful. Eleven years ago, Anna thought, women in
their thirties were hasbeens and now, well, now she was just
beginning her own life. Would there be time to discuss this today?
Would they think her plans were crazy? It wouldn't be the first time.

'Let's have a drink in the living room,' said Teddy, ducking into
the closet for sherry and soda pop. Anna and Wanda walked ahead,
arms around each other, chatting. Leah carried in dishes of nuts and
popcorn. Teddy paused in the doorway, remembering those
Saturday mornings when they all lazed around the house after
chores. She was grateful they each had come back to her in one
piece. Would Moira make it today? How many times had they all
tried to get together over the years? Six or seven and always someone
was sick or out-of-town. Well, there was nothing to do about it, she
would just wait and see. Teddy checked her watch: 12.30. She
wouldn't think about Moira for fifteen minutes.

'Papa grows younger.' Anna smiled. 'Why this morning he and
Leah were outside at – what was it, love – eight o'clock – planting
the garden. And he's never going to retire from the factory.'

Teddy poured them each a drink and handed Leah a glass of Coca
Cola.

'A toast,' said Wanda. 'A toast to old friends.'

'All old friends,' Anna sighed.

'Speaking of which,' Teddy leaned forward, 'have you heard from
Reuben lately, Anna? It seems ages since we talked about him.'

'Yes, actually.' She rubbed her neck. 'Just last week. He says he
wants to come this summer. Wants us to meet in Yosemite, to go
hiking together in the High Sierras.'

'Sounds idyllic,' Wanda commented. She felt a twinge of
jealousy. What was getting into her today?

'Yes,' Anna sighed, 'and maybe just the tiniest bit impractical.'
Eager to change the topic, she asked, 'What about Betty's music?
She was applying to schools the last time we talked.'

Wanda smiled. 'She got into the Academy and she's doing
beautifully. There's a recital next month – the fourteenth, I think –
I'll be sending you each invitations. Mama would have been so
proud. She came around at the end and loved Betty's music.'

Anna nodded. 'I was sorry I couldn't make the funeral. We had a family with impossible problems and I was tied up for days. But you went, didn't you, Teddy, and Moira went too.'

'And a lot of people from camp.' Wanda spoke quickly against the lump in her throat. Although it had been two months since Mama's death, it was still hard to talk about. 'She would have been pleased. She had more friends than she knew. Many people spoke about her strength.'

Wanda sipped her drink and considered how they were trying out difficult topics. She couldn't help changing the conversation again. Maybe they would feel more secure as the afternoon progressed. 'So how's work, Teddy.'

'Well, you'll be surprised to hear I have news. Nothing's happened at that office in ten years and now the best of all possible things. . . .'

'A promotion?' asked Anna.

'No, but Mr Whitney is leaving – for a store down in Los Angeles. He has been a real trial, you know. Never did stop pestering me.'

'But,' Wanda looked puzzled, 'doesn't that mean you can move up – into his job? You know it backwards.'

'I'm not interested.' Teddy shrugged, understanding this would bother her friends. 'I'm happy with my job, with the hours. The pay is enough. I get along with everybody – or at least I will now that Mr Whitney is leaving.'

'But who knows who your next boss will be?' Wanda bit her lip. This wasn't her business. It wasn't inconceivable for Teddy to be content in the old job and the same house.

'Between us – Angela and me – we make more than enough money. This place is paid for. I know you think I'm foolish.'

Anna watched the two of them, so opposite in their goals. As much as she had learned about persistence from Wanda, she had learned about acceptance from Teddy. Interesting, this brief mention of Angela. She always entered the conversation fleetingly, as an assumption, as part of Teddy's life that was never fully acknowledged.

The doorbell rang. Teddy's eyes caught her watch. 12.40. She inhaled slowly and tried to relax. These butterflies were ridiculous. She had seen Moira last month. So what if they hadn't all been in the same room together for eight years? They were the same people. Relax, she told herself, just calm down.

Anna lit another cigarette. No, they wouldn't get to Angela today, not in front of Moira. What a relief last year when Moira finally told her about the relationship with Teddy. Teddy knew that she knew now, didn't she?

Wanda noticed how big Moira had got in the last month and she registered Teddy's surprise. Did Teddy know Moira was pregnant again? One difference in the group's friendship now was that one didn't know just what the others knew.

Tess and Clara skipped ahead of their mother into the living room. Both girls had Moira's curly red hair and wide eyes.

Leah rushed over eagerly and then halted, her hands on her hips. 'Hi there.' She waited for them to come to her. As the oldest child, she was entitled to deference. Anna watched carefully, wondering if Leah felt too old for these little girls – what were they – five-and-a-half and four years old? Finally Leah broke into a smile, herself, and waved them into the dining room where she had been drawing. 'Come on in. I've been waiting all day for you!'

Moira laughed. 'The only honest woman in the crowd. Listen, girls, sorry I'm late, but the frosting on this cake went liquid and. . . .' She turned to the front door where Randy stood uncertainly.

'Hi there, Wanda,' he called.

Wanda waved back. Anna advanced and waved as well. Teddy stared and eventually took a step forward. 'Hello there, Randy, how're you doing?' She tried to repress her animosity. After all these years, she admonished herself, but she couldn't help it.

'Well, I got to be going.' He waved again. 'You girls all have a good time.' Teddy noticed he seemed afraid to close the door. Moira stood in the hallway, her arms around an enormous chocolate cake, feeling like the cake, round and cumbersome and out of place.

Anna observed Teddy's paralysis and took over. 'Here, Moi, let me escort the cake to the kitchen. You take a seat and a glass.'

'Yes.' Teddy recovered. 'Let me hang up your coat. And I'll get the girls some soda.'

Moira sat tentatively on the elephant and accepted a drink from Wanda. She had been feeling woozy all day – why did they call this 'morning sickness'? – and maybe the alcohol would settle her. Either that or send her into orbit. Christ, it was odd to be back. Her attention was immediately drawn to the new apricot wall in the dining room. Probably Angela's idea. Not too bad. She would remember to say something complimentary about it.

Anna walked back and sat beside Moira. 'The girls look beauti-

– 452 –

ful. Clara isn't a baby at all any more.'

'No, not the way she runs away from me in the street! And did you notice Tess's blouse? Those clothes from Leah are coming in handy already. Sometimes I think that Tess is twice the normal size. But what's normal. As Mother says, she's healthy enough.'

Wanda sank into the couch, heavy with conflicting feelings. What happened to the old Moira who sparked and inspired her to be independent? But how could she be irritated with this weary woman who looked older than any of them. Also, the poor kid was married to Randy, a nice enough guy, but not exactly talented in the financial department. Wanda reminded herself that underneath it all Moira was the same quixotic, original person. 'They are both beautiful girls,' she joined in.

Teddy would not sit down. She was at once too excited and too scared. She would fiddle in the kitchen a while, get her bearings and then return.

'Teddy, let me help.' Anna got to her feet.

'No, you enjoy yourself. I just need to check on the meatloaf.'

'She looks terrific,' Moira said, '. . . in top form.'

'Yes, she does seem happier,' Wanda agreed. 'Middle age suits her.'

'Middle age!' declared Moira. 'Do you think we've really hit it? I feel like I'm only getting started.' She reassured herself that she was three years younger than Teddy. Still, she felt that she had faded away while Teddy, Anna and Wanda had come into their own.

Inadvertently Wanda glanced at Moira's stomach.

'Oh, I don't mean with the kids. This is the last one! Even if it's not a boy. How can I be the mother of three kids already? Middle-aged? I keep thinking I'll get back on the track. You know, like I did when I quit acting to work in the war. I thought I'd be off the market only a couple of years and then I might even get "mature woman" parts. When we decided to get married, I thought it would free me up from supporting Tess to go back to the stage and then Clara came and now here's little-what's-his-name, and well, I can't think of this as middle age, can you, Anna?'

Anna took a drag on her cigarette. 'I don't know. Sometimes I feel much younger than when I lived in London. Then I have to acknowledge that Leah is twelve already. I do feel like I missed part of my twenties, like I'm actually twenty-five or twenty-six.'

'Yes,' Wanda agreed. 'That's why I felt such urgency once I got to college. I still feel like I'll never catch up.'

Moira saw the distress on Wanda's face. 'That's what I was saying about not being middle-aged; I haven't finished my youth yet.'

'Guess we've all changed direction since our "youths".' Anna grew more pensive.

'Yes.' Moira drained her glass and poured another. 'I'm different in little ways. Like my relationship with Mother. I don't think I ever could have forgiven Mother if I hadn't had my own kids.'

Wanda winced at the reminder that she and her own mother would never reach that final truce. In this one respect, she had refused to be a model daughter. They had understood each other more during the last months. Yet so much still separated them, so much grief which they took out on each other.

'I wonder if this is just the normal aging process. How many of the changes in our lives came about from the war?'

'You're right.' Wanda tried to forget Mama momentarily. 'It's probably just the classic dwindling of goals. So Roy and I didn't get to Africa. Everyone has disappointments.' She was not convincing herself.

'Hey, hey.' Teddy returned. 'No more interesting chat without me. Lunch is served, ladies.'

The children seemed happy at their card table, Teddy observed. Leah was helping the younger ones, reminding Teddy of her own role in the Fielding family. People made eager comments about the *sushi, kugel*, salad, meatloaf and beans. Then there was silence. Teddy felt tongue-tied, unsure where to start. Should she try something like plans for summer vacation or would that set a superficial tone for the rest of the meal? She wanted to find out more about Reuben. But could they talk about such serious things with the children here?

Moira reconsidered the apricot paint. Yes, it did work well with the brown rug and the beige curtains. It added a little zest to the room. Why hadn't she thought of it herself? Could she mention it offhandedly or would Teddy think she was trying to be too friendly about Angela?

Wanda tried beans and was transported by memories of her first taste of Teddy's spicy, substantial cooking. Suddenly, she was tired and sad. The years in this house had been the most hopeful in her life. She had never since made friends like these. Even her relationship with Carolyn didn't involve the depth of feeling she had for

Anna, Teddy and Moira. It wasn't as if they were dead or had moved a thousand miles, unlike Roy's war buddies, who had disappeared in one way or another. Moreover, she got to see her friends every month or two. She would never be satisfied. Maybe Mama was right; she asked too much of life. But it was from Mama she had learned to ask.

Anna looked at Wanda's tight mouth and wondered how the girl was doing. She would try to find her alone later. She seemed distracted these last couple of months. Maybe she was having troubles with Roy. She wondered if the camp memories haunted her. They said that some of the Jews in Europe were now committing suicide. Of course the camps here had been different, but some of the effects were similar.

'Mommy, Mommy,' Tess called, 'Leah made the salad. Did you know that?'

'Delicious, dear.' Moira smiled. Leave it to Tess to break the silence. She might be the most comfortable person here today. She had almost been born in this house. Did she have any sense of that? Could she remember colors or objects from her first months here? Perhaps that striped scatter rug she used to lie on between the kitchen and the dining room. Moira glanced down, gratified to find the rug there.

'What's happening to Vivian?' asked Teddy.

'Still typing in Castro Valley.' Moira shrugged. 'That guy from Modesto didn't work out. We haven't been in touch for six or seven months.'

'We mustn't ever let that happen to us.' Wanda was struck by the force in her own voice. 'I mean, promise we'll alway stay in close contact.'

They each nodded solemnly.

Fearful of another silence, Teddy interjected, 'How about your sister-in-law, Carolyn?'

'She's teaching in Colorado now, high school French. She seems happy. I find it hard to understand. But she and Winnie like the snow and quite a few *Nisei* live in that part of the country – a number of people who decided to stay after their dislocation from the coast.'

'Once I saw Seattle, I could understand Dawn moving,' Teddy offered. 'She and Sandra say it's like what San Francisco used to be.'

'I can't imagine leaving the Bay Area for good.' Wanda looked around with concern. 'Could any of you?'

Anna glanced at Leah who was exchanging a piece of *sushi* for some of Tess's meatloaf. 'No,' she sighed heavily. 'There were times I thought we might go back to London. But I can't see it now.'

'Me neither,' Moira added. 'That's one thing that hasn't changed. We all live in the Bay Area.'

'A lot is the same,' Teddy said. 'We're basically the same people.'

'Oh, no,' Anna and Wanda answered in unison.

Teddy shrugged. They were right: here she was trying to contain things again.

'OK,' Teddy admitted. 'We're living differently than we anticipated.'

'And doing different jobs,' said Anna.

'Everything is different,' declared Wanda, 'everything. We have a smaller sense of possibility now.'

'Smaller or just different?' asked Anna.

'Maybe you're right,' Wanda conceded. 'Different. I think that one of the reasons I cherish our friendship is that it's a reference point. Everything has changed around me. So many of my friends didn't live here ten years ago. But you all understand who I was, and maybe, as a result, more about who I am.'

'Yes,' said Teddy, 'I agree. Angela and I have friends who – well, who have always lived like the two of us do. They don't understand all the stops and starts. . . .' She picked at the beans, too nervous to eat. 'I don't know, there's something about keeping up with people – people you choose – that holds you steady. When you're going through a bad patch, they remind you that you've endured before.' She sipped the water to stop herself from jabbering and almost gagged. She breathed slowly, relaxed and swallowed. She thought about Moira throwing up one morning. All of a sudden, she was flattened by sadness.

Anna started into her pocket for a cigarette and stopped herself – totally inappropriate behavior for the middle of a meal. It was surprising to hear Teddy being so self-scrutinizing. Sometimes she thought Wanda and herself were the only ones consciously moving, but they had all transformed, been transformed. Teddy's life was far more radical than anything she might have imagined for herself.

Wanda nodded. 'Yes, Teddy, I know what you mean.'

Moira stared at the *kugel*. It was wonderful hearing Teddy's commitment to them. She had promised that they would always remain friends, but Moira used to think of that as Teddy's moral idealism. Here, though, she could tell Teddy needed Moira as much as she, herself, needed Teddy. She was almost crying, so she tried for a lighter tone. 'Changes. Well, I've gone through some big ones. Cooking, for instance. Anna, you'll be disappointed to hear I still serve Campbell's chicken soup, but at least it's hot nowadays.'

'Mommy is a good cook,' Tess declared. 'We had beef stew last night.'

Teddy regarded the child with affection. How much did she remember of Aunt Teddy in the early days? Tess was always more affectionate than Clara. Was this because she was older and less shy, or was it because she recalled those first months in the house?

'Well, I still haven't changed my bad habits.' Anna laughed, pulling out her cigarettes. Everyone had finished the first course. And she needed reinforcement before embarking on Moira's cake. She thought about meeting Moira that first day of typing school and of the compassion she felt for the poor kid's tangled fingers. She could still see that brilliant red nail polish.

Leah and Tess were at Anna's elbow, taking her plate. She exchanged a pleased glance with Moira. Moira nodded, wanting to warn the children to be gentle with Teddy's favorite dishes but holding her tongue.

'Careful,' Leah whispered to the younger child, 'careful with the plates.'

Anna smiled to herself.

'Coffee?' asked Wanda. She needed to move around. All this casting for intimacy gave her the willies. Maybe they should have simply met for drinks. Maybe she was too self-conscious. 'Or tea?'

Teddy stood.

'No.' Wanda put her hands on Teddy's shoulders. 'You've been running around for us all day. Sit down and let me get the drinks.'

When Wanda returned, she was dismayed to find them on the subject of children's clothes. She tried to start a conversation about the Emporium, but Teddy was as immersed as Moira and Anna. It was boring and inconsiderate the way mothers went on and on about their children. However, she also knew she was jealous that they had settled into their families while she couldn't even decide to have children. Decide? Having children was natural. Why was this so hard for her? Was she unnatural? She sat down and thought about Teddy's courage in bringing up the subject of Angela and about the cowardice of everybody else in letting it pass. Maybe she would find an opening after this discussion of rapid bone growth.

'Terrific cake, Moi.' Teddy cut herself a second piece.

'Yes,' Anna nodded, filled with deep affection for Teddy. It wasn't so bad; the frosting was a little patchy, but it tasted better than anything she could remember Moira concocting. People usually manage as best they can, she reminded herself. For some reason, this recalled Mama. Memories of the parents' dinner here at the table without Mama. Of her weekly visits to the hospital, of her dreams about Mama in London.

Abruptly, Anna drained her coffee and turned to Wanda. 'How about you and me doing the dishes?' Had this been too quick? Would the others feel excluded? Still, she needed a break. She needed to talk about her plan with Wanda, who would understand better than anyone. She reached down for another cigarette.

'Sure,' Wanda nodded, disappointed that the four of them hadn't been able to have a long, serious talk. Well, after the dishes, there was still time. Did Anna have something urgent on her mind or did she just want to give Teddy and Moira some privacy?

The children insisted on clearing the table. By the time Anna and Wanda were alone in the kitchen, Anna lost her nerve. Wanda probably wouldn't understand either. She would say it was a self-indulgence, a superficial kind of work. Wanda wrote about urgent issues – poverty and education and racial discrimination – what would she think of her friend becoming a psychologist puttering inside other people's heads?

Wanda sprinkled Tide over the plates and ran hot water. She hadn't used Tide to wash dishes since she lived here. Was this Teddy's custom or something they came to together? Just one of the house idiosyncracies she had forgotten. She watched the soap suds rise into a sweet scent and waited for Anna to begin.

'I, I feel embarrassed.' Anna stared at the suds. 'I wanted to talk with you about work.'

'Yes,' asked Wanda, 'how's your job?'

'OK. But ultimately, I don't know how meaningful it is.'

Wanda nodded. She had expected Anna might quit once Reuben arrived. She probably wanted to have more kids. But why would Anna pick her to discuss this with? Because she thought her involvement in a career was equally strong? Wanda was not sure she wanted this intimacy. Perhaps she could develop a sudden allergy to

Tide. 'I think I know what you mean.' Wanda scraped chocolate frosting from the side of a plate.

'The problems are so deep. We've only started to help by finding decent housing. The traumas continue for months and even years. When you consider what some of those people endured in camp. . . .'

Wanda listened, at first relieved by Anna's intensity. She stacked plates in the rack while Anna leaned back against the sink, smoking and gesturing with the dishtowel.

'So I've been looking into a psychology program. It's a long haul, but by the end of it, I would become what they call a clinical psychologist and I could help people in a deeper way.'

'Like a psychiatrist?' Wanda leaned against the sink now, looking into the dining room where the children were racing around the table and into the living room where Teddy and Moira were talking intently. She cleared her throat to get back on Anna's track.

'Yes, do you think that's crazy?' Anna listened to her own hoarse laugh.

'No, I, I think if anyone has the sensitivity for it, it's you.' Wanda studied her. She wanted to ask if the decision had anything to do with Anna's mother, if she thought that helping other people before it was too late would compensate for . . . really, she rebuked herself, turn off the journalist.

'It will take years for the degree, going to school part-time. Living with Papa is cheap.'

Wanda shook her head, thinking how good Anna was to stay with her difficult father. Of course she would have done the same thing.

'What's the matter?' asked Anna.

'Oh, nothing. But what about Reuben? Does this mean he'll stay here? Have you worked that out?'

'No, as I said earlier, we have no plans.' She spoke more slowly. 'If anything, this is likely to end the possibilities. I'm sure he doesn't want to hang around waiting for me to finish school. He wants a home and a family.'

'You already have a home and a family!' Wanda argued. 'What more does he expect from you?'

'You think it's a crackpot scheme, don't you?'

'No.' Wanda was crying. She turned to the sink to avoid Anna's eyes, but it was too late.

'What's wrong, sweetie?' Anna put her hand on Wanda's

shoulder. 'Did I say something? What's going on?'

'Oh, nothing, nothing. Everything is so confusing. You giving up on Reuben. Moira having one baby after another without blinking an eye. And me with the job I've always coveted, unable to decide whether to have children.' She hadn't meant to reveal this, but she felt an immediate relief. 'How can I bring kids into this world? Would I have the spirit to raise them, after all that has happened?' She shook her head, refreshed by the tears. 'I think it would be better to adopt – like you did. But I don't know if I want to do that. Maybe I'm just selfish. I've got everything that I ever wanted and it's not enough.'

'Now, hang on, pal.' Anna watched the suds melting in the greasy water. 'Do you truly think you have everything you wanted? You are a freelance journalist, right, but you were saying at lunch that you had expected to be working in the South and going to Africa. You fought hard for what you have; it didn't fall from the sky.' Anna listened to these words with which she lectured herself every day. 'It's OK to sympathize with yourself, to acknowledge the things you've been through.'

Wanda stared at the sink for several moments.

Finally, she turned and hugged Anna. 'Yes, yes, I think you're right. One thing's for sure,' she sniffed, 'when you open your office, I'll be the first in the waiting room.'

Teddy glanced over Moira's shoulder at Anna hugging Wanda in the kitchen. What was going on, she wondered. Such familiar feelings: wanting to be everywhere in the house at once. She had been glad they were slow in clearing up the dishes. Moira was relaxed, chatting about her plans for the new baby, about how her mother would come up and help again. Moira looked so well today, happier than she had been in months. As much as she protested, having children agreed with her. Also, Moira was just as pleased as she with the reunion. Teddy smiled, thinking that they all acted as if they were humoring her, but they all wanted the reunion too. How wonderful to see them at the dinner table, to watch the kids playing together, to have a private time with Moira. Oh, she loved this woman. Dawn would say she was a fool, but she felt alive in a special way with Moira. It wasn't the same affection she used to feel. Angela lived in that part of her, but Angela didn't take up her whole heart. What did Moira feel? Did she ever miss the old days? Maybe some time it would be safe to talk about it.

'So tell me, Teddy, was the apricot wall Angela's idea?' Moira teased.

'Yes.' Teddy refused to be embarrassed. 'Do you like it?'

'Very much.' Moira reached for Teddy's hand. 'Wish I had thought about it, myself. Makes the dining room much more homey.'

'I always thought it was homey enough. We had lots of good times here. But Angela is strong on color. You should see what she did to the bedroom upstairs.' Teddy forced herself to keep eye contact. She hadn't intended to mention it, but now that she did, she would just leave the word between them. Bedroom. With all its softness and hardness. Bedroom. What was wrong with that? Moira had told her how she and Randy kept Clara in their bedroom until she was two years old. Everybody had bedrooms. 'All blues and greens.'

'I'd like to see that.' Moira smiled. 'You seem happy with her, Teddy.'

'Yes. She's a good person, Moi. Solid, reliable.'

'Like I wasn't.'

'I didn't say that.'

'You didn't need to.' She frowned ironically. 'What I want to know is, does she treat you well?'

'Oh, yes,' Teddy laughed. 'Often she acts like I'm a china figurine! Me, can you imagine?'

'Yes,' Moira said, then looked into the dining room after the children.

'Maybe you can come over for dinner – or lunch would probably be easier for you – some time.'

Moira nodded, understanding that lunch excluded Randy. Well, what did she expect? Randy would have a horrible time and he would never stop teasing her about the 'old maids'.

'And Randy,' Teddy sat straighter, summoning all her good will, 'he's treating you OK?'

'What do you think?' Moira smiled. 'Refuses to let me get a job, works overtime at the garage every night. Bought me the most gorgeous sofa for my birthday. A real family man, Teddy. Not the wild boy you knew before the war.'

'Yes.' Teddy sucked on her lip. She wouldn't like her mate working till late at night. Yet Moira did look OK.

'Teddy?' Moira reached over for her friend's hand.

'Yes?' Teddy felt as if she were sixteen. Moira could still do that to her.

'I want you to know I miss you. I hope you understand how much you'll always mean to me.'

'Yes.' Teddy nodded, catching sight of Wanda and Anna bringing in a fresh pot of coffee.

Moira noticed, too, reluctantly removing her hand.

'I should get going,' said Anna, setting down the tray. 'I've got shopping and then I have to drop off Leah at her art class. But I can't resist a final toast.'

Wanda poured the coffee, pleased that she remembered Moira took three sugars, that Teddy took hers black and that Anna – after her time in London – took a touch of milk.

'To next year's reunion!' said Anna.

'Yes!' Moira stood. 'Next spring, in this room.'

Teddy stood and exchanged smiles with Wanda. They all clinked cups.

'But this doesn't mean,' Teddy leaned forward, 'this doesn't mean we can't all meet before that – at a restaurant or somewhere.'

'No.' Moira rubbed Teddy's shoulder. 'It just means that we have a guaranteed reunion here, next spring, with one more baby.'

'OK.' Teddy laughed at her own solemnity.

'Without you, Teddy,' Wanda smiled, 'none of us would be here.'

'To Teddy!' Anna said, 'for bringing us together.'

'Again and again,' cheered Wanda.

'Mom, Mom.' Leah bounded into the living room. 'Can I play something for Aunt Teddy. Is it her birthday or something like that?'

'Something like that,' Anna grinned.

'Do you like "Heart and Soul"?' the girl asked Teddy.

'One of my all-time favorites,' Teddy answered.

Leah walked over to the piano and proceeded to play. Applause brought 'Peter, Peter, Pumpkin Eater' and then 'Twinkle, Twinkle Little Star'. The next round of applause drew Tess into the act. She climbed on the bench and insisted on a duet of 'Chopsticks'. The children continued to play, and gradually the adults turned back to their own conversation.

Anna looked at her watch and jumped up. 'So much for my shopping. Leah will never make her class unless I step on it. I can't bear to leave. This reminds me of that last morning before I went to

England and the breakfast you fixed for me. I always felt bad for not eating the toast.'

She looked up to find them all laughing. 'Guilt,' she laughed too, 'see, this is a family.'

Leah was buttoning her coat and waiting patiently by the door with the salad bowl and the *kugel* plate. She smiled shyly as her mother was buried in hugs by the three women. Tess walked up and threw her arms around Leah. Then Clara gave her a loud, wet kiss.

'It's horrible to rush the good-byes.' Anna shook her head. 'Listen.' She reached for the doorknob. 'We'll be in touch. Lunch in two weeks, right, Wanda? And I'll ring you both, Moira and Teddy.'

Wanda, Teddy and Moira stood at the door, Tess and Clara in front of them, waving good-bye. When the car was out of sight, Moira turned to Teddy, 'Are you still going downtown? Can you still give us a lift? If it's out of the way, we can take the bus, I mean. . . .'

'Of course,' said Teddy, concealing her disappointment, 'but do you have to leave so soon?'

Wanda knew it was her card. Teddy would accept her reasons more easily. Actually, she didn't want to leave at all. She wished she could go upstairs to her room and bury her head under a pillow for the rest of the weekend. But she made the responsible move. 'Yes, Teddy, Roy is expecting me. We're going to Betty's rehearsal.'

Teddy sighed, leaning into the closet for her jacket. 'OK, gang, all aboard.' Tess jumped into her arms. 'Train, Aunt Teddy, we haven't played train in a long time.' Moira walked into the kitchen for her dish and gathered up Clara with the children's clothes and dolls on the way back to the front door.

Wanda walked slowly to her car. She sat there, pretending to organize her belongings on the seat as Teddy pulled away. Tess rolled down the window, 'Bye, Aunt Wanda. Bye.' Clara leaned out, 'Bye-bye.' Teddy waved. Moira nodded her head, laughing. Wanda watched the circus roll down Stockton Street and told herself to leave. She put her key in the ignition. Everyone had gone; there was no point sitting here.

Her eyes went back to the house, upstairs to the window of her old room. Sometimes she thought these last five years had been the toughest, as they worked out the compromises the war had insinuated. Maybe life would feel simpler next time they met.

She looked down the façade, through the living room window

now. Teddy had left the curtains open and the dining room light illuminated the entire floor. Wanda was filled with tender sadness. There was something precious about the late thirties and even about the war itself. Then, you could blame the bad times on history; you could foresee a personal truce. The pain would pass. Some day. But the experiences of the war still pressed down. There was no conclusion. There was no some day. It was twelve years since they had met. Eleven years since they had moved into the house. She shook her head, noticing the shrubs that Moira used to trim. Eleven years since Miss Fargo and the Pacific Exposition and the first day on Stockton Street. There was no telling what lay ahead. What would they be like in another decade? Leah would be a woman in 1960. Anna might be a grandmother. It was going too quickly. She would never catch up. They would leave that to their daughters. Those who dared to have daughters.

In 1960 they would all be in their forties. Ten more years. It was almost unimaginable.